The Imaginings

Paul D. Dail

ISBN: 0615509266
ISBN-13: 9780615509266

Special thanks to my parents, wife and family.

Thanks also to Kimberley Cameron and John Paine,
both of whom helped me edit this book
while always respecting authorial choice.

Finally, thanks to Shawn Ekker of Ekker Design Build
(www.ekkerdesign.com),
who always gave me work whenever I needed it.
Support employers who support the Arts.

Cover concept by www.RicardoGuzman.com

Cover design by CO2 Graphic Design

PROLOGUE

From the dark of his apartment, Peter Blithe parted the curtains of his living room window just slightly. Just enough to peer outside. Even though the apartment was cool, sweat beaded on his forehead, pasting his greasy blond hair to his face. He had lost track of how many times he had performed this little ritual over the past hour.

Peter scanned the night outside. The other lights in the complex glared into the dark sky, but he could still detect a few stars above. The storm hadn't arrived yet, but still he hesitated. Because he knew it was gathering.

Peter really didn't want to leave the apartment. Not if he didn't have to go. But he needed the tow rope from his Blazer.

A small dust devil twisted across the parking lot. It whipped up a clump of leaves gathered against the curb, and in the instant before they were scattered, Peter swore that they swirled into the shape of a face. There was only darkness where the eyes should've been. Then it was gone.

No, he definitely didn't want to go outside.

The icy wind had started ripping though the Twin Cities just after lunch. The morning forecast had predicted an unseasonably warm day in Minneapolis, and the cold blast had caught people unprepared.

Peter had been at a used bookstore when it hit. After the optimistic forecast that morning, he had felt safe enough leaving his home. Hell, Peter might have even said he felt *good*, even though he knew that optimism had become something of a gamble the past month. When the wind kicked up that afternoon, he knew it had been a bad bet. People suddenly swarmed into the previously quiet store, shivering and pretending to be interested in the handful of new releases the store carried. Peter gently closed the book he had been skimming, *A Field Guide to Demons, Fairies, Fallen Angels, and Other Subversive Spirits*. Through the crowd milling around by the cash register, he could see others on the sidewalk hurrying past in a swirl of clothing and wind-tangled hair.

Who am I kidding? Peter asked himself. And at that moment, he knew it was decided. He would never have peace again. His shoulders dropped.

Nothing had ever come easy for Peter. Not grades. Or girls. Nothing. From trying to get a body that a girl might look twice at, to almost every test in high school and college, most of his life had been a workout with very little to show for it. But there had been a bright spot. Everything seemed to turn around for him when he moved to Minnesota.

It didn't last long. And by the time the real bad shit got started, he just didn't have any fight left in him.

Peter let out a quiet sigh, then looked around the store. He spotted a door at the back with an "Employees Only" sign. He crept across the aisle and tried the handle. Locked. He turned toward the front, studying the group that still waited for the weather to abate. No one seemed to be looking at him.

Or, more importantly, *for* him.

He had to take his chances, and he started forward, excusing himself through the crowd and leaving the store.

Outside, he had fought through the rushing masses until he reached his SUV and quickly drove back to his apartment. He stayed inside with the blinds shut for the remainder of the afternoon, even though he knew it was the last time he would see daylight. At least inside, he would be safe from the storm until he finished his business.

Peter checked out his window a final time, swallowed hard and took his coat from the couch. He tried to open the front door, but he quickly yanked his hand away in pain. The handle of the door was glowing red, the bronze coating smoking from the intense heat. Blisters rose on his palm where he had touched the knob. Peter clutched his hand into a fist and closed his eyes. When he opened them again, the door handle had returned to normal, and there was just a faint prickling in his palm.

Not much longer, he told himself, but still he hesitated at the door.

He remembered when the first hallucinations began almost three months earlier, minor harmless flashes of light or movement. Peter dismissed them as work exhaustion. It was winter in the mid-West. The cold and storms could get to a person.

Then it got worse. He started seeing faces in his peripheral vision, outside his windows, which would dissolve when he turned to look at them. He went to the doctor, whose only suggestion was to take some time off from work. Peter did just that, and after a week of rest and apparent calm, he returned to the office, but what he saw

it looked so real

made him run out of the building, stopping only to vomit in the parking lot.

At first, his supervisor had tried calling and leaving messages, but there hadn't been a call in two weeks, not since Peter had answered the phone and then hung up screaming. He knew his coworkers weren't actually being fed into a meat grinder on the other end of the line, but that's what it sounded like. No one else called him. And until this morning, he didn't leave the apartment.

Just as Peter tried the handle again, a gust of wind blew the door open, knocking Peter back before cracking into the doorstop on the wall. He forced himself onto the porch and descended the stairs. At the bottom, he glanced around the complex before crossing the parking lot. He didn't see anyone else around. Peter opened the rear doors of his Blazer, but he quickly retreated in horror as an avalanche of brownish-black insects poured out of the vehicle. Stag beetles. They were two to three inches long with pincers half the length of their bodies. They tumbled over one another as they cascaded out, their hard shells clattering on the asphalt, where they found their footing and rose up in defensive stances, pincers snapping in the air.

Peter hadn't seen stag beetles since he was a child in Georgia. On hot summer nights, the disgusting insects would descend on his family's porch like a minefield, causing Peter and his younger brother, David, to race from the front door to the yard.

David.

Peter hadn't thought about his brother in months. The last thing he knew was that David was living with some girl in Colorado, but Peter had stopped calling his family.

The stag beetles continued to stream out of the Blazer. Suddenly the group on the pavement scuttled around, grouping together. The groups formed into the shapes of letters. Peter stepped back farther and watched in horrid fascination.

D-A-V-I-D.

When the letters were complete, a final clump formed into a squirming question mark, the pincers waving like mad.

Shit, Peter thought. There was a reason he had stopped communicating with relatives. Or even thinking about them.

"It's not real," he said aloud and stepped closer to the Blazer. The letters scattered and the stag beetles took on a militaristic front line, all heads raised against Peter. He pushed back his childhood fears and continued, cringing as he crunched over the insects. The survivors quickly spread out and then surged forward. He could feel them crawling on his shoes and then his legs.

"Not real," he said again, but he rushed forward. The stag beetles continued to erupt like lava from the spot where his towrope was stowed. Peter clenched his jaw, closed his eyes and plunged his hand into the pile halfway up his arm. Hundreds of bites pinched his flesh as he groped around the back of the Blazer. He didn't need to open his eyes to see that the beetles had stopped surging out of the vehicle and were now swarming up his arm toward his shoulders, his neck, his face. Just as he was about to scream, his fingers found the rope and yanked it free.

The insects disappeared. Peter looked at the empty space, shuddering. Then he slammed the door and ran back to his apartment, only to find his last sanctum invaded. The wind continued to blow in his apartment, even though all of the doors and windows were closed. Newspapers and magazines swirled in the living room. A lamp next to the couch blew over, the bulb exploding in a flash of light.

The stereo switched itself on, and static blared from the speakers. Underneath the static Peter heard a gravelly voice whispering one word over and over:

"David." The voice started laughing, growing louder until it cut off, replaced again by static.

Peter didn't have much longer. He figured that the illusions would become reality soon enough, and he had one more thing to do. He had been tricked into setting this punishment on his brother. Whatever had been tormenting Peter had slipped in when he was weak and plucked out another victim. He didn't know how long until this thing would find his little brother, but Peter had to find a way to warn him somehow, before his mind shredded away entirely.

With the towrope still clutched in his hand, Peter rushed into the whipping debris, grabbed a newspaper out of the air and hurried into the kitchen. He yanked open a drawer, pulled out a black marker and scrawled a note across the front page of the *Minneapolis Star Tribune*. He examined his warning.

never disregard your imaginings.

Peter knew he should say something else, but the swirling maelstrom in his living room told him that more time was a luxury he couldn't afford. These hallucinations

but are they really hallucinations? If someone walked in right now, what would they see?

were the most realistic yet. The others had seemed designed just to break down his mind, but they wanted his flesh now.

Peter scanned his kitchen for somewhere to put the message where it wouldn't be blown to shreds and lost in the mess. His eyes stopped on the refrigerator. He opened the door and set the paper on the top shelf. Someone would clean out the fridge eventually.

As he stepped out of the kitchen, the torrent of periodicals came at him. He threw up his arms in defense, and the pages of the whipping magazines sliced dozens of paper cuts over his exposed skin. He swung the rope at the flurry, managing to knock a few issues to the carpet, but they were quickly caught up again. He fled to his bedroom, slamming the door. It kept out the printed pages, but the wind persisted in his room, tossing the bedding from wall to wall. Peter dodged into his bathroom and yanked back the forest green shower curtain. The rod supporting the curtain was hollow plastic, the kind with an expanding spring to hold it against opposite walls. Too weak, he decided. Back in the room, he slid open his closet doors and tested the wooden rod held in place by flimsy metal hardware screwed to a shelf made of particle board. The shelf flexed when he pulled down on the rod. No good, either. Shit. How could he not have thought of this?

Then an image flashed in Peter's mind, and he hurried out of the bedroom through the living room to the front door. He didn't hesitate this time as he opened the door and stepped out from one storm into another. Outside, sleet had joined the wind, pelting his right side as he stood on the porch. He pulled his hood up and fought the urge to race down the stairs. Instead he took the steps cautiously, careful to avoid slipping. The last thing he needed was to fall and break his back, ending up crumpled and defenseless on the landing below while whatever torture rained down on him.

At the bottom of the stairs, he sprinted across the parking lot and flung open the gate to the basketball courts. The backboards were supported by four-inch steel poles rising ten feet before elbowing parallel to the ground like an upside-down L. They were perfect. Peter approached the nearest one and tossed an end of the towrope over the elbow. As if taunting him, the wind caught the rope and blew it away from the bar a few times before Peter successfully grabbed the other end. The rope had been designed for tow hitches, each end sewn into a large, sturdy loop. He threaded the dangling end through the other loop and pulled until the loop slid up to the bar. He tugged a couple of times on the rope and then swung the loose end over the bar repeatedly until it dangled a few feet above his head. Then he started shimmying up the pole. Halfway up, he hugged the pole tight with one arm and grasped the rope with the other, sliding the loop over his head before continuing up.

For the first time since his imaginings took on a life of their own, Peter didn't feel any fear. A remarkable lucidity drifted over him. It would all be over soon. Relief finally. Suicide was supposed to be a sin, but surely God would understand this time, considering what Peter had been through the past month.

Halfway up the pole, he stopped.

Maybe it was a test.

Peter's grip loosened, and he slowly slipped back down as the other lessons of childhood Sunday school rushed back at him. There were all sorts of biblical references to people being tested by God. *He* had put a family on a boat for forty days, surrounded by the filth, stench and disease of a bunch of wild animals. Forty days and forty nights. For Peter, it had really only been bad for the past month. He had been broken after only thirty days. Amazing how long each day had felt like, living in fear of every passing second of it, awaiting the next horrific vision.

He strengthened his grip and started back up. He had failed. Or God had failed *him*. Better to end it now than to put more lives in danger. He wanted to pray that his brother would be stronger than he had been, but he knew his prayers at this point would go unheard.

At the top of the pole, Peter crossed the bar hand-over-hand, his feet dangling above the blacktop. The sleet made the steel slippery, and a couple of times he almost lost his grip. Halfway across, he stopped.

What the hell am I doing? I can beat thi-

His hands slipped on the ice, and he dropped, but not enough to break his neck. He clawed at the tow rope, his body thrashing while he suffocated. His body twitched a couple of times with his last fight, then went still.

As he died, the sleet stopped, and the wind died down to a whisper.

CHAPTER 1
COLORADO

The wind grabbed the screen door and swung it open with a crash. David cursed the landlord for not fixing the latch as he rushed out of the kitchen, past the living room and down the narrow hallway. He opened the front door, shivering when the chill rushed in. Rain pelted the side of his face, and the wind whipped his shoulder-length blond curls into his eyes and tangled it in his thick goatee. Lightning flashed, revealing thick black clouds. If he still lived in Georgia, he'd be in the basement by now. In the South, those were tornado clouds. In the Colorado mountains, it was just one hell of a storm.

David reached out for the thrashing screen. Another bang like that last one would surely break the upper glass section. He wrestled the door from the gusts, finally pulling it shut and making sure the latch caught. Then he walked back into the living room, making a point of wiping his dripping face. His roommate, Kathy, sat on the couch watching the television. As usual.

"Kathy, you know with the broken handle you need to make sure the door closes all the way when you come in."

Kathy didn't bother to look away from the television. "I thought I did." David shook his head and walked into the kitchen. Her excuse for everything was to play stupid.

"Maybe Ann left it open when she went to work," she hollered from the living room.

Or she blamed it on someone else.

8

David didn't respond. He knew Ann didn't leave it open. It pissed her off more than it did him. David went back to work in the kitchen on the lasagna. It was Ann's favorite, and he knew that his fiancé would need it when she got off work. Nights like these were always busy at the grocery store. People stocking up "just in case." It happened every time a big storm was predicted. There hadn't been a flood in Canyon City since 1965, but people weren't taking any chances, especially with spring having come so early this year.

Lightning flashed again, illuminating the nearly opaque plastic that covered the window over the sink. David looked up from the pan, startled. He swore he thought something had moved just outside the window in that brief flash of light. He paused, waiting for a knock on the door, but when none came, he dismissed it. Just the freaking plastic again. Last fall the only department store in town had sold out of the clear window plastic by the time they got around to buying some, so they got stuck with the heavy painter's plastic. It helped keep the heating bill down in the old house, but in David's opinion, the only way the house could've felt like more of a body bag would've been if the plastic were black.

But it came down to dollars and sense, as his Dad used to say. With the wedding less than four months away, David and Ann needed all the money they could get. Having to live with another couple whose main preoccupation was an old 20" RCA television was another example. It was a miracle the thing still even worked; both David and Ann often wished that it didn't. They had been looking for a place of their own for the past couple of months. Big house or not, there was no way they were staying here once they were married. After that, Kathy and Jason could watch television until their brains oozed out of their heads.

Headlights shone through the plastic over the picture windows in the dining nook just as David finished up the final layer of the lasagna.

Perfect timing.

He knew it was Ann, even though he couldn't see outside. The sound of her truck with the loose muffler that she wouldn't let David fix was unmistakable. But more than that, David just knew. Like how he could tell when she entered a room, even if his back was turned. Like a little rush of adrenaline, she just made him feel more alive.

David heard a low rumbling sound outside in the distance as the truck's engine died, but it wasn't thunder. It sounded more like a freight train tearing down the residential street. The growling of the gale wind grew as David heard Ann shut the truck door. The blast hit the house, shaking the already loose windows and flinging the front door open. An icy chill swept into the house, raising the hairs of David's neck. Even colder than when he closed the thrashing door the first time, a rash of gooseflesh ran down his arms. He gasped, surprised by the cold.

"You didn't close the door all the way," Kathy shouted from the living room. For a brief moment, David couldn't move. His feet felt like they had grown roots into the worn, green linoleum. Then the door slammed shut, breaking his paralysis, and Ann entered the house in a swirl of obscenities. David was pretty sure "goddamn screen door" was in there somewhere.

"Make sure the latch on the screen catches," Kathy said as Ann stomped in, shaking the rain off her slight figure. Ann ignored the comment and went into the kitchen. She stood in the doorway with a scowl, water tugging down the curls of her red hair before dropping and pooling on the linoleum around her feet. Like a drenched cat.

But a damn cute drenched cat, David thought.

He grabbed the pan of lasagna and showed it to Ann. A smile spread across her tired face.

"I'm going upstairs to get changed," she said.

"Can I come?" David asked.

"I was hoping you would," she said, her smile changing to a sly grin. "How long will that lasagna take?"

"About an hour," David said.

"Perfect. Put it in and come upstairs."

David slid the lasagna in the oven, did an excited little hop and followed Ann upstairs. She flipped on the lamp in the bedroom. David walked up behind her and wrapped his arms around her shivering body. Slowly he began unbuttoning her wet blouse.

"How long has she been watching today?" Ann asked.

"Since she got home." David peeled off the blouse and began working on her bra. "Let's not talk about Kathy, okay?"

Ann turned around in his arms and kissed him. They fumbled with one another's clothes, tumbling onto the bed, exploring each other's bodies and falling quickly into passion. The rain and wind rattled the panes of glass on the window above their heads. Loose shingles on the roof picked up and slapped back down. Ann rolled David over and positioned herself on top of him. The bedside lamp cast her slender shadow on the low-vaulted ceiling as she found her rhythm. That rain continued to pound the roof, but David barely noticed. He was too intent on Ann, their eyes locked, his hands on her hips, urging her on, yet wanting to make the moment last. God, he loved her. Soon they would be married. And together forever. Just as David climaxed, a burst of light blazed through the plastic on the window, and thunder boomed loud enough to shake the house. David opened his eyes as the lamp flashed blindingly bright. Ann's silhouette burned into his vision as she cried out in ecstasy.

And then there was darkness. And silence. David felt like he had left the room...the house... the earth entirely. All sensation disappeared as he floated, surrounded and lost in the blackness. Again he had the strange sensation of paralysis, but it was more pleasant this time.

Then Ann fell forward on his chest, and the two lay still, catching their breath as the room took shape in the dark. "You were amazing," she whispered in his ear before rolling off his body onto the bed next to him. "What happened to the lights?"

"Must have blown a fuse."

"The way I feel," Ann said, "I think we could've blown the power for the whole neighborhood." She giggled.

A voice squawked up from the bottom of the stairwell. "Hey, you guys, are the lights off up there, too?"

"Shit," David muttered, then louder, "Yes, they are, Kathy."

"Oh," she said. There was silence, and then, "Do you think a fuse went out?"

"Probably just the storm," David hollered.

"Oh. Well, do you think--"

"We'll be down in a second," Ann said.

"Oh, c'mon, baby," he said, but he knew that Ann wouldn't be swayed. He sat up and stumbled over to the bookshelves, feeling around until he found a book of matches and lit the two candles on the second shelf.

Ann wrapped herself in a white fleece robe, grabbed one of the candles, and left the room as David pulled on his jeans and a sweatshirt. He walked downstairs with the other candle just as Ann came back in from the entryway. "The whole neighborhood is pitch black," she said. "The lightning must've knocked out the power for this whole side of town. It stopped raining, at least."

Kathy had resumed her spot on the couch, wrapped in a blanket, staring at the television as if sheer willpower would bring it back on. "How long do you think it will be out?" she asked. "One minute, I was sitting here watching TV. Then I blinked, and it was dark. I was watching my favorite show."

"Heaven forbid," David mumbled. Ann elbowed him. "We could tell ghost stories," he said. "Maybe pull out the Ouija board."

"No way!" Kathy shrieked.

"David," Ann scolded.

"I was just kidding," David said and laughed. Kathy was like a five-year-old when it came to anything remotely scary.

"Well, it's not funny," Kathy said. "The last time I watched a horror movie, I had nightmares for three weeks. And that plastic doesn't make things any better. It scares me almost as much during the day as it does during the night. I feel closed in. I can't see what's going on outside, just blurs of colors and movement. You never know when someone might be standing outside your window."

David sighed. He had heard this complaint on a nearly daily basis, and he regretted that he had agreed with her when she mentioned it the first time.

Lightning struck somewhere in the distance, briefly illuminating the house and making all three of them jump. David pointed to the window next to Kathy. "Hey, was that bush there before?" he whispered.

"Knock it off, David," Ann said.

"I was just kidding-" David started to say, but then he saw movement again. Real this time. A quick blur across the plastic. Someone was outside. David stood from the couch. "There it is again," he said.

"There *what* is again?" Ann asked.

"I keep thinking I see someone moving outside."

"Stop it, David!" Kathy said. "It's not funny, okay?"

"No, I'm serious this time." He crossed over to the front door, keeping an eye on the windows as he moved.

"David-" Ann began, but he raised his hand to silence her. He swung open the door, half-expecting to see one of his friends messing around. But only darkness met him. He pushed the screen door open and cleared his throat. "Can I *help you*?" he asked. He tried to shout it, but the black night seemed to swallow his words.

David stepped out on the stoop. God, it was dead quiet. Even the wind had stopped blowing. Usually David liked the blackouts and the silence that accompanied them, the silence that made him realize how much sound just simple electricity creates, the hum of the streetlights and the buzz of life happening in other homes. Tonight David didn't like the silence so much. Tonight it felt like the sounds of life had ceased, like if he walked into the house of one of his neighbors, he would see something horrible.

David shivered and then laughed in spite of himself. Must be Kathy getting to him. He puffed up his chest a little and leaned back into the entryway. "It was nothing. I'm just gonna have a smoke." He said this into the house but hoped it was loud enough to be heard by anyone outside as well. In reality, David wasn't too worried. Canyon City was pretty safe.

David shut the door, being sure to latch it, even though the wind had stopped. Around here, it could start up again any second. He stepped off the stoop and turned the corner of the house, heading down the driveway to the detached garage. Dark as it was, he knew his way, and his eyes had adjusted enough by the time he reached the backyard for him to see that if anyone had actually been there before, they were gone now.

He reached into his jeans pocket and pulled out his cigarettes. Low thunder grumbled in the distance, but David didn't see any flashes of lightning. Maybe the storm had passed over.

Peter.

A lump rose in David's throat. As he had done during the start of almost every storm for the past two years, he thought about his older brother. It still didn't make any sense to David, and maybe that was why he couldn't let it go.

Was it like this? he wondered and took a pull from his cigarette. *A calm in the storm?* David knew that sometimes the calm could be an illusion, like the placid field directly under the eye of a tornado, or the seeming innocence on the face of a serial killer loved by all of his neighbors. But he couldn't imagine the storms raging around Peter in the last moments of his life. Storms both real, and in his head.

David had been the one to find the note in the refrigerator. Along with two pounds of rotting ground beef and bad vegetables. The apartment was a wreck. When their mother called him, she could barely keep herself together. First their father and now this. When David first saw the apartment, he felt sure that someone else had done this to his brother, trashed his place and then hung him from a goal post like some degenerate criminal, but the police only went silent at this suggestion.

He was still convinced that someone else was to blame when he came back a week later to clean out the apartment. Then he found the note.

never disregard your imaginings

David still had the scrap of newspaper in one of his drawers, but he never showed it to his mother. Even though David knew that something had gone terribly wrong in his brother's head, driving Peter to give up the most important fight of all, his Mom needed to believe, if only just a little, that something horrible had happened to her son, and not that he had done something horrible to himself.

David didn't think he'd ever forget the bruise marks showing through mortician's make-up job around Peter's neck.

He had killed himself on a night like tonight, except colder. David had overheard one of the police officers say that it was a miracle his brother made it to the top of the pole in the icy conditions. Pete had always been determined.

In the dark quiet of the backyard, David shook his head. It just didn't make sense.

What could've been that *bad?*

He took a drag from his cigarette but immediately coughed the smoke back out. Suddenly, the cigarette smelled like burning hair and… something else. David had never tasted burning flesh, but he grimaced as he pinched off the end and flicked the butt into the metal trashcan. He needed to quit smoking, anyway.

He climbed the steps to the backdoor and cut through the kitchen into the living room, still half-watching the windows.

"What was it?" Kathy asked from the couch.

Ann looked up from her spot on the floor. David leaned down and kissed her. "Nothing," he said. "Just seeing things, I guess."

Just then the television screen flickered like it had been turned on. In that brief instant, David thought, *oh good, it's over.*

A voice boomed out of the previously lifeless box, punctuating just three words. "Jesus Christ, Almighty!"

David stepped back. The three went silent, their attention drawn to the resurgence in the television. Outside the rain started up again.

"Yes, brothers and sisters, only Christ Almighty will save your *mortal souls* from damnation."

The man on the screen preached in a Southern drawl. The drawl of a rich Southerner. Crisp. For the second time tonight, David was reminded of Georgia and his boyhood. And his brother.

The camera pulled back slowly and the evangelist slid across the stage to a second podium. Then back to the close-up. His face was drawn with age and shiny with makeup, his receding hair plastered to his head.

"To the entire nation of sinners, I cry unto you, you that have been guilty of commerce with the devil, I pray unto you, *cleanse* yourself." The preacher raised both hands to the sky. "For the Prince," he continued, "Yes, brothers and sisters, the Prince of Darkness knows no preference. He is an equal opportunity employer. He does *not* discriminate based on gender or race. He will take you one and all for the sins of yourselves, and the sins you have borne witness to but been too weak to prevent. Yes, brothers and sisters, too pitifully weak."

A gust of wind rattled the old windows in their casings, and the rain started again, pelting the panes.

"Where's the remote control?" Ann asked, annoyed.

David broke from a daze. "Whoa. How about this guy?" He shook his head. "He had me going for a second there. I was right there with him."

"He sounds like my dad," Kathy said.

David and Ann laughed. They had both met Kathy's father, the itinerant Fundamentalist reverend. "Now, *that's* spooky," David said. "Where *is* that remote? Let's find something decent to watch."

For a moment Kathy sat staring at the screen, until David shot her a look. Then she joined the others in searching under couch cushions and pillows. The evangelist kept up his rant. "Complete repentance!" he continued. "Yes, complete repentance is the only way into the Kingdom of Heaven."

"To hell with it," David said and walked over to the television. "What did we ever do before remote controls?" The digital light on the television read channel sixty-six. He pushed the channel button repeatedly, and the screen went dark as the count ran up to ninety-nine. Then the numbers rolled over and David stopped pushing at channel two. CBS. The sound came in before the picture.

"For God does not accept the *foul* and the *dirty*." The old television always took a minute for the picture tubes, and as the color bled into the picture, the evangelist's face transformed from blue to green to orange to flesh.

David shivered. "Strange," he murmured and stared at the screen.

"Hey," Kathy said, "why isn't the street light back on?"

"Why aren't *any* of the lights on?" Ann asked. No one had noticed until now that the television seemed to be the only power in the house.

"The TV works," Kathy said.

"Not from where I'm standing," David said.

"Yes, brothers and sisters, you must atone for your *every sin*, for until you do, you are guilty in the eyes of the Lord. There will be no discrimination between the murderer and the man who covets his neighbor's wife. All are guilty in the eyes of the Lord."

"Enough, David," Ann insisted. "Change the channel."

"Yeah," Kathy agreed. She pulled a strand of her black hair around and started chewing on it. "It's a little too much like Daddy."

"I tried," David said. He demonstrated his previous failed efforts. The digital numbers rose and fell at David's touch, but the picture remained.

"That's not funny, David," Ann said. "Fix the VCR or whatever it was you screwed up for this little trick."

"That's the thing, babe. I didn't do anything."

The evangelist paused and stared into the camera, into the dead quiet living room. "Be prepared, sinners."

"Turn it off, David," Kathy whispered.

"Yeah, David," Ann said. "I don't like this very much. Why isn't the power on anywhere else?"

"I don't know," David snapped. "Christ, how the hell should I know?"

Kathy cringed into the corner of the couch. "You shouldn't take the Lord's name in vain."

"Don't start with me, Kathy. Not now."

Ann rose from her spot on the floor, the deck of cards dropping from her hand and sprawling across the floor, and stood on the other side of the room, clutching her shoulders. "God, it's cold in here," she said.

David felt it too, but he didn't say so. The last words he had spoken sounded slurred to him. He tried to blame it on a creeping chill that was settling into his joints, his jaw included, but why was it so cold all of the sudden?

"Ann, don't take the Lord's--" Kathy started.

"Not now, Kathy," Ann said. "Turn it off, David!"

David looked at Ann, confused. His vision blurred for a quick moment. What was she talking about? David had to shake off the stupor. What the hell was going on? He couldn't keep focused. He tried to lift his hand to hit the power button, but his muscles felt sluggish, like he just woke from a long sleep. He had to flex his fingers out in front of him a couple of times, could almost hear them creaking with each bend, then he reached for the power button. With a push, the screen went blank.

"Thank God," David muttered. He swayed a little in place.

"Yes, my brother and sisters, thank God, indeed!" The evangelist's face crept back on the screen. He looked different, though. Worse. His hair was even greasier, his face paler.

David concentrated on the face. It seemed to be changing before his eyes. Slowly, to be sure, but definitely changing. The hair growing longer, the face turning sicklier.

But that's crazy.

"God dammit," David said, "what the hell is going on?" He knocked on the side of the television and felt a wave of warmth rise up his arm from the contact. When he stepped back, the cold seeped back into his body. He stepped forward and banged on the top of the television with his palm, jarring the picture, and again the heat surged into his body. "Must be something wrong with the television," he said, and started banging harder and faster. At this point, he didn't want to fix the picture as much as he wanted to feel warmth in his body.

"Knock it off, David," Ann whispered. "I can't see."

David kept pounding. Kathy had all but fused with the corner of the couch. She huddled in a ball, her feet pulled up beneath her body. She kept shaking, despite how tightly she had wrapped herself in the comforter.

"I know what's happening," she whimpered, but David ignored her.

"Knock it off, David," Ann said again.

"I should've known," Kathy continued, but no one was listening. "Had a bad feeling all day. Momma was right. The devil's finally come for me. I've been bad, and now the devil's come for me."

Soon the transformation on the screen became so obvious that David knew he couldn't change it even with all of his banging. He stopped, his hand poised a couple of inches above the television. He let out a heavy breath like someone had punched him in the stomach when he saw the aberration. "Holy shit."

"That about sums it up, son." The evangelist's hair had grown about six inches slimier and now hung over a face of mottled skin the color of buttermilk. Black, filmy, pebbled eyes rolled toward David, and the mutation broke into peals of guttural laughter. David staggered back a couple of steps before falling over. Ann backed up against the wall. It couldn't be possible, but David could swear he was looking at-

"A demon," Kathy whimpered as she continued to disappear into the couch. "David, please turn it off."

"He can't do that, sweetheart," the demon said and turned its attention on Kathy, its gaze sending her deeper into the upholstery. "You've been living in sin, little girl. You and your man. We know what your daddy would think, but what about your momma? What would *she* have to say?" Kathy let out a gasp. Her last words were sobbing apologies to her dead mother. Then silence.

"So easy," the demon said.

"Turn it off!" Ann shrieked.

David shook his head. "I can't," he stammered.

"Then I'll do it for you." Ann rushed over and threw her entire body against the side of the entertainment center, knocking over videos and framed photographs. She stumbled back and threw herself at it again. The television crashed to the floor, landing on its side with a sharp crack and a flash of sparks. But the screen remained intact. The picture on the television slowly rotated ninety degrees until the demon's face leveled again. "There's a lot of fire in that one, David," it said and nodded in Ann's direction. "I'd hold on to her, if I were you. For eternity." It chuckled.

Ann attacked the television again, this time kicking it. She kept up the assault, even after the blood seeped through the toe of her slipper. She wouldn't stop. Finally David grabbed her and pulled her away. She struggled briefly and then fell against him, sobbing and dragging him to the ground.

"Time to go, kids," the demon whispered. A murky red glow radiated from the kitchen. Apparently the television wasn't the only appliance that still worked. Thin threads of black smoke snaked up from the oven and curled around the doorframe into the living room. "Time to go."

"Wait!" David shouted. "Just wait one goddamn minute."

The demon smiled.

"Why us?" David asked. "Why us? What did we do that was so wrong?"

The creature on the television started laughing. The laughter rose to a screech of delight that sent a spider web crack over the entire television, splintering both the screen and the plastic shell and distorting the demon's face into a nefarious Picasso. "That's just it, boy," it said. "You haven't really *done* anything."

Ann stopped sobbing. David looked down into her vacant eyes and knew that she had left this place. It was a trick she learned from childhood, a trick any child of abuse knew. Ann told David about her secret place once. It was her grandmother's swimming pool in Virginia. A thick grove of oak trees surrounded the back yard, their reflection shimmering on the surface of the water. David knew Ann was there now. The only thing left of her in the living room was an uncontrollable shaking. He wished he could be there at Grammy's with her.

David held on to her as tightly as he could. The room grew colder. David could see his breath in the crisp air. He couldn't see Kathy at all, however. Just a lump of blanket stuffed in the corner of the couch. Of course, he couldn't be sure with the strobing light from the television streaking patterns in the rapidly thickening smoke and mixing with the growing scarlet haze from the kitchen. Had Kathy really been there before? Nothing made sense anymore. Not since the power first went out. Something had happened. David was starting to lose himself. Blackness bled into his periphery. "Ann?" he called, but no one answered.

The red intensified in the kitchen, the ribbons of smoke more like rivulets of blood. David could feel heat coming from the kitchen. Warmth. Comfort.

"Why did I pick you, son?" the demon asked. "Why you and your little monkey friends? Because you are Innocents. Because Hell lacks Innocents." The demon chuckled. "We need innocence to return the balance, and I will be the one to bring it about." His voice lost the Southern accent, the volume growing into a roar. "And when it is done, the name Mashart shall be revered in the Books of Eternal Damnation."

David's head felt heavy. He grew weary of resisting. "I'm not that innocent," he mumbled. "What about the children?" His eyelids drooped and then closed. "There must be someone else."

Light flashed beyond his eyelids, and David opened his eyes. Power had returned to the house.

Was it ever gone?

David sat on the floor in the middle of the living room staring at the blank television. Kathy still sat on the couch, and Ann was positioned with her back against the wall on his right, the game of solitaire still placed out in front of her. Thick black smoke rolled out of the kitchen, and the smoke detector beeped frantically, but no one moved. David tried to rub at his eyes, but he couldn't move his body. Then darkness started to return, running down the walls and over the furniture like a stain. When the shadow passed over the blank television screen, the demon's face reappeared. It looked curious. And a little uncertain, and when it spoke, the drawl was gone.

"Interesting," the demon said. "You *are* stronger than the others." It paused. "There is another reason I'm here." The demon's drawl seeped back in, the confidence returning. "Just as there was a reason I killed your brother, and that girl in your arms just made it sweeter. It will be done. But you needn't worry yourself about that anymore."

A dozen sets of hands stretched through the plastic on the windows. The arms pushed farther into the room until the heads appeared and then shoulders. The plastic seemed to melt around the spectral flesh. David didn't like the looks of that. What he did like was the blood-red blossom that seemed to radiate from the center of the kitchen, so bright and beautiful and welcoming. He gathered his strength and pushed away from the floor and stood up, cradling Ann in his arms, and turned toward the crimson bloom. He carried Ann clear of the mutations birthing themselves through his windows and walked toward the glow.

"Wait!" the demon shouted. "You aren't supposed to move!"

David stepped into the kitchen just as the red seed in the oven exploded, sending its fleshy core flaming across the kitchen. The clumps spattered against the walls, the curtains, the cabinets. As the kitchen burst into flame, David thought he could smell lasagna. He smiled.

At least it would be warm.

* * *

Excruciating pain took over all thought, shocking David back to his senses. He didn't know what had just happened. The last thing he could remember was standing in his kitchen, waiting for Ann to get home from work, when the door blew open. And now...

My God, the pain.

Colors flickered behind clenched eyelids, but the excruciating agony kept them shut. David was burning everywhere. Especially his right side, as if his skull itself was on fire. Muscles strained all through his shoulders and upper back, but he couldn't move his arms to put out the flames. His limbs felt like they were being pulled from their sockets, like he was being pulled into the earth. His body was rooted in place; he couldn't move away from the torment, but he didn't understand what brought him to this place. Was this a dream? Was he in Hell?

My God! What have I done?

Then David smelled something. Beyond his own cooking flesh and singed hair. Something faint but familiar, mixing with the stench. He opened his left eye as much as he could bear and realized what the smell was. Lasagna. Ann's favorite.

The rest of the evening's events rushed back to David, quick flashes of images that were immediately shattered by his brain screaming at him to escape. But still he swayed heavily in the kitchen and watched the flames through a slit eyelid as they climbed the walls away from the blackened pasta and marinara splattered on the peeling wallpaper. The fire had spread quickly. The black smoke rolling off the burning cabinets filled his lungs and burned his eyes, even the one still clenched shut on the side of his face which he was certain was aflame. Tears blurred his narrow vision, rolling down his cheek. His whole body wanted to recoil from the heat from the flames. Man-made material seemed to burn so much hotter than firewood, but still he couldn't move his feet to escape.

My God, the pain.

But the torment wasn't just on the surface, where he could feel the fire eating away at his face. Suddenly he understood the tearing muscles in his shoulders and arms, which felt like he was being taken apart and reformed in a forge, and the realization twisted the whole of his insides around on themselves. He knew why he couldn't lift his arms, why he hadn't simply dropped to the ground. Because he had believed that the kitchen was safe. And now he was burning to death because of it. Now *they* were burning to death.

David looked down at Ann. He cradled her in his arms, but her own limbs dangled toward the floor. He stared at her in spite of the flames that engulfed her upper body, climbing up her robed arms from the burning linoleum and licking at his face, igniting his hair. He had only wanted to save her.

He lifted his head toward the ceiling, but still he held on to Ann's body, even though her death was killing him as well. Bubbles of skin swelled and popped as the burning shreds of his shirt fluttered to the ground. Every muscle tightened in David's body in response to the trauma. His neck went rigid, straining from his skull into his back. His jaw clenched so hard that he thought he would surely grind his teeth into shards as the fire climbed the right side of his chest. Tears of pain welled at his eyes, but they evaporated before they could fall from his lids. Then he dropped to his knees.

Ann's body was slipping through his arms. He couldn't hold onto her any longer.

David lowered her burning body down on the melting linoleum even though his mind screamed to take her outside into the rain.

Maybe he could still help her. Maybe she wasn't dead just yet. If only he had been strong enough. That *thing* had poisoned his mind, and he had been too weak to fight back. What if he had moved sooner? Instead, he had just stood there while she died in his arms.

His brain rallied with his body, but the agony won out. Ann wasn't moving, and if he didn't get out, he would be dead too. He knew he couldn't lift her again. He could barely keep himself from falling over on top of her. They would never make it out of the house.

David rose slowly on shaky legs and looked down at Ann, the robe having burned away, her naked figure hardly recognizable anymore. His whole body trembled and threatened to give way beneath him, sorrow and pain racking his body. Finally his thoughts stopped racing long enough to issue one definite command.

Get out!

The decision had been made. Still he found it difficult to look away from Ann, feeling a final rip when he turned his back on her, like his heart being pulled through his throat, and sought an exit. The living room didn't look much better than the kitchen. Sparks shot from the cracked television screen, spreading the inferno across the carpet. The heavy plastic over the windows softened and stretched from the heat, dripping burning blackness where other pieces had caught fire. David looked toward the raging couch where Kathy had sat. No movement. No life in the room except his own. It took a moment to get his bearings and locate the door across the room, but now his body had changed its plans. Suddenly, he just wanted to lie down, surrender. What did he have left to live for?

But his mind wasn't giving up the fight this time, and he summoned the last of his energy, launching across the room into the entryway. He grabbed the door handle with his right hand, but charred skin pulled away from his clutch. He looked down at pieces of his skin stuck to the door and blackness started dropping over his vision. He beat the unconsciousness back and yanked the door open with his left hand, bursting through the doorway into the night. The rain from the storm washed over his burning body with a hissing sound. He dropped to the yard, rolling in the muddy grass.

Overcome by the rush of clean air, David was seized by gagging coughs, expelling the smoke. He caught his breath, gasping, and pulled himself to his feet. The world seemed to go gray. His legs wavered beneath him, but he fought the wave of nausea. Unsuccessfully. Doubling over, his stomach retched only fluid. Wiping his mouth, he straightened up, and he scanned the neighborhood for any sign of life. The only light in the area, though, was the growing glow emanating from the burning house.

Instinct took over, and his thoughts finally found focus. He realized that whatever had been in the television could still be around. He had lost the fight. Now it was time to run. His eyes adjusted to the darkness beyond the edges of the glow cast from the house, and he noticed dull light from the east side of town. Power was still on over there. The mountains were that way. Big yards. Lots of property. He could hide until morning.

First he would have to find something for his burns. He could break into a store while the power was still out. Something.

Anything. *God, it still burned.* His flesh was still cooking. He could feel the heat chewing toward his center.

And in the morning? He would run. The rest would have to take care of itself. There were places he could run, places to hide, people who could help him. He looked back at the house, and his chest hitched hard enough to almost put him back to his knees. There would be no help for Ann.

The tears came then, and blurred his vision as he turned away and stumbled across the street and out of his neighborhood.

CHAPTER 2

In the nightmare, David was running through the woods, but it was unlike any forest he had ever seen. The trees were barren of any green, their branches low to the ground, twisted and contorted into each other. A thick rain spattered and stained the trees black.

Something was chasing behind him. He could hear it. Even though his brain knew that the demon had only been pursuing him for a few months since fleeing the burning house, in the dream David felt like it had been his whole life. He stopped running and looked back. In a flash of lightning, he saw a dark writhing mass that seemed the size of ten elephants, but with the swiping claws of dozens of wild animals. And countless heads to match. The creature seemed to devour the very forest itself as it tore after him.

David looked down in his hand. He held a .38 revolver, even though he had never personally owned a gun. Knowing already that it wouldn't help him, he still raised the revolver against the monstrosity, but the weapon was replaced by a cap gun with paper strips, like the kind his father bought for him when he was seven. But the paper was all wet, and the gun only made a soft click. David dropped the toy and tried to run, but the muck underfoot sucked at his feet, and tugging felt like he was trying to free his bones from flesh. Finally, he pulled free and dashed through the mud toward one of the trees that grew wider and taller than the rest. At the base, he looked up and thought he could see bright green at the top, silhouetted against the black clouds.

The sounds of growling and gnashing teeth and the splintering of the trees grew louder behind him. Maybe if he could just get above the thing.

The dead tree was bare of any bark, and the rotten branches, slick from the pounding rain, made the climbing difficult. A couple of times David lost his grip, nearly falling, but finally he gained some height, and indeed life started to reappear, sprouts of green and patches of bark for better purchase as he climbed. But with the life came death. There were other people in the tree. Like the gallows trees of old, the branches were populated with the dead, but in this tree they were still squirming. Some were definitely worse off than others, barely recognizable as human. They ripped at their own flesh, trying to pull off scabbed, burned, and rotted strips. They howled at their own pain. Others, those who appeared to have died more recently, screamed and wept and clawed at the tree instead. When they saw David, they closed in on him, lifting their bodies and sliding the ropes across the branches toward him, those who could still speak begging for his help, saying they shouldn't be there. They put their cold, bloody hands on David as if he could save them, surrounding him with their stench. They tried to pull him away from his clutch to the main trunk of the tree.

A woman in a western-style suit coat and jeans skittered across a branch, her cowboy boots dancing on the rotted, slippery wood. She looked like she might've still been warm to the touch if it weren't for the death in her eyes. David turned away from her and hugged the tree tighter, but a moment later he heard her raspy, gurgling breath by his ear.

"Where's my gun, boy?" she whispered, her breath reeking of decay. "You're gonna need it."

Then the whole tree started to shake and vibrate. David looked down and saw hundreds of yellow eyes, like fireflies swarming the tree below. The predator had caught up. It hadn't passed him by. The tree swayed as the crunching of wood continued. There was a loud *crack*, and then the top of the tree began to fall to the darkness. David expected to plunge into the grinding maw of the beast below him, but instead he landed hard in the mud. A voice whispered in his ear.

I'm coming.

David tried to push away from the mud, but he was sucked into the soft surface. His arms sank up to his shoulders. For a brief moment he was reminded of hiking along wet riverbeds in the late spring, of his old job taking troubled teens on wilderness retreats. The image slipped away as the mud covered his face, filling his mouth and rushing up his nostrils.

* * *

David awoke with a start, coughing and gagging in a small puddle of muddy water. He quickly pushed himself up, taking ragged breaths as the pain shot through his aching body. He sat back against the large pine tree where he had dropped to rest.

How long ago? Hours? Days?

He cursed himself for losing consciousness, even though he knew he must have needed it. The forest was so thick he would only be given a few seconds warning of an attack, but David's body didn't seem to care. Maybe his mind didn't care anymore, either.

Dear God, how long have I been running?

The bark of the tree scraped against his raw back and the bed of pine needles stuck him, but David focused his attention on his battered shins and abused feet.

Has it been weeks? Who was the last human I saw?

Even with his wilderness training, the passing of the sun and moon meant nothing to David anymore. He woke and moved when he could, and he stopped and slept when he could move no farther. Dreams had become his reality as he stumbled through the thick forest, and often he didn't know where the line was drawn. He had seen so much horror during his waking hours. So why should he doubt the creatures creeping through the brush in the middle of the night?

David's feet throbbed in their boots, like his heart had relocated to his legs and was trying to make its escape out of the ends of his toes. He had been weighing a decision for days, but staring down at what felt like clubs at the ends of his legs, he knew what he had to do. He reached over for his pack, but it was gone. David wondered if he had it with him when he had stopped or if it was something he had lost long before today. Didn't matter now. Luckily, he still had his Leatherman multi-tool attached to his belt. He opened it up, pulling out the blade. Some time earlier, he had tried pulling off his boots, but the pain had been so excruciating that he had given up.

He had to do something; otherwise he wouldn't be able to continue moving. Each day, the pain in his swollen feet allowed him less distance.

Each day, he thought as he cut into his boots. *How long can this last?*

When he first fled the inferno in Canyon City, David tried hiding out in various parts of town. He attended to his wounds first, thankful for his wilderness EMT training even though he knew his condition was far beyond "first aid" and that he would never look even close to himself again. Half insane with the grief of losing Ann and with the pain of his burned flesh, David attempted contact with friends, but each time it turned out to be a mistake. On one occasion, an old roommate, Erik Janes, had been so insistent on contacting the police, or at least getting him to a hospital, that David slipped out in the middle of the night after convincing Erik that he needed to sleep on it. Erik woke the next morning to find David gone, but two other friends, Jeff Burns and his girlfriend, Nancy, weren't so lucky.

The mountains surrounding the Canyon City valley had boxed in the storm from that first night over the town for several days, and apparently the evil in with it. It was late the night David showed up at Jeff's place. He was going to just let himself in and explain himself in the morning, but hearing sounds coming from their apartment, David had knocked on the door. When there was no response, he stepped off the stoop onto the lawn and peered in one of the windows. He could see the shifting colors from a television cast on the walls of an otherwise dark living room. Circling the complex, David hopped the short fence surrounding their patch of backyard. Through the sliding door, he could see Jeff sitting on the couch with an arm over Nancy's shoulder, the TV flashing on their faces. He rapped lightly on the door, glancing around to make sure he wasn't drawing any other attention. Neither of the two moved from their spot on the couch.

David tried the door, and it slid open. He had already prepared his story to calm his friends' shock at seeing him in such a state, but when the stench of rotting food assaulted him from the apartment, he guessed it didn't matter what he had to say. Flies were gathering on two plates of crusted-over, half-eaten beef stroganoff on the coffee table in front of the couch. Just beneath the smell of the decay, David picked up another scent, faint traces like burnt gasoline. He stepped into the living room, already suspecting the worst, but still he spoke their names, hoping to wake them from wherever they had gone. Their bloodshot eyes never wavered from the flickering television screen, even when David stepped in front of it. He turned and looked at the set. He doubted they were watching the Carlton Sheets infomercial. He stepped around the coffee table, leaned over and lowered their eyelids.

David turned off the television and stood in the dark. He didn't want to believe that this was the same thing that had happened at his house. Or even worse, that he was the cause of whatever had happened to his friends here. His mind reeled. Then the moon broke through the clouds, briefly casting a blue glow into the room, and for the first time since his flight from the inferno three days earlier, David had a moment of clarity. He needed to get into the woods. The wilderness had always been a favorite place for David, so much that he even found work in Colorado hiking and camping out with troubled youths. He never really considered his passion for the wilderness a link with "God," was actually never convinced there even was a God. But he believed in nature, and in nature, he believed in himself. His comfort in the wild felt like more of a connection to the powers of the earth, the natural flow without the interference of man, a place where he could be invisible, his mind free and clear.

With a sudden renewed energy at the prospect, David left the apartment. On his way out, he paused and looked at the keys to Jeff's pickup truck. He hesitated only a moment before pocketing the keys. He couldn't go back to his house for his own vehicle, and if Jeff was alive, David knew he would have let him take it. It was survival at this point.

He drove out of their apartment complex to the outskirts of town, where he broke into a sporting goods store. With the bare minimum necessities for staying alive, David drove away from civilization. He wound into the mountains, taking unfamiliar turns, intentionally trying to lose himself, until he came to a dead end, a Forest Service gate crossing the rutted dirt road. He backtracked until he found a short turnoff leading down beside a creek, hidden from the main road. He camped there for the night and the next morning abandoned the truck.

It had worked. He lost himself in the mountains. He knew that he could only make it so far before either the demon or the weather caught up to him. He would never survive a winter in this condition, and that was just fine. Every day, he cursed himself for running away from the inferno where his love had burned to death, but he couldn't go back now, and he wouldn't give up without some sort of a fight. He would keep moving until he was overtaken or until he simply dropped.

Leaning against the tree, David wondered how much farther that point would be. He finished cutting off his boots and tossed them aside. The boots had put up a fight, but the relief was immediate, and he let out a heavy sigh as he fell back against the tree. Movement next to him caught his eye, and he twisted his body to the right, his hand drawing the knife, half-expecting to see a predator drawn to the smell of a wounded animal. Instead, his older brother stared back at him from beyond the grave.

Peter's eyes were sunken and ringed in black, his skin otherwise pale underneath streaks where it appeared tears had washed away the mortician's makeup. And his thick, bruised necktie showed through even starker than the day at the mortuary.

Not much longer at all, David thought.

He dropped his arm and sighed. He sat back and closed his eyes. This wasn't the first time he had seen his brother since fleeing the house in Colorado. "Never doubt your imaginings," David mumbled, his voice falling away in the dead quiet surrounding him. The forest felt like a black hole. Nothing moved. Not a whisper of air. Not a bird or insect. He wondered if he actually spoke aloud at all.

"Never *disregard* your imaginings."

For a moment, David wouldn't open his eyes, couldn't believe it to be true. It was the first time the vision of his older brother had spoken to him, but in truth, he just wanted Pete… hallucination, ghost, whatever… to go away. There had been so much loss, so much pain. He didn't want to see his brother. He didn't want to think about Ann. He just wanted to forget. He just wanted to die.

But his brother didn't care.

"This is not your time," Peter said. His voice was barely above a whisper, but it sounded rough, like he had gravel in his throat. Finally David opened his eyes and looked at him. "You have to push on," Peter continued. "Not much farther now."

Peter winced as he spoke, and David could see that even in death, his brother hadn't been spared the pain.

David shook his head. "I don't want to go on," he said, instantly ashamed of how childish he sounded, but he couldn't contain it. "I just want to rest. I'm seeing things. Night, day, awake, dreaming. I don't know what's real anymore. I don't even know if I'm really in these mountains." David's own voice cracked. A tear escaped his right eye, where his vision was still hazy from the fire. "Maybe none of this is real, and I'm still in Colorado," he said. "Maybe there's still time to save her." He waited for his brother to respond, to say something. Anything. Even just a comforting clasp on his shoulder. But Peter only stared back. "Am I dreaming now, Pete?" David asked.

"Does it matter?"

David considered his brother's question for a moment. After airing out his feelings, hearing his own words aloud to someone else, real or imagined, he felt better, if only just a little. Maybe he wasn't ready to die. "No, I guess it *doesn't* matter."

"You're alive because you were supposed to make it to this day," Peter said. "You have to keep going. Not much farther now."

A clap of thunder broke the unnatural silence surrounding the two. David looked up through the canopy of branches. Thin clouds had softened the previously stark blue sky. When he looked back, Peter was gone. Time to get going.

There were no thunderheads yet. He still had some time, but not that much. Dream or no dream, the storm didn't care. And neither did its rider.

David cut strips from his already tattered jeans, and wrapped them around his feet. Every muscle in his back seemed to tear as he pulled himself away from the tree and rose to his feet. Instinctively, he staggered to his left and started moving again, the forward momentum of his upper body dragging his legs along to keep up. The thinning of the evergreens gave him hope that he was moving in the right direction, toward a road maybe. Or a ranch.

The trees continued to thin until he broke through them completely and stood looking into a huge valley. Sharp granite peaks jutted up in the distance above a lush tree line. The ridge on his side sloped quickly down to form the oblong bowl of the valley. Not exactly a cliff, but steep. At the base of the slope, about four or five hundred yards away, stood a cabin. Two vehicles were parked there, and a thin trail of smoke rose from the chimney.

So that's where it would happen. That's where the demon would try to come through again. Not that much farther. But experience had taught him that time grew short. The clouds had arrived faster than David anticipated, and the sky turned dark. Against the will of his screaming legs, he started to clamber down the ridge to the cabin, just as he felt the first drop of rain.

CHAPTER 3

Dr. Robert Marrick thought that the feeling in the Jeep could only be described as electric. He felt happier than he had in months as he bounced over the dirt road, twisting through the mountains with his family on the way to the new Montana cabin. His fifteen-year-old daughter hadn't complained once since leaving Boston, and a couple of times he even caught Judy looking over at him the way she did when they were younger and more carefree. They exchanged sly smiles. Maybe now everybody could be happy.

"How much longer, Daddy?" Jeannie asked from the backseat, "This bumpy road makes me need to pee."

"Now, honey," Judy said, looking over her shoulder at their daughter, "that's not very ladylike." But when a giggle escaped Judy, the scolding was lost between the two. Judy turned back around. "How much farther, Bob?" she asked.

Robert looked down at the odometer and then at his watch. He frowned briefly and then smiled. "Probably about five more miles," he said. "We should be there in about ten minutes." He looked in the rearview mirror at his daughter. "I think you can wait ten minutes, sweetie."

Jeannie tried to look put out, but Robert just laughed.

Only your mom can pull that one off, kiddo, he thought.

Actually, Robert wasn't exactly sure how much farther it was to the cabin. Surprisingly, he had lost track of the mileage since turning off the paved road. He had made the trip a few times before the actual purchase and had already started his mental map of the area. A familiar curve here. A rotted log there. But now he realized that he wasn't sure where they were or how far they had gone.

The Jeep took a hard dip into a pothole on the left side and then quickly hopped out again. Jeannie let out a whoop from the back seat.

"You're supposed to be watching out for those, sweetie," Robert said to his daughter. "Or maybe you'd rather drive, and *I'll* be the one watching for the holes."

"I'm not old enough to drive," Jeannie said. "Yet."

"Thank heavens for small favors," Robert said. "We better enjoy the last couple of safe months of our lives." He started laughing. Again Jeannie tried to put on a sour face, but it barely masked a grin.

Judy managed a chuckle, but Robert sensed that it was forced. A year earlier, to Robert's astonishment, Judy had told him in counseling that she felt threatened by the attention he doted on Jeannie. Robert had tried to be understanding, but he wasn't about to ignore the fact that Jeannie was special. Every father likes to think this about his child, but it wasn't until sixth grade, when Jeannie's teachers told the Marricks that they should think about not only advancing Jeannie *at least* one grade but also seriously consider a private school, that Robert knew his daughter would do great things. Judy and Robert had argued that night for almost two hours before deciding to go ahead with the advancement.

Still, Robert knew Judy didn't like it. It was definitely an issue they were still working through. Judy just had to understand. Robert looked over at his wife, but he didn't catch her eye this time. She stared out at the thick patches of evergreens rushing past her open window. She shivered, then reached over and pushed the dial on the control panel to *warm*.

"Are you kidding?" Robert asked. "It's the middle of the day."

"I just got a little chilly," Judy said.

"Then roll up your window."

"But I like the smell of the air," Judy said.

Robert shook his head. "Jeannie, sweetie, if you get too hot back there, let me know and I'll put down the other window."

"I'm okay, thanks."

Judy huffed and looked back out of her window as the edge of the woods receded from the road and the valley widened.

"There it is!" Robert exclaimed.

In Robert's opinion, they couldn't have found a better place. It was as if God had cupped His very own hands and let the earth grow up around it. The dirt road broke out of the mountain pass and opened up to the most beautiful place on earth. The jagged landscape retreated almost immediately and gave way to a lush green meadow that spread out in front of them for almost a mile before sloping up about three hundred yards to a forested plateau that ringed the small valley. Only a handful of trees actually dotted the base of the bowl itself. Their realtor, Barbara Stack, told them that it was the result of a microburst, a small-scale, severe storm downdraft that acted like a steamroller down the slope many years ago, taking the trees with it.

Robert slowed the Jeep to take in their new view. It matched almost precisely the image in his mind's eye when they started talking about buying property in Montana two years ago. The log cabin sat at the far end of the meadow, built closer to the base of the slope. A stream, maybe five feet wide, ran along the side of the dirt road. Barb Stack told them the creek originated at a lake farther up in the mountains.

"Say, kiddo, have you ever wanted to catch a fish?" Robert asked Jeannie. "I'll bet we could dam up this creek and make ourselves a nice little pond." Robert looked at his wife. "What do you think, babe?" he asked. "You haven't fished in years."

"It has been awhile," she said and smiled.

Robert reached across and rested his hand on her thigh. "It will be better," he said. "I promise." Judy put her hand on top of Robert's.

"Hey, look," Jeannie said. "Somebody's already here."

Robert returned his attention to the road. Sure enough, as they wound up to the cabin, he saw the dark-blue Jetta parked on the side. So Barb had already arrived. It never ceased to amaze Robert that the Jetta made it up the road without busting an axle.

"Who is it?" Jeannie asked.

"It's Ms. Stack," Judy answered. "She's the woman who sold us the house."

"And made a healthy little cut for herself," Robert muttered.

"Oh, Bob," Judy sighed. "Barb worked hard to find us this place."

"I know, I know," Robert said. "I was just hoping we could get up here a little bit before her."

"She won't be here long."

"I still don't understand why we couldn't take care of this without having her on our first day."

"She likes to be at a property when the new owners arrive for the first time. You know, hand over the keys. It's part of her charm."

"Just because she's a friend of your boss's wife doesn't necessitate congeniality. And besides-"

"Wow, look at that!" Jeannie interrupted as they pulled to a stop in front of the cabin. "Eagles. Check it out, Mom, eagles!" She pointed to the sky just above the ridgeline. Two birds looped around and over each other.

Robert looked up and squinted. "I think those are just hawks, sweetie," he said. "They're too small to be eagles. Pretty cool, though. Don't see *those* in the city." Robert watched the birds as their circles grew larger, then wound tighter. Each time they neared each other, the two birds seemed to attack before the circles widened again. The sky had started to darken. Gray clouds were rolling in. Robert was amazed by how quickly they were moving.

"Hey, y'all!" It was Barb. She walked out of the house, crossed the deck and started descending the steps. She wore a dark green suitcoat with jeans and cowboy boots.

Only in Montana, Robert thought.

"I thought you'd never make it," Barb said and laughed. "I'd swear you city folks don't know how to drive that fancy rig you got there."

"Hi, Barb," Robert said and got out of the Jeep.

"Howdy, Bob." Barb walked around to Judy. "Hey, Judy," she said and hugged her. "How are you doin', lady?"

Judy looked surprised, then hugged Barb back. "I'm well, Barb."

"I think I'm going to walk around a little," Jeannie said. "Just take a look. Is that okay, Mom?"

"Sure, honey," Judy said. "Just don't go too far, okay?"

"She might want to wait on that, Judy," Barb said. "We got a storm comin' in real fast. Why don't y'all come inside. We'll have a cup of tea and I can go over the last of the details. By then, the storm should've passed, and I can get outta' your hair."

"Aw, do I have to?" Jeannie asked, sounding younger than her years. She quickly corrected her tone. "I mean, that's just boring adult stuff. Besides, I don't care about getting a little wet."

"I don't know about a *little* wet, darlin'," Barb said. "We're fixin' to have ourselves a good burst of rain. We'd have to put you in the dryer after this one. Besides, it'll be a lot more fun *after* the rain. The sun will come back, and if you're lucky, you might be able to chase down some toads."

"Gross." Jeannie scowled, clearly not convinced that it was going to rain, but as the group crossed the pebbled driveway toward the cabin, a low rumble rolled into the valley. Robert's first thought was subway train, but he quickly dismissed his city inclinations. *Probably not many passengers looking for a ride out here.* He chuckled.

Barb looked to the sky. "This is my favorite time of year. Storms roll in about mid-afternoon, cool everything off, and then roll right back out. You can almost set your watch to it." Another clap of thunder filled the valley, much louder this time. "Looks like the ol' 4:15 is a little ahead of schedule." Barb laughed again.

Robert looked up the slope before stepping onto the porch. Most of the sky had already darkened. A fat drop of rain splashed on his left shoulder. Other drops rustled the grass around the house.

"C'mon in," Barb said. "I've already started a little fire. Temperature'll probably dip about ten, maybe fifteen degrees here in the next little bit, but we'll be nice and cozy."

Robert stepped into the house. Jeannie edged past the adults and down the hall to her new bedroom, already pulling out one of the teen magazines from her backpack. Robert stood in the main living area of the house and smiled. It had been a couple of months since they last saw the place, but it already felt like home, and the great room was Robert's favorite part. The living room and dining area had high vaulted ceilings. A flight of stairs led up to the master bedroom and an open den that overlooked the downstairs. A fireplace was on the wall opposite the main entrance with a stone chimney running all the way up. Four skylights were installed in the ceiling of the great room, and Robert watched as large drops of rain exploded on the glass panes. The storm was picking up.

"You ain't seen nothin' yet," Barb said. Robert wondered if the thick drawl might also be part of Barb's "charm," part of the show for the city folk. She walked over next to him and followed his gaze. "This is going to be a big one, I think."

As if in confirmation, another clap of thunder filled the little valley, rattling the windows just slightly.

"What did I tell you," Barb said. "Come have some tea, Bob, and we can take care of those papers."

"I think I'll go for coffee," Robert said. "I have some out in the Jeep."

"Now you're getting into the Montana way." Barb gave him a playful slug on his arm. Robert chuckled, a little in spite of himself. She could be annoying sometimes, but Barb was a good enough woman. And even with her commission, they had made out like bandits.

Bandits, Robert thought. *I really am in Montana.*

Robert stepped out onto the porch and down the stairs. The rain still fell light enough that it wasn't completely drenching, even though it felt close. He walked to the Jeep and rummaged through the things until he found a box that was marked kitchen. He pulled the box out, shut the door and walked around the Jeep toward the cabin, looking at the slope that ran up behind the house to a forested ridge. He stopped in his tracks and watched in amazement as a curtain of rain swept over the tops of the trees and then dropped off the ridge, rolling down the slope toward the cabin. The few drops of rain hitting Robert now were nothing. That moving wall carried the real storm.

He was about to continue inside when movement up on the slope caught his eye. Something about three-quarters of the way up was making its way down. The storm followed just behind it. Robert squinted and tried to focus his vision, but the rain kept hitting his face and making him blink. And then the thing disappeared. The front line of the storm had overtaken it.

Probably just a deer or an elk.

He quickened his step up the stairs and joined the two women in the kitchen. They stood by the industrial stove, the gas flames licking the sides of the tea kettle. Three mugs and a package of Montana Sunshine herbal tea rested on the island in the center of the kitchen. Barb hadn't missed a trick.

"How's it looking out there?" Barb asked.

"Tremendous," Robert said. "Something big coming in." He plugged in the coffee maker and filled the pot at the sink. "It's amazing, babe," he said to Judy. "When it tapers off, you should go outside and stand in it. It's so..." Robert searched for the right word, "refreshing. So much cleaner than the city."

Judy smiled. "I'll have to do that," she said. "Maybe we can go for a walk."

Robert laughed. "Is it time for *the walk* already?" He knew that it was Judy's solution to getting Robert to relax on vacations. It usually took him at least three days of being away from his patients before he could start to unwind. Judy had said in more than one counseling session that she thought if he didn't slow down, Robert would end up in the hospital himself before he was fifty.

Barb clapped her hands together. "Well, let's get wrapped up so I can leave you folks alone," she said.

Just then the rain really hit the cabin, pounding violently on the metal roof. Judy jumped a little, and Robert rushed over to the windows. The rain fell so heavy that he could barely see the vehicles in the driveway.

The storm had arrived.

"There it is," Barb said and sipped calmly from her cup.

Judy let out a nervous laugh. "Is it always like this?"

"More or less," Barb said. She stood from her stool and peered out the kitchen window. "I've got to say, this is one of the stronger bursts I've seen. At least it's not hail, which isn't completely uncommon for this time of year. Why, it wasn't more than three years ago that we had a blizzard that swept across Montana at the beginning of June. Dropped snow as low as three thousand feet." She shook her head, as if still in disbelief. "Don't worry, hon. You'll get used to it. And like they say around here, if you don't like the weather, wait fifteen minutes, and it'll change."

Judy shivered as the din grew. "I'm going to check on Jeannie," she said and left her spot by the counter. She made it halfway down the hallway when she heard a crash from the front of the cabin. She rushed back to the living room just as Robert ran in.

"What the-" Robert started, but stopped when he saw the ragged person lying face down in the entryway. The figure lay sprawled halfway across the threshold; the wind bounced the door between the doorstop and his right shoulder. He was half-covered by tattered clothes, and thick, dark mud was clumped on his body.

Barb nearly ran into Robert when she hurried from the kitchen, and the three stood motionless until Robert's professional side kicked in. He kneeled down beside the man. He rolled the emaciated body over, and both women gasped. Even Robert was taken aback. The young man's face was horribly scarred on the right side. Robert thought they looked like burn scars, but with no attempt at medical reconstruction. The man's eyes bulged and rolled in their sockets, one of them blue and the other a milky gray color. The man's right arm shot up and spasmed, his hand clutching at empty space. His breath was ragged, and he was mumbling something. Robert leaned closer to hear.

"Close the door," he gasped, "must close the door."

Rain was already starting to puddle in the room. "Judy, get the door," Robert said.

Judy rushed over and pushed the door shut against the wind. The man let out a raspy cough and clutched Robert's shirt. The tendons in the man's neck strained as he lifted his head from the floor, and he pulled Robert closer. "Must...not...open...again," he whispered, and then his eyes rolled back in his head and his body went limp.

CHAPTER 4

"He's unconscious," Robert said.

"What's going on?" Jeannie had stepped out of her room to peer down the hallway.

Judy rushed over to her. "It's nothing to worry about, honey," she said and tried to guide Jeannie back to the room.

"Who's that man?" Jeannie asked, looking past her mother.

"I don't know, honey," Judy said, "but he's very sick. Your father will take care of him, but you shouldn't be around. We don't want you getting sick."

"Yeah, but-" Jeannie started, but Judy managed to get her into the room and shut the door behind them.

As for the stranger, passing out had apparently done him some good. His breathing calmed. After checking his vital signs, Robert stood up and crossed his arms. "Is this normal in Montana, Barb?" he asked. "Did this guy just wander off a compound somewhere?"

Barb stared at him. "Your guess is as good as mine," she said. "Whoever he is, we need to call an ambulance. Do you folks have a cellular phone? I can't seem to get any service up here on mine today. Must be the storm."

Robert walked over to his coat and pulled out his phone. He turned it on, and after a moment, shook his head. "Nothing," he said. He walked around the cabin, holding it up and trying to get a signal, but the "out of service area" message remained. What was once another charming aspect of the new vacation home now took on a darker tone. "Okay, we're going to need to think about this."

"I don't see what there is to think about," Judy said. Robert hadn't noticed her coming out of their daughter's room.

"How's Jeannie?" he asked her.

"She's fine," Judy said. "Barely shaken up, but we need to get this man-"

Robert cut her off. "Barb, you're going to have to drive into town. Take Judy and Jeannie with you. I'll stay here and keep an eye on our friend."

"What if he wakes up and attacks you?" Judy asked.

"Try using your head, Judy," Robert snapped. She pursed her lip and turned on her glare, so Robert toned it down. "I don't see another alternative," he said. "He's not going to attack anybody. Even if he did, I would rather it be me than one of you. He's half my size. And besides, I'm the doctor. I don't think he's in critical condition, but just in case something happened, I wouldn't-"

"So why don't *you* drive him into town," Judy said. "Wouldn't that make the most sense if he's not in critical condition and you're certain he won't attack? It would certainly be the quickest way. And if he seemed to get worse on the way, like you said, you're the doctor."

"Yes, but..." Robert started. He clenched his jaw. "You're probably right. I'll go start the Jeep." He put on his coat and walked over to the front door, splashing in the puddle in the entryway. He stopped and looked at Judy with his eyebrows raised. "Could you get this?" he said and motioned to the floor. Judy tensed, and then headed into the kitchen to get the roll of paper towels. He was reaching for the knob on the door when Barb stopped him .

"Bob, wait. Maybe we better think about this," she said. "He's not gonna die just yet, right?"

Robert turned back toward Barb. "My wife is right, Barb. As a doctor, I need to get this man help. I don't see that there's much more to think about."

"Well, that's because you're from the city," she said. "No offense, but it's true."

"Really? What do we do in Montana, Barb? Sew up his cuts with a little horsetail hair and send him on his way?" Robert cracked.

"*Bob,*" Judy scolded on her return to the great room.

"It's alright, Judy," Barb said. "What I'm about to say might sound just a little crazier, but you got me thinking earlier, Bob. Now, there's generally only two reasons you find a young man in this poor of condition so far from civilization. One, he's a college boy that got himself lost in our little maze of mountains. The other possibility is that this boy's never seen civilization in the first place. Lots of families live in these mountains, I'd imagine. Someone may be looking for this kid, some backwoods family or even a cult. The last thing you want is for them to track him here while you're gone. I'm not saying that's the case. It's probably not. But why take any chances? And what did he say to you just before he passed out, Bob?"

"He said something about how we shouldn't open the door."

"You see? Someone's chasing this boy, and even if it's not some wacko, it could be the authorities, which means he could be dangerous."

"Well, I'm certainly not taking all of you in the Jeep," Robert stated. "You think I'd expose Jeannie to that?"

"That's not what I'm suggesting," Barb said. "I think your plan is a good one, but it just needs a little polishing. You folks don't own a firearm, am I right?"

"Not with Jeannie," Robert said. "I bought some bear mace before we left for hiking."

"That's a start. Now, here's what you're going to do." Barb stopped and looked at Robert. "You okay with this?" she asked, as if she'd known a man or two in her life who didn't take too kindly to being told what to do. Robert wasn't used to it either, but he just shrugged, and she continued. "Judy, you get your daughter ready to go. You two will be following Bob and me in my Jetta. I've got a .38 snub nose under the seat of my car. It's mostly in case I hit an animal and need to put it out of its misery. I'll ride with Bob and our new friend here, and keep the revolver trained on him just in case he wakes up and tries anything funny."

Robert thought about this for a moment. "Maybe it would be safer if *you* drove, and I held the gun."

Judy laughed. "How many times have you ever held a gun, Bob?"

"*He* doesn't know that," Robert said.

Barb stepped in. "I appreciate that, Bob, but I think we should stick with my plan. I'm pretty familiar with the .38, and would prefer handling it myself."

"Fine," Robert said.

No one moved for a moment. "I'll get Jeannie ready," Judy said and hustled down the hall to her daughter's room.

Robert and Barb just stared at each other, before the realtor broke the silence. "I'll go get my .38 in case he wakes up sooner."

Barb opened the closet and pulled out her raincoat. Robert couldn't believe the words he was hearing from the realtor. He had to force back a crazy grin that threatened to break loose.

Life in Montana, he thought. And people called New York wild.

Barb put on her coat and was reaching for the handle of the door, when she stopped and turned around. "Bob, if you give me your keys, I can move the Jeep closer to the porch."

"They're on the table next to you," Robert said.

Barb pocketed the keys. She stared at Robert, as if she expected him to do something, but for a moment he couldn't figure out what she wanted. Finally it hit him. "I'll get some dry clothes and get him ready to move."

Barb nodded and opened the door. A burst of cold air rushed in, threatening to put out the fire in the living room, but she pushed out into the storm, tugging the door shut behind her.

She stepped onto the porch and shivered. This was actually one of the worst storms Barb had seen, but she hadn't wanted to say it to Judy earlier. She rushed down the steps in the rain to her Jetta and quickly pulled the .38 from under her seat and slipped it in the front pocket of her raincoat. A flash of light, followed immediately by a crack of thunder, almost sent Barb to the ground for fear of being struck, but she kept her footing in the muddy driveway and dashed over to the Jeep. Locked. She cursed Bob as she fumbled with the keys. Finally finding the right one, she unlocked the door and hopped in. She put the key in the ignition and twisted.

Another flash lit up the valley, and a crack of thunder seemed to shake the earth as the Jeep's engine fired to life. Barb had her hand on the gearshift and was about to put it in reverse, but she froze.

As the only child in her family, Barb had been on more than a few hunting trips with her father. He always told her that she had "a good sense about her, even for a girl." More than just seeing or hearing an animal, when she hiked in the wilderness, she could almost *feel* when an animal was close.

Barb had that feeling now. And she didn't like it. Something was out there. She didn't think it was any deer or elk, but the rain fell so hard that Barb barely could see past the hood, even with the wipers on. Bear, maybe. If only she knew what the creature was, then she would know how to deal with it.

Barb pulled the .38 out of her pocket and undid the snap on the canvas holster just as a huge dark form crossed in front of the Jeep and faded into the rain just beyond the passenger side.

"Shit."

Bigger than a bear. Or maybe it just looked that way. What kind of animal wouldn't be seeking the shelter of the woods or its den in this kind of deluge? Maybe it just got caught in the storm. Barb removed the revolver from the holster, set it on the seat next to her and waited for a minute. Two minutes. When she didn't see anything else, she put the Jeep in reverse and turned to look behind her just as the black hulk passed behind the vehicle. Barb let out a surprised yelp. Something banged into the driver's side door, and she pushed herself out of her seat, over the center console, and scooted up against the passenger door with the revolver pointed in front of her. Another crash rocked the Jeep on its shocks. Barb looked behind her at the looming silhouette of the cabin. Whatever animal was ramming into the Jeep, it was on the driver's side. She thought she could make it if she did it right.

She was wrong.

She swung open the passenger door, dashed out a few steps and then swung around with the .38 pointed it at the Jeep. Nothing moved. She continued to backstep toward the cabin. Something above her caught her attention, and Barb looked up just as the darkness fell upon her and she dropped to the ground.

* * *

When the woman lying in the driveway opened her eyes, she smiled and stood up. The Jeep was still idling. She wiped the gravel off her backside, then walked over and closed the passenger door before crossing to the driver's side. Reaching in, she pulled the keys out of the ignition and popped the hood. She lifted it up and stared at the engine for a moment before reaching in and yanking out a handful of wires, which she tossed into the tall grass. She lowered the hood, and then proceeded to do the same to the green Jetta.

CHAPTER 5

Robert stripped the young man of his soaked clothing and dressed him in a pair of sweat pants and an old t-shirt from Stanford. The scarring on the young man's face continued down his upper chest and forearms.

Robert was surprised to see how fit the man was once he was cleaned up. His earlier diagnosis mistook emaciated for the thin physique of a marathon runner, but something told Robert that this guy might have run one mile too many. Something wasn't matching up, and the pounding of the rain on the metal roof didn't help his concentration. Hadn't Barb said these storms usually rolled in and then right back out? Where was Barb anyway?

And who was this poor kid on his floor? Robert searched the wet clothes for any identification. Clothes? More like rags that were barely held on his body. They fell apart without much prompting. Robert didn't find any clues to the man's identity. None of this made any sense.

Barb rushed in the house, holding the .38 and panting, drenched and dripping on the floor. Never very comfortable around guns, Robert felt relieved to see her set it on the table to take off her coat. "What took you so long?" he asked. "You're soaking wet. What happened to you?"

"I've got some bad news," she said.

Judy walked out of Jeannie's room. "Are we ready to go?" she asked. "Barb, what happened?"

"We're not going anywhere," Barb said. She picked up the revolver and started toward Robert and the man on the floor. Robert stood.

"What's going on, Barb?" he asked.

Barb stopped with a questioning look on her face and pocketed the .38. She put her other hand in her pocket and pulled out a set of keys. "I was just giving these back to you, Bob. But at this point, it doesn't matter *who* has them, seeing as we're all staying here."

"Is this the new plan?" Robert asked.

"Apparently, it is," she said. "Neither of the vehicles will start. Engines won't even turn over. Damnedest thing I've ever seen. You weren't having problems with the Jeep on the way up, were you?"

"None that I'm aware of."

"What are we going to do now?" Judy asked.

Robert looked at Barb, again stricken by the feeling that something wasn't right. "We wait," he said finally. "Once the storm has passed, I'll see if I can figure out what's wrong with the Jeep."

"What if you can't fix it?" Judy asked. "I didn't know you were so talented in the art of automotive mechanics."

"You're not helping, Judy," Robert said. "We'll just have to cross that bridge when we get to it. For now, we wait until the storm passes."

"I think it might be a long one," Barb said. The hint of a smile curled on one side of her mouth.

The slight smirk irritated Robert. If anything, a big storm only proved her wrong. "I thought you said-" he started, but Barb cut him off.

"How's our man?" she asked.

"He's stable. He looks like he's been through hell, but his unconscious state just seems to be a result of extreme fatigue. He's a little dehydrated, but other than that he should be just fine."

"So he's not gonna die just yet?" Barb asked, then added, "I mean, maybe he can tell us what's going on around here."

Robert paused, stymied by the wording of the question she had asked twice, now. "No, I don't think he's going to die," Robert responded. "But he could be out for awhile."

Barb sighed, then turned to Judy. "How's that little girl of yours doing?"

"She's okay. It was everything I could do to get her to stay in her room, but like all kids, I think sometimes her show of bravado is just masking fear. But I think it helps her to know that Bob's a doctor and it's his job to help sick people."

"Well, maybe I'll go and talk to her anyway," Barb said. "Sometimes it helps to hear that everything's okay from someone besides your parents. You know what I mean? Besides, I can tell her a couple of *happy* stories about the area that'll ease her mind a touch."

"Thanks, Barb," Judy said.

"My pleasure." Barb started to walk down the hallway, then stopped. "Sounds kind of like the storm's letting up." She cocked her head to listen. "Maybe not. Must be my imagination."

Barb opened the door to Jeannie's room and walked in, closing it behind her. Jeannie lay sprawled across her bed, pretending to read a magazine while looking obviously put out that she had been confined to the bedroom.

"Whatcha reading, darlin'?" Barb asked.

"Nothing," Jeannie said without looking up.

Barb leaned down and read from the cover, "*Teen Pop*. Interesting stuff?"

"It's just a magazine," Jeannie said. She set it on her pillow and looked at the realtor. "What's going on, Ms. Stack?"

"Not much, darlin'." Barb sat down next to Jeannie on the bed. "Not much at all. The vehicles aren't gonna to start, so nobody's going anywhere, and meanwhile our Daveyboy is still out cold."

"Daveyboy?" Jeannie asked.

"It's actually David, honey. He's ol' Mister Scarface in your new living room, and he's a special one, he is. He's the last, you know. Oh, but you haven't seen him, have you? You really should get a look at him. Pretty scary."

"What happened to him?" Jeannie asked, then narrowed her eyes. "And how do you know his name if he's unconscious?"

"Aren't you the smart one," Barb said and patted her on the head. "You'll just have to ask him yourself. If he ever freaking wakes up." She stood and paced the small room. "I mean, how tired could that little shit be? I'm the one who has to do all of the work, and he gets the royal treatment out there by the fire."

"What are you talking about, Ms. Stack?" Jeannie asked, rolling into a sitting position.

"Don't you worry about it, babydoll. Tell ya what we're gonna do. We're gonna spice things up a little bit. I'm getting bored."

"Maybe we need to get some help," Jeannie said. "We should just get in the Jeep and go."

"You don't want to do that, darlin'," Barb stated. "That's where this one made her mistake. But you and I are going somewhere soon. I've gotta get rid of this woman first, though. That's not gonna be real pretty. She's an older one. Probably won't have fared the trip too good." Barb sat back down and rapped on her own head with her knuckles. "But you're a strong child. If everything goes like I want, you'll be just fine. Probably bounce back in no time. I just want the boy." Barb pulled out the .38 and held it in her lap.

Jeannie slid quickly back on the bed. "What are you doing with a gun, Ms. Stack?"

"You should ask Ms. Stack what she's *plans* to do with the gun," Barb said. "But you'll find that out soon enough, too. Ms. Stack and I are gonna go into the living room real quick, but don't you worry, sweetheart. I'll be right back." The woman stood up from the bed and walked toward the door. Jeannie stayed on the corner of the bed.

"Ms. Stack?" Jeannie whispered, and the woman stopped. "Did you get sick, too? Was it that man in the living room... David?"

"You could say that. And believe me, you don't want to catch it. Unfortunately, sometimes disease finds you no matter how hard you try to hide." With that, she left Jeannie's room.

On the way down the hall, the thing that had taken over Barb Stack's body let her come back to the surface. It pushed itself away from her consciousness just far enough to see the show, but still close enough to move when it needed to. Switching bodies could be difficult if the timing wasn't just right, but the demon had become better at the trick since first meeting David. The boy wasn't the only one with power.

The demon laughed as Barb stumbled down the hall like an old drunk, suddenly having regained control of her body.

* * *

Barb knew that she should recognize the familiar looking man and woman in the heat of a discussion in the living room, but they didn't even notice when she stumbled into the living room. Maybe she wasn't actually there. She wasn't really sure if this place was real. A young man was unconscious on the floor.

Him.

Barb trained her focus on him and scowled. Her mind had dissolved to a filthy slush pile of horrific images.

The last thing she could remember that seemed sane was being outside in a Jeep.

But I don't own a Jeep.

She was in the mountains. There was a storm. And something wild outside. She was just a little girl in the Jeep with a toy pistol. Something dark outside.

And then it invaded her.

The things that had filled Barb's mind since then left her dead on the inside, even though she apparently still occupied a living body. But she didn't want to be alive, didn't want to remember what she had seen. She only hoped that her own death wouldn't be so full of pain, but she was willing to take that chance. Barb started to surrender. Her body wouldn't last long without her. She wavered, her body slackened, and the darkness blurred the edges of her vision. Then a voice spoke in her head, the voice that temporarily could drown out the screams of anguish she heard from all around her. The voice that brought relief at the same time as terror.

You're not done yet, Barbara. One more thing you must do.

Barb tried to push away from the voice, and the life in the cabin, like a child fighting being woken from sleep, but she wouldn't be released.

Not yet.

The muscles in her body tightened, starting at her hands and feet, working their way up her arms and legs, over her torso, wrapping around her breasts and up to her shoulders, pulling her to attention, finally snapping her head upright. Her vision cleared and once again she focused on the man on floor.

The boy.

His name was David, but Barb didn't know how she knew this. The one thing she *did* know, even with her mind so shattered, was that he caused all of this, whether he meant to or not. She knew what she was supposed to do. Just one more thing.

The Marricks finally noticed Barb staring at the man on the floor. She swayed as if it was everything she could do to stay on her feet.

But her attention never wavered from the man. The gun dangled loosely in her hand.

"Are you alright, Barb?" Judy asked. "You don't look so good. Is Jeannie doing okay?"

Barb turned toward Judy, but her eyes darted around until she could focus. She staggered a couple of steps toward the Marricks.

"Maybe we should put down the gun, Barb," Robert said. "You look like you should sit down yourself." He made a tentative movement toward Barb, his hand outreached. "Let me help you."

He took another step and Barb snapped to attention, her body taut, the .38 pointed at Robert. "Don't come any closer, Bob," she warned. "I don't need to sit down. Don't reckon I could even if I wanted to." She managed a strangled chuckle, but it broke off in a seizure of coughing. Robert tried to shift out of the way of the shaking revolver, but Barb gained control and steadied it on him again. "Y'all aren't goin' anywhere," she said. "He may say that he'll let you go, but he won't." Her eyes welled up, and a couple of tears ran down her cheeks. "I'm sorry," she said. "It was probably me that let him in, and I'm sorry."

"What are you talking about, Barb," Judy asked. "You let *who* in?"

"But you can save yourselves," Barb said. "You don't have to go through the misery. You can save yourselves. Let me show you the way." She aimed the .38 at the man on the floor.

"Barb, no!" Robert shouted, but before he could move toward her, she put the barrel in her own mouth and pulled the trigger.

* * *

"Oh my God!" Judy screamed.

Just steps away from the realtor, Robert almost made it to Barb before her body hit the ground, but it didn't matter. Her aim was true. Robert couldn't do anything at this point, and he knew it. He dropped to his knees next to the body and clutched his head. Judy kept screaming, echoing Robert's same confusion. Only louder.

"Judy!" he said finally. She stopped screaming.

"My God," she stammered. "She just shot herself. What are we going to do? What's going on?"

Robert knew he should stand up and comfort his wife, hold her and tell her it would be okay, but that sort of behavior wasn't exactly second nature to Robert. Judy would see right through it. Instead, he stayed on his knees. "I don't know."

The words coming from his mouth surprised him. He was usually the first one to come up with a plan in tricky situations. When something went wrong in the operating room, Robert always had the quick solution, but this one had caught him completely off guard. It isn't exactly every other day that your realtor shoots herself in the living room of your new house. But there was more. Robert hadn't been able to think truly clearly since the young man burst through the door.

"Just let me think for a second," he said.

He looked at the body of Barb Stack lying on the floor. Blood pooled on the hardwood around her head. What could have possibly caused her to go so crazy? She had seemed perfectly fine, and then she went into Jeannie's room.

"Oh, dear God," Judy said as her train of thought reached the same stop as Robert's. Certainly their daughter would've heard the shot.

Robert almost fell over Barb's body as he stumbled to his feet, and then he sprinted down the hall.

"Jeannie!" Judy cried from behind him. Robert threw open the door, a thousand fears of what he might find flashing through his mind.

His daughter was sprawled across the bed, unmoving, one hand hanging limply off the side, her teen magazines in a heap where she had dropped them. "Oh God, no," Robert said and rushed over to her, kneeling next to the bed, relieved to find that her breathing, though soft, still rose and fell in her chest, and her pulse was normal. He automatically reached for the penlight that always hung in the pocket of his work smock, but then he remembered where he was. "Judy, flip the lights," he said.

"What?"

"Just flip the lights a few times! Slowly."

While Judy switched the lights on and off, Robert checked Jeannie's pupils. Then he dropped his head on the mattress next to his daughter and let out a heavy breath.

"Bob?" Judy whispered from the doorway.

"She's okay," he said, his voice muffled through the blanket. *Alive, at least.*

"What the hell is going on?" Judy asked. She knelt down next to the bed and took her daughter's hand. "Why won't she wake up? She's breathing. Her hands are warm. Why won't she wake up?"

Robert pushed his hair back on his head and straightened up. "She's just unconscious. It's going to be okay. I'm going to figure this out. We'll be alright." This time he did take his wife in his arms. Judy looked like she was about to lose it *big time*, but more than that, he didn't want her to see the fear in his eyes.

"What's wrong with my baby?" Judy asked. Her voice cracked, and Robert felt one of her tears run down his neck.

"I don't know, but we're going to find out." Robert stood up, leaving Judy sitting against the bed.

"Where are you going?" she asked.

"Stay here with Jeannie. I'm going to try the Jeep."

"Barb said it wasn't working," Judy said. "Neither vehicle."

"And Barb just shot herself," Robert said. "Maybe we shouldn't take her word for it. Just stay in here. I won't be a minute."

Robert shut Jeannie's door behind him. At the end of the hall, he stepped over Barb's body, almost slipping in her blood. As he crossed through the great room, he pulled his cell phone out of his pocket and checked it again. Still nothing. He grabbed his coat from the closet. It seemed like the rain had let up, but black clouds still filled the sky, darkening the valley. Wind whipped across the tall grasses, rolling like waves, and Robert figured there would be more rain before this cleared entirely. He dashed out into the cold, down the porch and over to the Jeep, stopping suddenly when he rounded the corner of the vehicle and saw the passenger door. Most of the lower half was dented in.

"What the hell?" Robert walked over and examined the door. A few tufts of what appeared to be hair or fur stuck to red smears in the crumpled metal. "What did she *do?*"

Robert opened the door and climbed in. He stuck the keys in the ignition. Nothing. He sat for a moment and then tried again. The engine didn't even turn over. He reached down and pulled the lever under the steering column, then stepped out of the Jeep and popped the hood. He stared for a moment, but realized he had no idea what he was looking for. The engine was still there. Battery still seemed to be hooked up. He had the oil changed before they left. Beyond that, he was at a loss mechanically. The rain started again, harder this time and without any warning. Robert slammed the hood and rushed back to the cabin. In Jeannie's room, he found Judy still sitting on the floor, watching her daughter as if waiting for her to speak. She looked up when he entered.

"Anything?" she asked.

Robert shook his head. "Let's get Jeannie into the living room," he said. "It'll be warmer by the fire. And I can figure out what to do next."

"What about Barb?"

"I don't think Barb will mind," Robert said.

"Bob!" Judy gasped. She cupped her hand over her mouth and backed away from him.

Robert bit his lower lip and took a deep breath. "I'll take care of Barb," he said. "If anything seems to change with Jeannie, shout for me." He turned and left the bedroom, trying to push back the questions still rushing at him and keep a level head.

The blood around Barb had started to coagulate. "Shit," Robert muttered.

He thought for a second and then walked through the kitchen into the garage. There was still a roll of the old carpet from the house. Robert had asked the workers to leave it just in case he decided to finish part of the basement. He grabbed a large section of the carpet and went back to the living room and unrolled it just beyond the blood. He dragged Barb's body onto the carpet and wrapped it around her. He started to pull the bundle toward the entryway but stopped halfway and changed direction back toward the garage. He may not have figured out the mountains yet, but one thing he did know was that you didn't leave a carcass on your front porch.

With Barb's body safely tucked away in a corner of the garage, Robert attacked the task of cleaning the blood, brain and bone fragments. He had seen worse in the emergency room, but he never had to clean it himself. Twenty minutes and all of their towels later, the job was done. Robert was actually shocked he hadn't heard anything from Judy. He guessed that the slightest hitch in Jeannie's breath would send his wife scrambling out of the room. Robert figured Judy must have been holding Jeannie's wrist, checking her pulse and her watch this whole time.

Robert walked back down to his daughter's room to find Jeannie still unconscious. Judy sat on the bed next to her, lightly stroking her forehead. Robert thought he might have been a little hard on his wife lately. Well, not exactly *hard* but certainly not easy. He had let work weed its way into their marriage, the stresses from one bleeding over into the other. As a result Judy pulled away. And Robert pushed. Looking at her now, though, he realized how much he still loved his wife. She looked up and smiled. "I think she might have snored a little," she said. "That's a good sign, right?"

"She's gonna be just fine, babe. Let's get her into the living room, and we'll figure out what to do next." Robert walked over and gently lifted Jeannie from the bed.

"What did you do with... with Ms. Stack," Judy asked.

"I took care of it."

"Oh," Judy said. "I just wanted to know so I didn't accidentally stumble across-"

"Don't go in the garage."

"Okay."

In the living room, Robert placed Jeannie on the couch and slid the piece of furniture closer to the warmth of the fire.

"We can't just stay here and wait out the storm, Bob," Judy said.

"I know."

"What do you think we should do?" Judy asked.

"I'm not sure," Robert said. "I was trying to think of something when I was out here, but I kept getting distracted."

"Why don't you try the Jeep?"

"Have you looked outside, Judy? It's pouring. I don't think my novice monkeying around under the hood in a downpour is going to accomplish anything."

"That's not what I'm talking about," Judy said. "Why don't you just go outside and try it again."

"It wasn't even turning over," Robert said. "Not a sound."

"Just try it again. Maybe it will work now. You've given it some time."

Robert started to say something but stopped. He turned away from his wife, swung the door open, ran out into the rain and tried the Jeep again with the same result. Just before getting out, he tried his cell phone. Still nothing. On his way back inside, he noticed something metallic in the driveway. He bent down and picked up another set of keys. Volkswagen keys. He looked at the Jetta, surprised he hadn't thought of it before, but it didn't matter much. Barb's car wasn't starting either.

Robert tried to suppress his "I-told-you-so" face when he walked back into the cabin. Instead, he just shook his head. Judy looked over at her daughter on the couch. "We'll just have to walk," she said. "We'll wrap Jeannie up, find something to keep her dry. The shower curtain, maybe, and then we'll walk down to the main road."

"It's almost twenty miles back to the highway," Robert said.

"We can't just stay here," Judy said. "I'm sure I saw other houses along the way. Certainly there will be someone able to help us. We have to go, Bob."

"I wouldn't do that," a voice said.

CHAPTER 6

The Marricks hadn't noticed the man on the floor turn over and sit up, but now he was leaning against the wall next to the fireplace, nursing his right wrist and wincing. "I think it's broken. You're a doctor, right?"

For a moment no one spoke. The sudden intrusion into their argument had apparently rendered the Marricks incapable of thought. Robert finally broke the silence. "It's not broken. And you're lucky I *am* a doctor. Anyone else might have thrown you back out in the rain."

"Thank you," the man said. "I wouldn't have survived out there. I can't believe I made it here, down that slope."

Robert remembered standing outside just before the storm hit, seeing what he had thought to be some sort of wildlife, overtaken on the hill by the rain. He shivered, suddenly unsure of himself. Then he remembered his advantage. "You're not out of the woods just yet," he said. "Would you mind telling us what the hell you're doing here? Or would you rather tell it to the local police?" Robert pulled the .38 from his pocket and pointed it at the man.

"Jesus, Bob!" Judy gasped. "What are you doing?"

"Don't worry, Judy. I've got everything under control." Robert prayed that Judy wouldn't blurt out something about how often he had actually handled a gun. "It seems to me that everything went bad just after this guy broke through our door. Now our daughter is unconscious, a woman is dead, and I haven't the faintest idea why.

Maybe he can explain it." He turned back to the stranger. "So, what's it going to be?"

"You don't need the gun, Dr. Marrick," the man said. "I'm not the one you need to be afraid of. Unfortunately, I *am* the reason your family is in danger, and for that, I can understand if you want to kill me." He looked over at the girl on the couch. "I apologize for invading your lives, but if there's one thing I've come to believe lately, there are certain events in this life that we have absolutely no control over, but which still happen for a reason. I have to believe that is true."

Robert's aim on the man had slowly drooped. He quickly corrected himself. "What are you talking about?"

"Well, it's not everything in life," the man said. "There must be certain destinies that we can direct by our actions and thoughts. But there are certain things, terrible things that can never be constrained. These forces roll across the land, and when they hit, there's nothing you can do but ride it out. Kind of like a really bad storm. For whatever reason we're all in the eye of one now. I tried to keep it out, but I was too weak." As if in confirmation, lightning flashed outside, illuminating the rain-stricken landscape like a photograph, accompanied by a crash of thunder. Robert jumped, accidentally pulling the trigger of the revolver. The bullet exploded one of the rocks on the chimney just a foot above the stranger's head. Judy shrieked. The man didn't flinch when the bullet shattered the stone, but he stiffened. Robert looked at the gun in his hand in horror, as if it had shot itself.

"My God, Bob," Judy said. "Put down the gun."

"Or at least put it in your waistband, Dr. Marrick," the man said. "If it would make you feel more comfortable."

Robert didn't have to think long about where the gun would be pointed by sticking it in his waistband. He nodded and set the .38 on the table in the entryway. He thought for a second, and then slid the little table over to where he stood with Judy.

"The gun wouldn't have done you any good anyway," the man said. "Unless of course, you wanted to take Ms. Stack's way out."

Robert was about to counter when he realized the young man's comment had given something away. He *knew* about Barb, which meant that he must have been conscious for longer than any of them thought.

58

He's been lying in wait. Gooseflesh rose on his arms. "Let's start at the beginning," Robert said. "What's your name?"

"My name is David."

"Fine. So tell me, *David*, what are we supposed to do if we can't use a gun and we can't go outside?" Robert asked. "What's out there? I don't know much about Montana, but I do know that however big an animal is, a handgun will at least make it think twice."

"We're not talking about some bear," David said. "Oh, you could go outside just fine. You could even get in your Jeep. Maybe it would even start next time. But don't think for a second that you would make it to a town."

Judy walked over and sat next to her daughter on the couch. "Why is that, David? What's out there?"

David sighed. He looked out the window at the rain beating against the panes. "My brother, Peter, called it the Imaginings, like your worst imagination come to life."

Robert raised a clinical eyebrow. "Called *it?*"

"Your brother has seen this thing, too?" Judy asked.

"Well, kind of," David said. "Peter died almost three years ago, but I've seen..." David trailed off and looked at the Marricks. "That's not important," he continued, "because Peter wasn't exactly right. I think he was only given a glimpse, just enough to torment him until ... until he died. This thing does feed off your imagination, as well as your deepest fears, regrets and suspicions." He hesitated to use the word "demon" because he didn't think the Marricks were ready to hear it, but also he wasn't sure that's what it was himself. *Demon* had just been Kathy's assessment. "But it's far worse," he continued. "I don't even know what it is exactly, but I was shown more than Peter. Maybe because I wasn't supposed to survive that first night in Colorado. Maybe it was just showing off."

Robert looked at Judy and Jeannie on the couch. Then he glanced at the .38 on the table and the young man on the floor. "Showing off?" he asked. "Alright. I have no idea what the hell you're talking about. I've had enough of this cryptic bullshit. We're leaving."

"But what about-" Judy started, but Robert cut her off.

"If you want to stay here and talk crazy with this guy," he said, "that's just fine. I don't know what's going on around here, but you were making more sense before he woke up. You were right. We need to go. If we have to walk out of here, we'll walk. But I'm not going to sit another minute and listen to this nonsense while our daughter's life may be at risk."

Judy slumped slightly on the couch. "I thought you said she was okay. I thought..."

Robert ignored her. He headed for the hallway. David reached for him, "Dr. Marrick, please," but Robert skirted around him and continued down the hall. Clanging and tearing sounds echoed from the bathroom, and Robert walked back into the great room dragging the floral shower curtain.

"That was a good idea, Judy," he said. "We can wrap her in this."

"Bob?"

He set the shower curtain on the floor in front of the couch. "Help me out here," he said to her. "We need to lower her down on-"

"Stop!" David shouted. "Just stop!" Robert froze, and Judy cringed into the corner of the couch. David lowered his voice. "Please, Dr. Marrick. I've seen enough death. I don't want to see any more. If you leave right now, you will die. And your daughter will die. You need to think now, and listen. For the sake of your daughter. Right now, the safest place to be is inside."

Robert straightened and looked through the streaked windows at the Jeep in the driveway. Those red spots on the dented side panel had been blood. He knew that. He sat on the couch and took his wife's hand.

"Okay," Robert said, "you want to talk? That's fine. Talk. But you better talk straight. What's out there?"

Lightning flashed, almost immediately followed by the crack of thunder. This time David flinched. A tear escaped his right eye and ran over the ripples of his scarred cheek.

"The first attack came..." David paused. "I'm not sure really. Six months ago, maybe. Before I looked like this." He lowered his head, looking down at his hands, and another tear dropped on his forearm. "I might have been able to save her." He put his face in his hands. "She could've still been alive. But I ran."

* * *

When David finished telling the Marricks his story, the living room of the Montana cabin was quiet. Even the rain seemed to have let up, falling only lightly, as if it were weeping for his lost love. But if the demon had anything to do with the storm, David knew there was no mercy in the reprieve. Only a trap, if anything.

"I'm so sorry," Judy finally said.

Robert looked incredulous at his wife. "You have got to be kidding me."

"Bob-" Judy started, but Robert cut her off.

"You expect me to believe that you're being chased by some demon?" he asked. But David didn't pay any attention to him.

"Whatever it is travels on the winds, faster with the storms," he said to Judy. "Funny thing about the wind, that it can have so much force but remain completely invisible."

Robert laughed. "And this *demon* wants you in particular because you escaped somehow?" he asked. "Are you saying it's some sort of pride thing?"

"I don't know what it is," David said.

Judy leaned forward toward him. "You mentioned something earlier about your brother."

"Peter."

"Right," Judy said. "You said he knew about this thing as well?"

Again Robert regarded his wife in disbelief. When she wouldn't acknowledge him, he huffed and crossed his arms. He took out his cell phone and checked for a signal before returning it to his pocket. David ignored him, even though he knew the doctor was thinking about another attempt at getting out of the cabin. "Peter tried to warn me before he... before he died, but the police told us that he must have gone crazy. Even I thought he was crazy. But in the past six months..." David paused and looked at the family. "I'm pretty sure it just wants me," he said. "I'm sorry I've brought this down on you, but if I can just get some water, I'll be on my way. The storm is letting up. I can't promise to get these clothes back, but-"

Robert stood from the couch and strode over to the table with the revolver. "You're going to be even sorrier if you don't give me a straight answer," he said and set his hand on the table. "This is some amazing story you've told, but now I want the truth. And you can start with what's happened with my daughter."

There it is, David thought. The Marricks' true reason for listening to him for this long. Their concern for the child trumped everything. They didn't really care what had happened to David. Mrs. Marrick seemed a little more receptive, but David suspected she was just being diplomatic, handling the crazy guy with kid gloves while she, too, worked around to that one question.

Did he know what was wrong with their daughter?

The truth was, he didn't. But he had his suspicions

"I wish I could tell you what happened," he said. "But I can only tell you what I know. You have to trust me." Robert started to speak, but David cut him off. "And if you can come up with a better explanation for what's happened here today, Dr. Marrick, I'd love to hear it. Really, I would. I would love nothing more than to know that this has all been my imagination, and we can all go back to our normal lives." David shook his head. "If only I could tell you how much time I've wasted on *that* delusion. Your life has just changed in a way that you would've never imagined. You can either deal with it now or surrender to it."

"Like you did?" Robert asked. "Your girlfriend dies in a fire that one of you probably started with all your candles, and you run away."

"I didn't..." David clenched his jaw, then turned to Judy. "We don't have much time. I'm pretty sure it's growing stronger with every life it takes, and it can probably move more effectively in a body." He glanced at the teenage girl, then stood up, surprised at how much the short rest and warmth had revived him. "You can shoot me if you want, Dr. Marrick. That might make things easier, actually, but one way or another I'm leaving. Maybe it will leave with me."

"Talk, talk, talk," the girl on the couch said. She sat up. "Yet all your talk won't make any difference."

Robert backed up in surprise at his daughter's awakening, bumping into the small table. Judy had been staring at David, but she blinked a couple of times and turned to Jeannie just as Robert rushed over to the couch to hug his daughter.

"Dr. Marrick, no!" David started, but it was too late. Robert was already to the girl when she lashed out, arms swinging in every direction. One clawed hand found Robert's face, her fingernails scratching trenches across his left cheek. Robert leapt away in shock. Judy threw her arms up in defense, but the girl knocked her off the couch.

"*Don't touch me!*" she screamed. Then she stopped thrashing and looked at David. He was wound up and ready to spring, like a cat ready to dart out of the danger's way. She narrowed her eyes. "And you," she said. "Why don't you just sit back down, circus boy? You wouldn't make it far, anyway. I've got all these fresh, healthy bodies to catch you."

David thought for a moment, then slid back down to a sitting position, his shoulders slumped in an effort to conceal the energy he believed *would* allow him to elude any of the three Marricks if need be.

"Jeannie?" Judy whispered.

The girl turned toward Judy. Her eyes narrowed and a malicious grin formed. "Jeannie's not here, Mrs. Marrick." She chuckled softly, the laugh grew louder and more grating until it sounded more like the cawing of a raven than childish glee. Then it stopped abruptly. "Actually, she is here," the demon said in Jeannie's voice. "Just far away. Your world is like a pinhole of light to her right now, the sounds echoing down a long tunnel. But I imagine your world is the least of her concerns right now. Don't worry, though. She's in good company. She's got some friends of David's with her."

Judy's eyes widened and she shook her head, fighting back the tears. "Not my baby."

"Go ahead and weep," the demon said to Judy. "You've been through so much today. And so much these many years. It's okay. Crying will make you feel better. Let out your heart."

The girl fixed her gaze on Judy, and suddenly the older woman clutched her chest, her body stiff. She gasped and then broke into racking sobs. Then the girl turned to Robert. He was still holding his wounded cheek, the blood seeping through his fingers. The look from the thing that used to be his daughter backed him up against the wall.

"Jea- Jeannie?" he asked.

Judy rose to her feet. The demon watched with one raised eyebrow of amused interest. "I just want my daughter back," Judy said. She looked over at David, and he could see the pleading confusion in her eyes. Then she returned her attention to her daughter. "That's all I want. What do *you* want from us?" She glanced at David again. "We just want our lives back."

The girl smiled. "I like this one, David. So full of hope. Do you think she ever had the faintest notion that this place, where she invested so many of her dreams, would turn out to be her demise? And to think that it would be brought about by her own daughter, the little girl of which the grown woman has grown jealous."

"Goddammit!" Judy shouted. "What do you want?"

The girl swung her feet around, and both of the Marricks flinched. "At first I just wanted the boy. He was the end of it, and he's been giving me some chase. But now I want you. I want you all. I want each of your souls. Every bit." She hopped off the couch and walked toward Judy. The woman retreated until she was backed against the wall. The girl reached out and stroked Judy's shaking arm. "Such a tasty little meal you'll be."

Robert gritted his teeth and removed his hand from his face, the skin pulling where the blood had started to clot. He looked at his crimson palm for a second and then rushed at the thing touching his wife. "Stay away from her!" he hollered as he knocked the demon away from Judy.

David saw his opportunity and scrambled for the gun, but the girl was closer. With a surprising grace and agility, she turned the blow from Robert into a roll toward the little table, kicking out the legs and catching the weapon as it dropped toward the floor. She quickly righted herself and pointed the gun at David. He froze just a couple feet short of the barrel.

"Back over by the fire," the girl growled. David rose to his feet, the girl mirroring his movement while maintaining her aim. He backed up to the fireplace and sat down on the hearth. "In fact," the girl said, "why doesn't everyone go sit by the fire?"

In the ruckus, Robert had positioned himself in front of Judy, and they maintained this pose as they circled around the room to the opposite wall and stood next to David.

"How touching," the demon said, waving the gun at the Marricks. "No, it's better than that. _Heroic._ The man rushes over to save his woman. So brave." She chuckled. "Except something isn't right. There's something wrong with this picture." She sighted down the barrel of the revolver at Robert. "The man acts like a husband at all the wrong times and only when the situation forces him to act. Just like he forces himself to love the woman. Is it hard to lie to yourself, Bob?"

"I don't have to lie…" Robert trailed off.

His grip on his wife behind him loosened and his arms dropped to his side. Judy pulled away slightly.

"You'll be an easy one," the girl continued. "And slightly disappointing, I must say. Hell is what you have coming. I'm just speeding it up a little."

"Bob?" Judy asked. She moved farther away from him, but the girl held her sighting on Robert.

"Uh-oh, Bob. Didn't you tell your wife about the other woman?"

Robert finally noticed his wife was no longer behind him. "Judy?" He reached toward her, but she jerked away.

"Mrs. Marrick, don't listen," David said. "This is what it does." But in Judy's eyes, he recognized the truth the demon spoke.

"Oops." The girl giggled. "Guess not. Well, don't worry, Bobby. You'll get to meet your wife again. So much sweeter indeed."

She pulled the trigger.

The kickback of the .38 knocked her backward off her feet with a delighted "*whoop!*" But she held onto the gun, and her aim was true. Robert staggered, clutching his chest. His eyelids fluttered as he looked first at his daughter, then his wife and finally David. Then he collapsed on the floor.

"Oh God, no!" Judy screamed and dropped next to Robert's body. David reeled backward, grabbing his own chest. An explosion burned in his heart, but ice spread out from his chest to the ends of his fingertips. He knew that he was experiencing Robert's death. Maybe this was how his own death would come.

Finally.

His vision wavered and his eyes started to roll back in his head. Then he caught sight of the girl sitting on the floor, and he summoned the last of his energy to come back. There was something about her, something in her eyes. This wasn't over, after all. He wouldn't give up on this family yet.

The cold in his chest subsided, and feeling returned to the rest of his body as he focused on Jeannie. She seemed confused. The malicious smile was gone from her face, and a tear ran down her cheek. The girl was fighting it. Her bottom lip quivered. The gun had slipped from her hand to the floor. She shook her head a couple of times and then started swatting in front of her face, as if she were being buzzed by flies.

David looked at the gun on the floor. *Maybe*, he thought, but it was as if he spoke aloud. Jeannie stopped swinging her arms and looked at him, her eyes still those of an innocent kid. She looked down at the gun, picked it up by the barrel with her thumb and forefinger, and dangled it out to David. Then her body shuddered and her head jerked back. Her body stiffened, the dainty hold on the barrel of the .38 turning to a clutch. Then she folded forward. When she raised her head, the smile had returned and she righted the revolver in her hand.

"Now, let's see," the demon said. "Who's next?"

David stood. A mirror hung on the wall across the room next to the entryway, but instead of his own reflection, David saw Peter standing by the fire. It was only for an instant, and then it was gone, but now David knew what he had to do. He didn't know why, or even if it would make any difference… if it would save the lives of the Marrick women… but he knew. And he hoped.

"Take me," David said to the demon. "That's what you really want." The girl rose and cocked her head at David as he continued. "Won't I taste good to you? The one who eluded you all this time. I wonder, will you be too greedy to share me with your friends? I think so."

"I already have you," the demon said, but something in the voice sounded uncertain. David didn't respond. The two stared at each other before the girl spoke. "Why, boy? Why now, after so much fight?"

David glanced again at the mirror, and the girl followed his look. She turned back to him with her eyes narrowed. "What are you thinking?"

"Take me," David said again. "But leave the girl. And her mother. I'm a much more suitable reward."

The girl looked at Judy, who had stopped crying but still held her husband. Judy had been watching, and now she nodded at David's suggestion.

"Hmm," the demon said. The girl flopped the gun from hand to hand, from Judy to David and back again. "I get you *and* the mother," she said finally, "Then the little girl lives."

David looked over at Judy. She lowered Robert's body down on the floor and stood up, clenching her hands to control her emotion. "It's okay," she said.

"No, it's not," David said. "But it's the only way. I'm so sorry."

"If it will save my baby…" Judy stopped, and took a shaky breath.

The demon walked over to David. "But you have to do it yourself."

"I won't kill this woman," David said.

"Not that," the girl said. "Give yourself freely to me." She held the revolver in her palm. David stretched out his own hand. She put the gun in his hand, the steel cold against his skin. "But not like that," the demon said, grabbing his hand with both of hers and sandwiching the gun between the two. "You'd be worthless to me dead."

A burning sensation spread from the little girl's hand into David's, rapidly spreading up his arm. David tried to jerk free, but it was too late.

* * *

The girl fell unconscious against David as Mashart left her body and entered the boy. The demon stood steady in his new form, clutching the girl against his chest. Then he let her drop to the floor. The mother rushed over and wrapped the girl in her arms.

Mashart looked down at the two girls. The younger one was still breathing. Yes, she was a strong one indeed. Good. He might need her again

"The boy was part right," he said and smiled at Judy. "I am greedy. I do want him all to myself, but not like he thought. Through him I can do so much more. Something about this one draws people to him, and I'll use that." He reached up and trailed his fingers down the lines of scars on David's face. "They must pity the circus freak." He seemed to reflect on this for a moment. "Now," he continued, "let's finish this."

CHAPTER 7

It had been almost a hundred years since Mashart escaped from Hell. The ritual which had released him, carrying him out of the frozen underworld on the back of a storm, was the same one the demon used to transport the souls of the innocent down to Hell. But today was the first time the words had been spoken through human lips since Mashart's deliverance. There had never been a survivor in the past. Only the dead had been present, the sacrifices to the underworld, and the words had carried on the gales of the wind and the cracks of thunder.

But now the demon had the boy. The last of them. Finally.

However, just underneath the elation, Mashart sensed something else. A subtle unease that he couldn't quite grasp. He had never experienced insecurity, but rather reveled only in anger and terror. He decided that it must be some filthy residue from the boy whose body he now possessed. Still, the ritual felt different coming from the boy's mouth. The incantation had a different tone, even though the ancient words were the same. If the demon didn't know better, he might think he was opening up another door.

After he finished the rite, Mashart stood back and looked at the dead bodies of the man and wife. After taking the life of the woman, he had moved the girl into the bathroom while he carried out the ritual in the living room. She was still unconscious. There was something different about the girl. She possessed a strength greater than her years, stronger than her parents.

She would have to die, of course. He sensed a threat in the girl, perhaps a challenge similar to the boy, but there would be no survivors this time. Mashart needed to finish the ritual with the parents first, and after their innocence had coursed through him on the way to Hell, he would be strong enough to sacrifice the girl.

A high-pitched whine started to rise in the living room of the cabin. The windows seemed to flex inward as the din grew louder. Then a hissing perforated the edges of the windows and around the front door. A grayish-green mist sprayed into the room, forcing through the seals and seams of the cabin. The mist swirled above the bodies, expanding into a thick cloud. Small bits of the chinking between the logs in the walls exploded inward with popping sounds, and the gray oozed between like heavy smoke. Soon the cloud filled the entire space overhead. It formed a rolling, bubbling ceiling just above the demon. The smell of decay pervaded the cabin. The storm had come to take the dead.

The cabin grew colder, and the air felt as thick as the cloud, almost as if the room was being compressed by the murky mass above. Even the previously raging fire sputtered to a collection of broken blue flames on hissing embers. Flashes sparked in the cloud overhead, currents of electricity shooting across it, like the insides of a diseased mind. Finally the cloud broke and a sticky rain poured from the filth, spattering over every inch of the living room and rapidly pooling around Mashart's feet. The noxious stench of the rain, like ammonia mixed with gasoline, drowned out the stink of death and covered the bodies of the dead, forming a shiny coating over them, refusing to run off like normal water.

Then as quickly as it had started, the deluge stopped. A crackling noise filled the air. Mashart reached up and felt the hairs on the neck of the body he had taken over. They tingled at their roots. The hair on his arms also stood on end, pushing through the slick that had also covered his body.

"Interesting," he said just before a flash of light blinded him. A surge of lightning erupted from the black mass, striking the man and woman on the floor, igniting the viscous film on their bodies. The fire spread from their forms, consuming all traces of the fluid until the entire room raged with flames. The boy's body also caught fire, but Mashart smiled as the cold flames licked around his head. The inferno devoured all that was pure and innocent in the room and started to diminish.

"Another gift for you, my Dark-" Mashart started, but he stopped when he saw the boiling cloud. It had turned black, like a bubbling oil slick. Mashart frowned, and then a blast of heat from the cloud sent him reeling into the dining room. He clutched his chest as the souls of the dead entered his body and the last flames sputtered out. It had never happened this way before.

He stood and walked back into the living room. To the human eye, nothing had changed. No fire scarring appeared in the room. Not on the cabin walls or the bodies. All of the black rain, as well as the clouds that spawned it, had incinerated.

Only Mashart could tell that the souls were gone from Robert and Judy Marrick. Except they weren't gone as far as they should've been. The ritual usually funneled the innocence directly to Hell through Mashart's dark soul. Today it had been injected into the body of the boy. Mashart sensed the man and woman squirming somewhere deep in the flesh like blind infants.

The demon smiled. Yes, he had made the correct choice in keeping David alive. Mashart had been right about the boy's abilities to attract prey. Even defeated, his body no longer under his control, the boy had drawn in their innocence like a magnet. And with it a guilt for their deaths. Oh yes, this was so much better of a reward than the demon had hoped. For years Mashart had traveled at the whim of the winds, chasing down this end, but now that he had his final prize, he wasn't ready to give it up. The boy had power. More than the others. He would bring the monkeys to them. The demon had a new purpose, a new direction.

Before that, however, he would finish the rest of the business. Mashart walked down the hall and opened the door to the bathroom. The little girl still lay crumpled on the tile floor between the toilet and the tub. The demon grabbed one of her ankles and dragged her out to the living room. He looked at this small child for whom David had given his life and wondered why.

In the corridors of his mind, Mashart felt the boy stumbling around in his own confused agony. "Doesn't much matter, now," Mashart said. He reached around and pulled the .38 from its spot in his waistband just below the small of his back. He hoped David was enjoying the Hell he had created for himself.

* * *

70

My God, the pain.

David burned everywhere. Especially his right side, as if the wounds that had finally started to heal had suddenly erupted open again. His arms felt like they were being pulled from their sockets. Muscles strained all through his shoulders and upper back, and his whole body seemed heavier.

When David smelled the sweet tomatoes and burning cheese above the stench of his own cooking flesh and hair, he knew what was happening. He was back in Colorado, six months earlier, and dinner was being served. He had been here before in fevered nightmares over the past months, but this was no dream.

It was too real. He had experienced physical sensation in dreams before, but this was much more. Once again, he choked on the black smoke filling his lungs. His body desperately wanted to recoil from a burning which he thought he could never survive again. In the dreams there had been pain, but mostly in his heart. This time David was actually dying again. And he couldn't move to put out the flames. He looked down at Ann just as he had that night.

In the Marrick cabin, David had surrendered to the demon. He hadn't thought of the consequences, only thought it was the right thing to do, the only thing to do. Now the weight of his sacrifice descended on him.

Oh God, please not again.

David should've died in Colorado. He knew it had been the demon's plan. And now, not even a year later, he found himself back in the house, reliving the moment when Ann died in his arms. Every aspect of his memory had brought it back to life.

He lifted his head to the ceiling, his neck muscles tightening until he knew they must certainly snap, and flames rose around his body. Then he dropped to his knees.

Just as he had done six months earlier. Everything the same. His punishment for escaping the demon. It was all happening again.

David knew this was his hell, to relive this moment for eternity.

He laid Ann's burning body down on the melting linoleum even though his mind still screamed to take her outside into the rain, and as he rose, he realized the worst part of this torture, beyond the physical pain. He would have to see her burned body for eternity, be reminded that death had replaced her life. He would never see her smile again, and soon even the dimmed memories of what she looked like would disappear, replaced by a burning skull. And just as he done before, he fled the kitchen into the rainy night.

No. Don't leave the house.

Much as David wanted to run back into the house, to at least *try* to pull Ann's body out, to change his future, he could sense his past thoughts trying to rationalize through the pain of that night, find a solution... somewhere to hide from further damage.

David was a prisoner in his own mind, and he knew that he was about to set off again on the past six months with no control over anything. He would have to see good people die again, friends and strangers alike, and all because of him.

Or even worse. Maybe like a broken record, he would only make it down the street before finding himself back in the burning house with Ann's body in his arms.

While his body tensed for flight as it had that night six months earlier, David's soul slumped inside, and he surrendered. The past would not be denied. He had fought all this way only to be rewarded in Hell. When the tears came, they were of little comfort. This was the exact moment when he had wept that night for the loss of Ann.

David could almost feel the launch signal his brain sent out to his body telling it to run, but he only made it as far as the curb when he heard his name screamed out from the house. This was new. There had been no cry that night, but now it rose over the rain and the rage of the fire, over the sirens in the distance and the shouting of neighbors from down the street who had finally noticed the burning house. The pleading cry split the night and stopped David in his tracks. So abruptly, in fact, that he sprawled forward off the curb.

Put out your arms!

This time, David's body listened. He caught his fall and sat up, stunned by the sudden recovery of control, and heard the scream again. She cried out his name.

"Ann!" he shouted and waited for confirmation. But he knew it wasn't Ann. Ann was dead. He couldn't have done anything to save her.

The realization rushed over him for the first time since that night like a crescendo in classical music. Like angels might sound, maybe. When the music broke in his head, it was cleansing. He finally believed that there was nothing he could have done. At least about *that* night.

72

But he could do something right now. A voice calling his name. David wasn't sure how he knew, but it was the Marrick girl. Somehow she was in the house and still alive. But she was in danger.

David raised his hands in front of his face, flexing his fingers, pleased that he had the ability back. He pushed himself back to his feet and faced the house.

Neighbors started coming out of their own homes, but no one noticed David. People had gathered on the street around and behind him, but not a soul acknowledged his presence.

Because I'm not really here, David thought. He was seeing what happened at the house after he fled. He looked at the house before him. The front door still stood open to the entryway, and the screen door thrashed in the wind. A strong gust grabbed the door, swinging it closed with a crash as the glass section finally shattered. Then the wind shifted, throwing the door open again and ripping it from the hinges. Flames spread out around the door jam, leaving just enough of a mouth for David to run through. This was the chance.

He ran back into the house. The wall of torridity he encountered almost pushed him back out. The heat seemed to reignite his still simmering flesh. He stumbled back into the entryway and patted at his body, but this only sent shockwaves of pain as his hands displaced the melted skin.

David gritted his teeth, held his arm in front of his face and charged forward. He barely recognized the living room. Flames had devoured everything to indistinction. Anything of character or identity had simply charred or melted.

David momentarily forgot his mission as he stood fascinated by the destruction while flames encircled him, watching as the last substance of that life incinerated. A burning whisp of curtain drifted across the living room, landing on the back of the imitation leather recliner. The chair caught immediately, black smoke billowing out toward David, breaking his mesmerism.

He dropped low and scrambled into the kitchen. The Marrick girl, Jeannie, was sprawled unconscious on the floor where Ann had been previously. A blackened circle of scorched linoleum surrounded her body, with small flames dancing on the perimeter, but they kept clear of her body. In fact, besides being unconscious, she didn't seem harmed at all. There was something about the girl, but David couldn't put his finger on it. He had given himself over to the demon because he didn't want to be the cause of any more death, but now he was starting to wonder if there wasn't something more. After all, her voice crying out into the darkness had broken him from the spell of repeating his past. And now here she was in Ann's place.

Tendrils of smoke rose from the circle surrounding Jeannie's body and filled David's nostrils, bringing more tears to his eyes and distracting him from trying to rationalize the situation. He didn't know what was going on, but he did know that he had to get Jeannie out of the burning house. He patted out the small fire around her, the adrenaline numbing the pain in his palms. Then he bent down and picked her up, slinging her body over his left shoulder. When he turned to leave the kitchen, though, a wall of flames filled the doorway.

The first thing he noticed about the obstacle was the color. The flames blocking his escape burned bluish-gray. Figuring it was a result of whatever paint or plastic was burning, David pulled Jeannie forward in his arms to protect her when he ran through. He didn't have a choice. It was the exit of least resistance. He prepared for a dash when suddenly his whole body shuddered under a wave of cold that rolled out of the doorway. So cold that David gasped. His joints started to ache, expanding like balloons, and he almost dropped the girl. Fortunately, Jeannie seemed small for her age, and he kept his balance. He backed away, but the chill wrapped around him and trailed after. He thought he would rather jump through a kitchen window than face that cold.

David tried to think of other escape alternatives, but his uncontrollable shaking seemed to rattle his brain. The fire in the doorway flashed white and then changed to solid gray. The flames circled toward the empty space in the center, spiraling to a focal point. A burning hand emerged from the inferno. David clutched Jeannie tighter and backed farther into the kitchen, his conviction suddenly weakening that the demon had left the house.

A burst of heat in the kitchen from behind David scalded his back and pushed him toward the hand reaching from the gray flame. Jeannie lifted her head from David's shoulder. "It's the only way," she mumbled and then dropped her head back down.

The arm rotated until it was positioned palm up, like a beckoning lover. David started to reach out, then pulled back. The fiery hand remained, and the heat grew more intense behind him.

Death stood behind that gray flame. Maybe not the demon, but death nonetheless. David knew that, but he also believed what the girl said. And he wasn't afraid. What did he have to lose that he hadn't already lost? Finally he closed his eyes and took hold of the gray fire.

Like grabbing frozen metal with wet hands, David's skin stuck. He automatically tried to pull away, but the skin pulled with it. Then he felt nothing at all as the flesh numbed and the cold spread up his arm and into his chest, the gray color seeping out of the flaming hand onto David's body. The freezing paralysis veined out from there, spreading into his chest, and then it found David's core. He sucked in a sharp breath, and found he couldn't let it back out. Yes, this was death. He was suffocating.

David thought of his brother.

His eyes widened, and a cacophony of noise, like the twisting and grinding of metal and tortured humanity, erupted in his head. Then he was yanked through the flame just as the kitchen fire found the gas line and the house exploded.

* * *

The demon stood over the girl's body. He felt that something was wrong, but in his elation, it took a moment to figure out what was happening. Something the demon had first sensed when he had control over the girl, a moment when she slipped back to the surface. It was happening again. This time it was the boy fighting to regain control of his body. Mashart recognized the struggle. Very few gave up with out some sort of fight, but the boy fought harder than the rest of the monkeys.

The demon glared at the girl's body. Definitely an Innocent. One of the finest examples the demon had seen over the many years, but that also meant danger. The threat he felt from her brought almost as much fury as the anger that had consumed him after losing David in the burning house. Mashart didn't like feeling threatened. Finishing her off with David's own hand would wrap things up perfectly. Then Mashart could continue in his body. With the girl dead, the boy would give up the fight.

The demon raised his arm, holding the revolver and looked down the barrel at the girl. Then he lowered the weapon, walked into the kitchen, rummaged through the drawers and returned with a fillet knife.

He would carve her up like a fish. It would be much more satisfying.

"*The labor of the righteous tendeth to life; the fruit of the wicked to sin.*" he said.

* * *

David opened his eyes.

Where have I been?

He didn't know, but now he was back in the cabin in the mountains, crouched over Jeannie. It took a moment to realize he had returned to the present. Relief flooded over him that the girl was still alive. Then he saw that her anime character T-shirt had been slit up to her sternum, and his own hand held a knife with the point just starting to draw a bead of blood above her belly button. The girl's mother was lying motionless next to her, a crimson pool already drying under Judy Marrick's head. David knew that the demon had used him to pull the trigger. He also knew that while he may have been back in the cabin, the demon still controlled his body in this world. David could only watch.

Then Jeannie opened her eyes. She blinked a couple of times, then spoke. "David?" Her voice was weak. David stared down at her and realized that she could see him beyond the glare of the demon.

His body shuddered, and the demon shrieked in his head, apparently just as surprised that the girl had sensed David's return to the flesh. David seized the opportunity and strained to regain control of his body, forcing down the demon. Pin pricks ran down his arm, like blood rushing to heavy, unused limbs after waking from sleep, and he used the momentum to pull back the knife and jerk his body away from Jeannie. He fell backward, and the knife spun across the hardwood floor toward the entryway.

David righted himself and followed the path of the knife, heading for the exit. The girl was alive, but the only way to assure she stayed that way was to escape the cabin. He scrambled across the room and had his hand on the knob of the front door when the demon pushed back, literally freezing David in his tracks, one arm extended forward, before taking control again.

David could only bear witness and taste hatred like copper on his tongue as the demon spied the knife, which had slid halfway under the door to the entryway closet. He released the doorknob and opened the closet instead. He reached down for the blade, straightened up and smiled at Jeannie.

"David?" she asked, but more uncertain this time.

The demon advanced toward her. Her focus switched between his eyes and the knife. She pushed herself up on her elbows and scooted away, giving a little shriek when she bumped into her mother, then breaking into tears when she saw her father.

"Please don't kill me," she whimpered.

The demon paused, and his body convulsed as David once again fought for control. The expression on his face morphed from fear to confusion to savage glee as either side took momentary advantage. This time David had the choice of determining his own future.

The noise he had heard from beyond the gray flame started in his head again, low at first, then rumbling louder, and a memory from what seemed to be another lifetime came back to him. David remembered the first time he survived death. Halloween. His last year of college. One of his first dates with Ann. They had gone to Jeff Burns's house for a couple beers before a dance. Leaving the house, David had pulled the car out into traffic without looking to his left. When Ann shouted at him, he turned to see the grill of a black truck inches away from his face, separated only by the thin window.

The truck smashed into the side. The sound of crunching steel and shattered glass screamed in his head, and time seemed to slow to a stop. Blackness and silence followed. It was amazing how easily David accepted the idea that he was dead. In that hush just after impact, all fear disappeared, and he only prayed that everyone else was okay. Then the sounds returned and light bled slowly back into his vision of life inside the crumpled vehicle as it spun off the road and up on the curb.

Ann had said that if they could survive that wreck, they could survive anything.

The sounds David had heard that day screeched in his brain now, but they provided comfort this time, as if the twisted metal blocked out any other thoughts but survival, making him stronger. And somewhere, underneath it all, a voice. Or voices, rather. Whispering.

But much as David strained he couldn't make out what was being said. Then he heard it.

hold on to the girl.

And he knew that it wasn't over yet. If nothing else, the girl would make it out of this place alive. Scarred, but alive.

David surged against the demon, and the scales tipped. Senses returned again to his right arm. He felt the knife in his hand and knew that the demon was losing control, but he still needed the rest of his body. He brought up his reanimated hand and pulled the blade across his bare chest, cutting a deep swath into the unfeeling flesh.

The pain awoke the rest of his senses.

David cried out as the shockwaves surged through his body. It was enough to regain control. He straightened, but he stood as if the earth moved around him. His grip on the flesh was tenuous at best. It felt as if his body was shutting down from the struggle, like he just needed to sleep. He could feel the demon's dark threads weaving back into his muscles, and he knew that when his body surrendered-- which he thought could be imminent-- everything would be lost. There was only one way to be sure.

Must end it while the demon is still restrained, David thought, and turned up his left wrist. At least the girl would survive.

"David, no!" Jeannie shouted.

David paused, the blade shaking, anxious to finish the job, and stared down at the girl. She didn't look like a kid anymore. Could he blame her? The demon had possessed her body as well, and David couldn't even guess what her Hell had been like. No, he could only blame himself. But it didn't look like Jeannie blamed him. There was no hatred in her eyes. It seemed more like compassion.

Her face showed no fear. She had drawn herself up into a sitting position.

"Not like this," she whispered.

David started to weep. "I'm so sorry."

"I know it isn't your fault."

"But I can't keep it back for much longer."

"Then run," Jeannie said. "You have to run."

David dropped the knife. Thunder boomed in the distance as the knife clattered on the floor. Jeannie collapsed, her arms thrown over her father. David turned away from the ruined family and started toward the door. He didn't slow as he caught sight of the mirror next to the entryway. He didn't look back at the reflection of his older brother, still standing where David had just been and looking down at Jeannie.

David opened the door. He looked up at the sky, and the words of the dead echoed in his head, the dead that he now carried with him.

...my favorite time of year... storms roll in about mid-afternoon and then roll right back out...

The wind started to die down, breaking up the dark, clouded sky. Patches appeared that were so blue, David thought the world might've flipped over and the sea had replaced sky. The sun shone through, and the warmth on his face gave him strength.

The way I feel, I think we could've blown the power for the whole neighborhood.

David even managed a smile. Then he heard a gurgling from the depths of his gut. He doubled over in pain, clutching his stomach, as a trail of fire burned a path from his stomach into his throat, and a voice other than his own forced its way from his mouth.

"See, boy, aren't they all great? All the souls we've gathered together?"

David vomited out the demon's laughter.

"I told you it was fun."

David swallowed back the bile and uncurled himself.

"Run, David!" Jeannie screamed from the cabin. And he did, as fast as he could.

Jeannie wouldn't say another word for two years.

CHAPTER 8
MONTANA

Mary Rose Mulaney sat on her futon pretending to read the latest copy of *Art Digest*. As the resident manager of the Atlantic Apartments, she usually left the door to her apartment open if she was there during business hours. Currently she was eavesdropping on a couple of tenants just outside her door in the "Un-commons" area talking about their ceramics class final.

Someone brushed past her door, obscured behind a large stretched canvas carried by mystery legs as they hurried down the hallway. The breeze caught on her door, rattling the manager plaque hung on the front, a collaged sign that Mary Rose had made, adding various pictures and changing it to say "WoMan-ager."

"Slow down, out there," she admonished.

"Sorry, M.R.," Bane called. His real name was Jeremy Leavitt, but he went by Bane. He did dark paintings, mostly about the ruin of civilization, past and future. Mary Rose didn't care much for his work, but she supposed there was a place for everything, and there was no doubting that he possessed some talent. But she never said he could call her "M.R."

Mary Rose heard a *crack* from the hall, probably as he knocked into one of the plant shelves, followed by a muffled "*Shit.*"

"Bane of my existence!" she called out, not for the first time, and went back to looking at her magazine. The girls in the Un-commons laughed, but Mary Rose didn't laugh back. As more of an artists' commune than an apartment building, she could discriminate against a potential renter for their profession without really getting any heat, but she knew she couldn't get away with turning away people based on their gender. Even though she wanted to do just that.

Mary Rose Mulaney didn't trust men.

She knew it stemmed from her childhood. She didn't need any shrink to tell her that. Her father, Samuel Mulaney, had worked in the mines in Butte. When he wasn't working, he was drinking… and beating up her mother. When Mary Rose was seven, Ruth Mulaney took her and her three younger sisters in the middle of the night and left for Missoula. Mary Rose had been the only one old enough to know what was going on as the bus rolled through the frozen mountain valleys. She had asked her mother if Daddy would come after them.

"I wouldn't worry about that, sweetheart," Ruth had said, and there was a look in her eyes that Mary Rose trusted. Her mother would protect her. Mary Rose fell asleep with the moon jittering in the dark sky outside the moving bus window.

Ruth had been right. The story Mary Rose heard when she grew a little older was that Samuel had woken in the middle of the night, still half-drunk, and set out to find his family, but apparently the brakes in his truck went out, and he spun off the highway, careening into an icy river.

When Mary Rose was in college, she asked her mother why she never went back to being "Ruth Dennis." Mary Rose had been considering changing her own last name to her mother's maiden name. Ruth gave her a look both sad and ashamed. She reached out and put her hand on her daughter's blonde head, like when she had been a little girl. "Why'd you have to cut your hair so short?" she asked. "You have such pretty hair when it's long."

"Mama."

Ruth took her hand away and sighed. "You can't change where you've been, Rosie," she said. "Only where you're goin'."

At the time, Mary Rose didn't think that she wanted to be going *anywhere* that involved a man. Almost a year later, just before she graduated with her art degree, she figured it out for sure, thanks to Kate Osbourne. Katie. They had been friends through four years of college (six for Mary Rose) and lovers ever since.

Another streak caught her eye as it passed her door. She looked up but wasn't able to identify the resident. Then the smell wafted into the room, and she knew. Not exactly a bad smell. Mary Rose had known her share of young tenants who had decided not to shower in their pursuit of being "artistic," so she knew body odor, but this was just *different*. A little sweet at first, but then it kinda pinched up the back of the throat, rising through the nasal passage. A quick little rush, like the wasabi they gave out with sushi.

David Blithe. He had lived in the Atlantic for just over seven months. Mary Rose hated the fact that she would feel herself go flush slightly when he was around. Katie had been the one to convince her to let David move in.

"Have you read his poems?" Katie had asked a few nights after David dropped off his application. They were having dinner at Katie's house outside of town, where Mary Rose stayed during the weekends when she wanted to get away from the hotel.

"I haven't," Mary Rose said, setting down her piece of olive bread. "Have *you*?"

"Listen to you," Katie said and laughed. "Like a jealous schoolgirl. As a matter of fact I have. I was catching a quick snack for lunch yesterday. He stopped by looking for you. He was carrying an old, beat up portfolio. When I told him you weren't there, he started to leave, and then I asked him what was in the case."

"Nosey," M.R. said.

Katie playfully poked at her with her fork.

"Well?" Mary Rose asked. She picked up the bread and pretended to act uninterested.

"Well, he looked down at his shoes and said that someone at Charlie's told him it might help. Of course I goaded him until he pulled out a few pages of his stuff."

"Charlie's," Mary Rose huffed. "What a meat market."

"It's also where half of your tenants hang out," Katie said.

"And?"

"And what?"

Mary Rose shook her head. "What was his stuff like?"

"As rough as his face," Katie said.

"Kate Osbourne!"

Katie giggled and covered her mouth. "I'm sorry, that's horrible to say. Must be the wine. But when it comes to poetry, you *know* how I like them to rhyme."

"Of course," Mary Rose said and rolled her eyes.

Katie ignored her. "But in my opinion what he lacked in style, he made up for with emotion. I've gotta' say, one of them caught me a little breathless, and you know how I don't understand most of that stuff you call 'art.'"

Mary Rose pulled at a strand of her blond hair, wrapping it around a finger and inspecting it. She had let it grow out since college. So much more gray than there used to be. "Breathless, eh?"

"There it is again," Katie said. She laughed and narrowed her eyes. "I'd swear you're jealous, but I'm not sure of whom."

"Oh, really?"

"I think so." Katie stood, walked around the table and turned Mary Rose's chair out, planting herself in her partner's lap.

"I think you just feel sorry for him," Mary Rose said, even though she herself had seen something in David's eyes that made her feel sad inside.

"He probably has some interesting stories to tell," Katie said and kissed Mary Rose on the forehead.

"If you could get them out of him. They're probably painful." The words just slipped out, but Mary Rose knew from the moment she spoke the words that she had decided to let him move in.

Over seven months later, she still didn't know if she had made the right decision, which is to say that she hadn't heard any stories yet. She hardly saw him at all, as a matter of fact. Occasionally she would walk out into the hall and know that he had been there; she could almost taste him, but she rarely heard him come into the building or up the long flight of front stairs that were so old they creaked if you even thought about using them. No one else in the building seemed to know much about him, either.

Mary Rose didn't like it. But what she *really* didn't like was the fact that she didn't know if her steadfast mistrust of the male species made her wonder what he did with his life, or if she was actually drawn to him by fascination.

M.R. stood, crossed the room and flipped the sign on the door, now instructing tenants to "knock or call." Then she shut the door and went back into her bedroom. Mary Rose lived in the only actual apartment in the Atlantic Hotel. Like an old-fashioned boarding house, the rest of the tenants rented just rooms basically, sharing common bathrooms, a kitchen and the "Un-common areas" with each other.

In her bedroom, she shut the door and opened the bottom drawer of her dresser. Pulling out her grass, she sat on her bed and rolled a joint. She took the lighter from the lap of the female Buddha she had sculpted her third year of college, lit up, and then turned her window fan around to draw air out of the apartment. She took a deep drag and dropped back on her bed. Autumn had settled in Missoula, and the afternoon was a comfortable, just slightly brisk, cool.

Mary Rose exhaled the smoke, watching it rise toward the high ceiling, and her mind drifted back to David. What could have happened to him? She took another drag. Was his whole body as scarred as the half of his face?

Mary Rose hadn't been attracted to a boy since… well, never. As a young girl, she tried to pretend when the other girls talked about boys, but at best, it was more curiosity than attraction.

And it's not attraction with David, she reminded herself. *Like his smell, or his pheromones, or whatever you want to call it. It's just different.*

Kind of like, if he would let anybody near, she wanted to be someone close to him. But at the same time, part of her was downright scared of David Blithe.

Mary Rose had never given this much thought to anyone, let alone a man, and it infuriated her. Maybe smoking the joint hadn't been such a hot idea. She stubbed it out in her ashtray shaped like a screaming mouth.

What can I do? He's quiet, and he always pays…

Suddenly she stood from the bed and went back into her living room. "Well, well," she said aloud, looking at her calendar. "Will you look at that? He's late." She popped in a piece of gum from her shoulder bag and filled a glass of water in the bathroom, ignoring the little voice in the back of her head reminding her that she didn't usually nag the tenants; if they paid late, they paid the extra fee. She swished the water in her mouth, then spat out the gum. She checked herself in the mirror, instantly scowling as she realized what she was doing.

"Just getting the rent," she said to her reflection.

She left her apartment and started down the hall. When she approached David's door, her hand was already rising to knock, but she stopped when she realized he wasn't alone. She caught the end of something he was saying as she reached the door. Then someone else responded, a male voice.

"You can't beat me, boy. You can't escape, you'll never escape."

Mary Rose's heart skipped when she heard the voice, and she reeled a little as if a strong gust had blown down the hall. It was unmistakable, even though she hadn't heard him in over thirty years, at least not in her waking hours. And in the nightmares, he had spoken nearly the same words she just heard... *you'll never escape.*

It can't be, she thought. She started to bring up her hand again, a little slower this time, but then the male voice came again.

"Can I help you?"

"What are you talking about?" David, this time.

"Shut up, boy." Then louder. "Can I help you?"

A chill swept over Mary Rose's flesh, and she held her breath, afraid to move. She felt certain that the other person in David's room

Daddy?

knew that she was standing outside the door, just inches away.

Suddenly the hall felt much smaller than usual.

Mary Rose broke from her paralysis and dropped her arm. The two girls in the Un-commons peeked their heads around the corner as she hurried back to her apartment with the laughter from a dead man echoing down the hall behind her.

CHAPTER 9

David thought he had won. Apparently he had thought wrong.

He opened his eyes to blue sky, with just a hint of wisps of white, and for a moment, he felt free, back in the mountains of Colorado, camping with the kids. Or even better, Ann.

Then David saw the crack that split the sky, the crack in the plaster of the ceiling that a previous tenant had painted in an attempt to give the small room in the downtown apartment building limitless possibilities, and he wondered if he would ever be free.

The demon had returned. Or caught up. Whatever. Maybe it had never been gone in the first place. Recent events led David to suspect the latter, and he wondered if he was alone even now.

He swung his legs over the bed and sat up. He looked out his window over the rooftops of the adjoining buildings and again questioned his decision to rejoin the world five months after running into the Marrick family. But he thought he had beaten the demon.

Apparently he had thought wrong.

When David first fled the cabin, leaving Jeannie Marrick with her dead parents, he simply ran, with no intention or direction except escape. In fact, he had *wanted* to lose himself. The cabin had been a mistake; three more people had died as a result and the demon inhabited his body. As he ran, he could feel it inside, and while the brief rest in the cabin had given him new strength, it didn't last long. As he thrashed through the brush, stumbling and crashing, he could feel the demon's icy tendrils weaving into his burning muscles, the strings wrapping around his flesh. The puppet master had awoken. David actually had relished the relief the cold brought to his aching body, and part of him wanted to give in. Almost an hour later, the choice was taken away. His body could go no further, his flight reduced to barely staggering. He started laughing, but the dark, maniacal sound from his throat wasn't his own.

"Just let go, boy," the demon gurgled.

And he did.

Blackness had followed like a dreamless sleep. There had been moments of consciousness in the wild, but barely recognizable from nightmares. He had thought it a dream when he woke, scratched, bloody and beaten, in front of an abandoned hunting cabin, but it had actually saved his life. He had just enough time to heal himself before the demon came back for its prize, attacking on the back of a late-winter storm, but David had also taken time to fortify the cabin. He held off the demon for two days, even surviving after every wild animal in the woods attacked the cabin, trying to claw or chew their way in to get to him. The structure was racked with the sounds of growling, scratching and thumping as the poor animals attacked, driven rabid by an unknown master.

But David had been able to withstand the onslaught. Just when he thought he would collapse from the exhaustion, the clouds broke. It was early afternoon on the third day, and it didn't take much of the sun's pervading heat in the thin, mountain air to scatter the rest of the storm.

David stepped out of the cabin amidst a scattering of animal carcasses underfoot and deep blue sky overhead. The glaring white reflecting from the ice and snow was only broken by spatterings of crimson surrounding the discarded dead, the smell of their blood crisp in the air. David's stomach grumbled and he smiled.

And he convinced himself that he had beaten the demon.

He was quite a sight when he showed up in Missoula, his beard grown in on the side of his face unscarred by the fire, looking haggard but hard. A nice woman at the Poverello Center, the local soup kitchen, had helped him get a job. David hadn't swung a hammer for a living since college, but it was a job he could get without his employer asking too many questions. Then he found the Atlantic Hotel.

David looked around his room. With the bed, a small desk, and a chair, there was barely much space to move. The sky-painted ceiling hadn't been the last resident's only contribution. She also painted the walls. Evergreen trees. And through a break in the trees, she had painted a jagged mountain peak in the distance. The manager told him it was supposed to be somewhere in Glacier National Park. It had been the only room available at the time of his application. Even in civilization, he couldn't escape the wild.

David threw on some jeans and a sweatshirt. Saturday morning. No work today. But he had plans nonetheless. He stepped out into the hallway, where plants hung from the high ceiling and filled in the spaces on the walls unoccupied by artwork, making the already narrow passageway almost impassable in spots if two people were coming from opposite directions. The Atlantic was quiet as he made his way to the kitchen. Saturdays were often quiet, as most residents were either nursing hangovers or already gone for the day in pursuit of some sort of outdoor activity.

David passed the door to the last room before the kitchen. The girl living there had affixed a white-washed picket fence to the wall on either side of her door. Strips of canvas in the shape of a house framed the door and hung down behind the fence. David had overheard her telling a friend that she called it *Home*. "With a question mark," she said.

Most of the time, David liked the fact that, for all intents and purposes, he lived in an art gallery. Most of the time, the creativity inspired David. It added a little color to a life that had been gray for too long.

Sometimes the chaos was a little too much. Sometimes his own memories provided him with enough torment to fill the hallways; he didn't need the constant reminder of others' pain, especially evident in some of the darker artwork that he had noticed during the previous winter.

More recently, since the return of the demon, David felt like an exhibit himself, or like he was part of one. Like he was being watched. Tested. Maybe by the demon. Maybe God. Maybe both. And more recently, "Home" only reminded him of something he may never experience again. Instead, as he walked into the open kitchen, a headless dressmaker's doll in the corner with feathers glued to her arms seemed to welcome him to another day on display.

He reached up for the cereal box that had his initials written on it. He was wondering when the demon would make another appearance when he heard a cough from behind him. Someone in the common area across the hall from the kitchen, or the "Uncommons" as they called it.

Is this it? he wondered.

He turned slowly around, still holding the box of cereal, but he relaxed when he saw a familiar tenant slumped on one of the couches in the corner cradling a mug of coffee in his lap. David thought his name was Bane. Or at least that's what he called himself. He had moved into the Atlantic just a couple months earlier. This particular morning Bane appeared barely awake and so much contoured to the furniture that David hadn't noticed him there when he walked past. His black hair looked not only dyed but also painted onto his face, his eyes just visible underneath.

"Morning," David said.

Bane grumbled something incomprehensible, but raised his coffee mug in greeting.

David turned around, pleased by the brevity of the conversation. He already had enough on his mind. He needed to think about the trip he was taking today, to a place he hadn't been in years. He finished pouring his cereal and put it back on the shelf. The milk, as well as quite a few other staples, was community. Everyone on the floor chipped in. Otherwise, they would need three refrigerators. David grabbed a spoon and started out of the kitchen.

"That was some night," Bane said. His body hardly moved when he spoke.

David paused. "Yeah," he agreed, even though he had spent most of his Friday evening in his room. He noticed the faint smell of alcohol and sweat coming from the Uncommons, then looked in the direction of his room.

"What's your poison, man?" Bane asked.

David let out a little sigh, probably undetected by Bane behind that hair. Normally he managed to avoid the other tenants without seeming rude. Off to work early. Back late, dirty and tired enough to excuse himself to shower, missing the main crowd at dinner. If he ran into anyone on the weekends, they were usually with someone else, and a simple greeting or nod would suffice.

But maybe this morning he could use a little company. "Depends on the day."

Bane chuckled. "I know what you mean."

David walked over with his bowl and sat on the futon opposite the couch. The morning sun shone through a window between them, casting Bane even more in the shadows. For a moment, there was silence, and David thought he might only be committed to the span of time to finish his cereal, which shouldn't be long. Then Bane spoke up.

"Mine's gin," he said.

Still a kid, really, he thought. Bane couldn't have been older than twenty-two or twenty-three, and even though David hadn't yet reached thirty, he felt decades older.

"I used to be a whiskey drinker," David said. "Um, Bane, right?"

"Aw, fuck that," he responded. "You can call me Jeremy. Just not around the chicks."

David couldn't remember seeing any girls with "Bane" in the past, but he still nodded knowingly. "No problem."

"You're David, right?" Jeremy sat up suddenly, and his hand shot out of the shadows into the column of sunlight faster than David was expecting, causing him to flinch and splash some of his milk on his jeans. Jeremy pulled his hand back. "Sorry," he said as David wiped at the spots. "I'm not very good with people. I mean, I don't normally-"

"It's okay," David said. "I'm just still waking up." He reached out his hand. "Nice to meet you."

Jeremy shook and then sat back into the couch again. "Yeah, you too, man. I've noticed you around and meant to introduce myself, but you're always gone before I get a chance. I mean, I'm not gay or anything, but... I don't know. You just seem like a cool guy, and I hadn't really seen you hanging out with anybody, and thought if you didn't have any friends yet..." Jeremy trailed off and took a drink from his mug, and once again only the muted sounds of an occasional car on the street below could be heard.

David was caught off-guard by the fact that someone had been keeping tabs on him. "I thought I was keeping a low profile."

"Well, no offense," Jeremy said, "but you're pretty hard to miss. I mean, man you got *fucked up*, if you don't mind me saying. What happened?"

David reached up and touched his face. It had been over a year and a half, but sometimes he still forgot. How could he think people wouldn't notice him? They were probably just too uncomfortable to talk to him.

Jeremy picked up on the action. "I mean, no sweat if you don't want to tell me. It's cool. I mean, I was just wondering, not to be sticking my nose where it doesn't…" he paused and shook his head. "Goddamn! I'm acting like I'm talking to a chick, here. You're seriously going to think I'm gay."

There was a moment of silence.

"So you were out on the town last night?" David asked.

"I don't know why I bother." Jeremy flipped up his hair and while most of fell back over his eyes, some of it clung in place. "Fucking chicks, man. You know, when I moved here, everybody said, 'aww, you'll meet somebody. It's real artsy there. All sorts of women.' But they're just the same here. They may not be as hung up on their appearance, but they're still stuck on themselves." Jeremy took a drink from his coffee and looked out the window.

"So where are you from?" David asked, surprised by the words coming out of his mouth. He quickly took a spoonful of cereal, as if to silence himself. Since rejoining the world, he had taken every step he knew to *avoid* conversation. Even at work, he just did his job and kept to himself. He did good work, so no one seemed to mind.

"Utah," Jeremy said. "Salt Lake City. But I'm not a Mormon, so let me save you the question. And whatever you've heard about Salt Lake, it's not true. It may be less-than-half LDS these days, but that just makes the ones who *are* Mormon even more obvious. You can feel it in their stares, like when you order a beer at a restaurant. There will always be at least one person at another table who won't even try to mask their look of disdain."

David thought that it wasn't just the beer that people were noticing about Jeremy, but he kept the thought to himself. Instead he continued to work on his cereal.

"It's like my cow theory," Jeremy said after a moment.

"Cow theory?"

"Yeah, man. Whenever you're driving, especially up here, watch when you pass a herd of cows. Law of numbers. You can almost guarantee that if it's a decent sized herd, more than just a two or three grazing on the hills, one of those cows will be either pissing or taking a shit. And they don't care that you're driving by. Just like some staunch Mormon trying to shit on your good time."

David laughed, and Jeremy smiled from underneath his hair, most of which had returned to covering his eyes. David thought that maybe he was an okay guy, under the cynicism. Possibly even a friend.

The idea vanished almost as quickly as David had thought it, as the reality of his life forced its way back in, souring the moment. Friends were a liability. David was in danger again, and that meant the same for anyone else around him. He stood quickly, and the smile slipped from Jeremy's face.

"Leaving so soon?" he asked.

"Yeah, I'm sorry," David said. "I just remembered an appointment I have this morning." He spooned down the rest of his cereal on his way across the hall to the kitchen. "It was nice talking with you, though. I just gotta go." He rinsed out his bowl and put it in the dish drainer. When he turned around, Jeremy still looked confused. "Hope you feel better," David said. "Drink lots of water." Jeremy managed a thin smile, then looked back out the window as David started down the hall to his room.

Yes, it was the right thing to do. He didn't know how innocent Jeremy was, but he couldn't risk another life at his hands.

But maybe another friend is what you need, he reasoned with himself. *Someone else on the outskirts of society who might not think you were crazy. Someone else to talk with.*

Even though there was something in Jeremy's demeanor that didn't jibe with David's, he couldn't deny that the conversation *had* been nice. More words than he had exchanged with anyone on just a casual basis since the woman at the Poverello Center who had helped him get his job. Even his first day at work, he had just shown up with only brief introductions, and then he strapped on his tool belt. Carpenters were like that. New guys came and went, and the others on the crew usually waited to see what a guy could do before they decided if they wanted to get to know him. But even after David had proven himself, he kept to himself. One of his coworkers, Steve Avery, was okay. Not quite old enough to be David's father, but not too far from it, Steve was still friendly with David. Not that the others were mean, but they just stopped interacting with him at all, except to tell him what to do next. Steve still said "good morning," and even occasionally invited him out for a beer with the crew after work, even though David always politely declined.

Back in his room, David again considered his options, unsure of how to proceed. Part of him felt that he should just stay put, see out the weekend and go back to work on Monday. In the small room, he felt safe. And alone, which he had previously convinced himself was the source of his strength. But this morning, the conversation made him feel that perhaps a little outside help was what he needed.

He grabbed his keys and left the room, going the opposite direction down the narrow hallway toward the balcony overlooking the alleyway. He didn't want to risk the awkwardness of possibly encountering Jeremy again. As he pushed open the heavy door at the end of the hall, crossed the plant-enshrined balcony and started down the metal stairs to the alley, he wondered what he might do the next time he saw the other tenant. They had exchanged too many words for a simple passing nod to suffice, but David thought maybe a few brief words would get across the idea that he preferred to keep to himself.

At the bottom of the stairs, he glanced at his locked-up bicycle but opted to walk instead. No need to rush. While he might have convinced himself to go where he was heading today, he still wanted a little time to think about it.

The morning air was chilly, and even though it had been a dry late-autumn so far, he knew that winter wasn't far around the corner. He pulled his sweatshirt hood on and started south, cutting through downtown. Few people were milling around this morning, and the ones who were out looked like tourists mostly. They were interspersed with a few locals already gathered at the tables outside Worden's Market. David recognized some of the faces sipping from steaming cups, and as he passed, he realized that some of them noticed him as well.

Usually when he was out on the streets, either on foot or on his bike, he just kept his head down and bee-lined to wherever he needed to be, but Jeremy's comment had set him wondering. Even though Montana was known for being a pretty good haven for people who just wanted to keep to themselves, juxtaposed with the social atmosphere of the college town, David suddenly wondered if he was the talk of the town. The local elephant man.

He took a less populated side street, pulling his hood tighter and trying to focus on the sidewalk… trying *not* to think about where he was going, suddenly unsure of the idea. But he was running out of options, and possibly out of time.

The sound of children caused David to raise his head again. He had made it to Caras Park on the northern side of the Clark Fork River. The carousel was running, and groups of families lined up outside for their chance to go on the Missoula landmark. He steered clear of the masses, staying close to the rear entrances of the buildings that flanked the park, then crossing to the pavilion and sitting down at a park bench far enough away to not be noticed. Children were honest; they stared without hesitation.

It pained David to watch the families. Even the parents who obviously wished they were anywhere else this particular morning incited envy in him. He had always been good with kids, especially younger ones, but now David was only afraid of them. Afraid *for* them. He had already ruined the life of Jeannie Marrick, taking away what was most precious to her. His presence was a threat, and he couldn't bear to scar another kid that way.

David stood from the table and turned away from the carousel. On his way out of the pavilion, he passed a table with two college-aged couples sitting at it. One of the guys looked up at him and smiled, watching him as he passed. It wasn't a friendly smile. A chill ran over David, but he kept walking. The hairs on the back of his neck rose, expecting an attack, but he fought the urge to look back or run. Only when he reached the stairs leading up to the bridge did he risk a glance at the table. The young man was still watching him while conversation continued among the others at his table. He turned and looked toward where David had been sitting, toward the groups of families, and when he turned back, the wide grin looked like it might split his face in half, revealing the dark thing inside.

David didn't know what the demon was thinking, but he knew that he was helpless. He couldn't exactly run over and beat the college student down, yelling at him to leave the children alone. That would surely land him in jail, bringing up questions about his past. He could only hope that the demon was taunting him, simply watching him. In effect, David could do nothing. He continued up the stairs to the Higgins Street Bridge.

This wasn't the first time David had walked away, resisting the urge to run. The demon had first reappeared almost a month earlier. David had been sitting in his room reading a book, actually relaxing, when the knock sounded at the door. His first thought had been that it was the apartment manager, Mary Rose. He had remembered earlier that day that his rent was late. He pulled out his wallet, removing the cash and opened the door, but instead of a woman, a burly red-headed man stood in the doorway, swaying slightly in place. The man's eyes were bloodshot, and the smell of whiskey crept across the threshold. *Great,* David had thought. *Some drunk wandered into the wrong building.*

The man looked down at the money in David's hand and smiled. "Interesting choice," he said. His voice was clear, clearer than it should've been for someone so visibly intoxicated. "Do you think you can pay me off, David?"

David didn't have to ask how the man in the overalls and flannel shirt knew his name. In that instant, he understood that he hadn't beaten the demon at the hunting cabin. But where had it been? Gathering more souls? Or just more strength?

"Put away your money," the demon said. "And let me in."

The man filled the door, too big for David to slip past into the narrow hallway; he briefly considered slamming the door. His window was only about fifteen feet above the roof of the pawnshop. But it was as if the demon could read his mind.

"I'll just break down this flimsy door. Now let me in. I'm not going to hurt you... yet."

David stepped back, and the man stumbled into the room, bouncing off the doorframe before shutting the door and finally plopping into a sitting position on the bed. For a moment David wondered if he could have actually escaped the possessed man's intoxicated body, if the demon had been bluffing, but he had seen drunken rages before, and they didn't require coordination. The door probably would've splintered under the man's large frame before David could even get the old window open.

Still, David remained standing, his mind running circles trying to come up with an answer as to what to do next, preparing for an attack or another attempt to take over his body. "What do you-"

"You can't beat me, boy," the demon said. "You can't escape, you'll never escape." He paused and cocked an ear toward the door. David had heard it, too. Someone treading down the creaky floorboards of the hallway. Then the sounds stops, seemingly outside his door. Maybe this time it actually was Mary Rose.

"Can I help you?" the demon asked.

"What are you talking about?" David asked. He could only hope that if it was Mary Rose, she would hear the talking in the room and wait to knock on his door for the rent. Of course, this was Mary Rose.

"Shut up, boy." The demon said. Then louder. "Can I *help* you?"

There was silence, and then David heard whoever was outside the door move away. Fast. The man sitting on the bed started to laugh then, a deep barreled laugh that filled the small room. David tensed his body, as if that action might somehow prevent him from being possessed himself. But instead, the man stopped laughing suddenly and sat forward, staring at David. "This isn't over yet, boy," he said.

Then the big man's body had slumped over and dropped off the bed. He regained consciousness quickly and looked at David with cross-eyed contempt. "Who the hell are you?" he slurred, staggering to his feet.

David stood as well, noticing that the man had urinated on himself. It was over. The demon was gone, and David still had control of his own body. "You just stumbled into my room," he said. "I think you might be lost."

"Fuck *you* I'm lost!" the man bellowed. "I've never been lost in my whole, entire life."

He swayed in place, and David followed his movements carefully. If this tree was about to fall, David didn't want to be in the way. But more than that, and a little strange in retrospect, he was more concerned about physical violence now that the demon was *gone*.

The man looked around the room until he located the door. "See?" he said. "There's the fucking *door*. I know where I am."

David saw a brief flash of confused fear cross the man's face as he probably tried to piece together what had happened to him, then it was replaced by drunken anger again as he fumbled with the doorknob a couple times before successfully swinging it open. He lunged into the hallway without looking back in the room, crashing his way out of the Atlantic.

David never saw the man again, but just as with the college kid in the park, he felt confident that he had seen the demon several more times since. The demon was playing with him.

On the other side of the Clark Fork, David continued past a row of shops and restaurants into the more residential part of town. His pace was slow, and not just because he wanted time to think. Even after sleeping in a little more than his usual weekday routine, David still felt like he hadn't slept in weeks. In truth, he barely slept at all the first few nights after the first visit, forcing himself to stay awake in case the demon came again. Finally his body succumbed to the exhaustion. Each day since, it was all he could do to stay awake after work long enough to eat dinner before passing out in his room, but even then his nights were filled with dreams, mostly of the same thing. He dreamt that he was working at a convalescence home, surrounded by the old and dying. The dreams felt so real that he might as well have been working two jobs. So vivid that he felt like he never received the deep sleep that his body needed.

David turned off Higgins onto one of the more residential streets, the same route he had been taking the past month to get to his current job site. The leaves on the heavily tree-lined street had changed a couple weeks earlier and already started dropping, and it pleased David that the only sounds this morning were his feet tracking through them. He tried to remember to find pleasure in the little things.

After a couple of blocks, he stopped and looked down the street. A modest house sat just a little farther back on its lot than the houses on either side. David passed it every morning, but if not for the sign hanging in the yard, he would have never known it was a church. An older man, probably late fifties, sat on his knees in the driveway, surrounded by a few plants, empty pots and a bag of potting soil. He wore jeans and, with gloved hands, worked a spade into one of the plants. Like the sign, if David hadn't seen him on a previous occasion sporting the white collar, he might have thought it was the gardener.

Suddenly he wasn't ready to approach the church. Not yet. He had it all planned out in his head, had pictured the scene. Approaching the house, the sun would be shining, and inside, David would find the preacher, or whatever he was called, sitting and reading reflectively. He wasn't counting on him being outside in a pile of dirt.

David looked around his immediate vicinity, then sat down on the curb, slightly obscured from the church by a gray Volvo, with just enough space so he could lean forward and watch, but where he would probably not be noticed if the priest stood up and looked around.

The older man, just starting to gray at the temples, finished repotting the plant he was working on and then started on an Aloe Vera. He was meticulous in the task, but at the same time he handled the plants delicately, filling in the soil and patting it down like a man tucking in his children.

After he finished with the aloe plant, he stood and brushed himself off. He paused for a moment, looking around the neighborhood. David quickly sat back, hiding behind the car, and when he leaned forward again, the reverend was gone. He waited a couple minutes, then stood and walked down the street to the church.

CHAPTER 10

Father James Oaks, or Father Jimmy, as he'd asked his parishioners to refer to him, was halfway through his Saturday morning chores. In the driveway of the St. Stephen Episcopal Church, a building that had been just another house in the quiet Missoula neighborhood twelve years earlier, Father Jimmy used his spade to delicately loosen the soil surrounding an aloe plant from its overgrown pot. He knew that at least four of the plants in the little chapel needed bigger homes, and today was a beautiful day for the project.

And what better way to complement this day, and this work of the Lord, than with a nice glass of lemonade? Father Jimmy thought.

But first things first, he reminded himself. He knew that he should probably get at least one plant repotted before getting distracted. He told himself it was the virtue of patience that he was working on, but he couldn't deny it was also absentmindedness. His chores usually ended up being his "afternoon chores" because he neglected them for some other bit of business during the morning hours.

Father Jimmy put his palm on the soil, with the base of the Aloe Vera situated in the crook between his thumb and first finger, and turned the pot upside down. The plant slid out in a solid clump. He loosened some of the dirt, freeing up the exterior roots, before putting it in a larger pot. He used his spade to scoop extra potting soil around the plant, and then packed it down.

Father Jimmy smiled. A plant just seemed healthier in a larger home with a new chance to spread its roots and continue to grow. He set down his spade on the driveway, wiped his hands on his blue jeans and stood up. Now for a little reward. He started across the yard, already thinking about the lemonade in the refrigerator, but then he stopped. He had the sudden sensation that he was being watched, not that uncommon when your church sat in the middle of residential neighborhood, but this felt different. Father Jimmy had been only twenty years-old when he went to Vietnam, but in the years since, he hadn't been able to shake the almost constant state of being on guard. In the jungle it always felt like someone, or some*thing*, could be watching.

He scanned the neighborhood, finally convincing himself that it was just the same lingering paranoia and that he wasn't about to get attacked. He turned back to the house and walked inside to the sounds of Bill Evans playing piano over the sound system. Jazz was one of Father Jimmy's guilty pleasures. After all, one couldn't listen to hymns *all* of the time.

On his way to the kitchen, he paused at the chapel, which had been built as an extension to the house seven years earlier. Full-length windows ran almost the entire eastern wall, looking out to a well-greened patio where fellowship was held after church. Father Jimmy loved this time of day, when the morning sun just filtered through the vine-wrapped trellis covering the patio and was softened by a thin, persistent coat of dust on the windows that the priest could never quite keep completely cleaned. The light lay gently over the pews, stretching out over the red carpeting and just catching the bottom of the pulpit.

If ever a house of the Lord there were, he thought.

But while the chapel was peaceful, Father Jimmy couldn't help but sigh. It may have been beautiful, but he often wished that his congregation, like the plants, required a bigger home. In his two and a half years as rector of the St. Stephen Episcopal Church, Father Jimmy's congregation had only grown by fifteen percent and that was mostly thanks to the birth of triplets to Matthew and Jennifer Aubrey two years earlier. It was a good flock, of course. Small, but strong in their faith. But he couldn't deny the fact that it was also an older flock, with not too many years before some of the members would be set out to their final pasture. What the church needed was some fresh blood, but in the college community, and with times being as they were, younger parishioners were hard to come by.

Father Jimmy was considering having some musicians play on Sundays. Sort of like a rock band, but a rock band for Jesus. He had visited other churches with these bands. Most of them seemed to have a greater turnout of younger members, and even the older parishioners got into it. Besides that, Father Jimmy thought it just seemed like more fun. It kind of reminded him of the sixties, a little more passion and a little bit of good ol' get-down-and-praise-the-Lord!

Father Jimmy continued down the hall past the meeting/independent study rooms into the kitchen. He opened the refrigerator and pulled out the pitcher of fresh lemonade brought over by Mrs. O'Myron. He was pouring a glass and thinking back on a production of *Godspell* he had seen in Paris in the summer of '74, when he heard the front screen door close. He set the pitcher on the counter and walked back into the hallway. When the priest saw the profile of the young man staring off into the chapel, his eyes widened, and he had to stifle a sharp breath of surprise. Instead he smiled and walked toward the scarred man who had entered his church. "Can I help you?" he asked.

The man turned toward him, and Father Jimmy saw that only the right side of his face had been burned. He looked to be about the same age as Matt Aubrey. Late-twenties, early-thirties maybe, but Father Jimmy could see in this man's eyes that he had been through harder times than Matt would even want to think about.

"I think I need help, Father," the man said.

The priest noticed the obvious difficulty he had asking for help. In Father Jimmy's experience, men usually had a harder time with admitting that they needed God. However, he suspected that this guy had something more to say than just expressing fear that his wife or girlfriend was cheating on him. No, he thought this was something very serious. While nothing of this nature had happened in his time at St. Stephen, he still recognized an opportunity to serve the Lord. "Can I offer you a glass of lemonade?" he asked.

"No, thank you," the man said.

"You aren't injured in any way, are you, friend?"

The man looked down at the carpet. "No, I just need to talk with you."

"Are you running from the law? It's okay if you are. As long as you don't pose a threat to me, I'll see that you find sanctuary in the house of the Lord."

The man looked back up and trained his gaze on Father Jimmy, who would swear the color of the stranger's eyes darkened just slightly. "Listen," he said, more forcefully. "I just want to talk."

The priest instinctively took a half-step back, but while something about the man made him nervous, he didn't think the stranger had come to cause any trouble. At the same time Father Jimmy felt an outpouring of compassion he hadn't felt in years, maybe since he took his vows. He couldn't explain it, but this was more than just his job. He couldn't shake the urge to drop to his knees and practically beg the scarred man to let him help.

You really are desperate for new members, old man, he told himself.

"We can talk in my office," he said. "Are you sure you don't want some lemonade? It's homemade."

The man smiled for the first time, and the priest realized how handsome he must have been before what appeared to be a fire. "No. Thanks, though."

"Well, c'mon in." Father Jimmy led the man down a short hallway to his office. Like the chapel, the office had a window with an eastern exposure on the only wall not entirely covered with bookshelves. However, unlike the airy chapel, the small office turned into an oven in the peak of summer if Father Jimmy didn't close the blinds and block out the sun, something he hated to do. Today the blinds were open.

Father Jimmy grabbed a box of books off one of the chairs situated next to his desk and set it on the floor beside two other boxes, also marked *books*. "Sorry for the mess," he said. "So much reading, so little time. And even less shelf space." The stranger managed another smile, but the priest could see this one was more forced. "Please, have a seat," he said. The man took the chair and slid it against the wall facing the windows, with the door on one side and Father Jimmy on his other side.

So he can keep an eye on everything, Father Jimmy realized. *All entrances and exits.* He may not have been in trouble with the law, but this man was running from something. The priest walked over and extended his hand. "You can call me Father Jimmy."

The man looked at the outstretched hand for a moment and then shook it. "David," he said.

"Ahh," Father Jimmy said and turned back to his desk. "King David." He slid his own chair out of the way and started running his finger over the books on the third shelf behind his desk. "Quite a character that King David." Father Jimmy found that people liked to hear things about their names; it was a good ice breaker. As opposed to many of the newer names couples were coming up with recently, "David" came directly from the Bible, and people seemed especially curious about biblical references to their name, more than just the origin of it.

"Do you really believe that?" David asked from behind him.

Father Jimmy turned around and leaned against the shelves. "The Bible?" he asked, as if the stranger had read his mind.

"No," David said. "The book you just passed over. *Holy Blood. Holy Grail.*"

"Ahh, that one," he said and smiled. "I forgot it was up there. Probably shouldn't have *that* one on display." He took the book from the shelf and put it on his desk. "A very interesting book, indeed. Have you read it?"

"Most of it. I never finished, but I had already heard the ending, you know?" He paused and cocked his left eyebrow, with just the trace of a grin. "So, do you believe it?"

"That's a good question," Father Jimmy said. "Do I believe that our Lord and Saviour, Jesus Christ, had a son and that the bloodline continues on even today?" Of the considerable other information in the book, from the Crusades to the Knights Templar, the revelation of a divine birthright had raised the most controversy. The priest scratched his jaw. "Well, it sure *sounds* like a nice idea," he said. "It would be comforting knowing that somewhere out there is a relative of that great man, howsoever distant of a relative. As to whether or not I believe it's true, well, that's a matter between my God and me. The important thing is to always keep our mind open to the possibilities."

Father Jimmy looked around the office and out the window and then leaned toward David and lowered his voice. "Just between you and me," he whispered, even though he knew the church was empty, "I also read a copy of *The Satanic Bible* not long after it was published in the late sixties." He waited for a reaction, but getting none, he straightened out and continued. "Whether you believe in it or not, I think it's foolish not to know as much as possible about those different from us, be it the Amish or the Satanists. *The Satanic Bible* actually dispelled many of the myths surrounding the religion, the most glaring disparity being that the true Satanist *didn't* believe in sacrificing children or animals like the media wanted us to believe. They considered those two creatures the finest examples of true Innocence, a state of existence that they worshipped in a sense. Of course, there were a few rituals in the book to be carried out without Christian ideals in mind, but those weren't much interest to me. It was the ideas behind the practice. They were closer to Naturalists, in my opinion."

"I like that," David said. "Not the Satan part, I mean. But nature. The innocence of the wild. Well, you know..." He trailed off.

Father Jimmy waited for a moment to see if he would continue, *hoping* that he would say more, again surprised by his own yearning to be of assistance, but David remained silent. Father Jimmy turned back to the bookshelves. "But as for me, I hold pretty good faith in another book." In his opinion, the particular version he reached for had been especially designed for times like this. "And as far as royal bloodlines go," he continued, "your name holds some pretty serious water in the kingdom of Heaven." The Bible he pulled from the shelf was twice the size of popular hardcover books. Intimidating at first, Father Jimmy knew that once most people got a look at it, they felt more comfortable, and many found it even more accessible than the traditional Bibles in the backs of the pews.

"That's one helluva Bible," David said.

Father Jimmy winced, but then chuckled. "Not exactly how I might have put it, David," he said. "But yes, it is quite impressive." He opened the book on his desk and slid his chair over.

"It has pictures?" David asked.

"It does," Father Jimmy said. "That's what I really like about it. It was published by Reader's Digest. I picked up this particular copy in a used bookstore, but it's in great condition considering it was printed in 1971. You see, what they've done is to put photographs of archeological sites, artifacts and landscapes from the areas referred to in the stories." Father Jimmy thought the book brought the stories to life, gave them substance in the real world, and seemed to appeal to younger parishioners who seemed more intent on "proof."

The man in the chair stared at the priest, but he didn't speak. That was fine. Father Jimmy knew David would say more when he was ready. "So let's see," he continued. "King David." He flipped to the back of the large Bible. "Here you are. 'The second and greatest king of Israel, a warrior, poet, and leader of men…'" Father Jimmy skimmed ahead. "'Despite grave blemishes in his moral character… his abilities and his virtues were such as to provide the model for the Messiah, the ideal ruler of the future, who it was believed would arise from David's descendents.'" Father Jimmy quoted from Samuel:

"Fill thine horn with oil, and go, I will send thee to Jesse the Beth'lehemite: for I have provided me a king among his sons."

"I know the story," David said. "I *have* been to church once or twice in my lifetime."

"Then you know what a great man he was," Father Jimmy said. "Even with a few minor shortcomings, he set the stage, in a way, for all of our redemption."

"He set the stage through blood," David said. "He was a killer. Don't forget that I know the story."

"Well, yes, but many of the books of the Old Testament are considered pretty violent. Again, though, perhaps it should be viewed *not* as the ritual, but rather the ideas behind the practice." He set the Bible on his desk and leaned forward on his elbows.

David leaned toward the desk. Father Jimmy flinched, momentarily thinking he should've kept up his guard, but David only shook his head and turned the Bible around. "It's a little more than just the honorable slaying of the uncircumcised Philistine." He flipped the pages. "Here it is. Second Samuel, Chapter 8. They've most appropriately paraphrased it as 'David extends his kingdom.'" David ran his finger down the verse. *"And he smote Moab… casting them down to the ground; even with two lines measured he to put to death… David smote also Hadade'zer, the son of Rehob, king of Zobah… David slew of the Syrians two and twenty thousand men."* David paused and looked up, his finger still poised at the end of the verse. *"And the Lord preserved David whithersoever he went."* He paused and looked at Father Jimmy. "Does this mean that it's okay to kill so long as it's in the name of God?"

The priest's knee-jerk reaction was one of defense, a result of previously having the pointed question fired at him from skeptics attacking past actions of the church. "Well, there were many…" Father Jimmy trailed off and relaxed back in his chair again. He narrowed his eyes and scratched his chin. Beyond the cynicism, he sensed that David was seeking a genuine answer, forgiveness maybe.

Father Jimmy had to say something. And that "something" had to be handled delicately if David was an actual threat.

Being a priest was more than just a job for James Oaks. He had heard his calling to serve the Lord not long after his return from Vietnam. It had come to him in a dream; he saw himself as an older man delivering a sermon from a pulpit. Once he started down that road, he discovered the truth about his intuition. His father once told him that he seemed to have a good sense about people, but James decided that intuition was actually God speaking. Father Jimmy believed that his basic ability to read someone, almost before they even spoke, and to know the right words to say to that person, was God's way of speaking to him. *Through* him, maybe. He wanted to comfort David, but beyond his obligations, he wanted to say things to keep David in the office because he knew he would feel a little empty if he left.

Father Jimmy reached over, closed the Bible and took a deep breath. "Why are you here, my son? Obviously God was in your life once, but I don't sense that you seek Him now. It does seem, however, that you are looking for answers."

David dropped his head. "I'm sorry, Father. I have a lot of anger in me. I do need help. I'm keeping my mind open to all of the possibilities, I guess. That's why I'm here."

Father Jimmy sensed that David was near to opening up. Just a little more persuasion. "You can tell me what has happened if you want. You're safe here."

David shifted in his chair. "I've seen some horrible things, Father," he said. "I've *done* horrible things. But... it wasn't really me."

Father Jimmy stood and slid the other chair closer to David. "It's okay, my son. You can tell me. And you can be forgiven by the grace of God." He reached out to put his hand on David's shoulder, but he pulled away.

"But I don't believe in God," David said. "Not like you. My God is the wilderness. I haven't found God in a building since I was a kid."

"That's okay, too," Father Jimmy said and slid his chair back slightly. "The important thing is that *He* believes in you. And even King David went to the wilderness and found God there." He started to reach for the Bible. "For example, in Samuel, Chapter-"

David whipped forward and slammed his hand down on the book. "Haven't you figured it out yet?" he asked. "Can't you tell that I'm not here to listen to old stories being recited? I need to know what *you* think."

Father Jimmy didn't know what to say. David was looking for answers, but he wouldn't ask any questions. He seemed to want validation, but for what? God? Did he want to know if God would help him get through whatever demons he was fighting? "Tell me what I can do," Father Jimmy said. "What do you need?"

David's chest hitched, and his body trembled. He lowered his head again, and Father Jimmy knew he was weeping. Then he dropped forward off the chair onto his knees in a position of supplication. "I just want a little help," he said. "I can't do it alone. I just need someone to help me." He looked down at the floor.

Father Jimmy stood and approached him. He reached out his hand, and this time David didn't retreat from him. He placed his hand on David's right shoulder, surprised by the warmth radiating off the young man's body. The heat only intensified in Father Jimmy's hand. Judging by the burns on his face, the priest guessed that the scars continued down the right side of his body, probably underneath the sweatshirt beneath his hand.

My God, it's like he's still on fire, Father Jimmy thought.

"I just want my life back," David whispered.

The whole room seemed to grow warmer. Sweat began to bead on Father Jimmy's forehead, and he tried to pull his hand away. More than just heat, he felt like his hand was actually burning. But he couldn't pull it away.

David looked up at him. "I shouldn't have left," he said. "Maybe she wouldn't have survived, but maybe I shouldn't have, either."

Suddenly Father Jimmy saw it. Flames consumed his office, but it wasn't his office anymore. He stood in another house. David was still on his knees, but now he held a naked girl in his arms, engulfed by fire. "I should've died there, too," David shouted over the flames surrounding them.

Father Jimmy found the strength to yank his hand free from David's shoulder, and the vision disappeared. He reeled backward, blinking in surprise. His body shook, consumed by David's pain. He could feel it as clearly as the ground underneath his shoes. Tears escaped his eyes beyond his control.

"I just want her back," David said.

Father Jimmy knew he was about to faint. Gray was leaching the color from his vision. He looked around and grabbed the arm of the chair behind him, falling into it.

"Can you bring her back, Father?" David asked.

Father Jimmy tried to speak, if only to convince himself that he wasn't dreaming, but his tongue felt swollen and dry, stuck to the roof of his mouth.

"That's what I thought." David stood and wiped away his tears. He left the office and was halfway down the hall when Father Jimmy finally found his tongue.

"Wait!" he called out.

David stopped and looked back at him for a long moment, but Father Jimmy didn't know what to say next. David turned away, and Father Jimmy slumped down in his chair, unconscious.

CHAPTER 11
CALIFORNIA

Dr. Samantha Brandt filled the Styrofoam cup with coffee from the staff lounge at The Rose Memorial Girls School. It was actually her second cup, and she cursed herself for waking up too late to make her own that morning. She grumbled to herself about the non-dairy creamer and flipped through the application of a new girl starting today. She scalded her tongue on the coffee just as a voice behind her made her jump.

"Dr. Brandt? Samantha Brandt?" the voice asked.

Sam set her coffee on the table and turned around. A girl who couldn't have been much older than some of the residents in the house walked up with her hand firmly in front of her. "Carly Shaw," the girl said. "Dianne at the front desk said you might be here. This is my first day."

Sam took a deep breath and extended her own hand. "Welcome to the Rose House," she said. "And please, Sam is fine. We try to keep the titles pretty informal around here. Less threatening to the girls."

"I've got to tell you," Carly said, "that's such a pretty name."

"Sam Brandt?" Sam asked and raised an eyebrow.

"No," Carly said and giggled. "I mean, Brandt's a nice name, but I love the name 'The Rose House.' I knew from the first time I heard about it that I would work here."

Sam just stared at the girl. It was shaping up to be a long day. "Okay," she said. "Let's get started. I'm sure you're familiar with the Rose Memorial Girls School."

"Well," Carly said and looked down at her worn sandals, "I know that the girls here are anywhere from thirteen years old to seventeen."

"Correct," Sam said. "Generally they're inner-city kids." She picked up the cup of coffee and took a sip. She winced and dropped it in the garbage can. "Rule number one," she said. "Bring your own coffee."

Carly giggled again. "I usually do."

Sam laughed. Maybe the girl wasn't too bad. With any luck she'd stay a little longer than most of the post-graduates. "Rule number two is to know who you're dealing with. So let's go meet some of the girls. With the holiday, most of them are here today."

The two left the lounge and walked down the carpeted hall of the house that had been converted to a school for girls by Theresa Rose twenty-two years earlier.

"We have twelve girls actually living here right now," Sam said. "You'll be wearing a few different hats. Your main responsibility will be as a sort of mentor for some of the kids." She paused and looked at the dainty girl beside her. "The younger ones, primarily. You'll be helping them with their classes, but we also want you to be something of a big sister. Some of the older girls have jobs, so occasionally, we'll have you driving them around in the van. Oh, and for one of the girls, you'll have to occasionally assist with bathroom duties. You don't have a problem with that, do you?"

Carly wrapped a strand of her brunette hair around a finger with a large turquoise ring on it. "Um, no," she said. "You'll just have to show me what to do."

"Good," Sam said. "You realize, most of the girls attend outside schools," Sam said. "Others need to be privately taught here. Kind of like forced home schooling."

The two ascended a second flight of stairs and continued down another hallway lined with doors. "Take for example," Sam continued, "a girl like Melissa Kent. She was living--" Sam stopped when she realized Carly was no longer beside her. She turned around and saw her standing in front of one of the rooms.

Jeannie Marrick, Sam thought, *how could I forget to mention Jeannie?*

"Wow," Carly murmured. She started to walk into the room, and Sam rushed over.

"Hold on, there," she said and put a hand on Carly's shoulder. "An open door isn't always an invitation." Sam rapped on the doorjamb. "Jeannie?" There was no response. "And in this case, we wait for her to return."

Carly stepped back from the door but kept her gaze in the room wallpapered with hundreds of pictures and articles. "What is it?" she asked.

"A year and a half worth of time," Sam said. "Life and death. Love and hate. You name it. It's all there. It's something of a work of art, if you ask me." Sam paused and looked past Carly. A girl with thick brown curls and deep blue eyes strode over to Carly and Dr. Brandt. "And here's the artist herself."

She could be a heartbreaker, Sam thought, not for the first time, *if she'll only give them a chance.*

"Carly, I'd like you to meet Jeannie Marrick," Sam said.

Jeannie smiled but didn't say anything. Actually, she hadn't spoken since she had arrived at the Rose House in the late summer of the year before, and more than a few staff at the school wondered if the girl would hold out the last seven months until she was old enough to leave the house.

"Carly was hoping to get a look at the masterpiece, if you don't mind." Sam said.

Jeannie stepped back and raised a welcoming arm in the direction of her room. Carly went in first, but didn't make it more than four steps before stopping again. Dr. Brandt and Jeannie had to step around her.

"I'd like to think it's helped you find a center, Jeannie," Sam said. She suspected there was something else to the collage, but she didn't say anything. "It seems like I notice something new every time I come in. Kind of like you."

Sam walked over to one of the walls. The first clipping to catch her eye was a tabloid article about a gorilla that was successfully mated with a dolphin to create "The Perfect Beast." Taped next to that was a cover of *National Geographic* with a photo of the snowcapped Andes. Under that was a newspaper article from Seattle about a prank caller getting murdered in his home.

And it went on like that. Stories, photos, and articles clumped together in a complex maze of patterns weaving along the walls. Sam wasn't kidding when she said she noticed something new whenever she entered the room. Another story about animals or people. Misdeeds and heroism. Tales of horror and visions of wonder. Rainbows and gravestones.

Jeannie cleared her throat. Sam turned around and saw that Jeannie was holding a couple of other clippings and a roll of clear tape that she had pulled from her drawer. She walked over to the window on the other side of her bed and held up one of the articles to a bare spot on the wall next to it, seeming to evaluate its place.

"Of course," Sam said. She turned from the section of mural and walked past Carly, who had yet to move from her spot. "Let's go, Carly. We've taken enough of Ms. Marrick's time."

"Huh?" Carly mumbled, and then, "Oh yeah. Nice meeting you, Jeannie."

Jeannie raised one hand, but didn't turn away from her project of adding the new articles. The two left the room and continued the tour, introducing her to a few more of the girls along the way. Sam continued her rehearsed routine for new employees of the Rose House, but while Carly listened, she seemed obviously distracted, and the older woman could guess why.

They circled back through the downstairs wing toward the main offices. "We just have some final paperwork for you to take care of," Sam said. Dianne looked up from the reception desk and smiled. Sitting behind her, coloring furiously, was her six-year-old daughter, Maren.

Dianne followed Dr. Brandt's glance at her daughter. "I didn't think you'd mind," Dianne said. "Day care was closed today, and Randy had to go into the office."

"Certainly not," Sam said. "Carly, you've already met Dianne, and this is her daughter, Maren. We usually only get the pleasure of Miss Maren on Tuesday and Thursday afternoons."

Maren looked up for a moment, smiled, and then quickly went back to her coloring. Carly walked around the desk and stood next to the girl. "You've got a very pretty name, Maren," Carly said.

"Thanks," she said without looking up from her paper.

"What are you working on?"

Maren slid the paper over on the desk, and the three women leaned in to examine the drawing of a yellow beach and blue sky. She had mixed blue and green for the ocean and was obviously in the middle of creating a palm tree. Off to the side, there was a huge house, but the girl had drawn it unfinished, just the framed skeleton. Sam shivered.

Dianne smiled, obviously pleased. "She's been working on it since yesterday."

"It's very good," Carly said.

"Thanks." Maren looked at Carly and smiled. "It's Hawaii."

"Really? Have you ever been to Hawaii?"

Dianne just chuckled.

"No," the little girl said, "but Jeannie has."

"She has?" Carly looked back at Sam, who only shrugged. "Did she tell you this?"

Maren pulled the paper back. "I don't know," she said, and blocked off the picture with her little arm. "I have to finish the coconut tree."

"Well, it's very pretty," Carly said.

"Yes, indeed," Sam said. She took one last look at the house, then made a mental note to talk with Maren later. Maybe Jeannie was talking with someone after all. "Okay, Carly, let's get down to the brass tacks."

Carly followed Sam to her office, the original office from the house when it had belonged to Theresa Rose. The woodwork in the room was beautiful; built-in shelves with cabinets underneath lined two of the walls. Sometimes Sam felt a little embarrassed by the clutter that took away from the polished craftsmanship that must've gone into the room, but it *was* an office, and work had to be done. Sam circled her desk, and Carly sat in the chair across from her.

"So, what do you think?" Sam asked. "Are you up for the challenge?"

"It'll be a pleasure," Carly said.

"Good." Sam turned and grabbed a stack of papers from a shelf behind her. "I'll need you to read through these and sign the last pages of each booklet. It's mostly just policy and procedure, but you should take the time to look them over. If you could fill out the W-4 now, we'll get you on the books and make sure you get paid for these hours."

"That would be great," Carly said.

"Paperwork," Sam sighed. "Sometimes I feel like I spend more time buried under the paperwork than I do with the girls."

Carly laughed and started filling out the W-4. "So I've been thinking about Jeannie Marrett," she said after a moment.

"Marrick," Sam corrected, "and I thought you might."

"Does she talk at all?"

Sam considered the question for a moment. "Jeannie hasn't spoken in a year and a half that I know of. Not since the death of her parents."

"That's horrible," Carly said. "Is it Post Traumatic Stress Syndrome?" she asked. "At first I thought childhood schizophrenia, but when you tell me about the parents, and the fact that it's only been the past two years, it seems... I mean, *she* seems like a case I studied in one of my college classes."

"You must have paid attention in class," Sam said. "PTSD is the closest we've come to diagnosis, although we haven't been able to really delve into her childhood."

"Where will she go when she leaves?" Carly asked.

Sam thought about this, rocking back and forth in her chair. "I'm not really sure," she said finally. "The truth is, she could go just about anywhere she wants. Dr. and Mrs. Marrick didn't have any other family, which is how she ended up here, and her father's life insurance policy has her well taken care of when she leaves."

Carly looked down at her papers, then back at Sam. "What happened to her parents?"

"Nobody is really sure." Sam stood and walked to a filing cabinet. She pulled out the dog-eared file. *Marrick, Jeannie L.* How many times had she gone over this file only to be left with the same questions?

She looked over at Carly. She definitely wasn't ready to be thrown in with the older girls, but she had shown a natural comfort with most of them, and Sam thought she would do well with the younger girls. If Carly Shaw was serious about social work, she just might do some good. She would learn all of the girls' stories eventually.

"Not even the police are sure," Sam said finally. "Besides her parents, a realtor at the house apparently killed herself. There was also evidence that Jeannie had fired the murder weapon at least once, but with other unidentified fingerprints and tracks around the house, the police figured she must have got a hold of the gun somehow and shot at the intruder. When the police found her, the parents had been dead for at least two days." Sam looked down at the file, started to put it away and then set it on top of the file cabinet and returned to her chair.

"My God," Carly said. "No wonder she hasn't spoken."

"But beyond that," Sam continued, "she copes fine in normal society. She's well on her way to finishing her high school degree a year early with honors, and even though she doesn't need a job, she has worked at the public library for almost a year. It has obviously been a great resource for her collection, but more than that, I believe she enjoys the quiet of the place, someplace where you're not *supposed* to talk."

"Do you really think the articles are helping her find a balance in her life?" Carly asked.

"Possibly," Sam responded. "But there's something more. If you really study the clusters and groups, it's almost like a timeline. Whatever it is, she's done her research. News articles dating back almost one hundred years wind that spiral through her room. Of course, there are some items thrown in that don't match the other dates, but I think she did that intentionally to throw me off the pattern."

"Is there something about the stories that ties them together?" Carly sat perched on the edge of her chair. "Some theme?"

"Not one that I've been able to come up with," Sam said. She thought about the room and its web of stories. There was something in all of that. *Something more than just a timeline but almost like a-*

"In school," Carly said, interrupting Sam's thought, "they told us that sometimes people collect things, external things, to try to make up for something missing on the inside… or something like that. So maybe-"

"I'm sorry, Carly," Sam said, standing and smoothing out her skirt, "but can we continue this later? I just realized what time it was. I have to meet with a couple of the girls." She walked around the desk and crossed the room, pulling open the heavy oak door. "Keeping to a schedule is everything for these girls, you know? If you could get me that W-4 by the end of the day, I'd appreciate it. For now, why don't you go upstairs and see what Amanda is working on."

Carly appeared confused that the conversation had been cut short… probably a little disappointed that she hadn't been able to further demonstrate the knowledge she had picked up in college. "Sure," she said and stood from the chair, managing a grin.

When Carly left, Sam returned to the filing cabinet, taking Jeannie's file and dropping it on her desk. Dr. Brandt really did have to meet with a couple of the girls, but she had a little time yet. She opened the file and leafed through the pages. She skimmed over printouts from her sessions with Jeannie, transcripts that matched up with computer printouts of word processor text, Jeannie's side of the conversation. The girl could speak, but she refused. That was how Dr. Brandt viewed it. PTSD was the closest psychological diagnosis, but Sam felt that Jeannie didn't speak because she didn't *want* to speak. Like an extreme version of the girls who wouldn't talk about their emotions, Jeannie wouldn't talk about *anything*. When she first came to the Rose House, she carried a notepad and only spoke to others using pen and paper. Her sessions with Dr. Brandt started that way, but Sam quickly realized that it was the girl's way of being very calculated about what she would reveal, choosing her words carefully. She convinced Jeannie that the sessions would go by faster if she typed her responses on the computer. The idea worked, and what Sam had hoped for actually materialized when the girl typed more than she would've written on the pad. Mostly.

While Jeannie may have said more in those pages, in a way it also seemed like she was just saying what she thought Dr. Brandt expected to hear. Typical teenage angst and confusion, of course. And thinly veiled anger at whoever had taken the lives of her parents. Sorrow at their loss. But not a single other clue as to what had happened that day at the Montana cabin. Jeannie would simply disassociate, and the responses always read the same.

I really don't remember... only waking up to find my parents dead... I didn't see anyone else, but there must have been...

As with the lack of speaking, Sam wondered about the truth of these statements. And when asked about the pictures and articles in her room, again Jeannie stonewalled her.

I don't know... it's nothing, really... I just think they're interesting...

Once, when she had attempted to get creative with her answer, Sam knew it was an effort to get the doctor to drop the issue.

I feel trapped in here. It's my way of seeing the rest of the world, of being free.

It was also a load of crap. Sam didn't say so directly, but she knew Jeannie must've picked up a psychology book at the library where she worked.

Jeannie Marrick posed an interesting dilemma, indeed. On the one hand, she would stay at the Rose House until she turned eighteen. That much was guaranteed. But beyond that, the choice in most other matters went to the girl. As an otherwise well-functioning member of society, when she became old enough, Jeannie could go wherever she wanted (Sam had been dropping comments to Jeannie that she should definitely consider the Art Institute. The money certainly wouldn't be a problem.). But until the day she turned eighteen, Jeannie also had the choice of whether or not she would verbally communicate with anyone.

Sam closed the file and pushed it away with a half-scowl. To Dr. Brandt, one's life was like a song, more than just the words, but also the way it was sung. And Jeannie wasn't giving enough of a performance to tell the story, much as the doctor wanted to know.

She rose from her desk, returned the file to the cabinet and left the office. Maybe she should go check on the Carly, see how she was doing with Amanda. The thirteen-year-old could be a little difficult when it came to new people. Of course, Dr. Brandt would have to pass Jeannie's room on the way. And if the door was open, and she was in the room, maybe Sam would stop in for a minute.

At the top of the stairs, she could hear a couple of girls down the hall talking and laughing loudly. Jeannie's door stood open. Sam walked to the entryway and raised her hand to knock on the doorjamb, but stopped. The girl stood on the other side of the room, facing away from Sam and staring at a new addition to her wall, a two-page photo spread from *Newsweek*. Sam didn't need to enter the room to recognize the picture. She had read the article about last summer's wildfires in the Northwest just a few days earlier. She had been amazed by the stunning photo showing a wildfire raging in a mountain valley at night with a few elk standing silhouetted in a river not far from the flames, the same photo currently holding Jeannie transfixed. The girl traced her finger slowly up and down over the picture, making patterns that seemed to resemble the flames themselves.

Sam wondered what Jeannie was seeing. More important, what she was thinking? Dr. Brandt started to raise her hand again to knock when a familiar child's voice shouted out her name. Sam looked down the hall as Maren bolted toward her from the top of the stairs.

"Hey, Dr. Brandt!" she hollered. "Whatcha lookin' at?"

Sam twisted back around just as Jeannie dropped her hand and spun to face her. Sam was too caught off guard to think of anything to say.

Maren crashed into Sam's legs in a child's version of a bear hug, somewhat uncharacteristic of the little girl. "What are ya doing, Dr. Brandt? Talkin' to Jeannie?"

Dianne rounded the corner just behind her daughter, and a little out of breath. "I'm sorry, Dr. Brandt," she said. "I had just gone to the bathroom, and she was gone when I got back." She looked down at her daughter. "Maren O'Shea, you know you're not supposed to wander around by yourself."

Sam glanced back in Jeannie's room. The girl looked back at her with a studying, somewhat skeptical, but definitely indecipherable expression, one of many that were perfected by kids in their teenage years.

The doctor turned her attention to the young girl wrapped around her legs, gently removing her from her knees. "Miss Maren," she said, "I think you better listen to your mother."

Dianne took her daughter's hand and led her back to the stairs. Sam didn't turn back when she heard the soft click behind her as Jeannie closed the door to her room.

CHAPTER 12

In the few weeks following the strange encounter with the priest, David didn't notice any activity from the demon. Life almost seemed like it had been before. Not like before *any* of this happened, but at least closer to when he had first arrived in Missoula, confident that he had won his life back. This time around, though, David remained more cautious than he had been before.

No matter how much he thought about it, he couldn't wrap his mind around what took place that day. Something had happened at the end, when he fell to his knees. He didn't know what had moved him to the action; his belief in modern Christianity was shaky at best. But he broke down, and when the priest touched his shoulder, he found himself in the burning kitchen for the third time. He could feel the heat, the burning and tearing muscles. Except this time, the priest stood in the burning house with him. David knew it to be true, confirmed by the frightened look on Father Jimmy's face when the priest pulled his hand away and the vision disappeared. What David *didn't* know was who had brought about the scene. His first thought in the moment following the vision was that it must have been the priest, the touch from a man of God, but Father Jimmy's expression of shock convinced him that this sort of bizarre confessional wasn't a regular occurrence in the priest's day-to-day life.

Since that Saturday, David had avoided any form of physical contact with anyone else, even being cautious of simply brushing past someone on the sidewalk, weary and a little frightened of this new development.

He also avoided Father Jimmy, much as a part of him wanted to go back, wanted to ask him about the vision. Wanted to believe that he could be saved.

He didn't necessarily believe that Father Jimmy had somehow dispelled the demon. He *couldn't* believe it. Not yet. But maybe the priest had scared it a little. And for the time being, it wasn't making its presence known. David had caught a few looks from people on the street, but nothing that appeared more than curiosity or sympathy for his scarred condition.

Instead, he threw himself into his work, taking extra hours whenever he could. The blue-collar work ethic ran strong in David's family. If all else fails, work harder. Or in this case, if nothing else makes sense in your life, there's always work, and if you do enough of it, you're too tired to think about anything else at the end of the day. It seemed to be doing the trick. The past few weeks David felt like he floated, only half-conscious, into the Atlantic every day after work, the sensation made even more surreal by the artwork, swirls of color and images surrounding him, blurring together, and even though he usually dropped on his bed before the autumn sun had set, David still woke the next morning feeling as if he'd barely slept at all. More often he dreamt of the convalescence home. Three and four nights a week. The dreams were still innocuous, just flashes of himself listening to their stories of times-gone-by and then wandering dark hallways while they slept. He kept waiting for something to happen, to stumble into one of the rooms and see the older version of himself, but every night was the same, and every morning he woke just as confused.

Thankfully, during the day, David had been working with Steve Avery on a smaller project, an interior remodel up Rattlesnake Canyon (in an already pretty nice cabin, in David's opinion). The two of them were onto the finish carpentry part of the job. Less labor intensive and more detail oriented, David knew that finish work often allowed for independent tasks with which one could take a little longer doing in the pursuit of "a quality job." He didn't *need* the extra time to do good work, but lately he had taken it anyway, giving himself the time instead to rest and adapt to his new schedule. He had put in long days before, even working two jobs when he had been engaged to Ann, and it took the body awhile to get used to it. It just hadn't seemed this hard before, but David knew that this was a different life.

His mind working on mostly auto-pilot during the day.

(*measure, cut, fit, nail, repeat*)

Today was no exception, but just before noon, David's mind wandered just a little too far from his task at the wrong time, and the finish nailer went off a moment before he could pull away his thumb. It was only a thin finish nail, surprising him more than hurting, and causing a shout probably louder than necessary. The nail must have ricocheted off a larger, framing nail behind the piece he had been holding up, bending the nail out the wood and hooking it through his thumb, like a fish caught on the line. He grimaced, pulling the nail back through his thumb with a yelp and automatically sticking his wounded digit in his mouth just as Steve Avery walked into the library. The older man didn't look concerned, even though he must have heard David's shout. In construction, no one came running unless they heard screaming.

David felt a little foolish standing with his thumb in his mouth. "Shot myself," he mumbled.

Steve looked at his watch and then hooked his fingers in the suspenders of his tool bags. "Close enough to lunch, I guess," he said. "Let's have a look at it."

"It's nothing," David said. "I don't even think it hit the bone." He wound the finger in his shirt. "But I could use a little help getting it wrapped," he admitted.

It definitely wasn't as bad as a framing nail. David had done that before as well, back in college. He had misfired on a board and almost nailed himself to the wall instead. Luckily it went through the side of his palm opposite the thumb and hadn't hit any bone then either. But the doctor had to pull that one.

Carpentry could be hard on the body. Compared to the constant hauling of lumber, lifting of walls or balancing on two-inch wide roof trusses while trying not to saw off the tip of a finger, a finish nail through the thumb was pretty minor, but David still knew it would hurt for the rest of the day and be a nuisance to have to work around.

"First aid is out in the truck," Steve said. "Maybe we'll eat out there, too. Doesn't look like it's still raining."

The day that David had been assigned to work with Steve Avery on the finish job, his supervisor, Ed McGinnis, pulled him aside after the crew meeting and made some smug crack about Steve's claustrophobia, saying that he didn't know how someone could be a carpenter if they couldn't handle a tight space every now and then. He said that he thought Avery would've been put out to pasture a long time ago if he wasn't a friend of the owner's father.

David didn't know why the construction supervisor chose to confide this little bit of information, although he had a few ideas. Not many people on the crew liked Ed McGinnis. Some of them thought maybe his book smarts didn't equal their time on the job swinging a hammer, but David usually stayed on the fringe, didn't involve himself that much with the other guys, so maybe McGinnis was looking for an ally.

Unfortunately, David thought McGinnis was pretty much an asshole. Just as bad as the carpenters who condemned his college degree, the young construction supervisor apparently felt his education surpassed their experience. David had already worked a little with Steve Avery, and he thought he was a pretty damn good carpenter, even with the claustrophobia (which Steve was too proud to admit). Maybe he didn't always do his work by the books, but he got it done, and it always passed inspection. And considering the fact that McGinnis had an occasional wandering eye, David didn't think he had much room to speak about job site qualifications.

When David didn't respond to the supervisor's attack on Steve, not with a comment or even a grin, but rather just stared at him, waiting for him to let him go, McGinnis huffed. David had been on his shit-list ever since.

Outside the cabin, the rain had stopped, even if it only looked like a temporary condition. The thick clouds hung lower in Rattlesnake Canyon, moving slowly up the canyon. It felt damp, and cool enough that David wouldn't be surprised if they showed up at the site tomorrow to see a few skiffs of snow.

At the truck, Steve opened up the first aid kit, tearing open an iodine swab and handing it to David, who wiped around the two holes in his thumb, wincing a little. He could feel it starting to swell.

"You know, if Buck was here," Steve said, "he'd tell you to dip it in some turpentine, save you from the second day throbs." He applied a bandage and started wrapping the thumb in gauze. "Course, I don't think this is too bad."

"I should be alright," David said. "Thanks for the help."

As much as he kept to himself, David had decided that he liked Steve. He thought that maybe the older carpenter was like what his father would've been like had Mark Blithe not died in a car accident when David was just a boy. He wished he could've known his father now.

They took their lunches to the porch of the cabin and sat on the steps. They didn't speak while they unpacked their food. For almost two weeks now, ever since the other guys on the crew finished their part of the job and moved on to the next one, Steve and David ate mostly in silence, except to talk a little about what still needed to be done on the job. Working alone with Steve had been a little awkward at first, but since the experience with Father Jimmy, David feared opening his mouth unless spoken to directly, and he kept it short when someone expected a response. For two weeks, Steve had never pushed it. Until today. Maybe it was the bonding over a bloody thumb. Steve's kids (*step*-kids, actually) were all girls. Maybe Steve wanted a son just like David wished he still had a father. For whatever reason, the older man chose today to break the silence.

"So, do you like working for A.C.?" he asked.

"Sure," David said. "He's a pretty good boss."

"His father was a good friend of mine. A.C. has some pretty big boots to fill, but I think he's doing a helluva job."

David didn't say anything, hoping the small talk would end there, and for a couple minutes, it did.

"So," Steve said, and David could tell he was grasping for something to say, actually trying to make conversation, "how long have you been working construction?"

"On and off since college."

"College, eh?" Steve looked at him sideways.

David waited for the typical "college boy" crack he often got from coworkers on a construction site.

"What sorts of things did you study?" Steve asked instead.

David looked over at him. The older carpenter actually appeared interested. It didn't surprise David much. He had heard some of the other conversations going on at work. A few of the guys were ex-cons, and a couple others should've been. Steve probably got a look at David that first day and made the same assumption, but now the "scarred, quiet guy" was a mystery.

"Business," David said, hoping it would break the spell.

"I'll be damned," Steve said. He took another bite from his sandwich, and in the silence, David examined the framework of the porch. It really was a nice place. And quiet.

Ann would've loved living in a place like-

"I always wanted to go to college," Steve said. "I would've studied history. I really liked history. Still do. That History Channel is one of my favorites."

David took a bite of his apple. He didn't want to think about history. It still hurt too much, and he was having a hard enough time holding on to the present.

"It's like that saying," Steve continued, "about those who don't learn from the past being damned to repeat it. You and me are sitting on a hundred years of history right now, with a hundred more before that. One day, somebody will be studying us, you know? Well, maybe not the two of *us* exactly, but you know what I mean. We can't screw up, let down all those people who died so we could be here today."

David's chest hitched, and he pretended to cough on his bite of apple.

Steve laughed and patted him on the back. His hand rested for a moment on David's shoulder, and a strange look passed over his face, like the older man felt or saw something when he touched him. David doubled over, breaking the physical contact, and pretended to cough out a chunk of apple. This seemed to break the moment, and Steve clapped him on the shoulder again. "Slow down there, son. You can't be *that* anxious to get back to work?"

David managed a smile. A light rain started tapping on the metal roof over the porch, and Steve looked up at the clouds.

"College wasn't in the cards for me, I guess." The older man continued as if nothing had happened. Maybe nothing *had* happened. "Instead I got two ex-wives and two kids to support." He scratched at the mostly gray stubble on his jaw. "Not to mention my old lady's kids now."

"Well, you may not have gone to college," he said. "But you seem pretty smart to me."

"Smart *now*, maybe," Steve said. "It took me a little while. But you, on the other hand. Business, eh?"

"I don't know what I thought I was going to do," David said, "but it sounded good at the time."

"That's what I said about my first ex-wife," Steve said.

David laughed. Yeah, he liked Steve, even if he tried not to.

"You should be able to do something with that business degree," Steve said. "Did you take any construction management classes? I bet A.C. would help pay if you wanted to take some at the university. Hell, you could take over that asshole, McGinnis's job. You'd probably do better than him."

"Probably so," David said. It was an interesting idea. Maybe one day.

"At least you would already have some experience to go along with your book smarts. I doubt McGinnis ever even put on a pair of bags. He's just a glorified secretary in my book. Kissing everyone's ass, especially A.C."

David thought that Ed McGinnis probably had to have *some* practical experience to get his degree. He also knew that a certain amount of ass kissing meant that they had another job when the current one was finished, but he didn't feel like defending the project supervisor. The rain picked up, louder on the metal overhead

"He couldn't be a carpenter anyway with that freako wandering eye of his." Steve pretended to swing at an invisible nail in his hand, each time missing by at least a foot. "Not a carpenter worth half a shit, at least. What's up with that eye, anyway? One minute I'll be talking to him, looking him in the eyes and the next minute one eye'll be gawking off in another direction. It creeps me out. I can never remember if it's the left eye or the right, and when I figure it out, he says something that makes me want to punch him in both of 'em."

"I think it switches," David said.

"What's that?"

"His bad eye. I think it switches."

"Well, whatever, he's a creepy little shit."

Suddenly David felt uncomfortable making fun of the supervisor's physical problem. Felt a little too close to home. He knew all too well how it felt to be talked about. The sounds of the rain filled the silence for a few minutes. Finally, Steve looked purposefully at his watch. "Guess we better get back to work."

They wrapped up their lunches and went back in the cabin. Steve went off to work on his projects without another word, leaving David with his thoughts. He didn't hear from the older carpenter again until the end of the day when it was time to clean up and head to the end of the week crew meeting in town.

125

In the conference room, David prepared to take his normal spot at the back, but Steve stopped him. "Why don't you sit up front with me and Hal and the other guys? We're both working on the same job, so we might as well take our lashings together."

David wasn't prepared for the invitation and as a result, didn't have a good excuse, so he consented and followed Steve to the front table, where Hal, Buck and Vince already sat. He had worked with these guys before. Besides Buck, a guy about David's age, they were all older local guys. Into their late forties or fifties. David still remembered the type from his time swinging a hammer in college. He had called them "Leatherbacks." They had been working in the sun for so long, it looked like you could make a motorcycle jacket out of them.

Hal had just delivered the punch line to some joke as they approached the table, and the other guys broke into laughter, but it tapered off as Steve walked up. David wasn't sure where he would fit in this group.

"I think you know the fellas," Steve said. "Now don't be fooled by that 'aw-shucks' attitude, kid. These good ol' boys are the best carpenters you'll meet."

Hal, the oldest member of the group besides Steve, turned to Vince. "He's buttering me up like he's gettin' ready to ask me out."

"I wasn't talking about you, shitwad," Steve said. "Now why don't you clowns slide over so we can have a seat."

The other three moved over to make room, and David looked around before sitting down with the veterans of the crew. Hal was just starting into another joke when A.C. and Ed McGinnis entered the room. David was surprised to see A.C. Usually the owner of Decker Built Construction was too busy to attend the meetings. He would make his presence known on the job sites occasionally to check on things, and he always showed up personally on Fridays with their paychecks, but he was rarely at the weekly meeting.

David had respected A.C. from the first. Brought up in a ranching family, at 22 years old A.C. had been the youngest person to get his general contractor's license in all of Missoula County, and eight years later, he was running one of the most successful construction businesses in the area. Steve's comment at lunch wasn't the first time that David had thought about the opportunities for advancement working for A.C. But for now, he knew that he had to concentrate on just doing the job he already had.

The two men made their way to the front of the room, and McGinnis dropped a stack of papers loudly on the front desk. "Okay, let's quiet down," he said. "Before we get started with this week's business, A.C. has something to talk about." He sat down behind the desk and A.C. came around front.

"Afternoon, everybody," he said. "And the end of another beautiful, clear day in Missoula, Montana." Some joking grumbling rose in the room as A.C. grinned and leaned back against the table. David guessed that it was more than just Steve being friends with A.C.'s dad that kept him working for Decker Built. The guys liked A.C., because he treated them like equals mostly and subordinates only when he needed to. "Well, let me get to the point," he continued. "I've got some pretty big news. It's a deal I've been working on for a while, and it looks like it's a go." He paused and the room was silent. "It looks like we're going to be doing a job in Hawaii."

Just after A.C. made the announcement, David's chest tightened, even as whoops rose from the other workers. Suddenly the room felt much smaller, more cramped. His body tensed, and he was painfully aware of all the other workers, cramped in the room with them, breathing their air. The walls felt closer, and David thought if he stood up he might hit his head on the ceiling. His pulse raced. He looked towards the single window in the room. So far away. He gasped, but it was masked by the jumbles of conversation that sprang up around him about Hawaii.

Then the moment passed as suddenly as it had started. David blinked his eyes, feeling a little dizzy.

A.C. raised his hands and the room quieted again. "Now don't everybody get too excited," he said. "I'll be the new general on this job, but as far as our part of the work, it's mostly just a finish job on a house that's already framed. Well, sort of, but that's a longer story." He glanced at Hal before addressing the rest of the group again. "What matters is that we can only take a few of you."

Groans sounded from a few tables. The framers.

"But if this job works out," A.C. said. "There should be more where this came from, and we'll try to get everybody over there."

Someone shouted out from the back, "So who's going, A.C.?"

Don't let it be me, David thought, even though he already knew they had chosen him.

While he couldn't deny his gut reaction that he didn't want to go to Hawaii, David had the conflicting feeling that maybe a remote island would be perfect. He could possibly escape the demon again, if only temporarily. Maybe there was a reason he was chosen to go to a tropical island where another, more tribal religion had existed before Christianity, beliefs which were still strongly exhibited in the culture. Maybe David could learn something there to expel the demon for good. The priest hadn't worked, but maybe he would find some other bit of magic to end it.

Still, something felt wrong.

A.C. looked at David's table. "I'm glad to see you all sitting together this afternoon," he said, "because if you can make it work out with your families, you'll all be working together with Ed on the Big Island in two weeks. Job is scheduled to take about a month."

"Shit, yeah!" Vince said, and the other guys laughed.

A.C. told the five carpenters that he would give them the rest of the details later and then went on to explain the changes on other jobs as a result. When he finished, he excused himself from the meeting and McGinnis took over with the immediate business at hand. David barely listened, although he pretended to be paying attention. Instead he thought about Hawaii, and beyond the apprehension, he tried to stifle a little excitement. He had wanted to go there since he was a little kid, used to stay up late to watch the old re-runs of *Hawaii Five-0*.

When the meeting ended, everyone filed out, the five of them pausing outside of the building on the sidewalk. Steve and Vince pulled out cigarettes and lit them.

"Hawaii," Steve said. "That could be interesting. I don't know what Alice is going to think about it."

"Or Laura," Buck said. "But it sounds pretty good."

"Hell yeah, it sounds good," Vince said. "You just need to convince your old ladies."

"Easier said than done," Steve started, but the conversation was interrupted when McGinnis stepped out of the office and walked up to the group. No one spoke for a moment.

"So how about this new job," Buck said. "Pretty cool."

"Yeah, well don't get too excited," McGinnis said. "It's not a vacation. We're going over there to work, so get ready for it. I don't want you guys thinking you're just going over there to fuck around." He looked at Steve. "Especially you, Avery."

He stepped through the middle of the group, forcing Steve backward into David. In that moment, David felt his own temper rise. Blood rushed into his face and he imagined himself catching up with McGinnis, spinning him around and punching him. The anger caught David off guard. He didn't like Ed McGinnis, but he had never wanted to get into a fight with him.

Steve regained his balance and apologized to David for bumping into him, but when David looked down, he saw the older man clenching his fists.

CHAPTER 13

On the drive back to the Atlantic with Steve, the words echoed in his head.

working together with Ed on the Big Island in two weeks

Except for the older carpenter saying that he would probably have to promise Alice that he wouldn't have any fun if he went to Hawaii, they didn't speak much about the possibility of going. Steve said he'd be surprised if they actually went to Hawaii, at all.

"Give it a few days," he said. "Then we'll see. Jobs like this come and go, and deals can fall through the day you're supposed to be getting on the road to wherever you're going."

Steve put the truck in park, the engine idling. "Seven o'clock, Monday?"

"Bright and early," David said and got out of the truck.

As he opened the door to the apartments, he could already hear the buzz of a crowd upstairs, and he remembered it was First Friday, when all of the art galleries in town hosted openings. The Atlantic was on the map for this particular event, known to be one of the less uptight places to visit. Currently, some sort of music that sounded like a mix between Celtic and dance club pulsed down the stairs from the UnCommons. David didn't need this right now, but took comfort in the fact that First Friday usually only ran a couple hours, time which he could just spend in his room if he could weave his way to the door. He briefly considered going back outside and around to the fire escape but figured it would be just as crowded back there with the smokers, so he started up the stairs with his head in the automatic "down" position. He almost reeled backward down the stairs when he nearly ran into the dressmaker's dummy, which someone had relocated from the kitchen to the top of the stairs. The creator of this particular piece of work (David thought it was the overweight girl a couple doors down from his) had affixed a mannequin's head on the shoulders, done up in clown makeup, and the feathers had been spray painted black.

He avoided eye contact with anyone in the Uncommons, seeing only dozens of feet as he bee-lined towards the hall, but before he could make it, a woman's feet stepped in front of him and stopped. The owner of the feet cleared her throat, and David knew who it was before he even looked up.

Mary Rose stood holding a plastic cup of wine. Her eyes narrowed for just an instant, then she saw someone behind David and the fake smile came on. She waved, but didn't move to let him pass.

"I see you still have your work boots on," she said. Mary Rose was the only one besides Steve Avery who would instigate interaction with David, but hers was usually negative. He didn't know why she didn't like him. Her girlfriend, Kate, had always been nice to him, but Mary Rose hadn't even smiled at him that he could remember since he moved in.

"Sorry, Mary Rose," David said. "But they were clean when I came in."

Mary Rose looked at the carpet behind David, then huffed. "Rent is due before the end of Monday."

"It'll be taken care of." David started to go around her, and Mary Rose flinched backward, as if expecting him to assault her.

Then she straightened out, skirting past him with the smile reaffixed. "I'll expect it," she said under her breath.

David lowered his head again and started down the hall, but he stopped when he brushed by another woman. When he came in contact with her, he imagined a rather plain woman in her forties walking into her bedroom to find her husband with another woman. Then the image was gone. David looked up to see the woman from his vision. She stared back at him with a dazed look in her eyes. He backed away from her, bumping into someone else. He turned around and saw a younger man, younger than David, and definitely dressed to the nines for the gallery walk. David had a flash of the young man in an office building, standing in the center of the room while everyone laughed and pointed at him.

David stumbled away, more frantic to get to his room, but he couldn't get down the narrow hallway without coming in contact with the mob. And each person he touched showed him something else. A scared child hiding in a darkened closet. A woman drowning in a lake. An intruder holding a family at gunpoint.

David reeled from it all. He thought he might vomit when a hand reached out and grabbed his arm. In the instant before he was pulled into one of the rooms, the image of a naked girl, face down and motionless on the floor, flashed in his mind. Then the door closed behind him, blocking out some of the sounds of the hallway and returning him to the present.

David stared at a large canvas showing a painting of a mountain valley at night. Steep evergreen slopes filled the painting, with a river running between them at the bottom. There was some wildlife in the river, deer maybe, although the animals were only small silhouettes. The scene looked familiar, but before David could place it, a shot of whiskey was thrust in front of him.

"It's a mad house out there," Jeremy said. "Stupid fucking First Friday." He held another shot in his other hand, which he proceeded to drink. "Now, there's a tongue twister. Fucking First Friday. Try saying that 10 times fast." He proceeded to attempt this very thing, making it about six times without much difficulty and stopping. "I guess it's not that hard," he said. "You want a shot?"

David didn't understand what had just happened in the hall. In fact, most of the afternoon suddenly seemed fuzzy. If he wasn't going crazy, imagining his trip to Jeremy's room, then what was it? He wondered if the visions in the hall represented things that had happened to these people or just things they were afraid of. David looked at Jeremy, a guy who didn't seem to have much luck with the ladies, and thought of the last image in his mind before being pulled into the room. What was Jeremy afraid of?

David had managed minimal contact with the angst-ridden artist since the morning before meeting Father Jimmy. The fact that David normally only came or went when he needed to gave him the excuse that there was something else he needed to be doing if he crossed paths with Jeremy. But tonight, he only briefly considered the alternative--going back into that crowd--before deciding he would wait in the room for a few minutes.

"I remember you saying that you were a whiskey drinker," Jeremy said. "You don't have to work tomorrow, right?"

David shook his head, and Jeremy mistook the gesture, handing over the shot. David stared at it. Would one drink matter? If it would help him sleep deeper tonight, he thought he just might have just one and then he would try to get to his room again. He took the shot from Jeremy and drank it, surprised at how easily it went down.

"I'm just about to add the final touch," Jeremy said and crossed to the canvas. He dipped the fingertips from his right hand in a red-stained paint can and his left in an orange can, trailing drops of the paint over his drop cloth. Then he ran his fingers down the canvas in jagged lines. He did this a few times while David watched, unable to move. The effect was like a mix of blood and flames over the mountains.

Jeremy turned around to face him, and David thought his eyes looked distant, like he had been looking *into* the painting and now was looking *past* David. Then he blinked a couple times and lifted a hand slowly towards his face, like he was going to rub his eyes.

"Whoa!" David said, taking a step into the room. "I wouldn't do that."

Jeremy stopped and looked down at his red fingers as if they belonged to someone else. "Oh yeah, right." He wiped his hands on his smock and his eyes seemed to clear as well. "Thanks, man. Must be the booze."

David had walked past Jeremy's open door a few times before, but this was the first time he had stepped inside. The room felt bigger than David's for some reason, and it took a moment for him to figure out why. Jeremy had hoisted his bed, an air mattress, off the ground using netting and a relatively simple rope and pulley system.

Jeremy noticed him looking. "Gives me a little more room to work," he said. "I just lower it at night. A guy who used to live in the building showed me how to rig it up."

Other than the suspended air mattress, a couple of television trays loaded up with painting equipment, a mini-fridge and a chair that looked like it might've been rescued from the Goodwill rejection pile, the room was bare of furniture. Smaller canvases in various stages of completion leaned against most of the available floor-to-wall space. David recognized a few of the finished pieces from display in the hall over the past months. One that had caught his eye was a futuristic take on Salvador Dali's "Temptation of St. Anthony." One of David's favorites. Except in Jeremy's version, the tremendous stallion and elephants bearing down on the ragged Saint with their multiple jointed legs were mechanical creatures, and instead of carrying more ancient architecture on their backs they carried skyscrapers, familiar city skylines. The voluptuous woman from the original Dali version, seemingly leading the march, cupping her breasts in her hands with her head thrown back, also made her appearance in Jeremy's painting with one difference. He had affixed a picture of a man's head on the body, the head of the President.

"What do you do, Jeremy?" David asked, still staring at the picture. "I mean, besides paint."

"You mean to pay the bills?"

David nodded.

"The work of the devil," Jeremy said.

David must have looked more surprised than he intended, because Jeremy saw the expression and started laughing. "Shit man, not seriously," he said. "I'm not a Satan worshiper or anything. I'm in market research, which is just a fancy term for phone surveys. Political stuff, customer satisfaction, that sort of thing." He made a space on one of the TV trays for the shot glasses, then quickly added, "But we don't sell anything. I'm not a telemarketer." He poured two more shots into the glasses. "What I do is probably worse though. I don't think the devil is that interested in sales. He already knows what you buy. It's the *surveys* that sneak in on you, classify you, find your likes and dislikes, but more importantly, your opinions. With surveys, you learn how to be someone's friend, say the things they want to hear to make them do the things you want them to do." He gave David his best evil-eye, then laughed again and picked up the shots. "My job sucks," he said, "but it pays the bills." He offered one of the drinks to David, who didn't hesitate as long this time. "What about you?" Jeremy asked. "You're in construction, right?"

David nodded, then downed the whiskey. Okay, *that* was the last one. "I guess I'm going to Hawaii in a couple weeks for a job."

"Hawaii, eh? Man, that would be *sweet*." Jeremy took the shot, scrunching up his face. "I sure wouldn't mind getting away from here for awhile. My shitty job. This gray town, and these frigid woman. Winter just makes 'em worse, you know?"

A woman in the hallway cackled loudly; the laugh on the other side of the door sounded as sincere as it was soft.

Jeremy rolled his eyes. "Bunch of pretentious assholes, anyway. Even the ones who come here." He filled another shot. Swaying slightly in place, he offered one to David.

David listened to the voices out in the hall and looked at his watch. People were still milling in the hallway, and he didn't think he wanted to try the path again to his room just yet. So he took the glass from Jeremy, but thought he had better sit down with it and wait a few minutes before drinking it.

Jeremy kept up his rant, something about a price tag on life imitating art. He was obviously drunk, and suddenly David felt like he was catching up in a hurry. He didn't particularly follow all of Jeremy's logic, guessing that much of his angst probably stemmed from some past incident of which David was unaware, but the young painter seemed content just to be talking to someone. David could relate. He lifted the shot to his lips and was surprised to find it empty. He looked down at his lap to see if he had perhaps spilled it on the chair.

"Hawaii, though," Jeremy said. "That would be cool."

David looked back up at the mention of the job, the quick motion briefly jarring his perspective of the room before bringing it into focus. "Whew," he said.

But Jeremy hadn't heard him. He stood with his back to David, looking at his recent painting. "Especially the Big Island," he said. "The volcano and the lava. Man, I could do some work over there." He trailed off.

Or maybe he was just mumbling. David couldn't be sure over the sounds of the people in the hall. The fatigue from the long workweek had returned, combining forces with the weight of the whiskey. He could barely hold his head up.

Jeremy turned around. "Don't ya think?" he asked.

"Huh?" David slurred. Then, "Oh. Yeah."

"Me, too," Jeremy said and returned his attention to the painting.

He was still talking. David could see that this time, but he sounded far off. And the sounds in the hallway could've been in another building, conversation blurring into a distant buzz.

Maybe he could just rest here for awhile.

David closed his eyes and as he drifted off, he heard someone speak from close by. Just two words.

"He's perfect."

* * *

A thousand miles away, Jeannie sat on her bed with the door to her room closed, holding a photograph. She could hear a few other girls talking and laughing in the hall. It sounded like Monica and Therese. They were about Jeannie's age. Pretty girls. They even talked to Jeannie sometimes, and were cool about her not talking back, patient while she wrote on her pad. Only Dr. Brandt pushed her to write more things, and the seventeen-year-old knew that was part of the plan to make her "better."

The truth was, Jeannie could speak. She had even spoken aloud to herself a few times without thinking about it, but no one had been around. And she wasn't just bottling it inside, as much as Sam Brandt wanted to believe that was the case. The problem was that she was *afraid* to speak, scared of what might come out. The events surrounding the murder of her parents were weird enough when it happened. At first, she actually had been too shocked to speak; the incident played back in her mind as an incomprehensible, jumbled horror of blood and confusion. And now, over a year and a half later, with the finer details of that afternoon starting to smear, it seemed even stranger. Jeannie worried that if she told someone what had happened as she remembered it, the things she saw that day, they would put her on stronger meds than her current prescription. Maybe even give her a cozy little coat. Jeannie didn't think white was her color.

But beyond her fear of being locked away, Jeannie just didn't *want* to talk. She didn't want to be a part of this world, and while she knew she had to function in it, she kept herself as distant as possible. Jeannie didn't really want a friend. She couldn't think about that, didn't want to grow close to another person. She was biding her time. And in a way, crazy or not, she was counting her days.

Jeannie looked down at the picture, a shot of her and her mom in the Black Hills of South Dakota. The trip to Montana. They had stopped at Mt. Rushmore earlier that day. Her father had taken the picture

Her Daddy.

The memories rushed back at Jeannie, and she took a sharp breath as her chest hitched and her eyes welled with tears.

Her Daddy. Driving out to the cabin. His smiling eyes in the rearview mirror of the Jeep. The looks he had shared with her mom. Like they were in love again.

Her Daddy had promised her they would go fishing at the new home. Everything was supposed to be perfect. She knew that her parents had been fighting for too long. The new cabin was supposed to change all of that. On the trip to Montana, her parents had been talking again like they used to. Smiling more, and even holding hands.

Then *he* showed up. David. And life turned upside down.

Ms. Stack went crazy or something. Jeannie didn't remember everything the woman had said in her room before she went out and apparently shot herself. Jeannie didn't even know until later that Barbara Stack had killed herself. After the strange conversation the two shared, the realtor had walked out of the room, and a few moments later, Jeannie blacked out. In her darkness, Jeannie dreamt of horrible things. She found herself in a huge, dark house with windows everywhere, and not a door in sight. Disfigured, tormented human beings broke through the windows, chasing her though the house that seemed to only have dead ends, and each time they found her they approached slowly, some only able to crawl, clawing at her...

Then she saw her father die. For a moment the clutching fingers of the intruders in the darkness vanished, and she found herself back in the cabin. And she saw her Daddy die. Actually, she saw her own hands shoot the gun.

She didn't believe at the time that she had actually killed him. It was just too much to take, so she convinced herself that it was all part of the nightmare, and that the words she heard before being brought back to consciousness, before seeing the bullet open up his chest, words about her father's infidelity which had echoed around her in the darkness while cold hands pulled at her body, were all in her imagination.

Later, she would try to convince herself that it was actually David who had killed her father, even though she knew it wasn't *entirely* the truth. He had been responsible. Of that she had no doubt. Before David had entered her life, like most teenagers, Jeannie wasn't really sure about the existence of a heaven or hell, but now she believed that he brought something evil into that cabin with him.

Something in the eyes, she thought. *They all have something in their eyes. Probably the same look that was in my eyes that day.*

Jeannie could still feel the weight of the weapon, the steel on her finger, the recoil of the shot that knocked her back. She still saw her Daddy stare at her in shock while blood spread across his shirt between his clutching fingers.

After he had dropped to the ground, everything went black again for Jeannie. The only thing she remembered was dreaming of a burning house. Lying on the floor of an unfamiliar kitchen surrounded by flames. David had been there. He had lifted her up in his arms; he had saved her. But when she opened her eyes again in the cabin, she saw him crouched over her with a knife.

Their eyes made contact,

His eyes were a clearer blue. Focused.

and in that moment, she knew that David didn't want to kill her. But she still didn't feel safe, even when he seemed to yank himself off her body. At that point, she still just thought he was insane, grappling with some inner torment. She backed into her father, dispelling the idea that she had dreamt it all. Her mother had also been shot. Jeannie could only guess that David was responsible for that as well, but she shelved all emotion except the desire for survival.

He came for her, but then stopped, and again Jeannie was struck by the feeling that he was fighting with himself. He even cut his own body. Whatever the purpose, after crying out in pain, his eyes cleared, and again Jeannie sensed that he didn't want to harm her. When he looked down at the knife and then at his wrists, the teenager knew what he was thinking and pleaded with him not to do it. She still didn't know why, but when she thought back on the afternoon, she knew that she had seen something in his eyes, beyond mercy. Something good, but also worn out and getting ready to give up.

Then he spoke. His first words to her since crashing into her life were an apology. He said something about being chased, then stumbled out of the cabin. Jeannie had thought it was over until she heard him outside. It sounded like he was retching on the deck, but then she heard a low, menacing voice underneath it all, and suddenly the pieces of the puzzle,

Two of the pieces, at least.

crazy as they seemed, fit together. There was something more going on than just a scarred lunatic battling some psychosis.

Whatever had forced her to kill her Daddy was trying to regain control over David. Probably the same thing that drove Ms. Stack to shoot herself, too. Another piece in the puzzle. And when Jeannie screamed at David to run, it was just as much out of her own fear, as it was concern for him.

Then she collapsed on the bloodied body of her father.

Jeannie had been changed from that day, more than just the trauma from having lost her parents. There were still moments when she doubted what had happened at the cabin, moments when she tried to convince herself that she had created these scenes to shelter herself from an already awful truth about the death of her parents, but the articles and pictures spread out over her walls in the Rose House served as proof of something else. She just didn't know of *what*.

Jeannie laid the photograph on her bed, stood and walked over to the collage. She knew exactly where to find the first article; she had affixed it on the wall next to her mirror.

She had first seen the headline in a grocery store just after her sixteenth birthday, only a few months after the incident at the cabin. Every week a few of the girls were chosen to do the shopping for The House. Frank Matsen, a security guard at the Rose House for seven years, would drive them to the store, where each girl had a portion of the list for which they were responsible.

Jeannie liked Frank. He had always been nice to her. He could be a little talkative, but in the time since she had shown up, he had never pushed for a response like some of the others at the Rose House.

On this particular day, Jeannie had been walking past the registers with her cart when the *Weekly World News* stopped her in her tracks.

THE END IS HERE! the tabloid cover proclaimed. *25 Recent Events Pointing to the Apocalypse.*

Jeannie couldn't take her eyes away from it. Everything else seemed to fade around the black and white cover, the colors of the fashion and entertainment magazines blurring while a sound rose in her head like when a fork accidentally falls in the garbage disposal.

A woman cleared her throat behind her, and Jeannie broke out of her daze, realizing that she was blocking the entrance to the checkout. She quickly grabbed the tabloid and put it in with her stuff.

She had returned to her room with the magazine, plopped down on her bed and flipped it open. Unsure exactly why she had picked out the tabloid (or why it had picked *her* out) she skimmed the pages, scanning over an article about a boy from Louisiana who was part-alligator and a brief piece on the world's fattest Siamese twins. As she continued through the pages, the grinding sound rose in her head again, and the same blurring of her vision occurred when she turned to the article advertised on the cover.

Twenty-five Bizarre Stories from Around the World.

Jeannie didn't know what she was searching for in the article, but she found it in the sixteenth story.

> Couer D'Alene, Idaho. Physicians at St. Luke's Memorial Hospital were stunned by a mysterious visitor at their hospital this past October. A young man, dehydrated, near starvation and severely scarred from what appeared to be a fire, walked into the hospital and stated simply, "Make this body healthy." He handed over a wad of cash, and doctors rushed him to the emergency room where he passed out immediately. "It was a miracle he was walking at all," Dr. Landers of the E.R. said. "And he seemed so aware."
>
> Police were called to the scene, and the unconscious man was fingerprinted from the hospital bed. When they couldn't come up with any connections, the police returned the next morning to question the patient, but he was gone.
>
> "He was talking all sorts of something crazy in the middle of the night," stated Elmer Jannsen, a patient sharing the room with the stranger. "Couldn't understand a thing he said. Kinda like them folks that speak in tongues or some such thing. Scared the bejeezus out of me. Thought I was rooming with the devil himself."

A review of the previous night's security tapes failed to show the young man leaving and, upon further investigation, there was no physical evidence of the man's presence at the hospital at all. In a most likely related story, the attending nurse on duty, Maggie Hinton, failed to show up for her shift the following day, and still remains missing.

Jeannie closed the magazine and stared at it for a moment. It had to be David. She was almost sure of it. He had made it to Idaho.

But was it David? Or was it something else?

She decided that she would start reading more. In fact, everything she could get her hands on. And she would save the stories.

Dr. Brandt was more than willing to help get her a job at the library, and in the year and a half since, Jeannie took any free moment to scan through magazines, newspaper and Internet articles. While there were a handful of recent stories, most of them were dated from before David had burst into her life. Forming a timeline dating back almost a hundred years, almost every story or photograph taped to her walls and ceiling had struck her in a different manner. Some hit her as drastically as the first tabloid article, blurring everything in the periphery. Others were as soft as a whisper, giving her pause long enough to continue past the first paragraph. The whisper turned to a buzzing like that of an insistent insect as she read on, growing finally to the familiar grinding sounds. But nothing in the collection since had given her as definite of a clue as the first article. Some articles had mentioned an unnamed witness, suspect or participant in a story, and Jeannie's skin had tingled. But nothing as clear as "a young man, severely scarred." And while most of them dealt with death somehow, some didn't make any sense at all, like a science journal article on claustrophobia and its causes, but she had been drawn to them nonetheless. Some told of horrible acts, while others mere accidents. Or were they? Recently Jeannie had started to wonder if there was such a thing. If life was predestined, she wondered what her path was supposed to be, and why her parents had to die.

Because of David.

The stories and pictures were Jeannie's connection somehow to him. Or whatever had possessed him that day. If everything was fated, she figured that the articles were a sign that she was supposed to find David when she got out of the Rose House. Follow the map trailed out in the recent articles, which seemed to be focused in the Northwest. But she was still uncertain of what she would do when it actually happened.

A big part of Jeannie recognized that David had fought that day to save her life, had almost taken his own life. But it hadn't ended there; the articles were proof of that. She didn't know why, but it wasn't over. More than that, though, he hadn't been strong enough to save her parents, and while she wanted to believe that he would be in control when she found him, if he had *lost* to the evil thing…

Jeannie couldn't think about the next part. Not yet. Not until she was certain, and she wouldn't be certain until she saw him. She may not survive the encounter. But she had to try. For her parents. Her Daddy.

The idea consumed her. And that was why she didn't talk to people. Her life in the present meant nothing more than preparing for the future. If only she could make the big connection in the collage, find the missing story. The Answer. To more questions than she could list.

Something in the eyes.

She just had to hold out until she was old enough to leave the Rose House. Hopefully by then she would know what she had to do.

A knock came at her door, followed by Frank Matsen's voice. "Time to call it a night, Jeannie," he said through the door.

Jeannie crossed the room and knocked back three times, her response to Frank.

"Sweet dreams, kiddo," he said from the other side, and then she heard him continue down the hall.

Jeannie walked back to the mirror and stuck the Mt. Rushmore photo in the corner, held in place by the frame of the mirror. Then she looked at herself. Her mother had been beautiful, and Jeannie wondered if she would grow up to look like her.

Jeannie brushed back her hair, pulling it into a ponytail before turning off her light and climbing into bed, surprised at how tired she felt now that she was actually in bed. Her mind started drifting not long after her head hit the pillow. Then she started dreaming. But the dream wasn't sweet.

After falling into darkness, she opened her eyes to a field of green. Jeannie instinctively knew this place. She stood in the tall, swaying meadow looking down the dirt road to where it cut in between the sheer granite faces.

Someone spoke from behind her. "Say, kiddo, have you ever wanted to catch a fish?"

Her Daddy. Jeannie spun around and shielded her eyes from the glare of the sun. The cabin stood in the distance, and her father was kneeling in the grass in between with his back to her.

"I'll bet we could dam up this creek and make ourselves a nice little pond." He reached over and grabbed a rock from a stack next to him.

Jeannie started to drift through the parting grass toward her father. Someone walked out on the deck of the cabin in the distance and called to her: "Jeannie, honey, time to come in for lunch." It sounded like her mother, but the closer she drifted to her father and the cabin, the less the woman on the deck looked like Judy Marrick. Then she realized who stood in her mother's place, who had once stood in the way of her family's happiness.

Over the years, Jeannie had created the woman now standing on the deck to represent the betrayal. Whenever she dwelled on the issue in the past, Jeannie tried to tell herself that whatever had happened between her parents wasn't worth her father's death, that he could've changed, but the imagined woman remained a focal point of her anger, even as she tried to convince herself that David had been lying.

Jeannie floated closer to her father, but then she saw the red stain on the back of his shirt. She tried to backpedal, but it was too late. She was being pulled in.

"Jeannie, honey?" the woman called.

Jeannie reached her father, stopping in front of the pond he had created. Bloated and distended fish, their glassy eyes covered by a milky film, layered the surface of the pond, floating belly-up. Robert looked up at Jeannie, and his eyes were the same as the fish. He plunged his hand into the pond and clutched a smaller one, which he stuffed into a gaping, fetid hole in his chest.

"We have to eat *something*, kiddo," her father said.

Jeannie let out a shriek, and the scene changed. This setting was familiar as well, except it was calmer. She had dreamt of the white sand beach before,

Hawaii?

the waves lapping gently on the shore of a blue-green bay, but before tonight, she had just seen snapshots, brief flashes before her slumbering mind raced somewhere else. This night she lingered. The palm fronds on the trees reaching up from the sand to the azure sky clacked together in a light breeze, and even in the dream, Jeannie could feel the warmth from the sun.

Then her skin went cold, and Jeannie felt a pulling in the pit of her stomach. A large house appeared just beyond the edge of the bay, looming on the brink of a black rocky shore where waves crashed violently. She had also seen this house in previous dreams, but tonight it pulled on her. She fought the feeling, wanting to stay in the calm of the white beach, but the pull twisted into a tug, and she was lifted off the sand and yanked forward, drawn across the bay to the house at the edge of the frothing ocean.

Much of the house was still unfinished. Jeannie saw workers filing in and out of the house like ants. Then she was propelled through a gaping opening on the ocean view side of the house where three men were installing full-length sliding glass doors. She swept through a maze of hallways and rooms, the outside light fading as she sped deeper into the mansion. Beyond the kitchen, she passed through a steel door and was whisked downstairs, under the ground. The only light came from bare bulbs hung from the ceiling, casting a white glare on the cement walls still awaiting finish. Then another maze of underground tunnels finally ending in a large, cold room. Metal framework had been started on the concrete walls, like the buried ribs of the house, and Jeannie had stopped in its heart. Two more bare light bulbs hung from the ceiling, flickering on and off.

Two men sat on a stack of steel building materials with their backs to her, but Jeannie didn't need to see them to know that one was David. He turned fully around and stared at her.

The fitful bulbs alternated playing light on opposite sides of his face.

"It's too late," he said, the light skittering on the scarred right side. Jeannie saw the same weary, troubled look from the day at the cabin. Then the light switched to David's other side. Smooth and definitely more handsome, but the smile and cold eye that stared at Jeannie made her shrink back. The lights flashed back to his right side. "It's already started."

The room went black, and Jeannie heard the gurgling voice in the darkness around her. The voice she had heard from David that day at the cabin. The voice of the other thing.

"What are you afraid of?"

CHAPTER 14
HAWAII

In the smoky hotel lounge, David and Steve sat in silence at the bar stools surrounding a high table. Silent, that is, except for an occasional comment on whatever karaoke song was being performed. Monday nights in The Anchor were reserved for Chinese karaoke. Apparently it was a big draw for the many Asian tourists on the island. For the carpenters, it was just the closest bar to their rooms.

David had gone to karaoke in college a few times, but this was different. And it wasn't like the more raucous Japanese karaoke he had seen in movies. People didn't even stand up to sing. Instead, a microphone was passed around to the tables, so David couldn't always see who was actually singing. Not that it mattered much. Chinese script ran across the bottom of the screen where English would have normally been. Only a few songs were performed in David's native tongue, but he didn't recognize those either.

Another glaring difference, and possibly the most surreal part, was the behavior after the songs. Complete silence. No one whooped or shouted, or even clapped. The first few times it happened, even though he didn't recognize the song, David thought the singer must've butchered it. He knew the rule of karaoke was that if you expected applause, you better give it to everyone else who tries. So he had clapped a couple of times, but after a few of the looks over the tops of raised glasses, he gave it up.

It was the same tonight, but still they stayed in the lounge. They were too tired from work to do anything else, so it was either this or sit in their small rooms, trying to decide what to watch on television. It was the way of this hotel. The carpenters weren't the only longer-term tenants. David recognized a few faces that he had also seen on occasion on the elevators going to the rooms. In a way, besides the fact that it seemed like the residents in *this* hotel lived there out of financial necessity, unable to afford much else in the Hawaiian market, it was like the Atlantic Hotel, except in the middle of the Pacific.

This particular Monday was even more subdued than the previous two times David had been. Even the group of local hippy kids he had seen both other times was quiet, and with the serious nature of the singers, the lounge felt almost somber. Must've been the weather. The guys said it rained most of the day, but David didn't need to hear it from them to know. He had felt it working down in the safe rooms, even that far away from open air. More humid and sticky than usual. Like it was seeping through the concrete walls from the earth surrounding him and Steve. The whole day felt damp, and the feeling had bled into the evening.

Vince had left an hour earlier to go to a different bar, frustrated after an unsuccessful attempt at picking up the cocktail waitress, and Hal and Buck, claiming the effects of a long Monday, went up to their rooms shortly after that. David was rooming with Buck and knew that he probably had actually left early to call Laura and talk to his two year-old son, so David decided to give him a little privacy and stayed in the bar with Steve.

Steve clearly wasn't ready to quit drinking. He hadn't seemed to be doing so well for most of the day, and David couldn't really blame him. Tonight was his last night of freedom.

David, on the other hand, felt better than he had in a while, even considering the underground working conditions. Maybe it was just a couple of weeks of being on a tropical island at a time when Missoula would be on the tail end of winter, swamped in thick gray clouds. It was the perfect time to leave Montana, and the whole crew had been excited when A.C. called everyone the Saturday after making the announcement to tell them that plans had moved much faster than anyone thought and that they should be ready to be on a plane on Sunday.

However, Steve had seemed the least thrilled when he and Hal picked up David to drive to the airport. Apparently Alice had made quite a stink, warning Steve of all the things that would happen to him if he even looked at one of those island girls.

"Would've been nice to have a little more notice," he had said to David. "Alice needs a little warming up for things like this, but leave it to the richies to stick it to the rest of us. I've worked for a few of these crazy rich types, kid, and let me tell you, they all think the rest of us are supposed to do whatever they want whenever they want it."

But apparently money talked. The crew was pulled from whatever other jobs they were working on to go, with A.C. shifting workers around like crazy, according to Hal. Steve said he had never seen a job this big move so fast. "They must really want us over there."

This last comment had given David that same suffocating feeling from the meeting when A.C. announced the trip, but since being on the island, things had definitely been looking up. David hadn't seen any sign of the demon since arriving. That fact aside, after the Friday night that he ended up in Jeremy's room, he was hyperaware again of physical contact with others, avoiding it wherever possible. So to a large degree, David was still on his guard, but deep down, a part of him wanted to believe that he had somehow escaped the demon. Maybe something about the perpetually erupting volcanic island itself. Or the tribal culture. Maybe he would stay here after the job was done. Vince had told him that union carpenters in Hawaii made a good amount of money. David liked it in Missoula, but he thought he could learn to like Hawaii more. It truly was a paradise, and maybe that was what he finally had coming to him. David knew that evil existed in the world. It was God that he doubted. But if there was a god, maybe this was his reward for everything he had been through. Whatever it was, for now, David felt good, and he wanted to keep it that way.

Steve, however, was a different story. David knew it had been a seriously rough week for the older carpenter. Actually it had probably started with the five-hour airplane trip over the Pacific Ocean. David hadn't needed to make physical contact with Steve to sense his unease at being trapped so long over water in the "flying tin can," as he had called it. He relaxed considerably once they got on the island, even seemed happier than David had seen him in the past few months, but one week after arriving, the proverbial roof caved in. Ed McGinnis assigned Steve and David to work on the Miller Mansion security rooms, a span of rooms under the gigantic house designed to be secure places for Jim Miller's valuables, and presumably in the case of any trouble, his family. They could only be accessed through the center of the house via a set of concrete steps leading into the earth and then a series of short passages connected by security doors, each requiring a key code before the next hall could be entered. This guy wasn't fooling around. David had heard that the owner of the unfinished mansion had been an arms dealer. Originally it had just been for the United States, but in the end, he was also selling to foreign countries. David could only imagine what sort of people he had met before retiring.

David knew that their new assignment was McGinnis's way of using Steve's claustrophobia against him, and the day the announcement was made was most likely when the fear of the roof *literally* coming down must have crashed in on Steve. David had paced out the distance early on, trying to keep his bearings with the outside world, and he thought the actual safe rooms were farther away from the seaside cliffs than the main house, possibly not even under the main structure, and probably not even that far underground. But that probably didn't matter to Steve Avery. While the others worked up in the sun, with the breeze passing through the open-air architecture of the Hawaiian home, the sounds of the waves crashing on the rocks below, the two of them worked in a cold, concrete block with only silence surrounding them.

However, that was just the beginning. At the end of a week that must've been torturous for Steve, McGinnis took it a step further and assigned Steve to stay overnight in the safe rooms as some sort of makeshift security guard. The older carpenter had been grumbling about McGinnis for the past week to the rest of the crew. At first, the others had tried to calm Steve down, saying that it was all part of the job, even though they knew that the supervisor had it out for him. Tonight, however, they didn't say anything. What else could they say besides, "Man, that really sucks"?

After no one had responded to his short rant tonight, but rather looked at their drinks or pretended suddenly to be interested in the older Chinese man singing two tables away, Steve had clammed up and not said another word since. Some carefully chosen small talk ensued among the other guys. Vince made another failed pass at the waitress and left, followed shortly by the other two.

David hung around. He thought that the older carpenter could use the company, whether he wanted to actually talk or not. David didn't mind either way. He had grown accustomed to silence, and if he got bored, he could always watch the karaoke videos and try to figure out what the songs meant. He was doing just that when Steve finally spoke.

"I'm getting too old for this bullshit."

David looked across the table, and Steve blinked in surprise, like he hadn't meant to speak aloud. He quickly covered it up. "But I'm also too much of an old dog to go looking for a new master." He raised his hand to catch the attention of the redheaded cocktail waitress.

"Two more?" she asked as she passed, and Steve nodded.

"You're not getting *that* old," David said.

"Well, I'm not gettin' any younger." He drained the last of his beer. "The drink doesn't help much, I suppose. Matter of fact, the drink and being on the road so much is probably what drove away Wife Numero Two." He started to light the wrong end of a cigarette, noticing just before burning the filter and correcting himself. "Can't say that I blame her."

David had heard Steve mention his second wife before, and he figured that she was Steve's "one that got away." She just left him one day without a word. David tried to lighten the mood a little. "I still say you're not that old," he said, "but this job may be the end of us both."

Steve snorted. "You can say that again, kid."

"This job may be the end of us both."

Steve laughed again. "Yeah, that's it. Maybe it's the damned house. It could be like that movie, *Amityville Horror*, you know? The one where the house is like a gate to Hell?"

"Except, instead of flies," David said, "we got mosquitoes. Big bastards, too. That's the one thing I don't miss about working up in the open air."

"Yeah, that's right." Even through the alcohol haze, Steve's eyes brightened a little. "And I tell you what," he said, "if Miller's Mansion ended up like that Amityville place, I sure as hell wouldn't go back for some goddamn dog like they did in the movie. If the freaking walls in *my* house are bleeding, I'm gonna be lucky if I remember to take my wife with me, let alone Scratch the Mutt."

David chuckled as the waitress appeared in a twirl of her mini-skirt and set the beers on the table. "This round is on the house," she said and smiled at David, who already had his wallet open prepared to buy the drinks. He pulled out the ten and set it on her tray.

"Then this is for you, I guess," he said.

"Thanks, sweetie," she said and smiled again.

They both watched her flit off to another table, then Steve shook his head. "I tell you what, kid. I wish I was your age again, just barely meeting your thirties, still strong. Able to work a full week and still screw for a full night."

David didn't know what to say. He was still surprised by the brief display of attention from the waitress. Not that she was necessarily his type. A few too many tattoos for his taste, but she was definitely pretty. However, like the few other moments since the fire when attractive women had acted extra-nice to him, if not downright flirtatious, he wondered about their motivation. Was it pity? Curiosity? Did they wonder if the scars went all the way down his body? Despite the stirring below his waist, he still wasn't ready to admit that it could be sincere interest from any of them.

Of course, he could never say all of this to Steve, just as the older man would never admit to his claustrophobia. "Yeah," David said instead. "It's pretty good stuff." He raised his glass. "Here's to women." It was a corny toast, but Steve clinked his glass on David's and took a big swallow. "Speaking of houses," David said, wanting to change the subject, "I was thinking. You're from California originally. Have you ever been to that Remington House up by San Jose?"

Steve set his glass on the table and scratched his balding head. "I don't think so. Never much cared for the northern part of the state."

"It's this crazy house," David said. "I was just thinking about it the other day. My great-uncle Pete was a plumber there for almost ten years."

"Ten years? Christ, boy, what sort of house takes ten years?"

"It was a helluva lot longer than that," David said. "They worked on this place for almost forty years."

"Oh, wait," Steve said and slapped the table. The glasses did a little dance, sloshing some of the beer out. "I've heard about that place. It's actually called the *Winchester* House. You got the wrong gun, kid. Old Lady Winchester thought there were spirits chasing her because her husband made the rifle that killed so many people. But some psychic told her that if she kept building on her house, it would keep the ghosts happy or some crazy shit."

David nodded. "That's the place. My Uncle Pete worked there on the night shift. I guess they had people working there twenty-four hours a day. My Dad took me there when I was a kid. It was wild. Stairways that would only lead up to a ceiling and just end, as if they might've gone to the next level originally, but a whole new room had been built over them since. You'd have to go back down and go a different direction."

"I heard that there are doors that open to a three story drop-off," Steve said and shook his head in disbelief.

"It was supposed to confuse the evil spirits."

"So whatever happened to your uncle?" Steve asked. "Did he finish the job?"

"He didn't," David said. "No one knows what happened to him. He just disappeared one day. With all the coming and going at the end of the shift, no one noticed that Pete didn't leave with the rest of them. Guys usually just wanted to get home to their bed. It wasn't until the next night when his truck was still parked at the job site that they started looking for him."

David leaned in closer to the table. "A hundred and twenty-two rooms they searched, but they never found him."

Steve sat with his mouth open. Then he shook off his stupor and laughed. "You're shitting me."

"No, I'm not," David said and laughed. "But I am being a little dramatic. It's probably nothing sinister. My Dad said it wouldn't have been the first job Pete walked off. He didn't have any ties in San Jose and might've just moved on to another job. It still didn't explain the truck, but my dad said it never ran that good anyway.

"But that's beside the point," David said. "What if *we're* the ones working on the Winchester House?"

Steve furrowed his brow. "I don't get ya."

"Well, we know where Jim Miller got most of his money."

"If you can believe Hal," Steve said. "He's been known to tell a tale or two."

"I wondered about that, too," David said. "But it's true. Unless Miller is lying to A.C."

"How do you mean?"

"The first week we were here, when A.C. was still on the island, I was working in the guest bathroom just off the office, doing shower backing, and I heard Jim talking about it to A.C. He said that one of the main reasons he quit was because he got tired of wearing a bulletproof vest."

David paused as a new song started, and again he had to search the crowd to find the singer, a younger girl sitting with three other women. Then he looked at the big screen. Some urban drama played out between a man and a woman, and the accompanying music led David to believe it must be a love song. Two lovers torn apart.

"So anyway," he continued, "you figure he's probably responsible for some deaths somewhere, just like Winchester. He used to sell weapons to foreign countries, for Hell's sake. And think about how long this house has been under construction before we got here. Five years almost? And we're still working on parts of the framing. They might be saying it's almost done now, but it sure as hell doesn't look like that to me." David looked around the bar. "And there's that whole curse thing."

"I don't buy into that," Steve said, but his voice betrayed him.

"Oh, c'mon, Steve," David said. "You can't help but at least wonder, right?" David had definitely wondered about it. "We're the third crew to take over the job," he said.

"I'm well aware of that," Steve said and took a drink. "If Miller didn't fire the first two, I probably wouldn't have to baby-sit his shit starting tomorrow."

"He's paranoid," David said. "Buck told me that when McGinnis sent him over to Kona last week to get that load of tile, he met the last contractor and said the guy was pretty cool." David didn't add that, considering Jim Miller's past occupation, it might not just be the previous construction crews that he had to worry about breaking into the house. "He also said that the guy told him that there was some bad mojo or something in the whole neighborhood. He said that the other house on the turnabout, you know the big one with the copper roof?"

Steve just nodded.

"He said they can't keep their hired help to stay longer than a month or two. They just up and split in the middle of the night. He told Buck that it had to do with the location, that the major points of land on the island that jut into the ocean, kind of like the one we're building on, are considered sacred areas. It's where they used to do their tribal rituals."

"Like what?"

"Apparently, lots of women used to give birth on the points, and if any baby looked screwed up somehow, one of the elders would kill it and throw it to the sea. We're surrounded by death." David thought about the ritual and again wondered if there was some sort of magic on the island for ridding the world of a demon. "Maybe we're all cursed," he said.

And not just me.

Steve stared at him for a moment. He blinked a couple times and looked down at his glass. "That's crazy."

"It doesn't make me crazy just because I wonder about these things," David said, maybe a little too defensively. "I mean, considering what we suspected he did for a living, didn't you give any thought to the fact that you were accepting blood money?"

Steve was silent, and David could see that the older man hadn't really thought about it. Until now. Suddenly David felt bad. He had been so wrapped up in himself that he hadn't thought about the older carpenter. He didn't know how superstitious the other man might be, but considering Steve's new assignment staying overnight at the site, the conversation probably wasn't helping.

"But hell," David quickly added, "someone's gotta do it, right? A paycheck is a paycheck, and this one is paying pretty well. Alice is probably pretty happy about that, right? It's going to be a pretty nice extra chunk of change you'll be taking home for doing the night shift. I sure wouldn't mind that."

"Well, you're more than welcome to take the job, then," Steve said. He laughed. "And Alice, too, for that matter."

David was glad to hear Steve make a joke. "Actually," he said, "I've got my eye on that waitress."

Steve chuckled. "I bet you do." Then his gaze drifted off. The singer finished her song, and silence filled the lounge as the DJ took the microphone to the next performer, a white kid with dreadlocked hair who stood up and went to the podium television. David didn't recognize the reggae song chosen but thought bemusedly that he might have fallen into the Twilight Zone. The lounge seemed to shimmer slightly. Or maybe it was just the smoke. Or the beer

beers

catching up with him. For a moment—and not for the first time since arriving on the island—his surroundings took on a surreal quality, almost like he was dreaming. This was understandable. Only two weeks earlier, he had been in the thralls of the Montana cold, and now he was on an island in the middle of the Pacific Ocean.

Steve interrupted the thought. "I don't know what I'm going to do down there," he said, looking into his drink. "I sure as hell won't sleep."

David didn't respond. It was the closest Steve had come to admitting to his claustrophobia.

Steve looked up. "It's already like a coffin down there during the day." He paused. "I mean, you think it's pretty closed in, right?"

David nodded. "Oh, yeah. I'd much rather be working with the other guys. No offense."

"Can't blame you." Steve took a drink. "And tomorrow night they want me to actually try to fall asleep down there. Oh, and I'm supposed to fight off any intruders, too. Although I doubt that any of the past contractors is enough of a super spy to break into *that* place. Alarm system hooked up or not."

"I'd switch with you if I could," David said, "but they seemed pretty specific about choosing you. They know they can trust you, what with you being on the crew the longest and all."

"It was McGinnis."

"Yeah," David said. "That, too. McGinnis stuck it to you. He wouldn't put me on the detail even if I asked. Sorry, man. What I don't understand is, why can't you just stay in the above ground part of the house? Watch for intruders that way?"

"How the hell should I know?" Steve responded. "This Miller guy's crazy. Or paranoid. Or both. Maybe he thinks they're going to tunnel underneath somehow, like rats. Chew their way into his safe. He must have some seriously important shit stashed in there."

"Or maybe it was McGinnis's idea."

Steve didn't respond. He drained his beer in a couple of swallows, then looked past David towards the karaoke screen. "I just don't know if I can..." His voice trailed off, and he sighed. In that moment, David saw the shackles around Steve Avery. Namely, his first ex-wife and kids to support, as well as wife number three and her girls. Steve didn't have any choice; he had to do what he was told. Probably at home as well as at work. David still didn't believe that Steve was "too old of a dog," but he knew that the leash didn't go very far.

Steve gave a short, bitter laugh and shook his head. "I guess it's like you said, kid. Somebody's gotta do it."

CHAPTER 15

With the exception of a single streetlight that burned a yellow haze in the mist blowing off the ocean that night, the neighborhood where Miller's Mansion was being built was dark and dead quiet. Steve sat in the company truck smoking his last cigarette of the night.

Maybe just one more in the backyard.

A few windows were lit in other houses, but the light was muted by closed blinds, and Steve didn't see any movement.

Probably just on a security timer, he thought. The neighborhood was full of vacationers and part-timers. "And one middle-aged carpenter," Steve grumbled.

For living on a tropical island full of beautiful women, Steve didn't feel nearly as good as he thought he should. Not even close.

It had all started with that unbearable six-hour flight from Los Angeles. Normally Steve would've downed enough drinks to sedate a cow, but the early hour of the flight had mingled with his nerves and set off his ulcer something fierce. Vince gave him a couple of painkillers, but that just made him feel numb and stupid… and still *very* aware of the confined space. The pills had actually made it worse. If anything did go wrong with the airplane, he knew he wouldn't be able to take any action as it plummeted to the expansive ocean below.

After they landed safely on the island, things seemed to look up. Hal had been right when he said that their wages would be twice what they were making in Montana. Steve hadn't felt the effects yet of what he had heard called "island fever," which he thought might get to him if he was claustrophobic. Even though the work had been hard that first week—mostly cleaning up all the junk from the last crew and stocking up the new building materials—they couldn't beat the job site, especially the view off the ten-foot rocky cliff to the sea. Not even Hal's story from their first night on the island could ruin his mood.

The whole crew had gone down to the hotel lounge that night, and after a few drinks, Hal told them about a conversation he had with A.C. the night before they left. Apparently, Decker Built was not just the third crew to work on the house. This was also the third time the house had to be rebuilt. When the house was nearly framed the first time, the inspector came out and said there was no way it would pass inspection. The architect apparently screwed up big time. So Miller fired the architect, razed the house nearly to the ground and started again. This time, as they were getting ready to put the roof on, a rogue lava flow from a volcano that had been erupting for twenty some odd years popped out a chunk of the hillside above the house. Nothing they could've done about it, and a week later the house was overrun. Melted all of the framing, and the whole thing collapsed on itself.

Steve was wondering what kind of cash flow a guy would need to continue past strike two. As if reading his mind, Hal answered the question, telling the group about Miller's past as an arms dealer.

"Talk about skeletons in the closet," Had had said. "This guy's probably got enough to fill a cemetery."

Steve hadn't let the stories get to him. Hal could be a real windbag sometimes, with a tendency for exaggeration, and Steve didn't consider himself to be that superstitious. Sure, he always avoided walking under ladders, but that was just good sense.

The first weekend on the island, they took the company truck and drove to Kona to see the more touristy beaches. Steve thought he might be in heaven, especially considering the fact that the crews in Montana were probably slaving under cold, gray skies. The fact that he didn't have Alice there to make a scene if he even glanced at another woman didn't hurt, either. But the following Monday, things took a sharp turn for the worse when McGinnis assigned him and David to finish up the work in the safe rooms. The past week had been torture for the claustrophobic carpenter, and then last Friday after work, he found out about the night duty.

That day before the meeting had been the worst claustrophobia Steve had experienced in years. His second wife, Marsha, used to say she thought he must've been left alone in the crib when he was a baby or locked in a closet by his older brother and then forgotten. Steve remembered the latter happening on a few terrifying occasions, but he had never called out for help because he knew his father wouldn't put up with the child's fear. That was how he felt at work that day.

When they had shown up to work that morning, he noticed dark clouds over the watery horizon, and a storm must've blown in that afternoon, because the humidity in the cemented cave felt like it was choking him. Because of his sour mood, he had worked mostly in silence Friday afternoon. He spent the last hour of the day checking his watch more than he worked, and fifteen minutes earlier than usual, he told David that they could roll up the tools. "We don't want to be late to the crew meeting," he said. "Seeing as we're the farthest away, it's only fair that we quit early."

The two had wrapped up what they were working on and left the largest of the three rooms, the command center of the house, closing a heavy steel door and punching in a security code. The main security system may not have been set up yet, but they had installed temporary punch-code locks on all of the doors. It took almost ten minutes to wind down the series of hallways, unlocking and locking the doors, until they reached the bottom of the stairwell that climbed to the main level. By this point every day, Steve had to fight the urge to run up the stairs to the fresh air that he knew was so close. On that particular day, he could barely breathe as they ascended concrete stairs that he thought would never end.

At the top, he told David to go ahead to the meeting room. "I'm going to see what Hal's been working on." He had watched until David rounded a corner, feeling a little better to be out of the stairwell but still trapped in the center of a maze. He hurried off in the other direction, following a quick series of turns until he came to the master bedroom. He slid open the glass doors and stumbled out. A light mist fell from thin white clouds. Steve stood in the backyard facing the ocean and took deep breaths of the cool air. His pulse slowed after a few moments, and when he felt calmer, he turned back to the house and went to the meeting.

He should have stayed outside. Hell, after the meeting that day, Steve wondered if he should've just stayed in Montana.

In the meeting, McGinnis informed them about some furniture and valuables which were being moved into the safe rooms. "Some of these things individually," McGinnis said, "are worth more than all of you put together. Miller's probably just being paranoid, but starting next Tuesday, he wants to have someone on the job overnight to keep an eye on things. We've chosen you, Avery."

Steve could swear that it had looked like the supervisor was pushing back a grin. He had tried to argue with McGinnis, but the little prick threatened him with a ticket back to Montana along with his last paycheck if he refused.

Steve had spent most of the weekend in the lounge, which, in hindsight, probably hadn't been such a good idea. And Monday night had been just a plain *bad* idea. After the other guys had left, leaving Steve alone with David, the kid had decided *that* night would be when he would start talking. Some crazy shit about curses and baby sacrifices. Suddenly Hal's stories from that first night carried a little more weight, and the next day at work dragged out as Steve found himself preoccupied with distractions.

However, when he pulled up to the job site for the first night, he felt okay. Pretty good even. He didn't even drink that much. A few shots at the bar and a couple beers. And just a few pulls off a new bottle of bourbon on the drive over. He could get through this.

Besides the ocean mist drifting through the neighborhood, the night skies were clear, the moon almost full. Without any city lights to dampen its glow, the moon's reflection off the ocean was all Steve needed to find his way through the gate and past the six car garage toward the main house, but as he keyed in the security code at the front door, he saw that the moonlight failed to penetrate much past the windows. Steve twisted the end of his flashlight and cast a narrow beam into the front room. He started down the dark set of hallways that led to the downstairs, taking the most direct route, but his racing heart changed his path to go through the exterior rooms with windows as much as he could.

Steve followed the rooms until he came to the main living room, where the seaside section of the house consisted of five panels of wall-length sliding windows looking out to the ocean. He pushed one of the panels aside and stepped out for a last breath of fresh air and to relieve himself one last time. Maybe have that *actual* last cigarette. He was immediately calmed by the bath of moonlight.

Steve set his things on the patio and went down the steps to the dirt that would eventually be sodded. Five or six industrial grade garbage bags were clumped together to the left of the pool, and Steve couldn't think of a better place to take care of the night's last business. As he stepped into the dirt, he heard a high pitched whine which seemed to be coming from somewhere in the distance beyond the bags. He paused and peered off down the shore, but a thin smear of clouds was passing over the moon and the rocky beach was darkened.

Steve disregarded the sound and started over to the pile of bags, unzipping his fly. The sound quickly intensified, definitely much closer than he originally thought and most definitely aggravated. In fact, the rising screech seemed like it was coming from the garbage just a few feet away. Steve jumped back and froze, his hand still holding the top button of his jeans. He stared in terror at the bags, and his mind took off in search of an explanation, rational or otherwise.

Sounds like a baby's crying, was his first thought, followed by an avalanche of others.

Not any healthy *baby. More like a deformed baby… Something in the garbage… Like maybe just a head. Still alive and screaming… Damn that David and his stories.*

The screech dropped a few seconds after Steve stopped moving, taking on the original lower tone that had fooled him the first time, but still he couldn't move. He had no idea what to do. Then movement in the tree behind the garbage bags caught his eye and he saw the silhouette of some critter scamper down the tree.

Steve let out his breath. "A freakin' rat," he said and laughed at himself. With few predators, the rodents thrived on the island. "Just a rat in Paradise."

Steve backed away from the garbage to the base of the patio stairs, but still he watched the pile of bags while he pissed in the dirt. The moon came out from behind the clouds but failed to reveal anything else.

He stood for a couple minutes before walking back into the darkness and making his way toward the center of the house. At the top of the stairs, he took two more swallows from the bottle of bourbon and started down, gripping the cold chain that had been bolted to the wall as a temporary handrail, slightly staggering down the steps. The beating of his heart began to fade under the dull hum of the liquor.

"Definitely not paying me enough money for this crap," Steve mumbled when he reached the bottom. He switched on the overhead bulbs that ran thirty feet to the first locked door. "Just until the job is finished," he said. Suddenly he envied the crews working in Montana.

He followed the passageways, extinguishing the previous hall's lights when he passed through each secure door. Darkened, empty rooms stood on either side of the halls. No doors, just gaping thresholds of darkness. Steve didn't look into those rooms; his imagination was sufficient to keep his eyes forward, focused on the end goal. He finally made it to the final door to the safe rooms, his hand rising to punch in the last code, when he heard a movement behind him. He spun around and nearly toppled over from the sudden motion. He briefly wondered if he had drunk more than he thought.

A cat sat in the middle of the hallway, licking its right paw before cleaning its head with it. The overhead light shone off its sleek, black coat. The cat stopped cleaning itself and meowed. Steve swayed in place and stared at it for a moment. Wild cats were a common sight on the island. One of the few things that kept the rats down. This one probably wandered in during the day when the doors were open. Or maybe it came through the ventilation ducts that still didn't have their covers screwed on.

Steve briefly considered the trip he would have to make all the way back outside to let the cat out before making his decision. He wasn't about to lock a stray cat in the saferooms with him, but he didn't really want to try to figure out how to get it upstairs, either.

"Sorry, blackie," he said to the cat. "You're gonna have to stay in the hall until tomorrow. I'm sure you'll be fine with these two rooms. Make yourself at home." He turned back around and entered the final code. At the same time as he heard the soft click of the lock, he felt the cat curling around his legs, wrapping its tail as it went. "Go on, now," Steve said and pushed the cat aside with his left leg. The cat skittered back down the hallway a safe distance and then crouched in the center of the hallway with a little growl. Steve opened the door and pulled it quickly shut behind him and punched the lock code. There was only one other door in the final room, one that looked much more reinforced than the previous doors, more like a vault door, but they hadn't given Steve the code to *that* door.

"Crazy sumbitch," he muttered, but still he wondered what was behind that door.

A rollaway bed had been pushed off to one side of the otherwise naked room. Steve set down his pile of stuff in the center of the floor, then rolled the cot over next to his things. He stopped when he thought he heard the cat meowing through the heavy security door, but that was impossible. Just the booze.

Steve unfolded the bed, and then stood looking at the concrete walls with their skeleton of metal-lined frames. This was no good. He took another drink, then he plugged the alarm clock into an extension cord and turned on the radio. A tinny voice came out of the little speaker announcing that the next song would be the Beach Boys "with a familiar little tune called "Surfin' U.S.A." Maybe you've heard of it."

Steve set the clock on the cement floor and turned the volume low. He didn't even consider turning off the lights in the room for sleep. That's where the bottle of bourbon came in. It didn't take long for him to drift off thinking about ocean waves that he rarely got to see, but his sleep was ragged and filled with nightmares of screaming deformed infants.

* * *

Almost 2500 miles away in San Francisco, Jeannie awoke in the middle of the night, gasping for air and grabbing at her throat. Her heart raced in her chest, and she had a terrifying moment lying on the bed when she believed that if she reached out into the darkness, she would feel the insides of her own coffin.

Then slowly, pieces of light filtered into her waking consciousness. Thin lines forming a rectangle around the doorway leading to the hall. The red glow of her alarm clock. The green light on the smoke detector.

Jeannie's breathing finally slowed, but she still trembled from the memory of the nightmare of being buried alive. In the dream, she had been unable to move as a man dumped her body into a box. She didn't recognize the older man, but something told her it was the same person she had dreamt of two weeks earlier sitting next to David in the basement of the giant house in Hawaii.

In this dream, however, David stood a little behind the man looming over her. His eyes were caved in shadows, but Jeannie knew he was watching as she lay paralyzed in the narrow, wooden box. She wanted to beg for her life, but the look in the older man's eyes told her that it was pointless. They were blank and vacant.

"It's the only thing I can do to save myself," he said. As he spoke the words, David moved his lips to match them exactly.

The man started to slide the lid over Jeannie and she woke up. Lying in the dark, she tried to shake the dream, but it wouldn't go away. Suddenly, she really needed the light on. Still halfway expecting to find herself interred in her sheets, she tentatively slid to the edge her bed. She walked toward the bars of light guiding her to the door and the light switch. But even though turning on the lights shed the illusion of entombment, she still felt imprisoned in her room. She looked at all of the articles and pictures she had taped to her walls and ceilings, and suddenly she felt her chest constrict again. She was surrounded, suffocated, by the tapestry of stories that covered the room. What had once been her only link to sanity now felt like it was killing her, and as Jeannie thought about the dream, she wondered where this next story would fit, the story of whatever ruination of which David was most certainly a part.

Jeannie didn't know how many more stories she could take.

The room started to spin, and she had to sit down on her bed with her head between her knees and take several ragged breaths. When everything felt steady again, she rolled onto her side, suddenly exhausted. She just needed to go back to sleep. But the light switch felt so far away. She pulled herself into a sitting position, stood and crossed to the door, but when she turned off the lights, her chest tightened again. The moon had already set, and with no other lights in the neighborhood to find their way into her room, the darkness felt like it was closing in around her. She quickly switched the light back on and was again confronted by the mural on her wall. She sighed, then trudged over and dropped onto her bed, thinking that maybe she could sleep with the lights on, but when she tried closing her eyes, she saw the images and headlines from her collection burned into the backs of her eyelids.

May 27, 1971. Railway accident in Germany claims 46 lives.
March 4, 1929. Man kills seven, then self.

A grainy photograph of a group of scientists in front of the Los Alamos Laboratory in New Mexico.

September 3, 1985. Local couple still missing. A photo of the couple from their honeymoon. The woman. Something in the woman's eyes.

Jeannie would never to get to sleep this way. Maybe a little moving around would settle her down. She needed to go to the bathroom anyway. She got up and put on her robe over her t-shirt and pajama pants, opened her door, and stepped out into the hall. The bathroom was just down a few doors, but as she walked toward it, something didn't feel right. She couldn't put her finger on it. Something different about the hallway. The lighting maybe. Even though Jeannie knew she was awake, something about the hallway felt like a dream to her. And not a very good dream. She broke out in goosebumps as a chill ran across her flesh. Part of her hesitated, unsure if she should just go back to her room. But that didn't feel quite right, either, and she *did* have to use the bathroom.

She had barely stepped into the bathroom—the small bathroom, no window, all white, glaring bulbs, no window, sharp lines and edges, no window—when her unease blossomed into something much worse. Worse than what she had experienced in her room, her much bigger room. A curtain of blackness closed in around Jeannie's vision, and she realized she had stopped breathing.

She stumbled backwards out of the bathroom and drew a deep breath, but back in the hall, she finally realized what it was that had seemed different. The hallway seemed smaller, suddenly much too narrow. And endlessly long. Jeannie needed to get outside, but the only exit in the Rose House that didn't set off the fire alarm was the main entry downstairs by Dr. Brandt's office and the front desk. She would have to go down the stairs at the end of the hallway. So far away. Breathing rapidly, she started down the hall. She knew Frank Matsen would be at the front desk for night security. What she didn't know was how he would react.

Trying to keep a calm appearance, Jeannie was still purposefully noisy, clomping down the stairs in order that Frank would hear her coming. She *did* not want this to look like an escape attempt. She just needed to get some fresh air. It was, in fact, all she could focus on; the idea of trying to do anything else, especially escape, was beyond her comprehension at this point.

Frank sat behind at the front desk reading a *People* magazine. He raised his eyebrows as Jeannie approached the desk. "I tell you what," he said, "some of these celebrities do the damndest things." He set down the magazine and looked at his wrist, even though he didn't wear a watch. "I think it's a little early for breakfast, isn't it?"

Jeannie tried to do a motion to somehow convey the fact that she felt like the walls and ceiling were closing in on her, holding her arms and hands out, then bringing her hands closer to her head and out again. Maybe he'd get it that she just needed some fresh air, but Frank thought she meant that her head was going to explode. "Headache?" he asked. "Well, I'm not supposed to, Jeannie, but I could give you a couple of aspirin."

Jeannie shook her head. She patted her pockets and realized that she had left her writing tablet in her room. She did the sign for a pen.

"Oh," Frank said. "Yeah, sure." He handed her a pad of sticky notes and a pencil.

Minor panic attack. Need fresh air.

Jeannie had never had a panic attack before, but it was the closest she could explain to Frank at this point. How else could she explain that, for the first time in her life, she knew what it was like to be severely claustrophobic?

"I dunno', Jeannie," Frank said. "I'm the only one on shift right now."

I'll just sit on the steps. Promise I won't run.

She drew a little smiley face, even though she thought she just might have to make a break for the front door if Frank didn't acquiesce soon. The front area of the house was more open than her room or the hallways, but she still was very aware of the edges of her confinement even here.

Please.

Frank sighed, then walked over and unlocked the door. "Don't make a fool out of me, kiddo," he said. "No farther than the top step."

It was all Jeannie could do to keep from bursting through the door, but she knew that wouldn't look good to Frank. Once through the door into the open, a wave of relief washed over her. She drew deeply from the cool night air and tried to slow her heart. With the exception of the light from Rose House cast out over the front lawn, the neighborhood was dark. After a minute, she felt better enough to sit down on the top step. However, she knew she would have to go back in eventually, and even though she was outside now, the Rose House felt like it loomed behind her, a living creature waiting to swallow her into its asphyxiating corridors. And she would have to go willingly. Jeannie could only hope that this newly acquired fear would abate soon, or at least enough to get her back into her room.

CHAPTER 16

When Steve awoke the next morning, the cat was gone. He called to it in both rooms, looked in the corners and tight spaces behind building material, but no cat. He figured it must've escaped whatever way it came in. He left the underground rooms, thankful to be back in the light of day, even though his head throbbed from the restless night as he climbed into the truck. The crew was outside waiting when he pulled up, but thankfully Vince was too busy talking about the girl he had met at one of the bars downtown for the other guys to ask much about Steve's first night.

Or maybe they just didn't want to hear him complain. Steve knew that he bitched a lot, but goddammit, he didn't have it *half* as good as the others.

When they drove up to the mansion gates, Steve was surprised to see the head electrician Frank Siolo's truck. He was parked next to the other electricians, five guys who Steve thought were all related somehow. Frank, or "Francis" if one of the cousins was ribbing him, was a mix of Portuguese and something else Steve couldn't remember. He spoke with an accent that was something in between Hispanic and what the locals called "Pidgin" or something. Even though they were speaking English, half of the time Steve needed a damn decoder book to understand the other workers because their Pidgin was so thick.

Frank didn't usually roll in until nine or ten, but today he was standing in front of his truck talking to his brothers or cousins or whatever. Steve parked the truck, and as everyone piled out and started toward the gate, Frank stopped talking with his workers and shouted to Steve. "Hey, Stevie, good morning." He ambled over to the carpenters. "My damn back again, don't ya know it. Musta slept bad." Frank took off his floppy brimmed hat and used a bandana to wipe the sweat already glistening on his bald head. "Not so bad as you, though." (This sounded to Steve like, "Nahsobadasyoo, dough.") "First you gotta work downstairs. An' now sleeping dere too, yeah? *Man.* How's *dat* goin'?"

Steve grunted. "Frank, I'd say that it's kind of like a big, dark asshole down there, and I'm sucking the big turd."

"*Suckin' da big turd?*" Frank repeated and burst into laughter. "I tell you what, bruddah. I think you're right about dat. Suckin' da big turd. That's funny stuff, Stevie." Frank looked past Steve at Hal and the other guys who had gone ahead, then he lowered his voice. "I tell you somethin' else, bruddah. I think that guy you gotta work for, the one with the eye-"

"McGinnis," Steve said.

"Yeah, dat's him. I think he got it out for you."

Steve just huffed, too tired to respond to the obvious. He started to follow the crew, then he hesitated. "Hey, Frank, you used to know the last contractor."

"Still do, bruddah. Yeah, Greg lives over on the other side of the island. I see him every couple weekends or so."

Steve glanced around to make sure there wasn't anyone nearby. "He told one of our guys that this place was cursed. Can you believe that horse shit?"

"Probably is cursed, bruddah," Frank said. "Whole area. It's dis location, man. Most spots that point out to the sea on Hawaii are sacred areas."

"So I've heard," Steve said.

"And this haoli, Miller, built his house right up da edge of one."

"That's just great," Steve mumbled.

"You don't got nothin' to worry about, bruddah," Frank said.

"Why's that? You don't believe in that stuff?"

"Oh, I believe," Frank said. "The trick is, you just gotta let dem spirits do their thing. This was their land first. So you gotta let 'em pass through when they want to pass through. They got no reason to mess with *you.*" One of Frank's workers called out to him from the supply trailer, and Frank nodded back. "Don't sweat it, bruddah," he said, then rejoined to his crew.

"Great," Steve said again.

As he went down under the house, his chest seemed to tighten more than usual. David stood waiting at the bottom, but he didn't ask Steve what he had been talking about with Frank. And Steve didn't offer.

They went to work as usual, but it wasn't until lunch that Steve decided to say something about his first night in the saferooms. Crazy as it sounded in his head, the surrounding silence was killing him, and he didn't have much interest in his sandwich. No matter how much mayonnaise and mustard he slathered on the bread each morning, his lunch still tasted bland in the dank, underground room. He rolled a bite of the sandwich around his mouth, grabbed his water bottle and swallowed hard.

"Damndest thing," Steve said. David looked over at him with his one eyebrow raised, and Steve proceeded to tell him about almost taking a leak on what he thought was a deformed baby. "It was all because of your damn story, kid. I just about pissed on myself," he said and laughed. When he didn't get much more than a forced laugh from David, he went on to tell him about the black cat. "What I need to do if I see that cat again is to put him on the rat, solve all my problems." He laughed again, but still David remained mostly stoic. Steve picked up his sandwich to try eating again when David spoke.

"You said you saw the rat run *down* the tree."

"Yeah. So?"

"But you said the sound seemed to be coming from the ground, from the bags. Wouldn't you have seen the rat going *up* the tree instead of down?"

Steve paused, his teeth clamped on the sandwich. He tore off the bite and chewed on it. "Well," he said finally, "maybe there were two rats."

"Maybe," David said. "Just seems a little weird. And have you ever heard of rats making that kind of noise?"

"I know they squeak," Steve said, pointing the sandwich at David matter-of-factly. "Other than that, I've haven't spent much time with the little bastards." He looked at the kid for a moment. "What are you getting at?"

David shook his head. "Oh nothing. Never mind. It's just interesting. Sounds pretty freaky, but you survived the night without having to fight off criminal masterminds, so that's good."

Steve let the subject go, but something in the kid's tone sounded strange. Like he was keeping something back, but if it was more stories about voodoo or some such shit, Steve didn't need to hear it. It certainly wasn't making his new assignment any easier. They finished their lunch in silence, and any conversation during the rest of afternoon was strictly work related.

After his previous night, Steve decided he would have a little more to drink this time before heading back to the house. Sitting in front of the main gate, he cast an eye on the bourbon bottle which was now half empty on the seat next to him but decided if he had another drink, he probably wouldn't find his way downstairs. He swung open the door of the truck, stepped out, and wove his way past the garage to the front door. The moon had already made its way to the western side of the island—Steve could never remember if they called that the windward or leeward side—and the house felt darker than the night before. As with the first night, he stopped again in the living room to step out for one last breath before going under, but he only stood on the steps for a few moments. He had purposefully gone to the bathroom before leaving the lounge this time.

No need to rile up the spirits by pissing on their path.

He almost fell twice on the stairs going down to the safe rooms. When he finally made it to the office, he started to close the final door, but a tightening in his chest made him drop his hand, and he left the door open to the small outer corridor. Nobody would know any different if just *one* door was left open, and Steve thought his head might explode if he was locked in the little room tonight. He opened the cot with a *clang*, yanked off his shirt and jeans, dropped on the cot and passed out.

In the middle of the night, Steve woke to the sound of his name being spoken. It echoed in the room, soft but persistent, like a woman. He opened his eyes and rolled over toward the voice. Through blurred vision, Steve thought he saw someone lying on the floor, propped on an elbow, watching him. Steve blinked. It kind of looked like...

"David?" Steve murmured. But the kid didn't talk like a woman. Was it a dream?

171

A damp breeze blew through the room, sending chills across his flesh. It was the first time Steve had felt the air move in the safe rooms, and he tried to remember if in his stupor he had closed *any* of the doors. He reached up and rubbed his sleep-caked eyes and deciphered the illusion on the floor. It wasn't a person. The black cat had returned and was sitting by the pile of discarded clothes. "Oh, it's you, kitty," Steve said. He quickly decided that he still didn't want to close that last door, and he started to roll back over. "Just be good, kitty."

"Not yet, Steve."

Steve's eyes popped back open. This time, it was the kid's voice. Steve sat upright and looked around the room, but no one else was in there with him. He fell back on the bed and closed his eyes.

Must be dreaming.

"Not quite."

"Shit!" Steve swung his legs off the bed. His head spun from the bourbon, and he had to steady himself before standing up. "That better not be you, David." He pushed himself onto his feet. The cat stood as well. Steve staggered into the hallway toward the other two rooms, but he didn't find anyone in either. He shook his head and went back toward the office, but he stopped in the doorway when he saw the cat sitting on the bed.

"You know what to do." The voice still sounded like David, but it was deeper this time, and more gruff. It also seemed to be coming directly from the cat. But the cat's mouth didn't move.

"Of course it didn't move," Steve said aloud, "because cats don't talk. It's a dream." Steve couldn't remember if he had ever felt drunk before in a dream, but he thought the best thing to do would be to just lay back down.

I said, not yet.

This time the command sounded in his head. The cat walked to the end of the bed and looked at Steve, who was starting to doubt that he was still dreaming. This felt too real. Sleep walking, maybe?

The cat hopped off the bed, trotted over to Steve and trailed figure-eights through his legs, its tail curling around his legs.

Wide awake, Stevie boy.

"Then I must be-" he started, but the voice cut him off.

You're not just imagining things.

Steve freed himself from the tangle of cat and stepped into the room. He turned around and stared at the animal.

Feeling smaller in here?

Steve looked at the walls and rubbed his eyes again. They seemed closer. Even the ceiling appeared low enough for Steve to touch if only he dared reach up his hand. And it was dropping lower.

"Just a dream," Steve whispered.

It had happened like this before. At hunting camp, in tents and cramped pull-behind campers, nightmares where he was being crushed alive.

The lights in the room started to fade as the walls closed in, and the door slid impossibly far away. He thought about making a break for the exit, but the cat prowled forward, growing larger and blocking his way until there was no more room for him to get past it. Steve drew a ragged breath and dropped to his knees as the ceiling lowered on top of him. He slid his body underneath the cot, even though he knew it wouldn't protect him.

Then the lights went out completely. Steve was curled in a pool of his own sweat, taking short, rapid breaths when he heard the cat's claws on the concrete. "Just a dream," he whimpered. He felt the brush of fur on the back of his neck, but he couldn't move.

You know what you have to do. It's only going to get worse.

Steve's breathing grew faster. His heart pushed to get out of his chest. The air was running out. He tried to slow himself down, but his body fought back, sucking in the last gasps of hot air until his senses faded and there was just the faint sound of his wheezing and the feel of the cold, hard concrete under his body. Then the pitch black turned to fuzzy gray and he lost consciousness.

CHAPTER 17

Steve woke in the morning on the floor, with a pounding headache focused where his skull seemed to have flattened in conformity with the concrete. He rose slowly and raised his arms toward the ceiling, with pops and cracks sounding from various joints in his body. He looked up at the nearly twelve inches of clearance above his outstretched hands and thought back on his nightmare.

"Just a dream."

On the way back to the hotel, Steve decided that he needed to lay off the drink a little. It didn't seem to be helping the situation. When he showed up at the hotel to pick up the guys, Hal asked how Steve's night went, but Steve's standard "fine" seemed to satisfy them.

The crew was pretty quiet on the drive, but Steve cursed aloud when he turned the truck onto the last street descending to Miller's Mansion and saw the tan Mercedes parked in the driveway. Ed McGinnis apparently had arrived early and was sitting in the car talking on his cell phone. Steve pulled up next to the Mercedes and nodded at him. McGinnis didn't return the gesture but rather continued talking on his phone. The crew got out of the truck and walked up to the gate. They were almost through when the project manager stepped out of the Mercedes. "Avery," he called.

Steve sighed and turned around.

"Good luck," Hal whispered under his breath before continuing on with the others.

"Morning, Ed," Steve said and walked back to the Mercedes.

"I wanted to know-" McGinnis started, but he stopped and scrunched up his nose. "Jesus, Avery, you smell like a distillery."

"Had a couple drinks last night."

"If you're going to be doing that nonsense, you need to find someone else to stay here."

Steve tensed up, the rush of blood to his head bringing back the sharp ache. "I'd love to find someone else," he said, his jaw tightening. "Why don't *you* find someone else?"

McGinnis stepped closer, a look of disgust on his face as he surveyed Steve. "Why don't you just find another job, old man?"

Steve clenched his fists.

Not here.

Steve knew a fight with his supervisor would be a seriously bad idea. He relaxed his hands and took a half step back. "What do you want, McGinnis?"

The supervisor's right eye twitched, and its focus shifted to Steve's shoulder, while his left eye remained trained on Steve. "What's the progress downstairs? We need to get the electricians in there to finish up by Friday."

"No problem."

"Good."

"Anything else?"

"No."

Steve started to turn, but McGinnis put a hand on his shoulder. "Actually, one more thing, Avery," he said. "If I find out you've been getting drunk before coming back to the house, I'll personally hand deliver your ticket out of here."

Steve jerked free. "Consider it done, *boss*." He walked away from McGinnis, pushing down his anger.

Not here. And not now.

Steve had his job to think about, but it still felt like rocks in his stomach to walk away from a young punk who would benefit immensely from a good punch to the jaw.

Or maybe more, Steve thought as he walked toward the house. He found David downstairs already in the office.

"How was McGinnis?" he asked.

"Don't ask." He walked over and unlocked the tool cabinet.

"He has seriously got it out for you."

"You can say that again," Steve said.

"Did you see the cat last night?"

Steve turned around. "What did you say?"

"I said that he has seriously got it-"

"No," Steve interrupted, "after that. About the cat."

"I didn't say anything about a cat."

Steve stared at David for a moment. "Oh." He turned back to the cabinet, shooting one last glance at the kid. "Well, I didn't see the cat again last night."

"Good," David said. "Congratulations on *not* seeing a cat."

"How about you just get to work, smartass."

Halfway through the morning, they had finished framing one of the rooms outside the office and had started to bolt down the bottom plate to the floor in the third room. Steve stood and headed out of the room to get more fasteners.

"Did you see the cat last night?"

Steve stopped and whipped around. The kid was crouched on his knees with his back to Steve, bent over a piece of steel.

"What?" Steve asked.

David turned on his haunches and looked at Steve. "What?"

"Did you just say something?"

"Not that I'm aware of."

"Oh," Steve said. David went back to cutting the piece of metal, and Steve backed out of the room. He stood in the middle of the hall, and his eyes darted around him. Four doors surrounding him. Three doors leading only to dead ends and one door which opened to another door, and another, and another. Narrow passages with locked doors. Walls and edges and corners cut through his vision, but no windows. Rooms with no exits.

Steve dug his fingernails into his palms and bit down hard on his tongue until the faint taste of copper spread in his mouth. He hadn't needed to use the technique to drive back the panic since childhood, to push away the fear and hide it from his father. Steve was a man now. He could beat this.

The pain helped him focus, and finally he regained his composure. He wiped the sweat from his forehead, took a deep breath and retrieved some fasteners from the other room. Thankfully, the kid didn't ask any questions about why he had taken so long.

Unless I count the questions he's not really asking, Steve thought. He almost laughed aloud, in spite of himself, but as the afternoon progressed, his sense of humor thinned to threadbare. Two other times during the day, he imagined the kid talking to him. The final time Steve asked David if he was fucking with him, and the look of confused innocence the kid gave him made Steve feel like an idiot.

Or a lunatic.

On the drive back to the hotel, no one seemed to notice that Steve wasn't speaking to anyone. They all had their little stories about "life in paradise." Back in the room, he showered, but he didn't eat after. He just wasn't hungry.

Steve remembered stopping by the corner liquor store, but like being in a dream, the next thing he knew, he found himself parked in front of the entrance gate to Miller's Mansion with an empty fifth of bourbon on the passenger seat. He couldn't recall much about the drive over to the house. In the thick fog, both outside the truck and in his head, it was as if nothing else existed. And he couldn't remember finishing the bottle of bourbon, yet there it was, empty on the seat next to him. So much for laying off the drink.

Steve pulled out a cigarette. The fog which had crept off the sea in the cool night made a perfect match for his blurred vision. The air outside of the truck felt as thick as his head, pushing into the cab and smothering the cigarette smoke. Even the streetlight failed to penetrate the darkness much past a hazy yellow cone, and the closest houses were just outlines in his vision, with only blackness beyond.

The night seemed to close in around the truck like the heavy breath of the spirits. Then time hiccoughed again, and Steve stood in the living room looking out the wall of windows.

The fog had completely swallowed the ocean, and the waves breaking on the rocks of the point below sounded like ships crashing in the confusion. The outside air would give him no comfort tonight.

And then he was at the top of the stairs. Felt a little like he was floating. The claustrophobia was still present, but it was only a distant nagging concern.

Down the stairs. Through the segmented hallway, until he stood just beyond the final door to the last three rooms. The black cat sat directly between him and the office.

When Steve had been a junior in high school, an older kid had slipped something in his drink at a party, and it had been probably eight hours before Steve stopped imagining inanimate objects moving. He remembered hearing that sometimes people who do that stuff get flashbacks. Maybe that's what was happening. Then the cat spoke.

You can pet me if that's what it takes.

It was a different voice in his head this time. A woman.

The cat stood and walked toward Steve.

C'mon, Stevie, pet the pussy.

It sounded like the cute waitress from the Anchor, but it wasn't attraction that Steve felt now. He backed up against the last door he had passed through, but he couldn't make himself turn around to unlock it. He slid to the side and into the corner. "What do you want from me?"

I only want you to be happy. The cat continued toward Steve, but he kicked at it. almost losing his balance. The animal stopped a few feet away. *Don't you want to be happy?*

Steve closed his eyes and shook his head. "This isn't happening," he said. "I'm losing my mind."

Not yet. But it will get worse.

"This isn't happening," Steve said again, sliding down the corner to the floor.

You know what you have to do.

Steve passed out.

It felt like only a few seconds had passed when he heard his cell phone ringing, but he knew he had actually slept. He dared to open his eyes, afraid of what he might see, but the cat was gone.

never was there in the first place.

His phone stopped ringing, and he picked it up and looked at the display.

7:45 a.m.

He discovered that he hadn't moved from the spot in the corner, a painful realization his body made at the same time. Standing up was going to be difficult. His phone started ringing again, and Steve saw Hal's name.

"Shit," he said, then answered the phone. "I'll be there in five." He hung up and again made a pledge of sobriety.

Back at the hotel, Steve nodded a distracted greeting to the others. He saw the disapproving look from Hal, but the rest of the crew was so intently listening to some story that David was telling, they barely said good morning. It seemed strange to Steve that this kid who had barely said more than two words to anyone besides

Steve was now the center of attention. As they drove out of the hotel parking lot, he looked in the rearview mirror and locked eyes with David. There was something different about him. He couldn't put his finger on it, but he had noticed it more and more lately. Almost like he didn't recognize him.

"So, anyway," David said, "he looked at the other guy for a second, and then he says, 'Not even if that pig was solid gold.'"

Everyone in the truck started laughing. Except Steve. And David.

How'd you sleep last night, Stevie?

Steve flinched and returned his attention to the road. Everyone was still laughing. They hadn't heard it.

Or maybe they *did* hear it and were all in on it. Maybe when everyone was laughing and Steve was looking at David, one of the others said it. It was all one big trick, and they were all in on it.

"Yeah, right," Steve said aloud. The laughter stopped, and the attention in the truck changed focus.

"What's that, Steve?" Hal asked.

"Oh, nothing. That was just a funny story the kid told." Steve managed a chuckle.

"Are you feeling okay, pal?"

Steve wanted to shout out that he felt anything *but* okay, to say that he might have had some sort of drug flashback the night before. He wanted to tell Hal, who was not only a coworker but also the closest thing Steve had to a "best friend," that a black cat had been talking to him. More importantly, he wanted to admit to Hal that he was terrified that he might start listening to the damn thing. Instead, he said, "I'm right as rain. Just a little tired is all."

Hal furrowed his brow, put his hand to his face and rubbed his beard. Steve had seen this gesture before at work when Hal was trying to figure out a particularly difficult project.

Think away, friend, Steve thought, *because you'll never even get close to this one.*

Steve thought he *was* losing his mind, but he also remembered hearing that crazy people never think they're crazy… or some stupid shit like that. Steve sure as hell felt like he was going insane, but he didn't plan on letting anybody else know.

At the job, he set himself to work, letting his hands do their familiar jobs. He tried to stay focused on work, but his mind kept skittering into the dark to think about his boogeymen. As the day passed, though, he felt less scared of that darkness. Unlike the days of his childhood terrors, today something was shaping up in his mind, a way to escape the suffocating closet of nightmares and close the door on all the bad thoughts inside once and for all.

At lunch, Steve's food remained untouched. He couldn't remember even making it that morning. The kid had gone up to the main level to get a couple boxes of screws.

Boxes.

Steve picked up a scrap of cardboard and started sketching a rough schematic. A box.

When David cleared his throat behind him, Steve folded the scrap of cardboard and stuck it in his overalls. David stepped next to him and looked at him for a moment.

Nice design.

Steve heard it, but the kid's lips didn't move. Steve had been looking right at him, and he knew it this time. No one else was working in the basement.

"You okay?" David asked.

This time Steve saw the words being spoken. He thought about the piece of cardboard poking his chest through his overalls. "Fine."

David shook his head and walked over to the tool cabinet. Steve stood up and dizziness threatened to put him back down.

"This tight space is getting to me," he said before thinking about it. It was the closest Steve had come to mentioning his claustrophobia to anyone besides his second wife.

David turned around. "Really?"

"Well… yeah," Steve said. "Sometimes it feels like it's closing in on me, or like the whole house is going to drop on us down here. I know, it sounds crazy."

"Not at all," David said. "It happens to me, too."

"Down here?" Steve asked, feeling a little better, a little more confident now that David hadn't laughed at him.

"Not so much down here," David said. "But it has happened on other jobs. Long hours working in small spaces with no fresh air. Your chest starts to tighten, and you just feel like if you can't stretch out your entire body and move around a little without walking *into* something, you'll never be able to take a deep breath again." David stepped closer to Steve.

"That's it," Steve nodded.

"And you start getting these crazy thoughts," David continued. "Things you may have never thought before, like it's coming from someone else."

Steve nodded faster, and David took another step.

"You wonder if you're starting to lose your mind." David reached up and put a hand on Steve's shoulder, his palm warm even through the t-shirt, and he dropped his voice. "Let me tell you, Steve, you're not crazy. You're doing just fine. Your thoughts are all right. Your thoughts are *all...* right."

The warmth from David's hand spread out from his shoulder, and Steve felt his muscles relax, knots untangle for the first time in years. With the warmth came the calm.

"All of my thoughts are right," Steve murmured.

"Yes."

The two of them went back to working, and as they did, Steve found himself floating again. He watched his body work as if he were somewhere just outside himself. He welcomed the feeling, the sublime sense of ultimate freedom from the trapped confines of his own flesh. Nothing to box him in. His fear was gone.

* * *

THE FINAL NIGHT

Even though Steve still felt detached from himself at the end of the day, he knew that he was still in control, and as his other self pulled up to the hotel to drop off the crew, he slid back into his body. He knew exactly what he had to do, and the rest of the night would require cooperation and coordination. Flesh and soul.

Steve smiled and said good night when the others got out of the truck. Hal stood for a moment holding the door open and giving Steve the beard-scratching look again.

"Good *night*, Hal," Steve said.

"It's Friday," Hal said. "You could probably go back to the site a little late. Why don't you get a drink with us?"

"I don't think I need one."

Hal showed a quick expression of surprise, then he shut the door and stepped back from the truck, still staring as Steve pulled away.

After leaving the hotel, Steve stopped at a burger joint and allowed himself to eat. He didn't really taste the food, but he knew he needed the energy. Then he went to the hardware store. Finally, a trip to the University of Hawaii. The chemistry lab. Something told him that there wouldn't be anybody there when he showed up.

"Looks like I'll be going to college afterall," he had murmured.

Three hours later, the carpenter stood in front of a door marked 903 at the Hilo Bay Condominiums. In one hand, he held a rag and a white plastic bottle of some chemical he had never heard of; with his other hand, he tried the knob of the door. Locked.

Try the back sliding door. Nobody locks those around here.

Steve crept around the side of the condo to the backyard patio. He saw a little sign next to the glass door that read, "Hawaiian Tradition: Mahalo for taking off your shoes."

Good idea, he thought. Make less noise that way.

He unlaced his boots and tried the back door. It slid easily on the track. Steve scanned the dark living room until he found the hallway leading to the bedroom. The door at the end of the hall stood open, and a cool breeze billowed out the curtains on the other side of the room.

A man lay sprawled on the bed on his stomach in a tangle of sheets. The man in charge. He had to be stopped from building over sacred land. It was the only thing Steve could do to save himself. He unscrewed the cap on the bottle and drenched the rag before approaching the side of the bed. He stood for a moment and then jumped on the man's back and stuffed the rag in his face.

McGinnis's eyes popped open and he started to fight back, but Steve outweighed him by at least forty pounds and had him pinned in an awkward position. McGinnis's arms flailed to the side for a few moments before his resistance weakened. His eyes fluttered a few times before closing. When he stopped struggling, Steve removed the rag from his mouth. He wrapped the sheet around the unconscious man and dragged him to the truck.

As Steve pulled up to Miller's Mansion, the moon broke through the thick clouds, opening a hole in the night sky like a giant eye, shining light on the path to the main house as he pulled the body out of the truck and past the gate.

Upstairs. The fourth floor. Master closet where it won't be noticed.

The floor installers had only finished half of the hardwood flooring in the master closet, a space almost as big as Steve's room at the hotel, and when he dragged McGinnis up to the door, he saw that all of his tools had been laid out, although he didn't remember putting them there. The black cat that had tormented his nights for almost a week was there as well, sitting on a stack of lumber, but it didn't speak to him this time. In Steve's mind, he knew the cat *never* spoke to him, really. Because cats don't talk. He wasn't crazy or anything.

He let go of the corner of the sheet, and the foreman slumped out on the hardwood floor, still unconscious. Then he started carefully removing a section of the hardwood flooring. Next he cut out the sheathing, revealing the floor joints underneath. Steve didn't pay much attention to the younger man while he worked, except for a couple of times when McGinnis seemed to be coming around. Steve would soak the rag, and after a brief struggle McGinnis would be still again.

Two hours later, Steve finished building the box in the narrow space between the floor of the second level and the ceiling of the lower level. It was six feet long, two feet wide and a little over a foot and a half deep. McGinnis started to shift and tried to roll over.

"Perfect timing, Ed," Steve said and grabbed his legs. He dragged McGinnis next to the hole in the floor and rolled him into it with a *thud.* "You don't look so comfy there, Ed. You might want to resituate yourself."

McGinnis's eyes focused on Steve as his predicament clearly started setting in. Then his right eye rolled away and seemed to be examining the box while the other watched Steve. McGinnis opened his mouth to speak, but Steve cut him off.

"Good night, Ed."

Steve took the final piece of plywood and placed it over the frame of the coffin and nailed it down. He ran strips of duct tape over the seams, sealing out the air. Then he started replacing the flooring.

Finally, Steve thought. *Some real carpentry.*

CHAPTER 18

Early Saturday morning, Jeannie awoke in a sweat. She bolted upright in bed, gasping for air, and switched on the light, but the terrified eyes of the man under the floor still burned into her mind. She knew that this was more than a dream.

For three nights in a row she had been plagued by the same nightmare of the older man dumping her body into some sort of box while David stood behind watching. The dream was always short and startling enough to wake her just as the lid was being put on. And each night she woke in a panic, which she had to force herself to swallow. She knew that Frank wasn't going to let her outside again. It was getting harder each time. Last night she had gone to sleep with the lights still on, hoping for a reprieve. In a way, she was granted one.

This night, she was back in the dark room, but she was standing on her own two feet. David was absent this time, and the older man was turned away from her, on his knees working on something. He turned to reach for a tool, and Jeannie saw that he had cut a hole in the floor. No, that wasn't exactly right. He had built something. It was a box. Built under the floorboards. The fear set in as Jeannie stood paralyzed, waiting for the man to grab her and dump her under the floor, but instead, he walked over to a bundle of sheets against the wall. But that wasn't right, either. There was a person under the sheet. The older man grabbed him and dragged his body over, rolling him into the small space he had created.

The younger man's eyes blinked a few times and then opened. She saw the fear in his eyes, and then she took his place, helpless, staring up from inside the box as the lid was secured in place, closing her in darkness.

It had been enough to yank her into the waking world, and now she tried to slow her racing heart. "Not just a dream," she whispered. Even though she had suspected that the recurring nightmare had been a part of her link to David, her main fear was that it was some sort of premonition, that the older man was coming for *her*. Now she knew that someone else's life was on the line.

Maybe she could still help. Maybe there was still time. Her clock radio read just past four a.m. She turned the radio on with the volume low. Even if it hadn't been so early, the television in the common area of the Rose House required a passcode for use.

Jeannie sat by her small radio and listened while her breathing settled and her pulse calmed. She knew the chances of hearing anything were slim. This early in the morning, most of the radio stations were on their pre-recorded programming; there wasn't anyone actually sitting in the studio. But she had to try. She grabbed her green notebook from her dresser and started scribbling out the details from the dream still fresh in her head.

the same man. Older. 60's? Construction.

Avery? but that's a girl's name. Last name?

Other parts of the dream started coming back to her. The shock of being buried alive had made the most lasting impression, but now she discovered that there had been more to the dream this time than just being in the room.

standing outside in front of a door. 903. holding a rag and a can of something.

A younger man sleeping. Mick something. The eye

Jeannie wrote as much as she could recall, stopping with her pen paused over the paper as she recalled the final part of the nightmare, when the younger man realized what was happening to him. She felt the panic that he had felt, more than just being sealed into the tight confinement, but the terror of facing imminent death.

Jeannie's head started to spin and her vision blurred, and then she let out the breath that she hadn't realized she had been holding. She set the notebook on the bed and listened as the ghost DJ reported only on the weather forecast for the weekend and upcoming events. A phone could've been ringing in the studio with breaking news about the suspicious disappearance of someone named Mick, but no one was there to answer it.

The nightmare had been real. Jeannie didn't know why she felt so certain of this, but like the articles and pictures covering her wall, she knew that somehow it had been a connection with David. Or the demon. She thought she could remember enough to save the man boarded up alive if only she could get the spark to fill in the gaps.

Jeannie grabbed her notebook and scribbled a name.

MacGuiness

She sat by the radio and waited, holding the green notebook in her lap. She had already filled two other notebooks with such notes since seeing the first article in the tabloid magazine about the scarred man who disappeared from the hospital. Actually, it was the dream from the night *after* seeing the article that prompted the journal.

In the dream, Jeannie found herself on a round, empty stage surrounded entirely by black curtains that seemed to extend up and far beyond the glaring lights overhead. The lights dimmed, coming up brighter on the other side of the curtains, and through the fabric haze, Jeannie saw a familiar setting taking shape. The greatroom of the Montana cabin. A figure lay curled on the floor in shadows, but Jeannie didn't need to see in order to know the person. He stirred, then pushed himself upright, but while light shone on the rest of the scene, he remained blurred in silhouette as he walked over and stood just on the other side of the curtain. Jeannie remembered that she had wanted to hate him then. A year and a half later, she was still trying.

"Is this real?" she had asked David.

"It feels like it," he responded.

"Has it all been real?" she asked.

"I'm afraid so."

A spotlight opened on Jeannie's side, and David parted the curtain and stepped into it. But it wasn't the same person who had been at the cabin. His scars were gone, his body clean, and in the bright light, Jeannie thought he almost glowed.

She had felt something in her dream. Something she didn't write down, but which she had never forgotten. She tried not to think about it. She was just a confused girl, and after all, he had sacrificed himself to save her life that day. But she had felt something that she had not with any other person.

Then the lights came to full brightness outside their circle, and Jeannie saw her parents sprawled on the floor. Everything else around them drained of color, and their blood shone bright against the dullness.

It had all been too much for Jeannie. Tears welled up in her eyes. She covered her face in her hands. "Make it go away."

"I'm so sorry," David said.

When Jeannie pulled her hands away, the vision was gone, and they stood alone in the circle, surrounded by the black curtains with nothing visible beyond them. The look on David's face confirmed what she suspected from that day at the cabin. David hadn't done these things, wouldn't ever do such things. There was something else controlling him.

But the fact remained that people were dying because of him.

"It can't go on like this," David said.

"I can't let you go on like this," Jeannie said. "When I get out of here, I'm going to find you."

A ripple rolled across the curtains surrounding the two, settling into a shimmer like water.

"Do you know where this is going?" David asked.

"I just want to know where *you're* going."

"I don't even know where I am."

"It's okay," Jeannie said. "I'll find you."

The curtains shimmered again, but this time from top to bottom, like a waterfall.

"It knows we're here." David said.

The curtains started growing longer, bunching on the floor, the extra material at the bottom softening and coiling like thick molasses. The black ooze piled up and closed in around the two as the curtains continued to melt, filling Jeannie's nose with a burning stench. She started toward David, but her feet were swallowed by the blackness. David tried with the same result. The flowing of the curtains sped up, the room filling with the tar. It was almost up to their stomachs.

Jeannie reached out to him, and he took her hand, but as she pulled, she felt David's skin coming loose from the bone. His arm stretched out like elastic. Then Jeannie heard a tearing sound. David's eyes widened, and then he split in half, his skin dropping away to reveal a pulsating column of the black filth. Jeannie shrieked and dropped the limp glove of his hand, and his flesh was swallowed in the pitch with a slurping noise. Then she awoke.

She had bought the journal the next day, and ever since, after any especially vivid or bizarre dream, Jeannie would pay closer attention to the news, listen for the buzzing, and search the internet at the library computer with a purpose other than reading pleasure or education, until she came upon another piece for the collection. Most of them predated the article in the tabloid, and in these older stories, it was usually the faces that brought on the sensation, more specifically, the eyes. Sometimes it was the person featured in the story—anyone from a soldier to an elderly grandmother—and sometimes it was just another face in the crowd at the scene of a crime or accident. Something in the look of hundreds of different faces, something not quite right, like the person was looking *through* the camera, almost through time, even. Like they were looking at Jeannie specifically. The noise in her head would increase, and the rest of the features on the faces would blur into homogeny, with only the eyes remaining. Looking at her. Challenging her. Taunting her.

She had seen that look in David's eyes the first time she looked into them, but in the dreams of him over the past two weeks standing behind the older carpenter, she had been unable to see his expression in the darkness. He hadn't been there at all tonight, but still Jeannie felt confident that he had something to do with what had happened. What she didn't know was to what extent. Much as she harbored a smoldering anger towards David, she also knew that some people just attracted bad things.

Jeannie sat anxiously listening to the radio, but in the early hours of this Saturday morning, she only heard classic rock broken by occasional commercials or promos. A woman DJ came on live at six a.m., but she didn't mention anything besides the fact that she needed a stronger cup of coffee, and then it was back to the music. Jeannie turned off the radio and tried to read a book, but she couldn't stop thinking about the dream.

Just after sunrise, stabbing pains, like splinters under her fingernails, shot into Jeannie's hands and up her arms. She drew in a sharp breath, her hands balled into fists, and all of her muscles seemed to coil tight around her frame, drawing her into herself. She tried to cry out, to release her breath, but her voice... air... life... was snatched away from her.

Then it was over. The pain faded. Her world came back into focus, and Jeannie knew that the man they called MacGuiness was dead.

Her body shook from the experience as her muscles unwrapped. When her breath came back to her, she broke into tears as the sun filtered through the trees outside her window.

Two days later, she found the story online. Her head had been buzzing all day, but by the time Jeannie found the article on one of the computers at the library (it was all over the news at that point), she already knew the outcome. Still she read to the very end.

> When Ed McGinnis didn't show up for work on Monday, the police were notified. A search at his rented condominium revealed signs of a struggle, and one neighbor reported seeing an unfamiliar truck in the area on the previous Friday night. When police questioned Steve Avery, he allegedly confessed to the kidnapping and broke into tears, saying that he could lead the police to the spot where the body was discovered. However, when the police removed the false floorboards, Ed McGinnis was already dead. Scratch marks on the underside of the boards indicated that McGinnis was still alive when Avery boarded over him.

The author of this particular article didn't mention David directly, but they didn't have to. Jeannie stared at the photo next to the article. It showed an older man in his late fifties

Steve Avery

being escorted in handcuffs across a driveway in front of a giant set of wrought-iron gates. A crowd of other reporters, photographers and a bunch of men in construction gear were gathered behind him, all of their faces watching the handcuffed man being carried off. All except for one worker toward the back of the crowd. Just the left half of his face, the unscarred side, was visible behind a heavyset man wearing a hardhat. He was a little distance back, and his own hardhat cast a shadow over part of his face, but Jeannie thought he was looking directly at the camera, a grin cocked on his face.

Jeannie trembled as she viewed what she considered to be the first *solid* evidence of David's whereabouts since the original article almost two years ago, but even that one had just been a hunch. There had been the dreams, of course, but this was an actual picture. She didn't know for sure that it was the crew that David was on, but the article said that Steve Avery had come from Montana. If they were on the same crew, it would confirm her suspicions that David

or whatever

had been hiding out in the Northwest. With the realization, the questions spun out in front of Jeannie. She jumped when someone spoke behind her.

"Are you okay, Jeannie?" The head librarian, Margaret.

Jeannie composed herself quickly and even managed a smile, something which wasn't too difficult when she thought about the fact that she might not be crazy, after all. She had doubted her sanity on more than a few occasions since that afternoon at the cabin, but now she *knew* that David was still alive. And maybe even back in Montana.

Maybe.

Jeannie gave Margaret the thumbs-up sign.

The older woman leaned over her shoulder and looked at the computer. "Horrible, isn't it?"

Jeannie let her smile fade, tightened her lips and nodded slowly.

"It's like something out of Poe." Margaret let out a dramatic shiver. "Ew, I can't possibly imagine it," she said, even though it was obvious that she *had* just imagined it. "Well, anyway, I was just coming by to let you know that Denise won't be coming in today, so it would be great if you could handle periodicals." She patted Jeannie on the shoulder, then walked off down the aisles.

Jeannie looked back at the computer. Yes, David was definitely smiling.

Not David, she told herself. *It's the other thing.* That was what was grinning at her from the picture. Now she just wanted to know if there was anything left of the man.

CHAPTER 19

After the arrest, work on Jim Miller's house halted for the third time, and the carpenters were flown back to Montana until things got straightened out. Hal said he heard that Miller might be calling it quits on the Big Island. Judging by the attitudes from a couple of the crews on the site, David thought that would be just fine with them. He gave his two weeks notice to A.C. after they got back from Hawaii, told him that it would just be too weird after what happened with Steve. That was only half true, but A.C. hadn't pressed the issue, only said he was sorry to see him go. David's other reason for leaving was self-preservation, and maybe A.C. understood that, too. Or at least he had seen it before.

David remembered the feeling in his stomach in Hawaii when he saw the police arrive on the job site. After discovering they weren't there for *him* and then hearing about Steve's confession, David had quickly weighed his options. Even though he wasn't guilty of anything, he knew that it wouldn't take them long to get around to questioning him. He couldn't run. He didn't know Hawaii well enough to survive in the wild as he had done in the Pacific Northwest on the mainland, and besides that, he was on an island.

After they took Steve away in handcuffs, the police told the Montana carpenters to go back to the hotel, and on the drive back in the silent truck, David tried to decide how much he should say when they came to him. Whatever he chose, he knew that it had to keep him as far away from the public eye as possible. He didn't know if

191

his name was in a database somewhere, or even if the police were in the habit of doing background checks on coworkers. He would just have to take a chance, but he was unsure of how to handle it.

The story was relatively easy to come up with, and when he was questioned later that evening by the police, he offered little information. He said that he hadn't noticed anything strange. He told them that he and Steve didn't really talk that much on the job except about what needed to be done. David didn't mention their talks about McGinnis. He chose to leave out the part about the day at work before it happened, when they were working in the safe rooms and Steve had finally approached him about the claustrophobia. And he definitely didn't mention the one possibility that he couldn't get out of his head. His own attempted words of comfort might have actually driven Steve Avery over the edge. David's memories of that Friday were hazy. It had been a long week, and thinking back, he recognized the feeling of working in a daze like before he had left Missoula. And not just that last Friday. There were other times, moments almost like sleepwalking. He would find himself in another room with no idea why he had gone there. Or worse. No idea *how* he had got there. He blamed it on the fact that Hal had been working them long days, and the saferooms were even starting to get to David. That Friday afternoon, he was only trying to make the older carpenter feel better, but he didn't remember much about the conversation beyond telling Steve that he was okay. Clearly he wasn't. But David didn't say any of this to the police.

He was even prepared when they asked what happened to *him*, where he got his scars. At least they were polite enough to finish their inquiries regarding Steve before asking him about his own condition.

"Car accident," he told them. "Lucky to be alive."

"Wish we could say the same for Edward McGinnis."

David nodded sympathetically.

It was a big story in the news, and A.C.'s company was in the spotlight as a result. David had managed to dodge the cameras and questions on most occasions, while the other guys practically stumbled over each other to talk to them. He drew enough attention as it was, and he figured it would only be a matter of time before some ambitious reporter would dig up the story in Colorado. He knew it was time to fade out of the picture, maybe even out of Montana.

At the end of his last day working for A.C., Hal offered David a ride back to the Atlantic. The weather had been decent enough since their return from Hawaii that David could ride his bike to work, but today a stiff wind blew through the valley coming down from the exact direction that he had to ride to get back to the Atlantic. Because of that, as well as the fact that he had to take his tool bags with him today, which meant he would probably actually be *walking* his bike back to the Atlantic, he accepted the offer from Hal and hefted the bike and his bags into the back of the work truck.

Traffic was heavy on Broadway this time of day, and the two sat in silence as they waited for their turn to make a left behind a line of cars. Two green lights had already changed before they made it to the front of the line.

"Damn traffic gets worse every year," Hal muttered. He turned off of the busier street, making his way through a residential section of town. David didn't know if the route was quicker, but at least they were moving.

Hal lit a cigarette, then he fooled with the radio, checking a few stations before turning it off again. "So what are you going to do now?"

It was a bigger question than Hal would ever realize. "I'm not exactly sure," David confessed. "I'll find something. Temp work, if nothing else. Maybe I'll try to get on a painting crew. That's pretty good pay."

"But you gotta breathe paint fumes all day," Hal said as he took a drag from his cigarette. "I haven't met a painter who wasn't a little bit crazy." He let out a little chuckle, but then his expression turned serious.

David could guess the reason. The mention of "crazy" had probably brought the image of his friend and coworker to mind. David knew that the moment Hal walked through the door of his home, he would turn on the television to find out any news on Steve. David just hoped that the older man wouldn't chose the last five minutes of the drive to bring up the uncomfortable topic. No such luck.

"You told the cops that you didn't notice anything," Hal said after a moment. "Was that to protect Steve?"

"Mostly," David said. "I didn't know *what* to say. I like the guy."

"So do I," Hal said. "But you're either blind or full of shit if you didn't notice anything different about Steve Avery those last few days. He changed. He got something in his head, and he went a little crazy."

"His claustrophobia sure didn't help," David said.

"Well, yeah, but that's not enough to make you kill somebody."

"I think it was much worse than anyone knew."

"He didn't tell *me* anything about it," Hal said. David thought he detected a hint of jealousy, but the older carpenter quickly added, "I mean, of course I knew he didn't like working in tight spaces, but I didn't think it was *that* bad. He should've said something."

He tried to tell me, David thought, but he pushed the guilt back. Steve was probably far enough gone by that point that it wouldn't have mattered what David said. Besides the claustrophobia, there was one other detail that David left out from his statement to the police, the fact that he thought he saw the design for Ed McGinnis's death box when he walked up behind Steve after lunch that day.

Hal drove the last couple of blocks in silence, pulling up finally in front of the Atlantic.

"Thanks, Hal," David said. "I appreciate it."

"Don't forget your bike."

"Oh, I won't." David opened his door, but the wind grabbed it and pulled it out of his hand and blew up a small dust devil of paper cups and receipts from the floorboard of Hal's truck. Hal started grabbing at things as David hopped out of the truck. "Thanks again."

"No problem," Hal said, catching hold of a piece of paper. "Good lu-"

David shut the door and waved at Hal through the window before pulling his bike out of the truck. He walked back toward the alley, but he didn't look back as Hal pulled away from the curb. He only wished the best of luck to the crew of carpenters, especially the one currently residing in a prison cell.

Luck? Or fate?

David locked up his bike in the alley and started up the fire escape. He felt a little anxious about leaving the security of the job with A.C., but he knew he could find something else, even if he had to leave Missoula to find it. Whatever he had to do, he knew that he couldn't have stayed on with A.C. When he pulled open the door from the balcony leading to the narrow hallway, Jeremy Leavitt confirmed this fact.

In his usual attire of black everything, Jeremy stood down the hall next to David's door. He whipped around when David walked in.

"*Dude!*" he attempted to whisper from thirty feet away. He looked the other direction, then started down the hall to David. "There were a couple people here earlier asking about you."

"Police?" David asked.

Jeremy grinned and pushed his hair out his eyes. "They didn't look like it. I think they were reporters. One was a chick. Kinda cute, too. I wouldn't have minded a little in-ter-view with her, you know?"

"What did you tell them?"

"They're still waiting down the hall."

"What?"

"I'm just kidding, man," Jeremy said. "I told them to fuck off. Said you didn't live here anymore. I don't think they'll be back anytime soon. Good thing Mary Rose wasn't here. She probably would've made them tea while they waited."

"Thanks, Jeremy."

"Hey, no sweat," Jeremy said. "I didn't think you wanted to talk with them."

"Not especially." David started past Jeremy toward his room.

"Say, do you want a drink?" Jeremy asked. "Nothing crazy like that night before you left for Hawaii. I just have a couple beers in my mini-fridge. C'mon, man. We haven't had a chance to talk since you got back."

David considered the offer, knowing exactly what Jeremy wanted to talk about, but he finally agreed.

"Cool," Jeremy said. "Just give me a second." He went into his room, closing the door behind him, and David heard some rummaging around for a minute before Jeremy returned to the door with a beer in hand.

David took the beer and stepped into the room. Jeremy had apparently finished the painting of the burning wilderness; it had been taken off the easel and was propped against one of the walls. The canvas on the stand now had a drop cloth over it. Jeremy moved the easel out of the way and cleared a spot on the tattered chair for David, who couldn't help but wonder about Jeremy's newest painting. But he didn't ask. The artist had obviously covered it for a reason, and David understood the concept of respecting privacy.

Jeremy's air mattress was lowered to the floor, and he proceeded to sit down on it with his back against the wall. For a minute, neither of them spoke. David couldn't think of anything to say which wouldn't just end up at the topic of Hawaii. Even small talk, an innocent question about how work was going for Jeremy, would lead to the subject. David pretended to be interested in one of the works-in-progress closest to him, a man slumped over the keys of a black grand piano in an all white room, hoping it would spark some conversation.

Jeremy saved him the trouble. "Man, that was fucked up what happened over there."

"Sure was."

"Did you see the body?"

David looked over at Jeremy, probably the only person who would ask that question. "Not until they took him out, but he was in a body bag." He went on to explain what he knew of the case, leaving out most of the same pieces of the puzzle that he neglected to tell the cops.

"Cool," Jeremy said at the end. "I mean, not cool. A guy is dead, and all. But nobody really liked him anyway, right?"

"Well, I don't know about *that*," David said, wondering how Jeremy knew about McGinnis's lack of popularity on the jobsite.

A gust of wind rattled Jeremy's window in the track, followed by a quick spattering of rain tapping on the panes. David looked out the window. "Something's blowing in."

"It was a dry winter," Jeremy said. "We could use it. Otherwise, we're gonna' burn this year again."

The rain tapered off, but the wind blew harder, whistling through the old window frame. Jeremy pushed himself off his bed and stuffed a t-shirt in the corner of the casing, silencing the sound before sitting back down.

"Wow," Jeremy said. "So Avery buried him alive. That's pretty fucked up. I mean, I've had some crazy ideas. Well, you know. We all have them from time to time, right? But I haven't carried any of them out. Like today, I see this priest hanging around on the sidewalk in front of the pawn shop downstairs, and I almost-"

"A priest?" David interrupted.

"Yeah," Jeremy said. "I wouldn't have known that he was a priest except for the collar. He was wearing jeans and this sweet black leather jacket. And as I walked up, I thought... well, never mind what I thought, because I didn't do it. I mean, you have to be able to control these things."

Jeremy kept talking, but David wasn't listening. Could it have been Father Jimmy? Surely the priest read the article in the paper or saw one of the reports and then put two and two together. He had come looking for David. But why?

"That's what *I* think, anyway," Jeremy said. "You agree?"

David just nodded. The wind continued its assault on the building, and thunder rumbled down from Hellgate Canyon. Jeremy downed the rest of his beer, opened the mini-fridge and offered one to David, who politely declined.

"So I heard," Jeremy continued, "that over in Phillipsburg, they still have a noose hanging in the town courthouse. I don't think they use it, but I bet that just having it around all the time means that they don't *have* to use it. Fuckin' Wild West."

A strong gust rattled the windows, and the lights in Jeremy's room flickered. He stood and looked out the window. "Man, it's blowing like a son of a bitch out there."

David felt a little nauseous. He had forgotten his lunch that day, and he didn't want to have to borrow money from anyone. Now he needed something to eat. He thought he would finish the beer and go heat up some dinner.

Jeremy turned back from the window. "So have you had reporters at your job?"

"A few, but I've managed to avoid them. You were right to get rid of those two today. I just don't want to deal with them. I don't want to be the next show in their circus. Hopefully I don't have to worry about that anymore."

"Why's that?"

"Today was my last day working for Decker Built," David said, and thought that besides hunger, maybe his nerves over being unemployed had unsettled his stomach.

"What are you going to do now?" Jeremy asked.

David repeated the plan that he had told Hal on the drive back from work, but with the recent developments, he thought there was a better possibility that he would have to leave Missoula.

Jeremy's eyes brightened. "Why don't you come work with me? There's a super high turnover rate, and they always need people."

"I don't know," David said.

"I know what you're thinking," Jeremy said. "There's obviously a reason there's a high turnover. The job sucks. And you'd be right to think that, but it's easy money fast. And you don't have to sell anything. It's just calling on surveys."

David thought about the possibility. He hadn't worked a phone job since he was seventeen years old. And he hadn't liked it then. Of course, he *was* good at it.

Jeremy seemed to hear this last thought. "And you'd probably make some nice commissions," he said. "You've got that low but quiet voice. In fact, there's a training starting tomorrow. I know the girl who does the orientation. I bet I could get you in, and you start making money tomorrow."

David's stomach relaxed. Maybe it *had* been the stress from quitting the job. But could he really work in front of a computer for eight hours a day? Jeremy answered the question for him.

"You can still register with the temp services," he said. "But one of the few things my father said that made any sense was that it's easier to find a job if you already have a job."

David felt his pants pocket for his last paycheck. Combined with his check from the previous week, he knew that he could get by for a little while, but if he had to leave Missoula, it wouldn't hurt to have a little extra padding.

"Besides," Jeremy said, "it would be good to have a friend there."

"Alright," David said. "Sign me up. Or whatever." Maybe a job where he could close himself into a cubicle and not have to really deal with anyone face-to-face would be perfect.

"Cool," Jeremy said. "Training doesn't start until ten o'clock. I've got to be there at eight, and I'll tell Katherine you're coming."

"Well, I better get going," David said. He stood up and heard a shuffling outside of the door.

Jeremy didn't seem to notice. "Right," he said. "I was getting ready to go to the bar, anyway. But I'll see you tomorrow. CRD is downtown, next to La Fiesta Grande restaurant."

David opened the door, and when he stepped out of the room, he saw Mary Rose ducking around the corner at the end of the hallway.

Nosey bitch.

David blinked in surprise at his own thought, even though he couldn't deny that he had grown weary of her narrow-eyed looks whenever he passed her in the building. He hadn't done anything to offend her, and it baffled him that she seemed to dislike him so much.

He started down the hall toward his room, but he only made it a few steps before his head started to spin and he had to reach out to steady himself against the wall. His legs felt shaky underneath him. He must have needed food more than he thought. He looked down the hall, and his vision grayed slightly around the edges as the kitchen seemed to stretch farther away. He stumbled a few more steps and then let himself into his room.

Maybe he would sit down for a minute. He pulled out his chair from the desk and plopped down on it.

In fact, maybe he just needed to lay down for a little while. David pushed away from the chair, the colors on the wall smearing as he rolled his body onto the bed, looking up at the blue painted sky.

David closed his eyes.

* * *

Alden Rowe sat in his studio apartment in the Hillcrest Retirement Home and waited for death.

At nearly eighty years old, he didn't fear death. He had long since exhausted that particular fear after fighting in World War II and in Korea. There were enough things about life and the world outside these walls that scared Alden without having to worry about death as well.

That didn't necessarily mean he looked forward to it. He had led a mostly good life. Longer than he would've guessed he would make it. And his mind hadn't given out on him yet. He still felt sharp, on top of things, even if his body couldn't always keep up. But he had heard about a pill that could remedy at least *one* part of his ailing body. And Rose Mayhern in 2701 *had* been smiling at him recently.

Alden thought there could be some life in him yet. But still, sitting in the quiet of the retirement home with the American Movie Classic channel on and the volume off, a plate of half-eaten pork chops and pureed *something* on the couch next to him, he waited for death. Hell, at least the idea was more exciting than waiting for whatever movie was coming on next.

They called it "independent living." Alden remembered not so long ago when he just called it "living." Now they had pinned a title to it, like a badge. As if to say, "Congratulations! You don't *usually* require someone to help you take a shit!"

Alden didn't think of life as a cycle, but more like a rubber band. Babies require assisted living, while toddlers are said to be more independent. You get to live a little while, stretch that rubber band, but then it starts to pull you back until you need assistance again. Alden just hoped his rubber band snapped before it went back to that limp place.

Like most people his age, he just hoped death would come quickly. However, while most of the residents of Hillcrest hoped they would go peacefully in their sleep, part of Alden still hoped for something dramatic. Quick? Yes. But dramatic. A bizarre elevator accident, maybe. Or kicking over at dinner. A loud gasp, then dead before his head hit the table, rattling the place settings. Maybe a couple of glasses would even fall off the table and break. He doubted that anyone would say it aloud, but he hoped at least one person would think, "Well, I guess Alden's done."

He just didn't want to go slowly. He had heard the "noble stories" of friends, or friends of friends, who held on to the last thread of life until a family member could travel across the country to see them one last time. He had also seen people still holding onto that thread long after the last family member had visited, after they had already started to mourn the inevitable, after it hurt more than healed to visit their dying relative.

No, sir. If Alden still had any family, he would've told them to wheel his bed to the top of Hillcrest when that time came and roll him off. It was only a three-story building, but he felt that should do it. Maybe he could convince one of the orderlies. A couple of them seemed like they might do it for the right amount of money.

Alden was jolted from his thoughts of soaring off the roof, white sheets flapping in the wind, by a sudden blaring of organ music vibrating through the wall next to his couch. Ms. Wende had obviously forgotten to put in her hearing aids again when she got up from her afternoon nap. Alden could've tried to call her or knock on her apartment to turn it down, but she wouldn't have heard him or the phone. The only thing to do would be to call the front desk, and he didn't feel the need to involve "The Authorities." Ms. Wende was a good lady, and didn't usually play too long.

Alden had to go to the bathroom anyway. He moved the newspaper from his lap onto the couch cushion. Like the television he wasn't listening too, he didn't really actually read the newspaper anymore. He figured he already had a pretty good idea of what was going on. He grabbed his cane from its resting spot on the arm of the couch. He still told people he only needed to use the cane occasionally, but recently it was only occasionally that he *didn't* need it. Autumn and winter were always the worst. Alden would swear that his joints would make better weathermen than those damn fools on the television. Judging by his left knee, Missoula would probably get rain tonight. Maybe even snow.

He made his way across the room and into the bathroom while "Amazing Grace" rattled the dishes in his cupboard. Some days, Alden could stand while he took a leak, but he didn't think his hip would put up with that nonsense today. He sat down on the toilet, glad to be off his feet. The organ music stopped mid-verse, and Alden stopped urinating mid-stream. He waited and listened. A moment turned into a minute, and he was starting to wonder if Ms. Wende was "done" herself, finished right in the middle of doing what she loved the best. Then the music started up again, but much lower in volume. She had put in her hearing aids.

Alden relaxed. Sitting on the toilet finishing his business, he wondered if there was anything *he* still loved. He loved the *idea* of quite a few things, but he couldn't think of anything he loved to do anymore.

"Goddamn weather," he muttered. "Got me in a funk."

He finished, rose from the seat with the support of his cane and flushed the toilet. He was leaving the bathroom when a knock sounded at the door. "C'mon in," he shouted. The door opened and Alden saw someone he hadn't seen in awhile.

"Hey, Dav--" he started, and then corrected himself. "Daniel."

The orderly had told him that no one else around Hillcrest knew him as David. He said it was like a nickname that he always wanted, and only his good friends called him by David. He told Alden if anyone else was around, his name was Daniel.

Alden hadn't fallen off the turnip truck just yesterday. He had a pretty good idea why the kid wanted to be called by a different name—something in his past he was running from-- but the truth of the matter was, he didn't give a shit. He liked the kid. David, or Daniel, or whatever. He was better company than the old man had shared in years.

The orderly was easy to talk to, and he actually listened. And not with that fake interest so obvious in some of the other employees of Hillcrest. Poor kid seemed like he might've lost some of his own fear of death. Too bad. He was too young for it. Not until Alden's early forties had the last shreds of his own fear incinerated--along with half his platoon--on a Korean battlefield. The kid looked like he had lost half his body to the flames as well, and a little bit of his soul. But he never talked about it, and the old man didn't ask. Alden was glad to see him back at Hillcrest, but David didn't have his uniform on.

"Where ya' been hiding yourself?" Alden said. "It's been a couple months. Some of us asked around after you, but the staff act like they don't know what we're talking about, like you never even worked here. They look at us like we're crazy or something. You must've really pissed somebody off when you left." The old man liked him even more.

"I got another job," David said. "This is probably the last time I'll be seeing you."

"Well, we better have a drink then."

The first time Alden had offered David a drink, it had been more of a joke, and he was surprised when the orderly took him up on it. He had wondered then about an employee drinking on the job, but the kid never drank more than two fingers worth, and Alden hadn't thought about it since. David, or Daniel, or whoever was more exciting than anyone else at Hillcrest, and Alden sure as hell wasn't going to disrupt his one pleasure by involving The Authorities. He just hoped that one day he would hear David's story.

Alden went to the cabinet and pulled out a couple of tumblers and a bottle of Irish whiskey. He plunked a couple ice cubes in one of the tumblers. The kid still liked his on the rocks. "So is this new job taking you out of Missoula?"

"Something like that," David said. "But it's been great knowing you, Mr. Rowe."

"Please, kid, I keep telling you, when we're drinking together, you don't have to be so formal. You can call me 'Sir'." Alden laughed and slapped his thigh. "You know you can call me Alden."

"It's the South in me," David said. "When I was a kid, most adults wouldn't even respond if you called them by much less than their formal name."

Alden snorted. "Yeah, well you can call me Mr. Rowe at my funeral." He handed David the glass. They clinked the two together.

"Cheers." Then he took a drink, relishing the mellow burn of the first nip of the day. "The South, eh?" he asked. "I spent a few years down there. Now *there's* a scary place."

"I can think of scarier things, I think."

An image flashed in Alden's mind, the same one his mind often wandered to when he wasn't preoccupied with something else, an image of wires and tubes, the rhythmic pumping of artificial air, steady beeps in the background. "I'll tell you what scares the hell out of me," Alden said.

"That's actually what I'm here to talk about."

CHAPTER 20

The next afternoon at Controlled Research Data, Jeremy sat in his cubicle holding his head. Even though he hadn't gone out to the bars the night before, a bitch of a headache had just snuck up on him. His headset was hanging around his neck, the black cord snaking down to his telephone, which was wired to his computer. It was a thankfully quiet Saturday at CRD. Kind of a skeleton crew. Most of the people that usually sat around Jeremy were missing. Even Jared, the Quality Control Monitor, was gone today. Jeremy called him Big Brother, but few of his coworkers understood the reference. And probably even fewer knew that Big Brother wasn't listening today. Katherine had told him earlier, even though she probably shouldn't have.

Jeremy looked up at the tall windows beyond the top edge of his cubicle. The crumbling brick building across the alley took up most of the view, but if he positioned his body just right, he could see a small slice of blue sky. The storm had passed with barely any rain, and it was probably beautiful outside. Most likely what accounted for the absences. Either that or the old bottle flu. Jeremy had fallen victim to that particular ailment on more than one occasion.

Jeremy felt a hand on his shoulder, and he turned, expecting to see a supervisor behind him wondering why he wasn't working. "I just got a serious head-" He stopped when he saw David standing there grinning. Something was different about him today. A look in his eyes. Jeremy had seen it a couple of times, like David was thinking a whole lot more than he was saying. Like he was trying to figure out Jeremy. Sometimes he looked like Jeremy's therapist. But Jeremy actually *liked* David. "Hey, man, how's the first day?"

"Just like I expected," David said. "I think I'll like it here. I'm looking forward to getting on the phones."

"Then you're one fucked up monkey. But hey, whatever floats your boat. Hey, did you hear about that nursing home?"

"No, I didn't," David said, but he still smiled, like he was expecting Jeremy to tell a joke. The grin was starting to make Jeremy uncomfortable.

"It's seriously messed-" Jeremy stopped when he saw one of the supervisors a few rows away. "Hey, man, I better get back to work. I'll tell you about it later."

"Well, I just wanted to stop by and thank you for getting me this job."

David clapped Jeremy on the shoulder again, his hand lingering for a moment. Warmth spread from his palm, loosening the muscles in Jeremy's neck. Then David leaned over and pushed a button on the keyboard. "I think this is your call."

Jeremy fumbled with his headset as the ringing started and mouthed the word "asshole" at David, who was already walking away.

One seriously fucked up monkey, Jeremy thought and chuckled. As the phone continued to ring, he turned back to his computer, pleased to discover that his headache had faded. His eyes still hurt, but that was par for the job.

Waiting for someone to answer, Jeremy thought about David. The artist in him was definitely intrigued by the most mysterious tenant of the Atlantic. Something major had happened to him. It looked like a fire, but David had evaded the question when the subject came up the first time, and Jeremy hadn't gathered the courage to ask since. Maybe David would just tell him.

The problem was, even if he tried not to, Jeremy still felt like he was trying to impress David whenever he saw him, and it baffled him. He had never been very good with people, trying to hide it by pretending that he didn't give a shit. Maybe this need to impress was what a good friendship felt like. Except, David didn't seem to want friends, but at least he would hang out with Jeremy. Without understanding why, the artist felt privileged. Maybe David would tell him what happened. More than curiosity, Jeremy's fascination with devastation inflicted either by man or by nature made him want to know what David had survived.

Jeremy's train of thought was cut short by a click sounding in his ear as someone answered their phone.

"Hello?" A man.

Jeremy quickly looked at his screen. "Hi, is this Gerard?"

"You got him."

"Mr. McNolty, my name is Jeremy Leavitt. I'm calling with-"

"I'm not interested."

"In *what*, sir?"

"In whatever you're selling."

click

Jeremy sighed and returned the phone receiver to the cradle.

"I'm not selling anything."

In general, more women were receptive to Jeremy's phone calls than men. It made it easier when they were nice. It wasn't as bad having to be there forty hours a week when they were patient, when they understood that he was just trying to make a living.

It was nice when someone listened to him for longer than fifteen seconds.

Jeremy took the handset off the phone and cued up the next call, setting off the ringing in his ear. The familiar throb returned, not from the hangover, but just from the job. The unpleasant sensation hit him almost every day. It started at the base of his skull and wrapped around his head. Jeremy thought it was the lights. And maybe the radiation seeping from the glowing blue computer screen. He had heard somewhere that he wasn't supposed to sit so close, but most days he had to lean forward to block out the noises around him.

There was a click on the line, and Jeremy prepared to speak, but a loud, high-pitched tone made him cringe and quickly hang up the phone.

Maybe the steady ache came from that type of call, the screeching in his ear when he dialed into a fax machine. It always reminded Jeremy of his grade school hearing tests. He was tempted to raise his hand to signal the examiner that he *definitely* heard that one.

But he wouldn't raise his hand. That would only draw the attention of one of the supervisors from the other side of the building, and Jeremy knew that they would miss the humor in the painful situation.

He knew that the joke was actually on him, an underling. An artist, forced to shackle himself to a machine, with a view of a narrow alley that smelled faintly of urine on its best days. Jeremy spent a good part of his time looking out those windows, watching that alley. Waiting for something to happen. *Anything.* But rarely did anyone travel down the alley, and nothing ever seemed to change.

Jeremy dialed another number and heard computer tones followed by an answering machine.

click

Followed by another answering machine.

click

An old woman. "Stop calling me, Godammit!"

click

Ringing. No answer. Ringing. *click.* Answering machine. Ringing. No answer. *click.* Ringing. Ringing.

Often Jeremy would forget that he was at work, on autopilot, his mind wandering while his body was confined, wired into a machine, automated movements, reaching out with his voice to thousands of silent, faceless names. He might go as long as twenty or thirty minutes before someone would answer. Sometimes he thought up some pretty crazy shit in that dead time. And then a human voice would bring him back to the world. Until today.

A woman answered her phone.

Jeremy blinked a couple of times, then sat upright. "Hi, can I speak with Jack, please?"

"May I ask who's calling?" A little rude.

"No." It slipped out before Jeremy could stop it. Normally, it would mean a write-up for sure, but he knew that Big Brother wasn't listening today, and Jeremy liked how it sounded coming out. He had always wanted to say it. He even felt a stirring in his crotch.

"Excuse me?" She sounded kind of young. Mid-thirties maybe.

"I can only speak with Mr. Henessey," Jeremy said. Then curtly, "Thank you, ma'am." He waited for her to berate him, demand a name, make up some lie or just outright hang up on him.

But there was a pause, then steps echoed off into the distance. Her muffled voice. "Honey?"

Full-on erection. Jeremy slid his chair farther under his desk as he heard a fumbling with the receiver at the other end of the line.

"Can I help you?" A man, this time.

"Yes, Mr Henessey, I'm calling with Quality Research on behalf of Tri-Star Insurance. We've been asked to call people who recently canceled a policy with Tri-Star."

"I don't have time for this nonsense."

You're losing him.

The voice Jeremy heard in his head wasn't his own. It sounded like David, but when Jeremy twisted around, he didn't see him. Had he imagined it? Sometimes the headphones could have that effect.

"Wait, Mr. Henessey, you really don't want to hang up."

"Yeah, why's that?" Wise-ass tone. Jeremy could almost hear the smirk.

Today, Jeremy would make something happen. "Because," he said. "Because your wife is cheating on you."

Silence. No click.

"Who is this?" Mr. Henessey asked, and the woman in the background repeated his question. He sounded a little older than his wife.

"I can't tell you who I am, Mr. Henessey, but if you want to find out *anything*, I suggest that you tell your wife it's just a survey. Auto insurance."

Another pause.

"It's just an insurance survey, honey." Then, into the phone, "Uh, yes, this is Jack Henessey. What can I help you with?"

"Very good. I'll guide this conversation from here." It was coming so easily now.

"Okay. Fine."

"So you're still listening to me, Mr. Henessey. Not so anxious to hang up on me. I assume you're not surprised by this bit of news. If I'm right, I want you to say, 'I would rate that a seven.'"

"I would rate that a seven."

"Very good. I find, Mr. Henessey, that infidelity is rarely a surprise to the significant other. I've heard it all. The frequent cold-shoulder she gives you. The looks of disgust you catch on her face when she thinks you aren't looking. No, sir, it's rarely a surprise. I would rate that a ten."

"I would rate that a ten."

"Well done. You're probably curious to know who the guy is, aren't you?"

"I would rate that at eleven."

"Well, the scale doesn't go to eleven, Mr. Henessey, but that was very clever. Now you're getting the hang of it."

"Yes."

"I can't tell you who it is, Mr. Henessey. But then, I don't really need to, do I? You already know, don't you?"

"That's a ten as well."

"Again, I'm not surprised. I'm going to hang up now, Jack. Now remember, the one important thing in a situation like this is to keep a level head. Violence doesn't solve anything."

"I would *disagree* with that statement."

"Really, Mr. Hennessey? Well, maybe you're right. You have a good weekend, Mr. Henessey."

"Thank you. Same to you."

click.

Jeremy hung up the phone and sat back in his chair. He slid off the headset around his neck and eyed the computer suspiciously. What had he just done?

You've stopped taking shit.

This time Jeremy didn't turn around to try and find David, but rather welcomed the voice of his friend. This idea of standing up for himself had been foreign to Jeremy for most of his life, but today, it sounded right.

That bitch was going to hang up the phone. And then they'd probably laugh about it.

Jeremy knew that he had pushed it too far, but at the same time, it had felt good. He slowly reached for the phone, and took it off the hook. A dial tone sounded in his ear. No angry customers on the line. He pushed himself back from his desk, looking down the aisle, but still no one seemed to be paying any attention to him. No one was rushing to reprimand him.

Just before sliding forward again, he glanced at the penny on the carpet three cubicles down, just barely exposed under one of the flimsy barriers separating the desks. It had been there for four days. Jeremy knew it was supposed to be good luck to see a penny and pick it up, but he didn't believe in luck. Jeremy believed in fate. That seemed to be a little easier to swallow, because there was no confusing "good" or "bad," like one could do with luck. Fate was fate. And today, Jeremy would stop being a casual observer of his own.

He relaxed in his chair, reached forward and pushed Enter on his keyboard.

A click sounded in his ear.

"Hello, may I speak with Glenda, please?"

"This is Glenda."

"Hi, Glenda, my name is Jeremy Leavitt. I'm calling with Quality Research on behalf of Tri-Star Insurance. We've been asked to call people who recently canceled a policy with Tri-Star."

"Okay, go ahead."

She let him in. No clicks, no disconnects, no profanity. Jeremy knew that if he could keep someone on the line for the first fifteen seconds, he could usually turn it into at least fifteen minutes. He switched into auto-pilot, droning off his scripted dialogue.

Sometimes Jeremy felt like his body was sucked into the earpiece, across miles of fiber-optic cables and into the home at the other end of the line. He tried to picture their houses. If they were on cordless phones, he would make his own mental map of their residence as they passed from one room to the next and the background noises changed. Glenda sounded like she had a nice home. In a quiet neighborhood.

Fifteen minutes later. "Thank you for your time and opinions."

Now for a little fun.

Next call.

"Hello, is Becky there?"

"This is Becky."

"Hi Becky, I'm calling with Quality Research on behalf of Tri-Star Insurance. We've been asked to talk to people who recently canceled a policy with Tri-Star."

"I don't have time for this. I'm late for work..." She paused.

Some of them paused before hanging up to see what desperate ploy a telemarketer would use to try to keep them on the line. David's face flashed in his mind. Today Jeremy went with the unconventional.

"Well, I guess I'll just see you there. Goodbye."

"Wait a minute, wait a minute. What did you say?"

"You heard me, Becky. I said I'll see you at work. Why should today be different from any other day?"

"Do I know you? Do you work in the Peterson Complex?"

Jeremy didn't say anything. He just waited.

"I don't think this is very funny. Peterson-McHally has a very serious policy about harassment."

After doing this job for almost a year, listening to people's often emotional opinions, Jeremy could read voices. Becky sounded confident, but a slight quaver gave away a little nerves. "Well, I guess I'd be in serious trouble if I worked at Peterson-McHally, but I don't. I just know that *you* do. I know a lot of things about you, Becky."

"How did you get my number?"

"Right out of the phone book. In fact, I'm looking at it right now. Not that I need to. I have it memorized."

Silence again. Jeremy could picture the scene. Attractive woman, from the sound of her voice. Probably worked for a big company. Lots of people. Lots of unfamiliar faces. She was racking her brain trying to think who possibly...

"My number's unlisted," she blurted out finally.

"It wasn't unlisted two years ago, Becky."

It was a shot in the dark, but the hush on the other end of the line told him that he was close enough to the truth to have her attention.

"This call can be traced, you know."

"You have a tap on your phone, Becky? Surely you're not that paranoid."

"Well, they can check the phone records and tell me exactly where you're calling from."

Jeremy laughed. "That will be a kick, Becky. You go ahead and do that, and I'll stand across the street and watch the cops bust some random Joe just for using this payphone. That would be a riot."

"You bastard."

"C'mon, now Becky. I spent my hard earned change to call you, let you know I care, and you insult me?"

A siren wailed from Becky's end, followed by car horns sounding nearby. Jeremy heard movement on the line and assumed that she was looking out her window to see if the driver of that sirened vehicle was available to her.

"So you're on a payphone?" She was stalling.

"Very good, Becky. You're quick. Do you want another hint? I'm within a half-mile radius of your home. Want another one?"

A pause. Then, quietly, "yes."

"My coworkers call me 'detective.' See how much fun it would be to trace this call?"

Heavy fumbling with the receiver, followed by a *slam*, then a *click*. Jeremy pushed a button on his computer.

Ring...

Ring...

Then an answering machine. "Hi, you've reached 555-0290. Leave a message."

Typical message for a household without a man. No name, just the number. But he knew she was listening.

"Hi Beck, I know you're still there. I did mention I was *within* a half-mile, didn't I? Boy, that could be just about anywhere. You know, my father always said, 'Never sign anything you're not sure about, and never let yourself be recorded.' A good rule of thumb, I think, but in this case, I'm just having a hell of a good time." Jeremy paused. "I can wait forever, Becky. I can wait forever for you. I could just keep calling, keep your line tied up so you would have to leave your house to call for help. Did I mention I was within a half-mile? But who would you call anyway? Who can you run to? I'm always around you, Becky. Going to work, going home or going out. In traffic, on the bus, in a cab. Strange thing about the city, Becky. The more people you know the smaller it gets. Why, you'd probably laugh if you could see who I was."

Finally, she picked up. "I doubt that, you son of a bitch." Feedback blared across the lines. She still had the answering machine recording.

Jeremy knew that he should hang up. Somewhere inside, a little voice told him that he was getting into deep shit. If he would just hang up now, he might be okay. But Jeremy ignored that voice. He was too fascinated (and more than a little pleased) by the words coming out of his mouth. "No, you would really laugh, Becky. Because you would swear that you had known me your whole life."

"Why are you doing this to me?" She sounded close to tears.

"Because I love you, Becky, and I think it's high time we meet."

Jeremy lifted the receiver and dropped it in the cradle.

click.

He sat in the chair for a minute, staring at the computer and waiting for the rush of footsteps to yank him out of his cubicle. But nothing happened.

And nothing will.

The voice was different this time. Jeremy shivered. It wasn't David. Lower, growling almost. It scared him at the same time as thrilled him. Such power. Still, he decided he should end on a high note. Go get drunk. Maybe call one of those escort services. Jeremy thought if he gave them enough money, they might—

There's one more call you need to make.

Jeremy looked at the clock on his computer. Five minutes to quitting time. Normally he could kill that time making his way to the timeclock. Instead, he lifted the phone receiver and pushed Enter. The phone rang until a voice mail. He hung up and dialed another. Same. And another. Again. And again. He looked at the clock. Two minutes. Just one more call, then the computer would shut them out of the system for logging off. Unless someone was still on a call. Jeremy only saw the number flash on the screen for an instant before it disappeared and the phone starting ringing, but he thought he saw a 406 area code. Somewhere in Montana. Then someone answered.

"Yeah?"

"Hello, may I speak with William?"

"This is Bill. What can I do for ya?" He sounded older. Late fifties, early sixties maybe.

"My name is Jeremy Leavitt. I'm calling with Quality Research on behalf of Tri-Star Insurance. We've been asked to call people who have recently canceled a policy with Tri-Star."

"Well, son, that'd be me."

"Outstanding. Now let me assure you that I'm not selling anything, and the survey takes under ten minutes."

"Well, I could probably speed things up a bit."

"How's that?"

"The reason I canceled my policy is because I got no car. Had to sell it when the wife left me. It was the only thing she didn't take. Hardest thing I had to do. Cherry red convertible Corvette. Built the whole damn thing myself. But I had to sell it. I sure as hell couldn't *live* in it."

"I'm sorry to hear that, Mr. Tifford."

"I'm sorry to say it, son, but what're you gonna do? Damn woman just went plumb crazy. Developed that schizophrenia. Craziest damn thing, no pun intended. One day she was fine, and the next she started asking me what the hell I was doing in her house. Then she started telling me all of these secrets. Dirty secrets, son. She told 'bout all these other men she slept with since we been married. Some stories so damned outlandish, I still ain't sure whether to believe her. Well, we went to a marriage counselor, and the counselor sent her to a psychiatrist."

Jeremy knew he wasn't going to get the survey. "Wow, Mr. Tifford. That's rough. And you say she took everything?"

"Every last red penny, son."

"But how did she get everything after admitting that she cheated on you?"

"It ain't that simple. She had everything from the get-go, son. She had more money than Ali Baba. Our premarital agreement was tighter than the wedding ring."

"I'm sorry to hear that."

Amazing, Jeremy thought. *Truth really is stranger than fiction.*

"Now, son, you wanna' hear the best part? The icing on this shit cake?"

"I'm not sure, Mr. Tifford. It's a pretty harsh story as it is."

"Well, it gets better. You're gonna love this last part."

"Alright, lay it on me."

"Well," he said, and then paused. "The truth is, I made the whole thing up. I just didn't want to do your goddamn stupid survey."

click.

The computer screen went dark. Jeremy stared at it for a few seconds in disbelief. Then he shook his head and stood to leave. He tried to spot David, but he didn't see him anywhere.

* * *

On the other side of town, William Tifford sat in a faded green recliner. The only sounds in the apartment came from next to him, a recorded voice from the handset of the phone which he had left off the hook. The nasally woman told him to hang up the phone and try again. Then the grating noise started, and Bill reached over and pulled out the plug. The phone went silent.

He picked up a picture from next to the lamp on the end table. Louise had given the photo to him three years ago for his birthday. It was one of those professionally done glamour shots. In the picture, Louise was clothed only in fur. Bill set the picture on his lap, and stared out the window. He could just barely see the top of Mount Sentinel to the east, over the trees in his neighborhood, and he watched the line of shadow climb toward the peak as the sun made its descent. He didn't turn on the lamp as darkness settled into the apartment. He knew he should get up and get something to eat, but he just wasn't hungry. Part of him wanted to go lay down, but he wasn't really tired either. So he sat in the dark.

Maybe tonight, he thought.

When a knock came at the door, Bill perked up, but he slumped again as he realized that Louise probably wouldn't knock when she came back. He reached over and turned on the lamp with a heavy sigh. He pulled out *People* magazine from the overflowing rack under the table and pretended to read it. "Come in."

Someone entered the apartment just beyond the periphery of the lamp light, crossed the room and set something on the card table, which also served as his new dining room table. Bill heard the clinking of bottles.

"You could use a little more light in here," the person said.

The voice sounded vaguely familiar, but for a moment, Bill had the intense feeling that he had just invited a complete stranger into his house. Then the light switched on over his table, and he remembered the person standing in his apartment. Bill couldn't forget a face like that. "Oh, it's you," he said.

"Of course it's me, Bill," David said. He pulled a folding chair out from underneath the table and sat down. "You expectin' somebody else?"

"No," Bill said. "It's just... for a minute there, I didn't know who... Never mind."

David look concerned. "So how ya doin', Bill?" he asked.

"I'm still on the right side of the dirt. So there's always *that*. How about you? I haven't seen you since you went to Hawaii. I bet that was nice. How long have you been back?"

"Too long," David said. "I wish I could go back. There was just something about that place. Like some kind of power, steeped and erupted from the depths of the earth itself. Just waiting to be molded."

Bill wasn't exactly sure what David was talking about; he thought the kid might be a little shell-shocked, but he still listened. Even though there was a look in David's eye like Bill had seen on some of the wilder members of his old platoon, there was something about his voice that was welcoming to Bill, like an old friend.

"And the *women*," David continued. "I tell you what, I've never seen so many..." He trailed off as he glanced at the unplugged phone on the end table, then at Bill's lap. "Did you hear from Louise again? Did she say where she was?"

Bill had forgotten about the picture. He felt shame color his face as he tossed the magazine on the floor and returned the photo to the table. "No," he said. "Just some goddamn telemarketer." He reached up and rubbed the back of his neck. "I fed him some cock-and-bull story just to mess with him, but he was asking a lot of questions about Louise." He slammed his fist on the arm of his chair, sending out a puff of dust. "What right do they have calling me at my home? Like I don't have to put up with enough shit every day at work from the guys."

Bill pushed himself up from the chair and started pacing the small room. *"Hey Bill, I heard your wife was taking it all up and down I-15. Maybe you should look for her at the truck stops, Bill.* And then I get this punk calling my house asking questions. What the hell does he want to know? I don't know where she is, alright!"

David watched him from the table. "I agree," he said finally. "He's got no right calling you, Bill. Come sit down. Have a beer." He twisted the caps off two of the bottles.

Bill stopped in the center of the room and turned toward the table. He swung out one of the metal chairs with a *clang* and straddled it backward, taking one of the beers. David stood and walked past Bill, clapping him on the shoulder as he passed, again like an old friend, and flipped on a couple more light switches. He crossed over to the small entertainment center with the twelve inch combination VCR/television on top and started flipping through the dusty cassettes on the shelf underneath. He picked one out. "How 'bout Charlie Daniels?" he asked.

"Perfect."

David popped the tape in the stereo and pushed play.

The speakers buzzed and rattled as the music blared. Charlie sang about the world needing a few more rednecks.

"Amen," Bill said and slapped his palm on the card table, rattling the bottles. This one was his favorite. He sang along about returning to the good old days of this country.

David smiled and crossed back to the table as the song continued on about a little less talk and more action. He glanced at the phone again and then sat down. "What I always wonder," he said, "is how they get my number."

Bill grunted. "Probably straight out of the phone book."

"I don't think so," David said, lowering his voice. Bill found himself leaning forward. "These big companies," David continued, "they get your name from some list somewhere. You might have signed up for a contest at your local grocery store, and next thing you know, somebody in southern California, *probably Los Angeles*, is calling you at home like he knows you. And he's got all your personal information on a little computer screen right in front of him. Every little detail about your life, what you like, what you don't like. They've figured out how to be your best friend. But it's a lie."

Bill glared at his phone. "It's probably some hippy, some goddamn kid who still doesn't know his ass from a hole in the ground."

"And you just know that he never served his country," David added. "Not like you." He turned away and ran his hand over his scar-rippled forehead. "Or me."

"Damn right," Bill said. "And this guy sounded old enough for the service, too. Like he coulda been over there in Iraq with you boys. Might've even been there to stop you from walking into that land mine. But what was he doing instead? Probably getting stoned with the rest of his worthless friends, talking about how we shouldn't even be over there." He guzzled the rest of his beer and stood up. "And he thinks it's okay to call my house? Like he's one of the boys from the platoon? I tell you what, the damned few that made it out of that jungle are lucky to be alive, and it's a goddamned *honor* to hear from *them*." Bill went into his bedroom, singing louder with the album now, and opened the closet. He returned to the living room with his 30.06 hunting rifle and a duffel bag.

"Whoa, Bill," David said and stood quickly. "What do you think you're doing there?"

Bill ignored him and kept singing. He pulled a jacket off the back of his recliner and pushed it into the bag. He picked up the picture of Louise, stared at it for a moment before setting it gingerly on top and then zipped the bag. "I'm gonna find that sonovabitch down there in L.A. Thinks he can call *my* house."

"Wait a minute, Bill-"

Bill stepped up to David. "Don't try to stop me, man. This guy is part of the reason this country is so fucked up."

David stepped back. "I'm not trying to stop you, Bill. I'm just saying you might not have to go all the way to California. Didn't you say he was calling for Tri-Star Insurance?"

Bill furrowed his brow. "Did I?"

"Their call center is right here in town. CRD, I think. Chances are, the kid lives here, too."

"Really?" Bill set down the duffel bag with the rifle on top. "I remember his name. I could look in the phone book. Jeremy something. Leavens, I think."

"Or maybe Leavitt," David said.

"Leavitt," Bill said. "Yeah, that's it." He crossed to his entertainment center, pulled out his phonebook and started flipping through the pages.

"I might be able to help you," David said.

Half a mile away, Jeremy was showering in one of the community bathrooms in the Atlantic. He felt pretty good, like maybe he would go out tonight. Maybe even get lucky.

He finished his shower, dried off and wrapped his towel around his waist. He walked down to the kitchen. He knew that Mary Rose would be pissed if she saw him walking around like this, but tonight, he didn't give a shit. And maybe the girl from apartment twelve would be in the Uncommons.

To his disappointment, the building was quiet. He grabbed a piece of frozen pizza from the refrigerator and went back to his room. The pizza was a few days old, but he would get something closer to real food at the Dino Cafe later. In his room, he took a couple bites of the pizza, then set it on a chair and wiped his fingers across his towel, leaving thin streaks of red. He reached underneath his air mattress and pulled out a magazine before plopping down on the bed. He flipped through the pages, briefly glancing at all of the women until he found the one he liked the best. She looked like the weekend bartender from Al's & Vic's. The crotch of Jeremy's towel started to rise.

A knock came at his door.

"Shit!" Jeremy hissed, quickly closing the magazine and fumbling with his towel. "Who is it?"

"Bill."

"Bill who?" Jeremy shouted, lifting the mattress and returning the magazine.

"Bill Tifford."

Jeremy paused, still holding up the mattress. He let it drop. "Well, I don't think I know you, Bill Tifford, and I don't want whatever you're selling, so why don't you fuck off."

The flimsy door splintered, and Jeremy jumped up, his erection still holding the loose towel. He saw the steel-gray of the rifle, just for an instant, his last and longest moment, knowing that he was about to die. Then he heard the explosion. He flew backward, as if someone had swung a sledgehammer into his chest. He crashed into the easel, splintering the covered canvas just before hitting the wall and dropping to the floor.

Jeremy couldn't move his body, but he had landed with his head twisted just so that he could see the paint-smeared canvas on the broken easel. The photograph which had been clipped to the side of the canvas dropped away, and the happy family drifted to the floor as blackness closed in on Jeremy.

CHAPTER 21

Jeannie was lying on her bed reading a textbook when Bill Tifford kicked in Jeremy's door, and as the rifle exploded three states away, Jeannie's own chest lurched inward, and her book fell to the floor. Then her body arched upward, and her jaw clamped down. She tasted blood, but couldn't feel the pain from her bitten tongue; the ripping in her chest took all her attention. Everywhere else in her body suddenly turned freezing cold, and she clawed at the bed. Then she dropped to the side and fell off. As she lay crumpled on the floor, taking short, quick breaths, the pain in her chest and ice in her limbs began to subside.

Jeannie knew it was more than just pain. As she shook uncontrollably, she knew that someone else had just died violently… another murder because of David. She pushed herself up on one arm and her stomach turned. Chills rose over her flesh, and thick saliva formed in her mouth as the bile threatened to rise. Jeannie didn't want to stand just yet, but she didn't want to throw up on her carpet, either. As soon as she thought her body would allow it, she pulled her traumatized frame upright and into standing. The shift in position brought forth an acrid belch. No more time to be careful. She flung the door open and ran down the hall to the bathrooms. With one hand clutching her stomach and the other hand over her mouth, she darted past Frank Matsen, who was on night duty.

"Jeannie?" he asked, but she only shook her head and kept moving. Thankfully, Jeannie found the second floor restroom unoccupied at this time of night, not that it would matter either way. The first heave hit as she was opening the door, but she managed to make it to the toilet stall before losing the contents of her stomach. She had a moment of panic seeing blood in the bowl, then she remembered biting her tongue. She vomited again. After choking through a few more dry heaves, she set her head on her arm and cried softly.

A knock sounded from the hall. "Jeannie?" Frank asked, his voice muffled by the door. "Are you okay in there? You didn't look so good."

Jeannie stifled her weeping, even though the sound of the older man's voice made her want to cry harder. She wanted to tell Frank that she was fine. Actually she wanted to say that she *wasn't* fine, that she felt like she had been run over by a truck. She wanted to say that she was terrified. Confused. And she wanted him to comfort her, like a father would do. Like her Daddy had done.

"Jeannie, if you don't want to talk, at least knock on the wall. Once if you need help, and twice if you're just feeling sick and want me to leave you alone."

She didn't want Frank to leave her alone. She wanted him to tell her it was going to be okay. But Jeannie had watched television. She knew what a seventeen-year-old girl was supposed to think about, the issues they would finally talk about with their parents, and this wasn't it. It would never be okay. It would only get worse. The low buzzing started in her head.

She heard Frank whispering outside the bathroom, followed by Elizabeth Horne's loud voice, "I'm not goin' in there if she's been puking and shit."

Then Frank. "*Elizabeth!*"

"Fine."

Of the girls at the Rose House, Jeannie liked Elizabeth the most, even though they had never talked. Elizabeth was tough, but funny, and she had been through some rough times. Usually dressed in black, she would boast of her eighteen piercings, only thirteen of which the boys got to see without taking her to dinner first.

Jeannie liked Elizabeth, but she didn't want to see her now. She reached up and knocked twice on the stall.

"See? She's okay," Elizabeth said. There was a long pause. Then, "Fine. I *will*."

The door opened, and Jeannie heard Elizabeth's heavy black boots clomp into the bathroom. "You okay in here?"

Jeannie knocked again. Elizabeth walked over the stall and lowered her voice. "Hey," she whispered. "If you need something, I got a bottle of muscle relaxers in my room. Bottom drawer in the back. One should do the trick for someone your size. Two at the most. Just don't mess with any of my other shit."

The sounds in Jeannie's head grew a little louder, like someone crumpling tin foil, and she had a crazy idea. She had to end it. It had gone too far.

Elizabeth's boots treaded away from the stall, and Jeannie heard her open the door to the bathroom, followed by the *click* of the door closing. "She's fine." Elizabeth said. "Just sick. I think it was something she ate. She told me in sign language or some shit like that."

"That's not the kind of language a lady uses," Frank said.

"I'll be sure to tell one when I see her."

The voices trailed off down the hall. Jeannie pushed away from the toilet bowl and stood up. At the sink, she rinsed out her mouth and wiped off her face. She looked at herself in the mirror as the noises in her head changed, like aluminum cans in a blender.

Who do you think you are?

It was the weakest she had felt in her life. What hope did she have for beating this thing? She was just a girl, young and naïve. She may have experienced more than most other girls her age, but surely nothing compared to whatever was killing these people. David *had* brought something with him into her life, and it was pure evil. How could she expect to defeat evil?

Suddenly, her crazy idea didn't seem so crazy,

It's the only way.

and desperation wrapped itself warmly around her shoulders. She would end it.

Jeannie took one last look in the mirror. A lump rose in the back of her throat. She wanted to cry again. Instead she spat blood into the sink and left the bathroom.

Out in the hall, she heard the other girls' voices from the TV room, and she wondered if maybe she should go down there, see if they would let her turn on the news. It was almost ten. She was pretty sure there was news on Saturday nights. But Jeannie knew it was just putting off the inevitable. She didn't need to wait for the news. She already knew. The grinding in her head confirmed the truth. She stopped in front of Elizabeth's door, looked around and then stepped into her room.

Posters of rock bands covered Elizabeth's walls. Jeannie hurried over to the dresser and opened the bottom drawer. Just as promised, at the back of the drawer, behind more black clothing, she found the bottle of pills. There appeared to be plenty. Jeannie stuck the bottle in her pocket and snuck out of Elizabeth's room.

By the time she made it to her own door, the noises in her head were so loud that she thought she might explode. In addition, images from the Montana cabin--more specifically her blurry recollection of seeing her father die, followed by waking to find both of her parents dead--repeated in her head. She flung herself into her room through a thick cloud of doubt, grief and despair that nearly filled her head, obscuring her concentration. She had to stay focused.

She pulled out the bottle and stared at the pills. She was scared, but she knew it was the only answer remaining. She couldn't go on. Not like this. She didn't know what else to do. She was just a girl. She couldn't do it alone, and her mind couldn't take it much longer. Her *body* couldn't take it much longer. This most recent experience had been much worse than when Ed McGinnis died. The next one might kill her, as well.

Jeannie had another thought. Maybe David would be the one who would kill her. Or torture her slowly. Certainly he could find her easily enough.

She wouldn't let it happen like that. This way she could just go to sleep.

Jeannie needed to sleep.

She popped the lid on the bottle and poured half a dozen into her palm. As the grating intensified in her head, she examined the pills for a moment, then plucked out a few more out of the bottle. She wasn't aiming for a coma. And she didn't want to have to wait long, either. She set the pills on her desk and used the base of her lamp to crush them into powder. She scraped it into her water bottle, shook it up, then drank it all, grimacing at the bitter, chalky fluid.

Then she sat on her bed and waited, wishing that in the last moments of her life she would be given peace, but the noises persisted, like an even *larger* blender, the size of a house, with the cans now replaced by cars. She clutched her head, wishing she could tear it apart. She had surrendered, and now she just wanted silence.

Jeannie pulled her hands away and looked at her walls, at her collection. The same noise grating at her skull, although never this bad, had led her to those scraps of paper. As she twisted her body to survey the extensive collage, the lines and colors from the articles smeared out in her vision. She started to feel dizzy, lightheaded. Just one more thing to do.

She stood from the bed, but her body pulled her back down. Suddenly she worried that she might have made a mistake in crushing the pills. It was happening too fast. She couldn't die yet.

Jeannie pushed herself from the bed, and the floor tilted under her feet. She grabbed her chair for support, and when the world stopped moving, she dragged it over and propped it under her doorknob.

Not much longer.

She staggered over to her mirror and pulled the first article off the wall. She crumpled it in her palm and dropped it to the floor. Then she summoned the last of her energy and began screaming, the first intentional release of her voice since arriving at the Rose House. The sound built into something akin to war cry as she tore at her collection, ripping the pages from the walls.

With a sweep of her arm, she sent the contents of her desktop clattering against the wall. She climbed on top of the desk and started clawing at the articles on the ceiling, gouging chips of paint and drywall. Somewhere at the end of her arms, she felt fingernails tearing.

Then her voice left her, as did her motor skills. Her body went limp, and she fell off the desk. She hit the floor hard and knew beyond the numbness that there was pain. But it was far away.

The noise in her head stopped. Finally there was quiet. Her mind cleared. Not a single thought of the past or concern for the future occupied her head. Only the final moment at hand.

Colors seemed brighter; the photographs she hadn't torn from the wall looked more vivid, the black text of the headlines more stark. Edges were crisper, more defined. From her dead still position Jeannie could make out every line in her periphery, the angles of the desk, curve of the chair, the Y where the ceiling met the corner walls, all of the lines converging into each other. The last thing she would see in this world. Pathetic.

With one final strain Jeannie flopped over on her back. She heard muffled sounds. Knocking. Then banging. The ceiling began to spin overhead, and darkness closed in around her. As she sank into the black depths, she heard a voice. *Voices.* The incoherent murmuring of a thousand low whispers. Like a swarm of buzzing flies. Somewhere in her mind, she knew that they had been there all along, just underneath the grinding cacophony, and just before the last thread to her life stretched and snapped, the whispers came together.

You have come to me.

* * *

David woke up shivering. Through gummy eyes he saw blurs of green, and his first thought was that he had awoken in his painted room in the Atlantic. But he felt so cold. And wet. He also knew that his bed was much softer than whatever was under him currently. As his senses returned, he discovered that he was lying on grass, and dew covered his body.

He sat up quickly, rubbing his eyes and looking around. Where the hell was he? It looked like someone's side yard, a stretch of grass that separated the house from a concrete block wall. The back yard was open to him, but access to the street was blocked where the block wall connected to the house. The gate must have been on the other side of the house. But how had he ended up here? Last thing he remembered, he had been talking with Jeremy. He had just half-heartedly accepted a job working on the phones, and then-

Suddenly, music started up inside the house. David jumped to his feet. Someone was home, which meant that someone could come outside. He was looking around for an exit, considering hopping over the wall, when the tone of the music registered with David. Organ music. His first inclination was that he was outside an elderly person's house, but then muffled singing started. Definitely more than just one or two people.

"Then sings my soul, my savior God, to thee. How great thou art."

David crept in the direction of the backyard, peering around the corner of the house and confirming his suspicion. He had seen the patio previously through the chapel windows the first time he entered Father Jimmy's church. The vines wrapping around the trellis had still been green that day, but after the winter they looked brown and fragile.

He stepped back between the building and the privacy wall, leaning back against the red bricks of the house where the sun shone to warm his body while he thought. The obvious question was, how did he get here, but before he could give it much consideration, the next question interrupted.

What day *is it?*

He didn't think that Father Jimmy's congregation convened on Saturdays. Could it be Sunday? He couldn't remember Saturday, at all. If it *was* Saturday, he was supposed to be starting a new job, but something in him suspected otherwise and knew that he had bigger concerns than missing the first day of a telemarketing job.

Whatever day it was, he had little doubt that the demon had played a part in his blackout. David cursed himself for being so stupid lately. So overconfident. Nothing in his life should've given him the impression that the demon was gone. In fact, the more he thought about it, the more he realized that everything around him should've made him aware to the contrary. The old saying about hindsight being 20/20 popped into David's head. He always hated that saying because it usually meant that he had screwed up.

Other signs aside, though, he hadn't blacked out since fleeing from the Marrick cabin in Montana. And when he came to consciousness that time, he was in front of the hunter's cabin. Sanctuary. David was skeptical about how much refuge the priest's house could offer, or for that matter, how much refuge *anyone* could offer, but he decided to wait out the service. Whether he believed in Father Jimmy's God or not, he felt safe there for the time being. He slid down the wall into a sitting position between a couple of hedges. The wet grass soaked through his dirty jeans, but the warm brick felt good against his back.

Inside the church, the hymn crescendoed, then ended, and silence filled the morning again. In the quiet, David remembered a dream from sometime in the night.

Friday night? Saturday?

He had dreamt of the fifteen-year-old girl from Montana. She would be almost eighteen now. Jeannie Marrick.

David had replayed that stormy afternoon in his head often, in both his waking hours as well as many a fitful night's sleep. He didn't think he would ever forgive himself for what he did to that girl, whether he was in control or not.

He knew he was responsible for the murder of Jeannie Marrick's parents, and it didn't do much to assuage his guilt when he told himself that it would've been *his* dead body if he hadn't stumbled into that cabin. But in the end, he at least saved *her* life, escaping from the cabin while he still held the demon down, and she had lived. David had done his research when he first came back to civilization. Jeannie had survived the experience, but with no other family, she had been placed in a girls home.

Severely traumatized.

Most of the articles that he read described her the same way, and the same excuses for his actions ran through his head, but they all sounded hollow. He may have saved her life, but to what end?

Alive, but severely traumatized.

In the dream from the night before, she definitely appeared severely traumatized. And older. In the other dreams she always looked the same age as that day, but this time she appeared how David guessed she would after a few years. More than just a few. She looked ten years older.

She looked like how I made her.

He could only remember fragments. Like being on the other side of an interrogation room, he saw the girl through a bathroom mirror. She looked pale and pasty, black rings around her eyes, her shoulders slumped. She had just been sick. He could almost still taste the stomach acid, and something else. Copper. She seemed to stare back at David.

She looked sad and then angry, spitting blood in the sink before leaving the bathroom…

The image of the dream slipped away when David heard a door opening to the backyard of the church. Apparently the service had ended. He looked around for a place to hide, but the bushes weren't big enough. Again he considered going over the wall, but he decided to take his chances. With no exit on this side of the house, he figured people were less likely to come around the corner. But beyond the lack of an exit, he had decided that he would rather get caught hanging out on the side of the church by one of the parishioners than run away again. He needed to see the priest. Such a strong urge was a little unsettling for David, taking into account his views of organized religion. But something had definitely happened at that first meeting with Father Jimmy, and now he had woken up next to his church. Maybe David just needed to give him another chance.

He closed his eyes, pretending to be asleep. He prepared a story in case anyone came around the corner.

Roommate locked me out of my apartment by mistake... Didn't want to wake the manager... I know Father Jimmy...

While he waited, he listened in on the conversations going on in the backyard. Fellowship. Someone's son off to the Middle East. Someone else lost their job at the mill, fallen on hard times. A younger couple disagreeing over whether or not the husband should take a new job.

David recognized Father Jimmy's voice in the mix, offering only a few words in between laundry lists of questions and dilemmas. While part of David wanted to be in on those conversations, talking about the issues of normal life over a cup of coffee, another part of him resented them for their trivial concerns. Some of the conversations illustrated the cause of some of his disdain for putting man's deities into another box. God was just a cheap therapist to so many churchgoers, something to ease their minds, make them feel better, for a handful of coins in the basket. There was no reverence. Only repentance and requests. Maybe that's why David chose the wilderness. If God dwelt anywhere, that was the place, and it was worthy of respect.

Conversations tapered off as David heard the parishioners saying their goodbyes and leaving the church, until only one voice remained besides Father Jimmy. A female voice. David thought he recognized it, and when the woman mentioned Mary Rose, he knew. The Atlantic manager's girlfriend.

Wo-manager's girlfriend, he corrected.

Kate Osbourne. By the direction of the conversation, he guessed that Mary Rose didn't attend church with Kate. Father Jimmy asked how things had been going, and David felt a little embarrassed to be eavesdropping when she mentioned the problems that the couple had been having. He liked Kate.

But that Mary Rose is a bitch.

Again, the malevolence of his own thoughts surprised him, even though he knew there wasn't much love lost between him and Mary Rose. At the end of his rope, courtesies had apparently fallen away.

Kate switched the subject to more surface topics and David tuned her out, focusing instead on the details of the block wall across the patch of grass where a perfect line of ants trailed their way up and down, in a quest for something very specific.

David remembered when he first discovered pheromones. He had been in grade school. He was sitting on the sidewalk in front of his house waiting for his mom to get home when Peter rode up on his ten-speed. The bike was still a little too big for Peter, and his rolling stop was almost a rolling crash.

"What's up, Doofus?" Peter asked.

"Watch this," David said. "If you lick your finger and smear it across the path of this line of ants, they get all screwed up."

"You're licking your finger and touching the dirty sidewalk?" Peter asked. "Weirdo."

"Just watch, Dummy," David said, feeling emboldened by his discovery. Sure enough, when he drew his finger over the line, the ants acted like he had built a little wall in their way.

"I already knew that," Peter said. "They're following a scent trail that leads to food. We learned about it in school."

"They can smell the food?"

"Not the food. It's a scent trail that they put down so the others know where to go."

David learned later that there were all sorts of chemical signals that insects and animals use to communicate with one another and that some animals can even detect a change in humans based on the person's reaction to fear. There was even debate that men and women responded to attraction pheromones released by the opposite sex.

The fight or flight reaction? Lust? These were all animal instincts, but as David leaned against the church, he wondered if other emotions could be boiled down to just chemistry as well. Hadn't he heard that eating chocolate releases the same chemicals in the brain as love. What if that was all that Love was?

And what about Faith? Waiting to see a priest, David couldn't help wondering if they weren't all being led around by their noses, just following the scent trail left behind by a select few who thought they knew their way to the goods.

And God?

Suddenly David became aware of the silence in the back yard. Kate must have just left. He was about to stand when Father Jimmy walked around the corner, holding a coffee mug that read "I ♥ Jesus." There was a brief moment of recognition, then the priest's eyes glazed over, and for a moment, he appeared lost. He swatted at something in front of his face, but David couldn't see what it was. Then he looked down at David. "What do you want with me?" he asked.

David stood. Seeing as he didn't even remember how he got here, he still wasn't convinced it was a good idea, and he figured he could make it over the wall blocking him from the street. "Father Jimmy?"

The priest reached up and rubbed at his eyes. "David?" The confusion seemed to clear and his wrinkled forehead changed to an expression of relief. He actually smiled, and then looked up at the sky. "Beautiful day," he said. "I think I was too distracted today to pull off my sermon." He took a drink from his cup. "Oh well. It's not one of my better ones, anyway." He looked back at David. "I'm glad to see you. I started thinking about you halfway through the sermon, wondering if you were okay." He paused. "Are you okay, my son?"

David considered the question briefly. "I don't know."

"Well, you don't look so great, but at least you're standing. Why don't you come in, and I'll get you a cup of tea or coffee. Are you hungry? We've got a few pastries left over from fellowship."

David's stomach rumbled. It felt like he hadn't eaten in two days. "That would be great."

A concerned look passed briefly over Father Jimmy's face, but he smiled again and started into the church. David followed the priest inside. The sun shone through the long chapel windows, and his body welcomed the warmth.

At the end of the hall, Father Jimmy stopped. "You can have a seat in my office. There are doughnuts on my desk. Tea or coffee?"

"Coffee," David said. He started toward the office, then turned back. "And thank you."

"It's my job," Father Jimmy said. "I'm glad you came."

David managed a smile, then went into the office. He thought he had made the right move staying at the church.

"I think we need to talk," Father Jimmy said from the kitchen at the other end of the hall. David's stomach growled again when he saw the box of doughnuts on the desk, and he reached in and pulled out a glazed one.

"Especially with everything that's been going on lately," the priest continued. "First there was Steve Avery. When I saw that you had been working with that crew in Hawaii, I tried to find you. It sounded like a horrible experience for such a beautiful place. Then there was the tragedy at the nursing home Friday night. I mean, what is going *on* in the world?"

David paused just before taking a bite from the doughnut. "Nursing home?"

Father Jimmy turned and looked down the hall at David. "You haven't heard?"

David could only shake his head.

Father Jimmy returned his attention to the coffee. "Oh, it's awful," he said. "They think it was some sort of mass suicide pact. The only other possible alternative is that a bunch of them all snapped at the same time. The detective they interviewed said it was one of the worst things he had seen."

As David listened, suddenly the office disappeared, replaced by a darkened apartment. Not his room from the Atlantic, but it looked familiar nonetheless. He dropped the doughnut and looked in the direction from which he had entered the priest's office. Beyond the door, he saw Father Jimmy at the other end of the hall, but this definitely wasn't the priest's office.

David heard a sound behind him, and he turned just in time to see an elderly woman in a nightgown leave her bedroom and shuffle to the window. Yes, he had definitely been here before. His dreams from before going to Hawaii had returned to him before his eyes. But this dream was different.

The old woman unlatched the windows and pushed them open, and David saw himself climb into the window. The other "him" took the woman's hand and led her back to her room.

Father Jimmy seemed oblivious to what was happening in his office. "Seventeen residents in all," he continued. "They're still trying to figure out what happened. A member of my congregation works for the newspaper, and she told me they found one man alive in his tub after a failed attempt to hang himself."

The room flashed white, and then David stood in another apartment. Similar layout. Different décor. He jerked like he had been shocked; his legs trembled beneath him. What was happening?

not just a dream.

Two figures sat on a couch in the darkness. One of them was heavier set, with hunched shoulders, holding onto the silhouette of a cane, and David didn't need the light to guess the identity of the other man sitting next to him. He heard his own voice whisper from the couch. "That's actually what I'm here to talk about." The other man's shoulders slumped.

"Apparently," Father Jimmy said, "he was sobbing one word over and over. He just kept saying, 'Alone.' Can you imagine?"

The apartment disappeared, replaced again by the office, as the priest came down the hall. "And then there was the incident at your apartment building last night."

David reeled in place, feeling like he might be leaving his body. He reached backward, finding the arm of a chair just before falling back into it.

Father Jimmy stood at the threshold to his office. He held two cups of coffee, but didn't make any movement closer when he saw David. He looked down at the doughnut on the floor. "David, are you okay?"

David just stared at him. Then he looked around the office, unsure of what actually existed anymore. The truth threatened to crush him.

"Were you there when it happened?" Father Jimmy asked.

"When what happened?" he whispered.

"That young man from your apartments. Jeremy Leavitt."

David looked back at Father Jimmy, and the expression on the older man's face supplied enough news for David to know something else bad had happened this weekend.

Saturday.

Suddenly, he didn't want to know why he couldn't remember the day before.

"Were you *friends* with Jeremy Leavitt?" Father Jimmy entered his office and set the mugs on a bookshelf. "Oh, David, I'm so sorry."

He walked over and put his hand on David's shoulder, and the office changed again, but this time nothing remained of the little church except the chair he sat on. Instead, walls adorned with artwork surrounded them on all sides. The Atlantic. The chair sat in the middle of the hallway, facing the exit to the fire escape balcony. David saw a figure standing in the shadows outside the balcony door at the other end of the hall.

Father Jimmy's clutch tightened on his shoulder, and David knew that he saw it too.

Creaking sounded behind them from the long flight of stairs, and David looked back just as a man walked past them and down the hall holding a hunting rifle.

Bill Tifford. He didn't know how he knew the older man's name.

The man with the rifle stopped and knocked at one of the doors.

Jeremy.

"Bill Tifford," the man said.

David heard Jeremy's muffled obscenities, then Bill Tifford stepped back and kicked the door in. As he barged into the room and out of sight, the figure on the balcony stepped closer to the glass panes on the door.

Like looking into a mirror, David saw himself smiling.

The deafening explosion from the rifle caused Father Jimmy to yank his hand away, and the office returned. The priest stumbled backward into the bookshelf, knocking over the cups of coffee. His "I ♥ Jesus" mug dropped and cracked on the floor.

After their first encounter like this, David had thought that the priest just seemed stunned, but today Father Jimmy looked afraid.

"That was… your apartment building," he stammered. "We were… you were… You were there."

David felt nauseous, the bile rising at the back of his throat, his stomach twisting.

Father Jimmy clung to the bookshelf as if the whole building might come down otherwise. "What happened? Who are you, David?"

David doubled over in pain, a gurgling noise rising from his gut. Then the demon spoke through him.

"I am the end of hope."

David summoned the energy to push up from the chair, but the world felt unsteady. He felt sick and dirty. He could feel the demon inside him. The frost in his bones, the twining of his muscles like rigor mortis setting into live flesh. Had he been so numb before? He wondered if the demon had been there all along. A voice answered in his head.

Whenever I needed you. Ever since you gave yourself to me at the cabin.

Suddenly David knew that the demon had been toying with him, pretending to be out of sight, so it could use him. Batting him around like the half-dead chewed up mouse that he was. What a fool he had been.

David's body twisted beyond his control toward Father Jimmy. He looked at the priest and felt shards of ice in the center of his chest as the demon spoke. "You wanted your answers. Here they are." He didn't know for whom the statement was intended, but Father Jimmy definitely didn't like what he was hearing.

The demon let out a peal of grating laughter. Like scrambling through mud, David pushed past Father Jimmy, stumbling down the hall. Suddenly the rest of his vision from the night before about Jeannie Marrick (and he was convinced now that it had been just that... a vision. Not a dream) returned to him. She had killed herself.

Because of him.

David lost his footing rounding the corner by the chapel. Gravity seemed to shift underneath him. His upper body went one direction while his legs tried to go the other way, and he careened into the chapel, cracking his head on a pew before crumpling to the floor.

Lying on the carpet, he lost sensation in his body as the demon took hold again. With the last of his strength, he lifted his head. A crucifix hung on the wall at the front of the chapel, but instead of Jesus, David saw himself hung on the cross.

Then the blackness swallowed his vision.

CHAPTER 22
HELL

An old man trudged barefoot over a narrow path of jagged stone. A cold gray hail rained down on him, and steep cliffs dropped off into darkness on either side of him. Shreds of clothing hung on the man's thin, sagging frame. All of his hair was gone except for a long, filthy gray beard that draped over his sunken chest. He looked rougher than the path underfoot, and twice as tread upon. Civilization had just turned into the twentieth century, but the old man had no concept of this fact. Last thing he remembered was 1857, lying on his death bed, surrounded by no one who loved him, and attended to by sterile physicians who barely blinked as he choked on his last breath. Toward the end, the old man hadn't cared that he was dying. Or at least that was what he told the nurses, who simply nodded. He was just ready to be done with life, but while his life on earth had ended, it was far from over. Ever since the man's heart finally seized in his chest, all he had felt was pain and freezing cold.

The old man's skin hung in flaps over his skeletal frame. Cuts and gouges ravaged his body, each oozing with a black substance-- the essence of the demon Mashart inside him. Only his feet were protected, as they had grown leathery over the years, but every now and then even his soles would encounter a particularly rugged shard sticking out of the ground, tearing the tread from his feet and leaving a streak of black slime as the demon forced him forward, like a cattle prod in the place his soul once occupied.

Mashart only allowed the old man the memories of everything that he had done wrong in his life, and the reliving of his final, lonely moments of dying. Over and over the demon pushed the tormented soul up the rocky path that would never end. The old man was only one of thousands whom Mashart had punished for his part of eternity, their fears and regrets splayed out in front of them like bloodletting from a severed throat, then frozen to their bodies in the icy pits. And when the last of the blood finally pumped out, Mashart's blackness filled the empty space and devoured their souls, just as he did now under the flesh of the miser.

The demon left the mind of the old man, ceasing any conscious thought patterns in the man, letting him simply stagger forward, aware only of the physical pain, occasionally stumbling on the slippery rocks and crashing down on them. Sometimes he would fall over the cliffs on either side, plummeting in terror before hitting the jagged glaciers in the dark void below. After the crumpled body died, the old man would wake again, back on the path.

The demon Mashart sought out another of his charges, a woman this time. Younger in age from the old man, but her physical appearance almost as bad. When she was alive, she had been obsessed with control over every aspect of her existence, usually including other people around her. When the control spun out of the woman's life--which it always did with that type--she ended her life. At least, her life on earth. But not before also ending the lives of those she blamed.

In Hell, she slowly drowned in a slushy, gray lake just off the steep slope of a frozen shore. The icy muck in which she sank was like cold porridge, with enough substance to push around in, but nowhere to gain any purchase as the chunks of ice gouged her frostbitten flesh. If she managed to make it close enough to the steep slope of the shore, the dead reeds she would grab for would simply break off in her fumbling, frost-burned fingers, and her hands would scrape across the frozen soil, leaving pieces of nail and tracks of black filth as she was pulled under by the muck. Her friends and family watched her from the shore, somehow holding their position like mountain goats on an impossibly vertical mountain. Finally the thick slush would fill her mouth like bites of broken glass, then her stomach, and finally her lungs. After the frost exploded inside her, she would wake to find herself slipping down the slope into the icy lake once more. It had only been six years since she killed her own family and found herself careening down the slope for the first time. She had just started her tour in Hell.

At some point, the flesh of the Damned, or at least what they considered to be their flesh, would simply break down, the mind finally completely collapsing. Or the heart, or the soul, or the "being." They called it all sorts of things in life. In Hell it amounted to at least a century before whatever remaining scraps of fear and pain would finally shred away and dissolve into the frozen flesh of the Dark Lord for eternity. They were resilient little monkeys. Mashart would give them that much.

The demon left the woman, who was frantically grasping at loose rock and dead weeds, fighting against the sucking chill of death wrapping around her body, and he traveled in the winds over the gray landscape of Hell before entering another body. This body served a different purpose, though. In the depths of a frozen cavern, the body of a handsome man, previously inert on the frozen ground lifted himself up. In life, out of vanity and pride, the man had put himself above their monkey god. While that sort of behavior was frowned upon in Heaven, they welcomed it here. The demons loved the misplaced sense of perfection, and they wore the beautiful bodies in the same way that the monkeys "dressed for dinner."

A giant throne of living human heads, twice the height of the demon, stood at the back of the cavern, surrounded by black ice stalactites. Dozens of sets of eyes watched Mashart as he approached the throne. While a few muffled cries permeated the room, most of the heads had stopped trying to make sound long ago, when they first discovered that their were lips sewn shut.

The demon frowned when he surveyed the chair. His throne was crumbling. Many of the heads were decayed almost down to just skull and rolling eyeballs. But Mashart dismissed this thought for the time being and sat down. He broke off one of the jagged spears of ice hanging from the ceiling and sliced the skin around his wrists. The fleshy hands slipped off like loose gloves, revealing black hand-shapes underneath which softened and stretched, oozing down over the heads toward the floor. Some of the faces tore their lips open with their screams. The new ones did that often.

When Mashart's black essence found the frozen floor, it sizzled and spattered before crystallizing into the ground. In this act, the demon could join with the core of Hell, the flesh of the Dark Lord surrounding and embracing the demon. Mashart merged with the darkness, absorbed in the cries of millions since the beginning of time. The pain, hate, regret and fear of all existence. The demon's daily charges--the old man, the woman, and all of the others--seemed mere playthings in the presence of his Dark Lord, simple bacteria in the greater host. This was purity. He must taste it all.

But something was wrong. The demon couldn't deny it. The misery wasn't as sweet, and it hadn't been for quite some time. A shift had occurred. After hundreds of years, The Seed had spread itself through the world, and even though the monkeys didn't have any idea, even though their old ones had hidden the truth from them, there was still hope. They could feel it. More now than ever.

And it was working. Mashart brought himself back to the flesh, returning to his chamber. Yes, something had definitely shifted. The monkeys didn't answer like they used to when the Dark Lord cranked the music box, and their antics weren't as funny as they used to be. Mashart's throne was crumbling, but the demon had a plan.

He just had to get out of Hell first.

CHAPTER 23

At the same time as David was dragging himself, barely conscious, in the middle of the night into the backyard of Father Jimmy's church, just as he dropped on the grass, Jeannie fluttered her eyes. She saw only a white haze. Then she heard voices, two women, and she closed her eyes again. The voices trailed off in the distance, but Jeannie kept her eyes closed and didn't move. She guessed by the mixed scents of antiseptic and sweat that she was in a hospital. A voice from above paging a "Dr. Harris" confirmed it. Otherwise, it was quiet. The middle of the night maybe.

After a few more minutes of waiting motionless, and finally deciding that she was alone, Jeannie opened her eyes. She had to blink a few times to get the room to come into focus. The curtain had been drawn around her bed, the doctors and nurses having moved on to the next emergency. But they had left her strapped down to the bed.

Jeannie heard someone else walking closer, and she closed her eyes just before they pulled at the curtain. The sounds of only one set of footprints entered and approached her bed, then she heard the curtain close again.

"You're alive," the person said. A man.

Jeannie didn't respond. Wasn't sure she *wanted* to be alive. The catches on the buckles of the restraints felt like they were piercing her wrists, every muscle in her body was twisted, her skull seemed to have fractured, and she was pretty sure that someone had taken a shovel and dug out her stomach. Her body still shook from the night's experience.

"They had to bring you back from the dead."

Jeannie still kept silent, but the impact of what she had done dropped on her. She couldn't remember much after throwing up in the bathroom except the grinding sounds, her own screaming and tearing down the walls. The grief and despair had been as heavy as a lead blanket. Jeannie had never felt so helpless and without hope. She knew that she was going to die, either by her own hands or David's. So why now did she have the feeling that she had succeeded by surviving?

"You're no longer at the Rose House."

It was true. Jeannie knew that getting out of the Rose House and the surrounding grounds was a practically impossible proposition under normal circumstances. She had thought about it before. Had her botched suicide been a subconscious plan to escape? There had to have been another, more rational way to get out. She felt like there was something else she was missing.

But she hadn't been thinking rationally. In her mind, she had no other choice. David would be coming for her. She had nothing left to lose, and only vengeance to live for. She didn't remember thinking about escape from the Rose House when she decided, on her knees in the bathroom stall, to take the pills, but at that point, her emotions were as torn apart as her insides. Now that she had survived, she had to believe that somewhere in her mind, she had been formulating a plan.

She had been so confused when she stepped out of that bathroom, yet so driven. Suicide had never before crossed Jeannie's mind, even after the death of her parents, but last night it made perfect sense. The *only* thing that made any sense. And the noises. The familiar grinding in her head.

Jeannie didn't want to think about it. She was ashamed of what she did, of what others at the Rose House must think of her. Then the words of the man standing over her echoed in her head. *You're no longer at the Rose House.* She must have drawn enough attention for someone to save her in time. The way her body felt, it must've been some ordeal. Two spots above her breasts felt like whoever used the shovel on her stomach had started with a sledgehammer on her chest. The paramedics must have used a defibrillator. Was the man standing over her now one of the people who had saved her? Whoever he was, he apparently wasn't buying the unconscious act.

"I'm here to help you," he said.

You can help by getting me out of here, Jeannie thought.

As if in response, she felt the man loosening the restraints on her wrists, and Jeannie dared to open her eyes. Again the room was mostly a wash of white through blurry vision, with only the silhouette of the man

doctor? he's wearing white.

standing over her loosening her restraints. "You've done a good job of getting yourself this far," he said, "but now you're in a bit of a fix, aren't you? Smart, but not *that* smart. So they sent me."

The words the doctor spoke didn't make much sense to Jeannie. What was he talking about? Then he leaned over her to get to the other arm, and Jeannie saw his face—or rather his eyes—and Jeannie's heart sank. If she were back in her room at the Rose House, she could pinpoint the article about the surgeon who had been arrested for sneaking into the rooms of his female patients and fondling them while they were passed out. It wasn't the same doctor as the man leaning over her now, but the look was there, the look that Jeannie could only describe as malevolence personified, and Jeannie knew her plan had been for naught. She waited for the worst.

But the doctor released her wrists and then straightened out. "Go find them," he said. "You know what you have to do." Then he parted the curtain and left.

Jeannie was confused. She waited for the doctor to come back with some frightening surgical device to kill her, but the longer she waited, the more she convinced herself he wasn't coming back. And in fact, she noticed a glass of orange juice on the bedside table that hadn't been there the first time she opened her eyes. Suddenly her stomach rumbled. She reached for the glass and took a large swallow, but it was everything she could do to keep from coughing up the burning citrus on her raw throat. Suddenly another image came back to her from the night before. A nurse standing over her. She couldn't see her face behind the white mask. "This isn't going to be pleasant," the nurse said. "But you're going to have to cooperate with me."

Then she shoved a tube in Jeannie's mouth. When it hit the back of her throat, she gagged, her stomach contorted and she had vomited.

"At least *that's* out of the way," the nurse said. "Let's give it another shot."

Then blackness. She had probably passed out.

Gingerly, Jeannie took another sip of the juice, knowing that her body needed it, and thought about what to do next. She had to get out of this hospital. At least she still had her clothes. She spotted them on a chair next to the bed. That was a step in the right direction, but she wondered if there would be nurses or security watching out for her. Maybe the doctor who had freed her was just setting a trap. Even if she made it out, what would she do once she was free?

If I lie here much longer trying to figure it out, she told herself, *it won't matter. First things, first. Get out of the hospital.*

Action, reaction. Survival. Jeannie winced as she plucked the I.V. from her arm and sat up. A wave of dizziness passed over her, but thankfully no nausea. She slid off the bed and got dressed as quickly and quietly as possible. Then she sneaked over to the curtain, slitting it just enough to peek out. Across the shiny linoleum floor were other curtained areas, some of them open and empty, and Jeannie didn't detect any movement behind the curtains that had been closed. In the middle of the aisle to her right, she spotted a counter situated in front of a glassed room. From her vantage, she could just see the ends of the shelves stacked with medical supplies behind the glass. A nurse stepped out of the room toward the desk, and Jeannie backed away from the curtain. She heard the nurses soft-soled shoes padding away, followed by a door opening. Then shutting.

Her heart pounded in her chest as she parted the curtain and stepped out. A man groaned somewhere across the way, but the area was otherwise empty. She slipped away in the opposite direction of the nurse, following the posted exit signs. She was almost to the door marked "Waiting Room" when she heard footsteps. She slipped into an empty room, hiding behind the door. She peered through the crack and saw a tired-looking nurse pushing a cart of medical instruments. Just as she was passing by, a commotion erupted in the direction from which Jeannie had just come. A man started screaming in pain. The nurse perked up immediately and rushed down the hall, leaving the cart unattended. Jeannie stared at the cart, more specifically at a scalpel on the top tray. She peeked her head out of the room just as another nurse rushed past. Jeannie stepped back, but the other woman didn't notice her.

Jeannie took a quick look around, then she grabbed the scalpel, concealing it in her sleeve. She didn't want to use the weapon. Not unless she had to. She hurried toward an exit sign.

She made it through the door to the waiting area without being noticed or stopped, but still her heart raced. A man with a blood-spotted rag wrapped around his hand glanced at her, but looked away, probably figuring that she had been discharged. She scanned the area until she spotted the sliding doors to the outside. Trying not to run, she quickened her pace with her head down and left the hospital. Beyond the glaring lights of the E.R. entrance, she cut across the grass, a more direct line to the full parking lot, where she would be less noticeable. She crossed a few rows of vehicles and then started down an aisle toward the street. She was within ten or twelve cars before the end of the row when someone opened their door and stepped out just a few cars down, facing the opposite direction. Jeannie realized that it was Dr. Brandt. The doc looked up at the sky, then took a drag from a cigarette. She hadn't spotted Jeannie yet, and Jeannie considered dodging in between the rows and trying to make a run for it. She started to turn on her heel, but the sound of the gravel drew the attention of the administrator from the Rose House. The two stared at each other for a moment.

The older woman looked in the direction of the hospital, then back at Jeannie. "I haven't smoked in almost three years," she said. She dropped the cigarette on the asphalt and snubbed it with the toe of her shoe.

Jeannie was still weighing her options, trying to figure her next move.

"I'm guessing you released yourself on your own recognizance." Dr. Brandt sighed. "Okay, let's go back in and make sure you're fit to leave." She started toward Jeannie.

"I can't go back in there," Jeannie said. Her first spoken words to another person since the death of her parents.

Sam Brandt was clearly stricken by this fact, but only showed it for a moment. She reached out her hand and continued forward. "I'm sorry, Jeannie. I don't know what you are thinking right now, or what you were thinking last night, and I'm not going to ask. Not today, at least. But for now, we need to get you back in that hospital."

"Please help me," Jeannie said.

Sam stopped again, and her arm lowered. "That's all I ever wanted to do."

"Then don't make me go back in there."

"Jeannie-"

"*Please*."

Neither spoke for a moment, and this time Sam broke the silence. "What do you expect me to do, Jeannie?"

Jeannie knew what she had to do. She was relieved by the idea, actually. "Just listen to what I have to say," she said. "Give me five minutes. Please."

"You don't have to talk about this right now, Jeannie. You've just been through a traumatic experience."

"But I want to tell you," Jeannie said. "I have to tell you now."

Dr. Brandt seemed uncertain. Jeannie's mind went to the scalpel hidden up her sleeve, and she added, "Just five minutes, and then I'll go back inside."

After what felt like an eternity, the older woman consented. "Five minutes."

"Not here," Jeannie said. "Can we talk in your car?"

Sam looked around the parking lot. "Fine. And after that, we go back inside."

"Right," Jeannie said. She followed Sam to her car, an older gray Subaru station wagon. Inside the car, a faint trace of fresh smoke mixed with vanilla. Sam put the keys in the ignition, and when Jeannie made a move to run, Sam quickly said, "It's just to roll down the windows. My husband would kill me. Well, not literally, of course, but you know what I mean."

Now that Jeannie was in the vehicle, she tried to think of where to begin. She had been over that day a thousand times in her head, but she had never imagined how to possibly tell someone else about it. Now she knew it might be her only chance.

"The cabin was supposed to make things better," she said finally. "Before that day, I didn't know why things were strained between my parents. I just knew that they were, but on that trip-" A lump rose in Jeannie's throat, and she paused. When she collected herself, she proceeded to tell Dr. Brandt everything. She started with the cabin, any of the details she could remember, even about her certainty that she had actually fired the shot that killed her father. She told her about the noises in her head ever since whenever she found another article, how she wasn't sure if she was going crazy until she saw the story in Hawaii.

"I dreamt about that house," Jeannie said. "And about that man, Steve Avery. I had that dream two months before it happened, just before the crew went over there. And I dreamt about him again on the same night that he boarded up that other man, Ed McGinnis." She shivered.

Dr. Brandt looked at her for a moment. "Jeannie, we've known each other for almost two years now--otherwise I probably wouldn't be saying this--but you can't be serious."

Jeannie didn't let the comment faze her. "And then tonight, something else happened. Someone else died because of him. A younger man in his apartment. Shot, I think. I think David lived there, too."

Something changed in the doctor's expression. "I heard something on the news," she said. "Just before they called to tell me that you had... that you were being brought here. There was a young artist-"

"In Missoula, Montana," Jeannie finished.

"Yes."

"That's where Steve Avery lived."

Sam stared at her, then shook her head. "I don't know, Jeannie. You could've heard a news report, gotten confused. You could've-"

"I didn't," Jeannie said. "I was reading in my room when it happened, and it almost killed me."

"You don't actually *believe*-" Sam started.

Again, Jeannie cut her off. "I don't know what to believe anymore. The only thing I know for sure is that I have been connected to this guy ever since he killed my parents. And it's only getting worse. *He* is getting worse. There is going to be more death, and I don't think I can take it."

"So you thought if you killed yourself, you would be free?"

"I don't know exactly what I was thinking," Jeannie said. "I didn't necessarily want to die, but I didn't want something horrible to happen to me, either. Maybe I just thought it would get me out of the Rose House."

Sam shook her head. "Teenagers," she said. "So reactionary." She looked out the window into the darkness before returning her attention to the car. "Let's say for a moment that I believe you."

Jeannie didn't respond. Sam Brandt would either believe her or not, and Jeannie thought that maybe the older woman was at least acknowledging the possibility.

"If everything you've said is true," Sam continued, "what do you plan to do next? No, wait. Don't tell me. You plan on searching him out."

Until this point, Jeannie hadn't decided whether or not she would tell Dr. Brandt where she intended to go, but Sam probably knew by the girl's silence that she had guessed accurately.

"Oh, Jeannie," she said. "What are you thinking? This man could hurt you. Or worse, kill you. If you really think he's somehow involved in these incidents, we need to contact the authorities."

"It won't do any good. He'll get away, and then he'll come for me. Or it. Or they. Whatever. It has to be me who faces this. I don't know why, but if this is all real, if David is possessed by some sort of demon or something, maybe he can still beat it. He saved my life. I have to at least see if there's any hope for him."

"And if not?"

Jeannie didn't answer, and after a moment, the older woman continued. "That's a pretty amazing story you just told. I have to admit, I always wondered what really happened to you that afternoon. More than what the police report and investigators stated. I've looked over your file more times than I can count, and something just never clicked. But I never expected to hear this story. Something else maybe. A jilted lover who followed your family to the cabin, maybe."

Jeannie drew a sharp breath and looked away. She hadn't told Dr. Brandt about the accusations against her father.

Sam misunderstood her reaction. "Oh Jeannie, I'm so sorry. I didn't mean to imply that either of your parents would ever do something like that. I was just looking for an answer. And now you tell me *this*." She looked out the window again. "And crazy as it sounds coming out of my mouth, what you've told me doesn't sound so crazy. I *want* to believe you because I know you believe it." She turned back and reached out her hand; Jeannie let her place it on her own. "But even if it's all true," she said, "you haven't thought through your actions. Given the circumstances, real or imagined, I can't blame you. But what did you think you would do if you got out of the hospital? How were you going to get to Montana?"

"I didn't know," Jeannie responded. "Until now. Dr. Brandt, I need to borrow your car."

Sam chuckled, but she stopped when she saw that Jeannie was serious. "Jeannie, you don't even have a license."

"I tried to kill myself tonight. Then I escaped from a hospital. And *that's* your reason why you shouldn't give me your car."

"That's just the start," Sam said and pulled back her hand.

Jeannie slipped out the scalpel. "Let me give you a reason why you should."

Sam looked at the small weapon, then at Jeannie. "I don't think you're going to use that on me."

"Probably not," Jeannie admitted. "But I'll use it on myself. And I won't mess up this time. Up one arm and down the other. Across my throat, if I have to. But I'm not going back in there, and I'm not going back to the Rose House." The idea of using the blade on herself terrified Jeannie, but she would do it if she had to. And she could see that the doctor believed her. "Please, Dr. Brandt," she said. "I'll be careful. Any sign of trouble and I'll get outta there. I'll call the police and come back to the Rose House. I promise."

Sam just stared at her. A car passed behind them in the parking lot, but neither of them looked back. "You know," she said finally, "I have a daughter. Just a little younger than you. A pretty girl. Just like you. She doesn't talk, either. At least not to her father or me."

Even though Jeannie was certain that the hospital would discover her missing at any moment and start the search, she didn't rush Dr. Brandt. She realized that if she couldn't convince her, she was out of options. Jeannie was trying to figure out what she had possibly been thinking by taking the pills in the first place when Sam spoke.

"They're going to come looking for you," she said.

"Just give me a little head start," Jeannie said. "And some help. Tell them I've done this before--run away I mean--but that I always come back after a day or two. Or tell them that you think I was heading South. Mexico, maybe."

"You want me to lie to the police?"

"Dr. Brandt, I was just kidding about Montana. I'm actually going to Mexico. There. Better?"

Dr. Brandt studied her. Jeannie knew that the other woman's mind must be reeling, trying to decide whether or not to believe what she had heard. If the doctor would accept the story, the law most likely wouldn't seem as important, but listening to herself relate what happened that afternoon at the cabin, Jeannie knew why she hadn't said anything about it before. She would've been locked up for sure.

Finally Sam spoke. "I don't know why I'm doing this when every fiber of my professional being is screaming at me."

"I promise that when I come back, I'll go along with whatever story you come up with."

"It's not just about getting caught, Jeannie. There are bigger questions here. *Much* bigger questions. But some small, irrational part of me knows that I have to let you go, as if I don't have a choice on this one."

"You always have choices," Jeannie said. "The question is which one is right."

Dr. Brandt gave her the clinical inquisitive look that Jeannie had seen many times. Then she shook her head, took her keys out of the ignition and set them on the center console. "I'll never forgive myself if something happens to you. Because I let you go."

"If you didn't, I would be dead anyway."

"Maybe."

"I would kill myself."

"Again, maybe." Sam opened her purse. "You have one week. If I don't press the issue with the police, I doubt they'll do much investigating, but if I haven't heard from you in a week, they'll know where to go looking for you."

Jeannie didn't argue. One week seemed like an eternity away.

"I'm guessing you don't have any money."

Jeannie let out a sigh. She could've slapped herself. This was the worst plan ever. Then Dr. Brandt pulled something out of her bag. A coin pouch. *Jeannie's* coin pouch where she kept her ID and bank card. She handed it to Jeannie.

"Frank Matsen insisted that the paramedics take it," she said. "He said he thought they would need it. Looks like *you* were the one who needed it, after all."

"Thanks," Jeannie said.

"Tell me again how I have a choice," Sam said. She opened her door and stepped out. Jeannie slid across into the driver's seat. Dr. Brandt leaned down. She looked uncertain again, and for a moment it seemed like she was going to reconsider her decision. "There's an atlas under the seat," she said instead. "Be careful." She shut the door.

Jeannie started the car and put it in reverse. In the headlights, Dr. Brandt still looked like she might change her mind and decide to call out for help at any moment, but Jeannie made it out of the parking lot without any commotion.

She drove until she felt like she was far enough away from the hospital before pulling over and looking at the map. She decided that she would cut through Nevada and up into Idaho. Heading north and then east would mean all interstate, and while she felt reasonably comfortable driving the car, she figured the less traffic and police, the better. She put the map on the seat and started out of the city.

CHAPTER 24

It wasn't until Jeannie was east of Oakland and the city lights started to fade behind her that she finally calmed down. Traffic was thin at this early hour. As she crossed the dark desert, she thought about what Dr. Brandt had said about choices. Jeannie really did believe what she had said about always having an option, but she couldn't deny that she also felt only *partly* in control of her actions. Like she was being pushed.

Or maybe pulled.

As the miles passed by, she had plenty of time to think about the fact that she could be getting sucked into a trap. Maybe whatever had control over David was reeling her in to finish what he had started two years ago. She had to constantly brush away the nagging feeling that she was crazy. If she wasn't crazy for thinking that David was possessed by some sort of demon, there was the fact that she was taking herself right to him.

Past Sacramento, the terrain offered a welcome respite to her restless thoughts, forcing her to concentrate on the road as she wound through the Sierra Nevadas. By the time she made it to Reno, the sun was just rising. With the tension from being an inexperienced driver on the road for four hours combined with the events of the night before, Jeannie knew she better pull over and get some rest.

She exited the interstate when she saw a Super 8 Motel and drove into the parking lot. She expected a swarm of police cars as she pulled into a stall, but nothing happened.

Yes, this was the right thing to do. She needed to rest. Otherwise, she might just end up falling asleep and running herself off the road. Dr. Brandt would be seriously displeased. Inside the motel, she had no problem with the bank card. No suspicious looks. The girl behind the counter barely noticed her; she was too busy talking on her cell phone.

An hour later, Jeannie stepped out of the stand-up shower in the modest bathroom. Although a tub would've been nice, the shower had brought her a little closer to human.

She had wept. She wept for her parents, the first time she truly let herself mourn them. And for herself. Alive, but still very scared. In the privacy of the shower, she let the tears come and let them wash away from her. When she had finally turned off the water, more than just her skin felt cleaner. She wrapped a towel around her body and stood in front of the mirror, combing out the tangles from her hair.

Looking at herself, Jeannie felt older than her almost eighteen years. She knew what an ordinary girl her age was supposed to be like, the things they should be worried about. She had watched TV. There were the three C's. Clothes, cars and college. Oh yeah, and college boys. A plastic existence compared to what Jeannie had lived through.

She thought about David, and wondered what he would look like after these two years. She had only seen a fuzzy image of him in the picture from Hawaii, and she wondered what sort of devastation the demon had caused. Would he recognize her?

Jeannie unwrapped the towel hanging from her breasts and let it drop to the floor. She stared at her naked reflection. Would David recognize the woman she saw in front of her?

Would he find me attractive? Under different circumstances, would he smile at me?

Jeannie ran her fingers over her chest and down the space between her breasts. She had never even kissed a boy. Quite a few had approached her in the library, but her silence had been like a stigma. David had been the only significant male figure in her late teen years, the sole object of her attention. Even with his scars, she couldn't deny she found him attractive. Even with all of the damage he had wreaked in her life.

Because he saved my life, she reasoned with herself. *And now I may have to kill him.*

Jeannie brushed away the thoughts. She found it relatively easy to do. The warm shower had loosened her tense body, relaxing her mind. The energy and adrenaline that had carried her from the hospital in San Francisco had drained out of her. She yawned heavily, pulled her wet hair back in a ponytail and left the bathroom. The walls in the bedroom were paneled in fake wood, and the floral pattern of the bedspread matched the curtains. She climbed under the covers on the bed and was asleep almost immediately.

Jeannie didn't stir at all until the next morning when the phone rang in the room. She bolted upright, disoriented, and then answered. A woman from the hotel asked if she was planning on staying another night. Jeannie mumbled that she was, then hung up the phone. She didn't feel like she had slept at all, and her body had regained the aches which had been relieved by the shower the day before. She was hungry, but too weak to get out of bed. She slid down the backboard and dropped into unconsciousness again, quickly slipping back into a dream state.

In the dream, she saw her father again. He was kneeling on the ground next to a pond with his back to her. Except this time, they were atop a frozen pinnacle and the pond was iced over. Black clouds filled the sky, and below them, a thick, dirty blanket of yellowed haze covered the valley. She couldn't see through those clouds, but she could definitely hear something horrible under the veil, could almost feel the atrocities committed below. The anguish erupted out of the valley in shockwaves.

Her father turned to look at her with his dead eyes.

"Not just a dream," he whispered. He turned back to the pond. He reached toward the ice and as he made contact, his flesh turned a bluish purple. His fingers connected with the pond, became part of the frozen surface. The color at the tips of his fingers seeped up his arms and covered his body until he stopped moving.

Jeannie heard a shifting behind her, and turned just in time to see a fissure widen. Then she was falling. Or sliding rather. The snow blew away from her feet as she dropped, revealing a giant chunk of broken ice. Her feet somehow clung to the frozen surface, seeming almost ice-like, themselves. The murky grayish-white color under her appeared to be spreading up her legs as she plummeted into the cloud bank. Blinded in the dirty haze, she could feel that she still sped downward, but could see nothing except for occasional flashes of white light. The tormented sounds grew in intensity, almost as thick as the moist air rushing past her body. Heavier, in fact.

Jeannie dropped out of the clouds, and realized that the slope of the terrain had lessened, and her speed decreased in half. Scores of tattered bodies littered this frozen landscape. They dragged their torn bodies in the direction Jeannie had come, as if trying to escape. Like a horrible amusement park ride, the chunk of ice cut a swath through them as it continued to slide. The poor creatures could barely lift their heads as she passed, but when they did, Jeannie felt their fear and pain clinging to her like leeches.

Then the scene changed, bodies much more animated and less broken, but not for lack of trying. Jeannie sliced a path through a tumult like a giant battlefield which seemed to spread out for miles in every direction. On the frozen hills in the distance, bodies clashed in rolling waves of violence while gray slush and hail stormed down from the clouds above. Except the death, destruction and torture surrounding her didn't take any recognizable order or direction. No side seemed certain. One group acted more like a mob, women and men viciously attacking each other without preference. Anyone within arm's reach was punched, clawed, kicked or bitten. Another group Jeannie passed appeared incapable of controlling their own bodies. Only their lungs seemed to work as they issued forth terrible screams while they lowered themselves on their swords or hacked away at their own limbs. In yet another part of the landscape, lines of victims waited like cattle for their chance to reach the front of the line where they were disemboweled then beheaded by beautiful naked men and women. The remains were scooped up and carried to the end of the line, where they were reanimated and joined the lines again. Pools of rippling black filth stained the frozen ground wherever Jeannie looked.

Just as she thought she couldn't take any more, the chunk of ice slowed, and she broke out of the pandemonium. The platform finally came to a stop, scraping over what Jeannie thought was a frozen lake. In the distance, the low-hanging clouds started to swirl, a lump at the center stretching toward the icy surface. It continued to funnel down as it grew larger.

Jeannie woke in the hotel room with a start, sprawled across the bed, her sweat-dampened clothes wrapping knots around her body.

She sat upright in panic and scanned the room. It took a moment to discern her new reality from the familiarity of her room in the Rose House. Or the landscape of her nightmare. She looked at the clock on the nightstand. Just after four in the morning. She thought it was Monday. Or Tuesday actually. She wiped the thin sheet over her face, took a deep breath and stumbled over to the vanity just outside the bathroom.

She tore the plastic wrapper off one of the glasses, filled it with cold water, then walked back and sat on the carpet and turned on the air conditioner. She shivered as the sweat cooled on her t-shirt and the nightmare dried from her salty body.

Jeannie got dressed and stepped out on the balcony. It was a chilly night, and she pulled her jacket tighter. The lights from all of the city's casinos cast a faded orange glow on the bellies of low clouds that seemed to trap in the noises of the traffic in the distance. Jeannie heard two men shouting at each other somewhere down the street. One guy shouted something about his "fucking dollar!"

She looked up to where a break in the clouds revealed a hazy night, but the stars were replaced by blinking dots of moving light as the jets carried people to and from the confusion of the city.

The shouting of the men below her turned more aggressive. Jeannie sighed.

When the planes outnumber the stars in the sky, perhaps it's time for good men to die.

She shivered and went back inside to the bathroom to clean up a little. She cursed herself for having slept so long—who knew what David could've done in that time—even though she knew that she must have needed it. Now it was time to go. She figured she had about ten or twelve hours until she made her final destination. Dr. Brandt had suspected that she was going to Montana, but she had been only part right. On the drive from San Francisco, Jeannie decided she wasn't going to Missoula. She was going back to the cabin. She would end it where it all began. She could only hope that if David really was coming for her, he would know to find her there. The plan sounded crazy in her head now, after the hot shower and rest, but it made sense at the same time, and she had to follow her gut.

CHAPTER 25

David woke in a hot, dark room. His sense of smell returned first, nearly gagging him with a thick haze of sex, smoke, perfume and sweat. A blurry light glowed from the other side of the room. He tried to rub his eyes to help them adjust, but both of his arms were dead-numb. When he pulled at them, he realized he wasn't alone in the bed, and even in the dark, the picture started coming together. The perfume came from two women on either side of him sleeping on his arms.

After almost three years, David still recognized the scent of the perfume on one of the women as being the same kind that Ann had worn. A tear escaped his eye, and his chest hitched, but he pushed back the emotion. He eased his right arm from underneath the sleeping form next to him. She rolled over as he pulled, and he felt his hand pinned briefly under her breast. He freed his hand and rubbed his eyes. The red glow from the clock on the nightstand came into focus. Four o'clock. Dark outside. But where was he?

He looked over the silhouetted curves of the back of the woman on his other arm. He slid his arm out, flexing his fingers as the blood rushed into his hand. Then he slipped off the bed. One of the women rolled over and wrapped her arm over the other. David was no prude, but what would ordinarily be most men's fantasy made him nauseous. Especially when he thought of what must have transpired the night before to bring about these circumstances. He could feel the abuse the demon had wreaked on almost every inch of his body.

His mind was muddy as well, and David guessed that it was from more than just being shoved back from his own consciousness. His nasal passages felt raw, his teeth tingled, and his jaw muscles ached like when he used to grind his teeth as a kid, leading David to the conclusion that the two women on the bed weren't the only things purchased by the demon the previous evening for entertainment.

What he didn't know in this state of confusion was whether or not the demon was gone, but for the time being at least, he had control of his body. And his body had needs. He stumbled over clothing on the floor on his way to the light in the bathroom. He recoiled back against the open door in surprise when he saw a painting of a huge clown on the bathroom wall. He steadied himself and quietly shut the door. Makeup and pill bottles cluttered the sink. He swept a pile of little plastic baggies off the lid of the toilet seat, confirming his suspicions about the night before.

David stared at the clown over the toilet while he urinated. Something familiar struck him about the jester holding the multicolored lollipop. An image from childhood. But his mind was still muddled, and he couldn't make the connection. David finished and turned to the sink. He turned on the cold water and splashed some on his face, then grabbed a towel hanging next to the vanity and dried his face. He was about to hang the towel back when he saw the writing on it. *Circus Circus* had been sewn into it. Of course. He hadn't been to the hotel since he was a little boy, on a trip with Peter and their mom, back in the days when it was the only place in Las Vegas where parents could feel comfortable taking their children, a place for the kids to play the midway games or watch the circus sideshows while the adults gambled.

So David was in Las Vegas. Even though he hadn't been to Circus Circus since childhood, he had visited the City of Sin quite a few times over the years since, most of them falling in his early college years, when his friends knew which casinos weren't as strict about checking I.D.'s. David still remembered the two rules of Las Vegas. Number one, the only thing illegal is getting caught. And number two, never stay on the strip long enough to see the sun rise. Not if you were partying at least. There weren't many things more depressing after a long night of imbibing than seeing all those casino lights outside still flashing the next morning. With daylight breaking over the littered city and its miles of concrete, the twinkling lights look dull and dirty. Las Vegas was skilled at finding weaknesses and preying on them. Whatever addiction, be it alcohol, drugs, women or gambling, it was all for sale. Open twenty-four hours. Anyone who spent longer than a three-day family vacation there knew this fact.

Those days were long past for David, predating even the tragic night in Colorado by a few years. Did the demon know about those troubled times? Had it pried into his memories? If so, it had made an excellent choice bringing him here. Even beyond the lingering effects of the drugs that the demon had obviously put into his body, David's *spirit* felt weaker here. The old scabs of temptation from those days still itched, even though he had long ago traded the chemical highs for the elation to be found in the wilderness. But the surrounding memories now smelled almost as sweet as sour, and David couldn't deny the stirrings, just below the righteous indignation, when he thought of the two women in the other room. He hadn't been with a woman in over two years.

He looked at himself in the mirror. Really looked. Maybe for the first time since losing Ann. He looked beaten, and not just in his eyes. His body was just one other thing which he hadn't been giving attention. He was too thin. Muscled from doing construction but gaunt. He had been working too much, pushing himself too hard even when he felt exhausted, an exhaustion which also had apparently resulted from the demon pushing him the rest of the time. David ran his fingers over the dark lines bagged around his bloodshot eyes, prodding skin that had once been taut across his cheekbones.

What have you done to me? And what have I done to all those other people?

David's mind ricocheted off the subject, his thoughts getting confused again. He couldn't think about the revelation in Father Jimmy's office right now. Not yet. Call it denial. Or repression. Whatever Freud may have called it, David's mind was doing it. Because whenever he started to think about the murders the demon had carried out in his body, he thought he might crawl into a corner, afraid to even move.

David's basic instincts took over. If nothing else, he knew that he needed to get out of this room. Maybe food. His stomach twisted at the thought.

Maybe not.

Even with the damage his body had sustained since leaving Missoula, he felt lucky to be in control at least. Maybe the demon had pushed his body too far, like the time David awoke in front of the hunting cabin. He didn't really care about the reason. He only wanted to try to figure out what he could do next.

He opened the door to the bathroom, relieved to see the two girls still asleep on the bed. Or maybe they were just pretending to sleep. For a guy who looked like David, he could only guess at how much the demon had been forced to pay them to stay. He squinted in the dark room and searched around until he found his clothing, or at least *men's* clothing. He pulled on an unfamiliar pair of slacks and a wrinkled shirt and slipped out of the hotel room. The hall was a bright wash of colors and David had to steady himself before continuing.

He wandered along the winding chain of patterned carpet toward a green exit light and stood in front of a sign full of numbers screwed to the wall, a map. It took his groggy mind a moment before he could figure out the location of the elevators. He laughed when he realized he had just passed them.

He stepped into the elevator and pushed the Lobby button, thankful for the lack of activity at this hour. When the doors slid open to the casino, cold air rushed in, and the sudden flashing lights brought David's headache on full force, followed by a wrenching of his gut. The demon had made quite a time of it, apparently.

He followed the signs for a café through the gaming area. There were no children out at this hour. The midway was closed, but not many of the remaining gamblers looked like they had children young enough to still take an interest in such a thing. Drab faces pored over cards and drinks while uninterested dealers dealt their fate. Only a few people took a second glance at the scarred young man passing their tables. This was Las Vegas, after all. David could be just another part of the show, as far as they knew.

The café was empty except for a slightly overweight man sitting at the counter with a suit coat hanging from his chair and a younger couple in a booth in the corner wearing all black, both of them wearing eye makeup. In high school David had called them Goths. The two kids glared at him as he walked past them toward the counter. The man at the other end of the counter turned and looked in David's direction when he sat. He wore his tie loosened around a white dress shirt. On the counter in front of him sat only a bottle of beer and a half eaten English muffin. David could tell by the man's swaying that he wouldn't remember David in the morning, except maybe as a drunken delusion. A tired looking woman with a nametag that read "Edna- Amarillo, TX" walked up behind the counter and leaned against it. She looked like she was either near the end of her shift, or that she wished she were. She didn't bother to ask David what he wanted, just stared at him.

"Coffee and a water, please," he said, then added as she started to walk off, "And an orange juice."

"That's the ticket," the man hollered from the end of the counter. He raised the beer in a toast, and David nodded.

"That's the ticket, alright," the man mumbled and picked at his English muffin.

David was pretending to read the menu when the waitress came back, even though he knew his stomach would resist the food. "Anything else?" she asked.

"No, thanks," David said, and then he noticed the newspaper behind the counter. "Is that today's paper?"

"Today's paper don't come out for another couple hours," she said and pointed at the clock on the wall.

"Right. Yesterday's, then. Could I take a look at it?"

The waitress grabbed the paper and set it in front of David. "I got the Entertainment section in the back, if you want."

"The front section is fine."

Mostly he just wanted to see the date, but it turned out to be the *day* which surprised him. While his body felt like it had suffered a week's worth of abuse, the date on the paper said that he had been in Missoula just a day and half earlier. It was Monday night, or Tuesday morning. Whatever. David downed the glass of orange juice, his body welcoming the vitamins, then started sweetening his coffee.

Watching the swirling cream, his mind returned to Father Jimmy's office.

Dear God, what have I-

His thought was interrupted by the man at the other end of the counter. "This here's the problem," he announced to the waitress, who was doing her best to ignore him. The man held up the beer. He turned to David and lowered his voice. "This here's the problem." He shook the beer in his hand, spilling some on the muffin. Again, David just nodded, but it wasn't enough this time. The man wanted more of a response. He pushed away from the counter and stumbled over toward him. He slid into a chair just a couple down. "The boy's tuition?" he slurred. "Well, the wife certainly won't be very happy about *that* little bit of news." The two kids in the booth snickered at the drunken customer.

"Sorry to hear that," David said.

"Hey, it's not your fault, pal," the man said. It came out more like *hey, snotyurfall, pal.* "The problem's right here in this little bottle." He scowled, then took a drink from the beer. "It's startin' to show up everywhere."

David thought that drinking was perhaps only part of the guy's problem, but he kept his mouth shut.

"They make it in my hometown," the man continued. "Righ' here in Milwaukee. Jus' popped up out of nowhere, and now I can't stop in a bar without seein' it."

Or drinking it, David thought. "You like beer, eh?" he said instead.

"I got a sof' spot," he replied and grinned, "but *this* stuff, I mean, c'mon. I used to think it was funny."

David tried to see the label on the beer. "What are you drinking?"

"You haven' seen this yet? Where you been, pal?" He slid the bottle over and David picked it up. A busty redhead on the label posed in a short flaming-red cocktail dress. She wore a mischievous smile and was propping up the ends of some sort of fur stole wrapped around her shoulders. Arched above her head in block letters was the name *Lucy's Fur Pale Ale* and below was the slogan in cursive. *Stop wanting. Start flaunting.*

"Lucy's Fur," David said aloud and laughed in spite of himself.

"Yeah, pretty funny, eh?" the man said. He reached up and smoothed over a long strand of hair that had fallen from its place over his balding head. "Jus' came out a few months ago, and it used to be a real joke ordering them at the bar, but sittin' here now, it doesn't seem so funny." He paused and looked at David, his head bobbing slightly as he tried to focus. "I didn't want to win that much," he said. "I jus' didn't want the kid's schooling to put the wife and me in the poorhouse. Bought one of those books, you know? All the tricks of gambling? But they still got me. Hook, line and sinker." The man turned the bottle in front of him. "*Stop wanting. Start flaunting,*" he mocked. "I'm in sales, pal, and lemme tell you, somebody's makin' a mint off this one." The man lifted the bottle toward his lips.

"Yeah, probably the devil himself," David mused and laughed again.

The man stopped, the bottle just inches from his open mouth. He set it down on the counter and stared solemnly at David. "The devil," he murmured. "Maybe you're right, pal." He pushed the bottle away and drifted back to his seat at the other end. He buttoned his collar and pulled his tie around his neck and motioned to the waitress. "Coffee, please."

That was easy, David thought, thankful that the encounter had been brief. He wanted to be more sympathetic, but he had his own problems, and Las Vegas wasn't the place to handle them.

David finished his coffee and temporarily panicked when he realized he hadn't thought of how he was going to pay. He patted the slacks and couldn't find his wallet, but he discovered a handful of gambling chips in his front pockets. Most were high numbered, but he plucked a couple of dollar chips and set them on the counter. He took one last look at the man at the other end of the counter, sitting with his coffee and staring straight ahead. The man's lower lip trembled, and he looked like he was about to break down, but he didn't turn to face David as he left. He decided he would go back to the room and see if he could find a set of keys. With everything else, he wouldn't be surprised to find a valet ticket.

Just as he stepped off the elevator on his floor, just as he was beginning to feel a little cognizant, able to think about his next step, David's senses started tingling, his limbs growing thicker and numb. The demon was awakening. Or taking over again. David didn't know which, but he knew that he didn't have the strength to fight. And if it was the former, he didn't want the demon to know he had been in control. Against the increasing weight of his body threatening to pull him to the carpet, he quickened his pace and slipped quietly into the hotel room, where he undressed and crept back on the bed. One of the women rolled toward him and flopped her arm over his chest, and he cringed at the same time as he felt a stirring in his groin. He blamed it on the waking demon.

David wanted to pray to see the light of another day, another chance to defeat the darkness enveloping him now, but the prayer sounded hollow in his head.

And then he was gone.

* * *

David's flesh welcomed Mashart with a headache and a hard-on. For all of its imperfections, the demon so loved the flesh. Over the past century he had killed using many of the hands of man. He had felt the warm lifeblood of another slick on those hands, tasted the copper twinge in his mouth. The flesh made everything else so real, especially death. What a thrill to see and touch the life as it flowed out of the living, to hear their last sounds before silence, to taste the sweat beading on their foreheads as a panic-stricken heart frantically pounded its last beats.

Oh yes, the monkeys wore well, indeed. And Las Vegas aimed to please. He reached over and ran his hand across the naked body of the brunette next to him. Her skin shivered under his touch, and she rolled away. Mashart started to pursue her, but stopped and smacked his lips, frowning at the bitter taste in his mouth. And something sweet, beyond the taste of a woman. Oranges. So the boy had been awake.

The flesh tempted the demon to ignore David's early morning adventure and continue the ravaging of the two women on the bed. Certainly he couldn't have gone very far in such a short period of time, but still Mashart was curious to see what David thought he could accomplish in this city. He pushed himself off the bed. The girls would be there when he got back. The money would guarantee that, but just to be sure, Mashart stuffed their clothes in a pillow case, taking it with him as he left the room. In the hall, he closed his eyes and drew out the flesh's muscle memory. The boy thought that just because he had control of his own body that the demon wouldn't be able to tell where he had gone.

When Mashart opened his eyes again, he turned to his left and saw the green exit sign. He followed the hall, glancing briefly at the placard of room numbers before heading toward the elevators. The door opened immediately after pushing the button. Mashart smiled, shoved the pillow case into a garbage receptacle and stepped onto the elevator. When he arrived at the lobby, he looked up at the arrows pointing to various attractions, but the café light blinked the brightest. Of course. The boy had nothing else left besides his physical urges. Mashart knew it was almost time to make his final move. Over the years the demon had convinced hundreds of the monkeys to kill, but the boy had been difficult, unwilling to kill with his own hands. Mashart had been forced to manipulate others. And it had worked. The experience with Jeremy had been better than even a demon could've guessed, and this world was full of Jeremys. Through David, Mashart was growing stronger, and with a new century of electronic communication, they would spread infection in the minds of millions of the monkeys before they even knew what hit them. But there was one final straw to be lain.

In the restaurant of faded oranges and yellows, the demon saw only three other customers. In the corner, two young punks looked up, confused when they saw him enter, but their expressions quickly changed to youthful disdain and distrust. Mashart pulled back his lips in a savage grin, chuckling when they quickly looked away. His feet carried him to the counter where he took a seat.

A haggard-looking woman behind the bar turned around. "Back again?" she asked. "Another cup of coffee?"

"Of course."

Mashart laughed aloud, but the woman didn't pay him any attention. The boy had done nothing with his moment of consciousness. He had been given a chance to do something redeeming, and he had gone to this dingy café. Things were working out just as the demon had hoped. Only the girl still needed convincing of this fact. Mashart had one more thing to do, the proverbial nail in the coffin. The *girl's* coffin.

He scrutinized the other customer at the counter, some fat guy in a cheap suit. The guy was trying to hold back, but every few seconds a choked sob would escape him. The waitress walked past him without even a glance. Yes, Mashart had one more thing to do, but he would have a little fun first.

"Actually," Mashart said to the waitress, "I'll take a Bloody Mary, and I'll take it down there with that gentleman." The waitress looked at the broken businessman, shrugged and then dumped the cup of coffee she had just poured back into the pot.

The man looked up as Mashart stood and strode over toward him. He wiped his eyes with the back of his hands as the demon slid into the seat next to him.

"How you doin', pal?" Mashart asked.

"You were right," the man said. "I think I've got a problem."

"C'mon now, Larry," Mashart said, watching as the drunk tried to figure out if he had told the stranger his name before. The demon patted him on the back, leaving his hand on Larry's shoulder for a moment like an old chum. "It's not your fault. Not really. The problem is in the bottle," Mashart said.

"I know, I know," Larry mumbled. "I've let the devil use my weakness for alcohol, and now I've got to pay the piper."

"No, no. The problem is very literally in the bottle."

Larry looked up. The demon could see his eyelids growing heavy as he stared at the scarred swirl of lines on his cheek, and Mashart continued. "You know, I heard that they put something in that beer."

"Really?" Larry slurred. His head dropped, but he quickly corrected it when the waitress wandered up and interrupted.

"Yeah, it's called alcohol," she said, setting the cocktail on the counter. Mashart shot her a look that sent her scurrying back to the kitchen.

Larry shook his head slowly. "They couldn't put something in the beer besides alcohol," he said. "Surely somebody would pick up on that. Wouldn't they?"

The demon leaned in closer. "No," he whispered. The other man's eyelids dropped lower. "But you can make things better, Larry. You'll be a hero. For once in your life. Let's go sit at a table. You think you can walk to a table?"

Larry shook his head again, but he stood anyway and followed Mashart to a booth where the demon told him what to do next. The drunken, whimpering slob made easy prey. When Mashart finished, he walked Larry out of the café and sent him on his way, smiling as the downtrodden businessman stumbled off to fulfill his destiny.

Speaking of destinies, the demon decided it was time to seek out the boy and put the gears into motion to finish this once and for all. He paid for his drink and left the café.

Mashart returned to the room to find it torn apart. The girls were gone, as was the bedding from the toppled mattress. The lamps had been broken, the phone yanked from the wall, and in the bathroom, one of them had smashed the mirror and ripped the curtain from the rod. The only thing untouched was the television. The demon laughed as he thought of the enraged hookers wrapped only in sheets, unafraid of the bad luck associated with breaking a mirror, but unwilling to smash a TV.

While he might have otherwise considered one more romp with the girls had they still been there, Mashart decided it was better that they were gone. The flesh possessed a distracting strength. He shed his clothing and stretched out on the bare mattress on the floor. He closed his eyes and sought the boy in his mind.

When the demon possessed a body, the shock of the experience, the raping of the soul, sent the mind to the darkest corner of its imagination. Fear, insecurities and pain. Mashart knew that he could have left David's body, possessing instead another monkey to confront the boy like he had done when he first found him in Missoula.

As the demon went deeper into David's mind, he thought back on their first encounter at the old hotel where the boy lived, with an incendiary rage. It had been all Mashart could do to not use the drunken man to tear David's head off. The boy was definitely stronger than the rest had been. He had given the demon quite a run after escaping the Marrick cabin, getting himself lost in the woods. When the demon finally took hold of the body, it was so beaten that Mashart had to abandon it in front of an abandoned hunting shack until it was healed. As a result, the demon had been banished back to the whim of the winds, but when the boy regained his strength, he barricaded himself in. The demon attempted another attack, sending every wild creature in the area in a possessed frenzy at the cabin, trying to get in, but in the end David defeated him again. The boy was powerful in the wild.

He should have stayed there.

Ever since finding David in the city, the demon had been able to come and go from the body as he had pleased, with the various distractions of civilization keeping the secret from the boy. Mashart had used him for his purposes, the main one being to break him down. Had the girls still been in the hotel room, the demon could've possessed one of the them, maybe even killed the other one while David watched.

But this moment needed to be more intimate. Lying on the bed, Mashart sank into the depths of his mind in search of the boy.

CHAPTER 26

When the demon had possessed Barbara Stack's body, her soul had gone to an earthen cell, a darkened crypt in her mind. But she hadn't needed the light to know what horribly mutated creatures gurgled and growled around her. She could hear the scraping of bone or claw and the slithering of flesh. She could smell the rotted death.

When the demon possessed the girl, she found herself alone in a vast, empty house with large windows looking out to a black night where a storm raged. But when the lightning flashed, she could see the faceless silhouettes looming at every window. She was fifteen; she knew what they wanted. When they crashed into the house, it didn't matter where Jeannie tried to hide. They always found her.

When Mashart first took control of the boy, David had condemned himself to reliving the night in the burning house, watching his love die in his arms. The demon was pleased to have been responsible for this created hell. But when he sought out David today, he found a room that looked exactly like the one in the hotel, but without any windows. And no furniture. Instead, in the center of the room was a mound of naked female corpses, ten or fifteen of them. A subtle movement shifted the pile, but the demon knew it didn't come from any of the bloody women. Mashart walked over, still wearing David's skin and started tugging bodies away, propping them in sitting positions against the walls. As he neared the bottom of the pile, he heard a muffled shouting, but the demon continued his meticulous setup. He was returning for another woman when the stack erupted and David pushed up through the bodies, gasping. Mashart stopped, shook his head and then knelt down and pulled David from the carnage. The boy stared at Mashart, obviously confused to be seeing his reflection in the demon.

"What are you doing to yourself?" Mashart asked softly. "Why are you torturing yourself?"

David coughed and spat. "I'm dreaming."

"Afraid not."

"Then it's you," he said. "You're torturing me." He struggled to free himself from Mashart, but the demon knew the resistance to be half-hearted. His arms could provide warmth to those tormented in the cold depths of despair. Even the imagination has its senses.

"The torture is your own," Mashart said. "Your own guilt. You carry the weight of too many dead girls. But more than that, you shoulder the guilt of the world. I want to show you something. It's time that you know why I'm really here."

David slumped like a rag doll when Mashart stood, and the demon dragged him over to the wall, propping him up between the legs of one of the dead women. Then he settled into the lap of the body next to David as the wall across the room shimmered. In place of wallpaper, a new scene appeared. The entrance to a cave, its dark maw just barely visible in the lush green foliage surrounding and draping over it. Huge leaved plants fluttered in a light breeze. The demon watched for a reaction from David, but the boy either still thought he was dreaming or was unwilling to give Mashart the satisfaction.

Two people wearing hiking gear and external frame backpacks entered the scene on the wall, a man and a woman in their early thirties covered in dirt and sweat treading through the knee-high ferns. They looked as if they were about to drop from exhaustion.

"It happened just like I knew it would," Mashart whispered. "Just after the turn into your twentieth century in South America."

On the wall, the woman stopped walking. "James," she said, and the man stopped as well. "Look." She pointed at the entrance to the cave.

The man seemed to come alive, rushing over to the opening. "My God, Tess, I think you're right." He spoke with an English accent. "I knew it was around here somewhere."

Like the lens of a camera, the image followed the two as they pushed aside the vines and entered the cave. As the cave stretched away from the light of day, they lit kerosene lanterns, continuing until they came to a larger cavern. The mummified remains of twelve bodies, indistinguishable in age, lay contorted on the dirt floor around a stone altar.

"Look at these bodies," James said. "They must be at least a hundred years old, but they've been preserved as well as the Egyptians. And without any visible preparation."

"It's amazing," Tess said. "And a little disgusting. If the book is here, let's find it and get out of here."

"Not so fast," James said and knelt down next to one of the corpses. "We've been searching for years, following the history and the path of the book. This is the last known tribe to have possessed it. We need to study every detail that-"

"There it is," Tess proclaimed, pointing to a figure just beyond the altar.

James almost tripped over the body he was examining, dismissing it in favor of the prize. He stepped over the others and leaned over a figure that appeared to have been a man holding an ancient leather-bound book. He grasped the book and pulled on it, but the dead man held firmly. A dry cracking sound resounded in the chamber as the arm was extended away from the body. "He doesn't want to let go," James said, and continued to yank on the book. The corpse's arm tore from the shoulder, and James stood holding the book while the severed limb dangled, still clinging on.

"James…" Tess said, but he wasn't listening.

"Even in death," he said. He snapped off the papery fingers, and the arm dropped to the floor.

"Now let's go," Tess said.

"This is the moment we've been waiting for," James said. "The possibility to change the world."

"It'll be a great discovery. Now let's take it back."

"It's more than that, dear," James said. "In this book is reputed to be a ceremony to return order to the chaos, bring life back into balance. For too long the seven deadly sins have corrupted the world. We can fix all of that."

"What on earth are you talking about?" Tess asked. "You're sounding a little off balance yourself."

James ignored her and gingerly opened the book on the altar. He turned through the pages. "Ahh, I think this is it."

Tess walked around the room, holding her lamp next to the bodies. "What happened to these people?" She set down the lamp and pulled a relic dagger from the chest of one of the corpses. "They seemed to have killed each other."

"I don't recognize the language," James said. "Some of it appears to be Latin. Maybe I can sound it out." He started reading aloud from the book.

A hissing emanated from the hole in the mummified body where the dagger had been, and Tess put her hand over her nose and backed away. She stepped on the arm of another, causing the body to roll up against her calves. She jumped, letting out a little shriek, and the body dropped back down in a puff of dust. Even without eyes, the body appeared to stare at her, and when she directed the lamp toward it, the skin glistened in the light. "James, I don't like this."

But he continued to read the incantation. More gases seeped from the corpses as the taut skin took on color, recomposing itself on the bodies.

"This is crazy," Tess said. "I'm getting out of here. With or without you." She started out, but James spun around and grabbed her arm.

"It's almost done," he said. Tess wriggled in his grasp, but he held tight and finished reading the passage in the book. A thick murky green cloud had almost filled the cavern. Finally Tess jerked free of James, but she looked suddenly confused.

"How do we get out?" she asked, stumbling around the cave, feeling her way around the walls. "Where's the exit?"

"What happened?" James looked around. "I didn't sense any change. Did it work? Where did this haze come from?"

"James?"

"We must get back to the world," James said. "It's the only way we will know if--" He stopped mid-sentence and grabbed his head. Then he dropped to his knees. "Oh, Jesus!" he cried. He dug his fingers into his scalp. "My God, it hurts!" Trails of blood seeped from his nose.

Tess stopped searching the cavern, swaying in place, and looked over at James. She blinked a few times, then swatted the air around her head. James thrashed on his knees, clearing a space in the mist around him. Tess gazed down at her hand and saw that she still held the ancient dagger in her hand. She walked over to James and put her free hand on his head. He stopped shaking and looked up at her with wide eyes.

"Tess?" he gasped.

She plunged the dagger into his neck, and he dropped to the floor. Then she reached down, pulled out the dagger and ran it across her own throat, falling on top of James.

David drew a sharp breath as the fog lifted from the bodies and withdrew from the cavern, back down the passage and out of the cave. In the light of day, it turned to black smoke and drifted up toward the sky. The rest of the hotel room faded completely, replaced by the foliage. Only the sitting corpses remained, their bodies held rigid by walls that were no longer there. David was staring up at the storm clouds filling the sky.

"James Ellison was a fool," Mashart said. "An idealist. He thought he could change the world, but his actions were steeped in selfish motivations. That's how I found him, and I watched and waited for the inevitable. James thought he was *ridding* the world of evil, but when he spoke the words, a passage to your world was opened, and a storm swept across the frozen underworld and carried me out with it."

"And then you came here to take innocent lives back with you to Hell. Like Ann."

"You are right. That's why I escaped hell originally," Mashart lied, "but then I met you and realized a better way."

"You used me. I know what you did in my body."

"You don't know the half of it," Mashart said. "You only know what I have *let* you know. And as far as using your body, you let me in. When you surrendered yourself to me to save that little girl, you gave me dominion over your soul. I *own* you. I will use you however I please. But you weren't so hard to convince. And you did so much of the work for me."

"I didn't kill anyone."

"Not yet."

"Not ever," David growled.

The boy strained to pull his body away from the dead "chair," but when the scenery around them changed, he stopped struggling. The demon knew that David recognized the office that had replaced the jungle. Ed McGinnis sat behind the desk.

"Why do you defend them?" Mashart asked. "Men like Ed McGinnis." The demon pushed up from the legs of his corpse and crossed to the chair across from McGinnis. "After all, he listened eagerly, grinning like a jackal, when we suggested the night security detail, specifically *your* man. He was more than willing to torture Steve Avery, to prey on his fears."

"That wasn't me in that office," David said.

"No, but you did so well from there."

The scene changed, the office replaced by the hotel lounge. The demon took the form of the older carpenter. He looked over at the boy still sitting on the floor, whose eyes widened with realization as the David across the table spoke about curses and blood money, finally ending with, "McGinnis stuck it to you."

"Imagination took over from there," Mashart said, speaking with Steve Avery's voice. "And in the end, I stuck it to Ed McGinnis."

The demon morphed back to David's form. "Of course, I helped it along a little. Never disregard your imaginings. Remember, David?" A black cat wove around the bar stools, and Mashart reached down and stroked the animal. "And then you wrapped it up so nicely on the last day. Telling that lunatic that everything he was thinking was perfectly sane. Nice touch."

"I didn't mean to-" David started, and the demon could almost taste the guilt when the boy dropped his head. Then he looked back up.

"But whether he deserved it or not," David said, "it wasn't just McGinnis punished. Steve will be convicted for the crime. He'll probably spend the rest of his life in jail."

"There's a saying about making an omelet," Mashart said. "But what have you really done? You have freed him."

"By locking him up? I don't call that freedom."

The boy still had a little fight in him, but the demon had expected as much. "I wouldn't exactly call his life before we met him 'freedom,' and that McGinnis was no huge loss. Besides, it was the law of man that put your old friend in his cell, while so many truly guilty walk free. We can change all of that."

"And Jeremy?" David asked. "Is he free now, too?"

"Ahh, Jeremy." The setting changed to the brooding artist's bedroom at the Atlantic, the demon now wearing the flesh of Jeremy Leavitt. The paintings came to life on the canvases. Fire burned through the wilderness. Mechanical elephants with spider-like legs lumbered across a desert wasteland. "You did so well with this one. You set it in motion; I just carried it through. He opened up to you.

He considered you a friend. Jeremy felt bolder because of you. He saw you as someone who had made it through so much and come out alive. He wanted to be strong like you, not to be afraid anymore." Mashart/Jeremy walked over to David, knelt down and began caressing the thigh of the dead woman holding up the boy. "But Jeremy was crazy. He would use the confidence he gained from you to live out the fantasies he had shoved back for his whole life, fantasies that should have stayed where they belonged... in the dark. He had called himself Bane around others. Left to his own devices, he would've lived up to it."

"I don't believe..." David let the words drop, and Mashart saw the look of recollection again.

"But certainly you remember," the demon said. "You sensed it that night when he pulled you out of the hall, when he reached out for you, the night we went out with him to the bar, the same bar where we met William Tifford after Jeremy left to go back to his room and masturbate. By the way, for the first time in his life, he orgasmed to the image of that naked girl pushed face down into the carpet, an idea that had scared him before he met you. You knew what he was capable of. You saw it. It had to be done."

Mashart brought to life the scene from CRD, on the Saturday when everything had happened. In David's guise, he entered William Tifford's phone number into the computer system. The monkey's technology was almost as easy to manipulate as they were. Then he walked over and placed a hand on Jeremy's shoulder.

David was silent for a moment. Then he spoke. "I thought that night in the hall, when he pulled me into his room, when I could see those things about the other people, I thought-"

The demon interrupted. "You thought that it was me."

"Or something. The alcohol, fatigue. Or... I don't know what to believe anymore."

The boy looked away, and the demon knew his plan was working.

"You have a connection to them. They are drawn to you. And you can see their fears."

"But how?" David asked.

"Don't worry about *how*. It is a gift. It is *your* gift. Does it matter from where it comes? What matters is what you do with it. I've come a long way to find you."

"What do you want from me?"

"I'm here to help you. We can help each other."

The demon took on the reflection of the boy, grabbed his arm and pulled him up from the floor as their surroundings changed again. They stood by the blackjack tables in a casino, but the life force had been drained from the gamblers, decaying bodies still pushing chips across the velvet. Only the dealers appeared to be alive, but the black orbs where eyes should've been gave away the secret. The boy's own eyes rolled back in his head as if he was about to drop into a darker, unconscious part of his mind, but the demon slapped his face. "Not yet," he said.

"No more," David said. "I can't take it."

"Just a little longer," Mashart said. "This is the easy part." He pulled David over and sat him at one of the tables. The demon set out a stack of chips. "I escaped Hell to find you." It was as close to the truth as the demon was willing to get. Now he would pound the final spike.

The dead Asian dealer grinned through teeth clamped down on a cigarette and the other players at the table gathered up their chips and rose from the table to leave. The boy just stared ahead.

"The balance is off. I told you that when we first met, and I meant it. But not in Hell. The balance is off in *your* world." Cards spun across the table, stopping in front of the demon, and without taking his eyes off David, he doubled-down. The dealer flipped a two of spades, then turned his own cards. Twenty. Mashart furrowed his brow as the dealer pulled away his chips. The demon saw the boy glance at the turned cards. It was just a glance, but it was enough. Mashart slid out another stack of chips.

"Take a look around," he continued. "Cruel injustice abounds. Decadence is worshipped. *Rewarded,* even. Murderers set free because of minor doubts in the minds of a group of twelve old men and housewives. The laws of man have lost sight of true Justice. You've known this. You can't lie to me. It's why you turned to the wilderness, the wild. You find your truth, your god there, not in some oversized box with a hand crank on the side."

Smoke curled around the dealer's head, but he didn't move until the demon stopped speaking. This time Mashart checked his cards, purposefully concealing them from David. He signaled for the dealer to hit him, and the dealer turned a nine of hearts. "Shit!" Mashart tossed his cards forward, and again the dealer took his money.

"What are you talking about?" David asked, and again the demon saw his eyes follow as Mashart put out more chips.

"James Ellison was a fool," Mashart said again. "He thought he could change the world, but he was wrong. Only you can change the world. *We* can change the world." The dealer dealt the next hand, winning automatically with a blackjack and taking more of the demon's chips. Mashart started to push out another stack, then slid them in front of David instead. "Why don't you give it a try? I'm not having any luck." David stared at the stack, then at the dealer, who narrowed his eyes. David placed the chips on the line, and the cards came out. He won with a blackjack.

"Those should've been mine," Mashart said and clapped the boy on the shoulder. David left the stack of winnings in place, and the dealer spun out new cards. Eighteen. The dealer busted. More chips. David let it ride and won again. He barely glanced over as the demon whispered next to him.

"Success is in your blood," Mashart said. "I've searched a hundred years to find you. You are the last of their hope."

The Asian dealt the boy an ace and a king of hearts. Another Blackjack. More cards. "Huh?" David asked.

Mashart smiled. "Even as you push the monkeys away, they come to you. It's in your blood. Together we can make things right. Form the world as it should be, where the guilty are punished and get what they deserve." The demon knew the boy was barely listening. "There is only one left in the way. The girl."

David flinched, knocking over a stack of chips in the middle of a game. Mashart reached over and flipped his cards, and again the dealer lost.

The boy restacked his winnings with meticulous detail, but instead of being engrossed in the game, the demon sensed that now he purposefully avoided his mirror's gaze. Mashart waved his hand, and the dealer stepped back from the table and bowed his head.

"It's too late," David said. "She's already dead."

"Not yet." Mashart said. He could tell by the subtle reaction in the boy that he believed it. "But you are mistaken if you think she can help you. She doesn't want to help you. Even after you saved her life, surrendering to me, she still wants to see you dead. Her little suicide attempt got her out of that prison of a school. Smart girl, that one. Now she is on her way to try to kill you. Are you going to let her?" The demon saw David's eyes narrow. Again, just a brief moment, but enough. "She is the cause of your suffering. And she's the last connection to your life. Your *old* life. You spared her from death once, and now you know the real reason why. It opened your eyes to your true destiny. You have tortured yourself long enough. Now it is time to move forward. Cut away the albatross. Give up your faith in her. Give up your faith in them all. You were never meant to live like the rest of them. Together we can shear down the wicked."

Finally David turned to face himself.

"You're lying," he said, but the demon wasn't convinced.

"It's you or the girl. You won't be able to sweet talk your way out of this one. She won't quit until you're dead."

"Liar!" David shouted.

Mashart's hand struck out like a rattlesnake around David's throat. In one quick movement, the demon rose from the stool and launched the boy backward in a clutter of chips and cards. They crashed to the floor with Mashart on top. David was no match for the demon, and Mashart tightened the grip around his neck until the room surrounding them started to darken. The boy was losing consciousness.

Mashart let go and lifted himself away from David. He wiped his hands on his jeans and righted a stool.

"I'm sorry, but you just don't listen," Mashart said. "But I think you fight it because you know it is true."

The boy rolled over on his side, coughing. Mashart kicked him in the back, and David cried out.

"Do you feel that pain?" the demon asked. "It isn't me, because I'm not even here. This is all in your mind. You fight against yourself." The bodies of the naked women returned, crawling out from behind the tables and chair, wriggling toward the boy.

"I can see that you're not ready," the demon said, disgusted. "But you will be. And this time, we'll give them a reason to be afraid of your bloodline."

The boy tried to pull himself away, but one of them, a brunette, got a hold of his ankle, and soon the rest caught up, hefting their dead weight on top of him.

David's screaming was muffled under the corpses as the demon pulled out of his mind.

CHAPTER 27

By six a.m., Jeannie had checked out of the motel and was back on the Interstate. She was pleased to find the roads relatively quiet as she drove away from Reno, continuing northeast across the desert. She tried to plan what she would say when she saw David, but there were so many uncertainties that she felt foolish even thinking about it.

The dream from the night before kept coming back to her, just at the edges of her thoughts. She tried to brush it away,

the spreading bloodstain on his shirt

but each time it came back even more vivid. Nor could she shake the fragments of images that she remembered of the multitudes of tortured humanity. Like she had dreamt of Hell itself.

Not far past the Idaho-Nevada border, her father's words from the dream came back to her, the words he had spoken just before freezing into the pond.

Not just a dream.

Jeannie swerved the car as the realization hit her. She almost hit a car trying to pass her. An older man in a Buick. His angry face etched in her mind as he honked at her and sped past, but Jeannie barely noticed. She pulled over onto the shoulder.

The desert around her started to fade as the dream,

not just a dream

as the events of Saturday night came completely back to her. Finally her suicide attempt made sense, even if she didn't understand it at the time. All she had known was that answers to her problems could only be found in death. But she couldn't just die. She had to kill herself.

The desert mountains in the distance blurred and darkened as the sky turned ashen-gray. The cold seeped into the car, and ice webbed out over the windows, the dashboard, the seats. Then the car crumbled, and again Jeannie stood cemented to the frozen lake from her dream from the night before.

Not just a dream.

No. It wasn't. She was remembering what had actually happened.

after I died. The doctor... or whatever... said they brought me back from the dead.

The giant funnel again descended from the black clouds, like a finger pushing down on the fabric of the sky, and suddenly the grinding noises exploded in Jeannie's mind. She grabbed at her head, as if trying to keep it from tearing apart. Then the sounds were gone, and a multitude of voices spoke in unison.

You have come to me, they said. *You heard me calling.*

The tornado touched down, and a bitter-cold gale of wind rolled over Jeannie, freezing her eyelids open. She clutched at her body, but she couldn't stop shaking. The wind blew away the snow, revealing the smooth, frozen surface.

"I've heard you for the past two years," Jeannie chattered. "I just didn't realize."

The twisting, writhing gray form rumbled closer to her. Bodies spun out of the upper part of the swirling mass, flung screaming through the dark sky. Jeannie could only guess they landed somewhere on the "battlefield" she had passed through.

"Why?" she asked.

That answer goes back to the beginning, the voices rumbled. *But your part, your fate, was sealed when the boy offered his life for you.*

Something flashed beneath Jeannie's feet, and she looked down at the ice. Just beneath the surface, the scene from the cabin played out. She saw her younger self, holding the gun that had killed her father, and talking to David, but the voice didn't belong to her. Jeannie realized it was what had happened in the cabin when she was unconscious, when she had been possessed.

"...And your last sacrifice," the girl from the past said, "your silly attempt at salvation will make it that much better." The girl from the past walked over to David. "But you have to do it yourself. Give yourself freely to me." She held the revolver in her palm. David stretched out his own hand.

The ice turned clouded again.

Mashart should have known, but his ignorance will be his demise. Only one other of the blood since the beginning has offered his own life to save another.

Suddenly, the cacophony of cries coming from behind Jeannie took shape. Two words stood out. Or maybe they had been screaming it all along. Two words, over and over. "The Seed!"

Then the screams erupted back into chaos.

When Mashart spoke the ritual through the lips of the living bloodline, a passage between the worlds was opened, and the boy carried you through, carried you here, sealing your fate. Now you have returned. We want Mashart back. We've been waiting for you to fulfill this. The boy surrendered his soul for you, and you are the one to finish it.

"I don't under-"

The ice flashed again, and beneath the crust Jeannie saw the silhouette of three crosses on a hill. Bodies hung motionless from them. Again the tormented cries took form again. "The Seed! The Seed that Didn't Die!" Below Jeannie, the scene changed to a Middle Eastern woman on the earthen floor of her home. She had just given birth to a child. Although his skin was much darker, and the infant's hair black, the eyes looked just like David's. The words that Barbara Stack spoke in Jeannie's bedroom just before killing herself came back to her.

"...and he's a special one, he is. He's the last, you know."

Jeannie shook her head slowly as a flood of questions threatened to drown her. She had heard the stories in Sunday school. Had they all been lies?

Yes.

The shrieks of the damned rose to a fevered pitch.

Mashart has killed almost all of your god's bloodline in your world, thousands over the past hundred years, but he is foolish and wrong. The scales must tip both ways.

Jeannie's head reeled. She wanted to put her hands over her ears to stop the voices, but still they continued.

At times there is more good than evil in the world. Other times, the dark side is just a little darker. And that little candle can't keep up with the fires of Hell. But now Mashart risks everything.

Under the ice, the baby's face morphed, growing older, fairer skinned. Scars formed over the right side of the face. David. A hush fell over the pits of Hell.

The only one of you we can't understand. The rest of you are open books, your fears splayed out on your faces. But we don't understand the boy. We don't know if he can fight Mashart. We don't know if he wants to fight anymore. He doesn't know of his true nature, his birthright. The boy doesn't know the strength he possesses, but Mashart does. And the demon corrodes the boy's conviction and compassion. You are the last link to his heart. Mashart dreams of his grip around your throat. We think the boy is almost convinced, and if the progeny of The Seed willingly serves Death, it will set into motion the end of all existence.

Jeannie's ears exploded as the air pressure plummeted. She clutched her head and dropped to her knees, but her feet wouldn't tear completely away from the ice, and she fell forward on the frozen lake. Pins of ice shot up, stabbing her.

The death of all of your kind.

The air continued to thin, and her chest felt like it was expanding, pushing to escape the cage of her ribs. Pounding racked inside her head.

Are you ready to die again?

"What... do you... want?" she gasped.

The ice cleared beneath her, and Jeannie saw herself scrambling around in the weeds in front of her family's cabin, looking for something. Wind whipped the hair around her face. Someone shouted her name above the gale, and her eyes widened, her searching more frantic, until she grasped something black. She pulled a long dagger from the dead grasses, and turned around. David ran toward her.

The ice clouded, and the air around Jeannie returned to normal, warmer even. She drew a deep breath, the pounding subsided, and she was able to lift herself back to her feet.

Which brings us back to you.

Again, the first scene from the cabin appeared beneath her. "Take me," David said. "But leave the girl."

He did it for you, child. You set it into motion, and now you have to end it.

"What do you want?" Jeannie asked, but she already knew. The voices answered her true question instead.

There is no other way. Mashart can only be defeated in the body of one of the bloodline. The demon must be expelled with the blood. Then we will take him back where he belongs. Your god has his tests. We have our tricks.

Jeannie started to say something, but a loud groaning from beneath silenced her protest. A spider web crack radiated out from where she stood. Loud snapping sounded under her feet. And yes, it definitely felt noticeably warmer. Jeannie heard another voice, a male, coming from somewhere outside her head.

"...took these pills... heart stopped..."

The man's voice sounded close, but no one else stood on the frozen plain.

It's happening already. In Heaven, the angels fall with frozen wings. No time for discussion. Time for you to go back. You have succeeded in the first step. A smart girl, indeed.

A bolt of lightning shot from the twisting clouds, striking Jeannie in the chest. Her vision flashed white, and she heard another voice. A woman this time. "Let's try again."

Jeannie blinked a couple of times, stunned and staggering on the ice. The swirling maelstrom sparked in front of her.

"Clear!" The woman again.

Another bolt of lightning crashed into Jeannie. Again she saw white, but with movement this time. The frozen landscape blurred into huge faces looming over her, the paramedics who must have yanked her back from death. The gray tornado retreated into the thunderheads until the scene disappeared entirely.

Jeannie sat in the car on the side of the highway and took a shaky breath. A semi-trailer roared past her, rocking the car, and she let out a shriek. Jeannie steadied herself, then reached up and touched the tender spots above her breasts where the defibrillator had brought her back. It had worked.

But dear God, what had she brought back with her?

A hundred questions and possibilities rushed her mind, almost too much for her to bear. Where to start? Which beginning? For Jeannie, it had all started with the desire to avenge the death of her parents, but that had all changed as of this moment.

She didn't want to have to bear the load of the future of mankind. She didn't think she could. Especially if it meant killing the one who possibly possessed all of their hopes. The last one.

We've been waiting for you to fulfill this. You are the one.

She wondered if it could really be true, but suddenly there didn't seem to be any other possible explanation for the past two years. She didn't know what to believe anymore. David, the scarred messiah?

Her own death at his hands? Or his by Jeannie's. Even if it meant freeing him from his torment, the idea of murdering another person had been hard enough to reckon with when she thought David was only human. But now...

A variety of scenarios blurred together in her imagination, seeming like everything from Creation to Armageddon. Suddenly the world around her started spinning. Jeannie fumbled with the door handle and lurched out of the Subaru. She staggered to the other side, dropped to her knees in the sand and short brush, and fought the nausea.

She focused on the earth below her until the moment passed, then she looked up. When she did, she saw the sign, maybe half the size of a commercial billboard. Wooden and hand painted, about sixty yards in front of her. Black letters in sharp contrast with a white-washed background.

Only 3 more miles 'til Buck's Shop or Drop.
We buy, sell, or trade almost ANYTHING!
Just off the next exit.

Jeannie didn't know where all of this was heading, but she had been foolish to think that the stolen scalpel would be sufficient protection. She stood and brushed herself off, then returned to the driver's seat and pulled back onto the highway. A few scattered houses appeared, and when she saw the clump of businesses coming up in the distance, she signaled and took the exit.

She drove down two blocks of what appeared to be a "downtown" until she found the pawn shop. Sandwiched in between a Christian bookstore and a corner drugstore, Buck's Shop or Drop had a maroon awning with white block letters making the same claim as the billboard.

She parked the car, stepped out and studied the store before going inside. A flaking painted scene on the windows depicted a cartoon deer hiding from an Elmer Fudd-like character in bright orange fatigues. *Get your hunting gear here!* was written above the cartoon. Jeannie attempted to peer in the windows, but the store appeared to be so full that they had stacked shelves against all available walls, including the front windows. The glare of the sun off the dusty windows, combined with the piles of shoes and radios and unidentified electronic paraphernalia shelved just on the other side, blocked out what Jeannie felt confident to be certain treasures inside.

She pushed open the glass door, knocking the bell hanging over the threshold. Even with the fluorescent tubes hanging from the open beamed two-story ceiling, the place still seemed dark. The sun barely filtered through the narrow spaces between the shelves lining the windows from floor to ceiling, diffused even further by a swirling cloud of dust when Jeannie let the door swing shut behind her.

A large black man stood behind the cash register talking to a white guy half his size wearing a cowboy hat. The smaller guy barely managed to hold himself up by the counter. They both paused to look at Jeannie when the she walked in, but were quick to go back to their business.

The little guy took a step forward, got his balance and pushed the tip of his cowboy hat back on his head. "C'mon, Big Jake, jus' this once." He drew out the ends of his words in a drunken slur.

The guy behind the cash register stepped back, waving his hand in front of his face. "Damn, Carl, how many times I gotta tell you? We buy *almost* anything. Bring me something that's worth half a shit." He picked up a cheap 35mm camera off the counter, scrunched up his face and examined it. The little guy watched him anxiously and sighed when "Big Jake" set it back down on the counter and shook his head. "I already got more televisions, cameras and alarm clocks than I know what do with," he said, "and most of 'em fetch more than this shit you bring me every week."

Jeannie turned away from the interaction and examined the wall of things nearest to her. She couldn't discern any specific order to the items on the shelves. Power tools were stacked next to stereo turntables, which were stacked next to lamps which were next to kitchen goods. Jeannie wandered through the narrow aisles, inspecting hundreds of pieces of other people's goods. She wondered how many of the owners brought in their wares believing they would eventually buy them back. Maybe they would forget they sold it in the first place. Someone like the intoxicated Carl, who she heard stumble out of the store in defeat.

Jeannie turned a corner and a giggle escaped her when she saw the display in front of her. One whole section of the back wall had been dedicated to Elvis Presley. Everything from signed photographs of the King to velvet paintings. There was even a life-sized cutout of Elvis from his younger days. He was holding the guitar with his knees bent together, his left foot kicked back on his toes, his signature stance. The more expensive items were locked behind a glass case on the wall. Elvis trading cards, collectible Zippo lighters and even knives. A handwritten sign tacked on the wall next to the case read, *Ask us about our Elvis costume rentals.*

Someone spoke behind Jeannie. "The owner's a big fan."

She spun around in surprise. For the size of the man, she was surprised she hadn't heard him walk up. He stood almost a foot taller than Jeannie, wearing a t-shirt pulled tight over his large frame with *Ricks College Athletics* stretched across the front. He reached past her and picked up an Elvis alarm clock and examined the curiosity in his large hand. "He's been collecting this stuff for over twenty years now."

"So I'm guessing you're not Buck," Jeannie said.

"Jake," the big man said. "And I'm guessing that you're not here looking for the Jailhouse Rock bobble head doll," the man said and set down the clock. Jeannie smiled and shook her head.

"In a place like this," Jake said, "you'll probably find what you're looking for faster if you ask me."

Jeannie had already guessed that what she needed was under the glass of the front counter. "What's the waiting period on a handgun?"

Jake raised his eyebrows and looked over Jeannie. Then he nodded. "Why don't you come look at what we've got?"

Jeannie followed him to the front counter. He squeezed through the narrow opening by the cash register and took the small step up behind the counter, giving him another few inches over Jeannie. A small television mounted on the wall behind the counter was playing a football game with the volume turned low.

"There's actually no waiting period in Idaho," Jake said, "and the law says that we don't have to run a background check since we're not a licensed dealer. Hell, you don't even need to register it."

Jeannie bent over the glass display case and looked through at the assortment of handguns, most of which were unfamiliar to her. She had heard of the .357 Magnum and recognized the .38 Special as the gun carried by law enforcement. One of the bulkier guns, the 9 mm Glock, she recognized from talking with a few of the tougher girls at the Rose House.

Jake followed along with her on the other side of the counter as she looked. "At first," he said, "Buck wanted to run state background checks, stay a little more reputable, you know? But the feds wanted to charge him something like ninety bucks a pop, so he said screw it. Pardon my French. You gotta be eighteen, though."

Even if she had been old enough, seeing the handguns laid out in front of her, Jeannie decided against it. She just didn't know enough about them and wasn't about to ask this guy what caliber she needed to stop a man. Since he had been wise enough to keep up conversation without directly asking *why* she needed the weapon, she surmised that he must have seen a few days in the pawn shop. Besides that, Jeannie had too much of a history with guns already. While she wanted to feel safe, she wasn't sure handling a gun for the first time since that afternoon in the cabin was the answer.

Where the guns ended, the next case held a rack with four Samurai swords laid across it. Each one had a different ornate sheath. One was wrapped in what looked to be snake skin, while another was made of finely polished wood painted red with black Japanese script running the entire length. An array of other decorated swords had been arranged very symmetrically on the red felt-lined bottom of the case.

"Yeah, he's kinda into that stuff, too," Jake said. "I think he actually bought most of that collection off one of them home shopping shows."

The rest of the knives were in the next two cases. Everything from smaller three-inch blades with black plastic handles to the longer hunting knives with a curved blade on one side and a serrated edge on the other.

Jake leaned sideways against the sword case and pretended to watch the football game, but Jeannie caught him watching her out of the corner of his eye. She was about to leave when she saw the dagger. A straight seven-inch blade, honed on each side, with a black handle, placed on a leather sheath that had two short nylon straps attached to it with clips on each end.

"Can I look at this one?" she asked.

Jake walked over and pulled out the dagger, setting it on top of the sheath on the glass counter. There wasn't anything special about the knife, but Jeannie knew it was the same one she had seen herself wielding at the cabin.

Jake flipped the tag. "Seventeen dollars with the sheath. A pretty good deal."

Jeannie didn't pick up the dagger just yet. She looked at the straps on the sheath. She couldn't imagine how it would fit around anyone's waist. A child's maybe, but that couldn't be right.

"What are the straps for?"

"They wrap around your upper thigh," Jake said. "You wear it there so you can get to it easier than a normal belt sheath."

"That's the one," Jeannie said.

Jake stuck the blade in the sheath, carried it over to the register and started punching keys. "You know, I heard once that the first thing police look for in a stabbing death is the direction of the wounds," he said. "That'll be seventeen dollars with tax."

Jeannie handed him a credit card. He swiped it and handed it back to her, and then he bagged her purchase. "Yep," he continued, still holding on to the bag. "Most of the time if the stab wounds go down." -- he imitated the motion of raising his arm, bent at the elbow and bringing down his fist-- "they say chances are it's a woman. But if the wounds go up or straight in, it's usually a man striking from the hip."

"Hmm," Jeannie said and wondered how far he planned on taking this discourse.

The credit card machine beeped a couple times, and a paper receipt printed out. Jake tore it off and handed it to Jeannie to sign while he leaned forward, propping himself on the counter with his huge hands. "But I don't suppose that's anything a pretty young lady like yourself needs to worry about."

Jeannie looked up at him. He was smiling, but she could see the seriousness in his eyes. "It's a tough world," she said and handed the signed receipt back to him.

"Maybe so." He handed her the bag. "You be careful with that thing."

Jeannie left the pawn shop and got in the car, tossing the bag on the back seat. She started the engine and picked up the map. For the tenth time today, she added up the mileage, then pulled away from the storefront. She would be at the cabin before sunset.

She drove north as the late summer sun cut across the sky.

CHAPTER 28

At her home across town from the Atlantic, Kate Osbourne prepped a salad to go along with the chicken marsala that Mary Rose had cooked. Even though, Joan Baez sang in the background, and candles were lit around the dining room and living room, it just didn't feel right tonight. It felt like they were trying too hard, and when Kate felt like that, it usually meant she shouldn't be trying at all. It meant M.R. needed her space.

Tuesdays were supposed to be their date night, but that day at work had seemed more like another Monday, souring her mood, and when Mary Rose suggested they do dinner at the Atlantic, Kate almost called the whole thing off. She suspected that the only reason Mary Rose wanted to eat at her place was so she could keep a watch out, make sure that she was there if David showed up. Kate wanted to believe that her partner just had a flair for the dramatic and liked to be in the middle of the action, but she couldn't help thinking that M.R. wanted to be there so she could call the police and turn him in if she saw him. That just didn't seem right to Kate. And after what happened with Jeremy Leavitt, it gave her the creeps being over there.

Beyond that, she wasn't nearly as convinced as her partner that David was to blame for all the strange things going on in town recently. She didn't understand why M.R. hated David so much. Well, hate was a strong word, but ever since he had moved in, Mary Rose had nothing but biting comments and general condemnations seemingly just because he was a… well, a "he." Kate knew that her partner had a rough childhood, even the fact that M.R. suspected her mother had tampered with the brakes of her abusive alcoholic father's truck on the night they left. And from the stories she had heard, Kate couldn't blame Ruth Mulaney. But she couldn't blame David, either, just because he had been in Hawaii and had been seen with Jeremy a few times.

More than that, for some reason, Kate felt the urge to protect him. David had clearly seen his fair share of trouble, but she didn't think he had been the cause of it. Some people just attracted bad luck. But beyond her instinct was something she didn't understand at all. Whenever he had been around her, Kate couldn't help getting flushed. Not attraction necessarily. Kate Osbourne hadn't been with a man since "The Mistake" in high school. But on the few occasions she had crossed paths with David, she almost felt like a kid. Like she wanted to impress him, say the right things to sound like an educated adult, like she was "cool," even though he was probably six or seven years younger. Maybe it was because he spoke so rarely to anyone, but whatever it was, Kate hoped that she could be the one for whom he'd open up.

Kate thought Mary Rose felt much the same way. She had even seen her partner blush at the mention of David not long after he moved in. But in M.R.'s case, it had turned to anger. Kate knew that she prided herself on her strength and independence, but lately Mary Rose's attitude seemed to be that anyone in pain, especially David, obviously did something to bring it on themselves.

Kate had never seen this side of M.R. before. She didn't understand it, and she didn't care for it.

And she almost cut off the tip of her finger for the salad because she couldn't stop thinking about it *now*. She knew they should've waited on tonight. Things were just too weird, right now.

Mary Rose sat at the table in the dining nook with a glass of wine. She had her eyes closed, pretending to be concentrating on the music, but Kate knew it was just her way of avoiding eye contact.

"Damn!" Kate said, and M.R. opened her eyes.

"What's the matter?"

"Oh, nothing," Kate said. "I just almost added a little finger to the tomatoes."

"Be careful, sweetie," Mary Rose said. "You know how much I like your fingers."

And that was when it happened. The moment when Kate decided it was probably over between her and M.R. They say every broken relationship has this point, when one or both people have a moment of clarity. Kate tried to brush it away. Certainly she was just having one of her moods, and the weather wasn't helping. It had been almost a week since the sun had broken through the clouds in the valley, but no rain. Just the wind.

As if reading her mind, Mary Rose chimed in. "I heard that something big is blowing in."

"Hmm."

"Of course, you never know around here, right? It might just be blowing over us."

Kate scraped the tomatoes over the salad. "I think we're about ready."

Neither of them spoke as they dished up their dinner and sat down at the table.

"How was work?" Mary Rose asked after a few minutes.

"Fine," Kate said, concentrating on her plate.

"Did you get that account for Rugged J Construction?"

"We don't know yet."

"Are you planning on being this grumpy all night?"

"Excuse me?"

Mary Rose set down her fork. "Are you still pissed because of what I said about David?"

Kate took the last swallow from her wine and refilled the glass. "I just don't understand why you dislike him so much. What did he do to you?"

"He didn't *do* anything that I know for sure," Mary Rose said. "But I don't trust him. Things haven't been right since he's been around. I mean, he knew that Avery guy in Hawaii. And he was all chummy with Jeremy."

"They're completely different incidents," Kate said. "Steve Avery murdered someone, and Jeremy Leavitt was murdered."

"My God, are you listening to yourself?" Mary Rose asked. "Why are we even talking about murder? Because of David. Because of two people he knew, and it doesn't seem like he knew that many people to begin with. I'd be a little worried to be around him."

"People die all the time. Are you going to say that they are all because of him?"

"I might," Mary Rose said, "if he knew them. His little disappearance sure isn't helping his case. And what do you think happened to him, anyway? Before he came to Missoula? We still don't know, but clearly it was something pretty fucking bad."

Kate started to respond, then changed her mind. "I think we should just eat our dinner," she said instead.

The wind howled outside the house, flickering a couple candles on the windowsill and reminding Kate that the old house could use new windows. Lightning flashed somewhere, and she waited for the thunder, but it never came. She hoped they would at least get a little rain out of this wind. It had been a dry winter and spring, and the newscasters were already talking about wildfires.

Kate let her mind wander over these things to distract her from the immediate. Neither woman spoke, and Kate only made it about a third of the way through her dinner before setting down her fork and deciding that the wine could finish things off. She saw that M.R. hadn't made it much further.

The last meal.

The random thought caught her off guard, but she disregarded it as exactly that, random. And a little brooding. She always got weird when the weather was bad.

Mary Rose reached across the table and put her hand on Kate's. "I'm sorry."

"It's okay," Kate said, even though she wasn't sure of the reason for her partner's apology.

"I don't hate him," Mary Rose said. "In fact, I want to like him. And it's almost as if, I want him to like *me*. It drives me crazy, especially considering the fact that I've tried my best to develop a sense of apathy when it comes to men's opinions."

Kate realized that she had been right about M.R., and she softened, taking her partner's hand in both of hers. "I know what you mean. I feel the same way about him."

"I knew you had a crush on him," Mary Rose said and grinned.

Kate faked a scowl, then leaned over and kissed her. She still loved M.R. It definitely had to be the weather. She stood and picked up the plate. "No offense," she said, looking at her unfinished dinner. "It was delicious."

"That's okay. I'm not that hungry, either. You should take the leftovers to work."

Kate pulled a plastic container out of a drawer and scraped the rest of her dinner into it. "What would you have done if we had dinner at your place, and we saw him?"

Mary Rose took a sip of her wine. "I don't know," she said. "The right thing to do would be to call the police." Kate started to protest, but Mary Rose cut her off. "And not just because he's a man, so don't even say it. If he's not guilty of anything, he'll be fine."

"All of us are guilty of *something*," Kate muttered, even though she agreed that if David was innocent, he wasn't helping his case by avoiding the police.

"But there's another reason," Mary Rose said. "Much as I wish I could deny those times when I wish I knew everything about him, when I wished that he felt like he could trust me enough to tell me. But there are also times, when I'm absolutely terrified of what he might say. Terrified of him in general. And those times I think we'd be a lot safer if he were locked up."

Kate didn't argue, but she didn't completely agree. Deep down, she was a little afraid of David, as well. But she didn't think a cage was the answer.

Thunder cracked outside, startling Kate, followed almost immediately by a knock at the door. The hair rose on the back of her neck, and she thought back on a science lesson from grade school about lightning. She had to resist the urge to drop as low to the floor as possible.

The two women stared at the door for a moment before Kate detached her feet from her place on the kitchen tile and went to answer it.

"Katie-" Mary Rose started, but Kate opened the door.

The porch light had burned out a week earlier, and the steps were dark. Someone stood just beyond the light cast from the house, but she didn't have to see the face to know.

"David," she said.

Then he stepped into the light, and she saw his eyes. And she saw what he held in his hand.

Lightning flashed, followed too closely by thunder, knocking out the power at the same instant that Kate was knocked backward. She came down hard on the tile, hitting her head, and blackness closed in.

* * *

Father Jimmy woke the next morning from a horrible dream. He had been standing on a platform in Caras Park. His congregation was all there, and more, it seemed. They filled the space under the pavilion. He had been pleased to see so many there to hear the Word of God, but when Father Jimmy tried to speak, his voice wouldn't come. Then the skies went dark, and the Angel of Death descended with wings as black as tar. But the angel had no head, and as it swept over the throngs of people, its scythe cleaved the parishioners' heads from their bodies, which dropped to the ground.

Father Jimmy woke just as the angel was raising the scythe before him.

At least he had slept last night, and for that he was thankful. But little else had made him happy since the previous Sunday. Something miraculous had happened that day in his office, but it hadn't been the miracle the priest was expecting. While the proof of the existence of evil only served to reinforce his convictions about the existence of holiness, it didn't necessarily mean that he wanted to be a part of that evil. Father Jimmy had seen enough in Vietnam to last him a lifetime, but instead of a choir of heavenly hosts proclaiming the glory of God some morning while he was sitting in the chapel with a cup of coffee, he had seen the mysteries surrounding recent horrific events unraveled before him in some sort of vision, as if he had taken part in the act himself.

But he *hadn't* really been there, not in the hallway of the apartments. David had, though. Of that fact Father Jimmy was certain. David had stood at the end of the hall while William Tifford shot the Leavitt boy. But why? And if he was involved, why would he show Father Jimmy?

The priest sat up in bed and rubbed his palms hard against his eyes as if to push out the images still fresh from the nightmare. He reached for his glass of water on the nightstand and took a drink.

But it wasn't David that night.

This was the thought which had tormented him the past few days. As a man of flesh, he wanted to believe that the lines weren't as clearly drawn between black and white, the darkness and the light, but every other part of being a man of the cloth told him that those lines had to be drawn *somewhere*, and whatever was going on, David definitely seemed pretty far past the blurry part.

But something in Father Jimmy sensed it wasn't evil *in* the boy, but rather *in control* of him. When David had lifted himself from the floor of the chapel after crashing into the pews, Father Jimmy saw something different in his eyes, something which made the priest back away and let the young man walk out of the building. The Episcopalian church definitely didn't make a habit of discussing possession or the rite of exorcism, and David didn't exactly act like the little girl from that movie, but something was definitely happening. More than just a deranged young man, when Father Jimmy suddenly found himself transported to the hallway of the Atlantic Hotel, it seemed like David, the *real* David who had been sitting in the office chair, was witnessing the events for the first time as well.

Father Jimmy swung his legs over the side of the bed and crossed to the window of the house which he rented across from his church. It wasn't yet seven a.m., but he could already see that it would probably be another day without the sun. The clouds hung low and unmoving in the grey morning sky. He looked across the street at his church. Suddenly it looked so small. He wished for strong pillars and thick panes of leaded stained glass rising up from a foundation older than himself. The 1970's converted house just seemed so vulnerable considering the things he had witnessed lately.

But what to do about it? What to do about David? The priest had no expertise in this arena. No practical experience had prepared him. He had been given these visions, and for some reason David had chosen to come to him for help. But he still didn't know his own role, if he was supposed to bring the boy back to the light or for the sake of his own safety, steer as clear away as possible. He wanted to believe that he could help David, help him back to grace, but he wasn't sure he could tread the dark waters on the other side to find him.

He just didn't know what to do, and in times of uncertainty, Father Jimmy had to fall back on the strength of his faith, his chosen path in life. Service in the name of the Lord. He was more than a little scared, but at the same time, he felt exhilarated. It was the most excitement he'd seen since taking the vows.

He got dressed in his jogging suit and slipped on his running shoes. Exercise always helped focus his thoughts, and he hadn't done anything along those lines since Sunday. His nights had been so restless that it was all he could do to drag himself through the day.

He stretched in his living room, stuffed an energy bar in his jacket pocket and left the house. He took a different path than normal, heading toward the university. It was quiet this time of day, and he cut across the campus, taking the footbridge over the Clark Fork into town. Five minutes later, he found himself in front of the Circle Square Pawn Shop, and he stopped to catch his breath. Next to the entrance of the shop was a wooden door with a center glass panel. The panel had been painted with some artist's abstract vision. Father Jimmy thought that the entrance to the Atlantic Hotel depicted either a rose garden or some sort of massacre. Given the recent events, he preferred to imagine the former.

He didn't know why he had come here. He doubted David would show up at the one place the police were likely to be watching. The newspapers hadn't directly said that the authorities suspected him of any wrongdoing regarding Jeremy Leavitt, but apparently the manager, Kate Osbourne's partner, had insinuated that he was a suspicious character with whom they should probably speak. She also pointed out that he had worked with that construction crew in Hawaii, where the older carpenter had killed his supervisor.

However, Father Jimmy didn't necessarily believe this was enough reason for the police to be staking out the place. Maybe David would come back. He could be inside right now, having snuck back to his room. Maybe it was fated that they should be in the same place at the same time, this exact moment, even if the priest had pushed "fate" a little.

He was looking at the door that led upstairs to the Atlantic, considering his options, when something floated down in front of him. He looked down at the sidewalk just as a light breeze blew the black feather away. Two more fluttered down to the cement. Father Jimmy shivered. He didn't really want to look up, but he did anyway and gasped at what he saw. Strung from the roof about twenty feet up was a dressmaker's dummy, painted black. Mannequin arms had been attached with black feathers glued to them. The arms were pulled out in the form of the Crucifixion. But it was the head, what appeared to be a real woman's head propped on the shoulders, that made Father Jimmy stumble back.

Someone shrieked behind him, and he spun around. A woman in a business suit and heavy coat stood looking up as well, her hand clutching her mouth. She looked down at the priest, her eyes wide.

Then she fumbled with her bag, pulling out a cell phone. She stared at it, as if wondering how to operate it, then dialed 9-1-1.

Father Jimmy blinked a couple times, then looked back up. The only thing missing from his dream was the scythe. As another feather dropped and was caught up in the wind, he staggered another couple of steps away. Then he turned and ran the other direction. He heard the woman with the phone holler for him to stop, but he kept running.

He knew how guilty he must look, but he didn't stop until he was in front of his house. He doubled over, gasping, and almost fell onto his lawn. Nausea came and then passed, and when his head stopped spinning, Father Jimmy straightened up. He started toward his front door, but stopped when he noticed an unfamiliar vehicle parked in the church driveway. A green Jeep covered in bumper stickers. He walked a few steps down the sidewalk to get a better view. The jeep was empty. No one stood in the driveway.

Father Jimmy kept his eyes on the church windows for some sort of movement as he crossed the street, but all of the blinds were pulled. He tried to remember if he had left them that way. The closer he came to the church, the more his hackles raised. This felt like an ambush. He had felt this way before, walking through the jungles of Vietnam. Today he had even less cover. But just as he didn't have a choice then, he knew he had to go now. David... or something... was waiting in the church for him. He treaded lightly down the driveway, thankful for the wind to hopefully cover the movement in the otherwise quiet neighborhood.

He paused only long enough by the Jeep to scan a couple of the bumper stickers, familiar slogans on bumpers around Missoula. *Love your Mother*, with a picture of the Earth. *Save the Clark Fork*. A pink triangle.

Under normal circumstances, Father Jimmy might have even chuckled at the sticker which read, *Eve was framed*. Instead he kept moving, thinking he might've seen this Jeep after all. He followed the driveway and checked behind the church. When he didn't see anyone, he crept to the side door. The spare key was lodged in the handle, and Father Jimmy could've smacked himself. Granted, putting the key underneath the planter by the door wasn't the greatest security measure, but he really only had it there as an extra in case he lost his own.

He opened the door, remembering a split second too late about the squeaky hinges on the door. He might as well have just walked in and hollered, "I'm here!" Now the priest really wished for a cathedral, with the high-rising, open spaces, as opposed to the tight, turning hallways of the old house.

Even though he felt confident that he wasn't alone, Father Jimmy resisted the temptation to search out a weapon. If he needed anything to defend himself, God would have to be strong enough.

Still, he made his way quietly, remembering the age of the house this time and avoiding the familiar creaks in the floorboards. He made it to the rear doors of the chapel without any surprises, but when he looked into the large room, he saw someone sitting in the pews facing away, with his head down.

Father Jimmy realized he wasn't ready to go in. He had been so preoccupied with sneaking in that now that he stood at the threshold, he couldn't think of what he might possibly say... or have to do. He started to step back from the chapel, but he froze when the person spoke.

"He isn't listening." David lifted his head and looked up at the wooden crucifix. "Why don't they listen?"

Father Jimmy stepped forward. "God is always listening," he said.

David didn't turn around. "And when I see only one set of footprints, that's when He's carrying me, right?"

Father Jimmy sensed the sarcasm in the question. "David, are you okay?"

"Depends on your definition of 'okay'."

"The police are looking for you. Where have you been?"

"I've been to Hell... Or Las Vegas. Whatever you want to call it."

Father Jimmy's skin crawled. At that moment, he wished he could be anywhere else besides standing in the chapel, and he was ashamed of himself. He tried to draw on his faith, but apparently that bucket had a hole in it, and it must have drained while he carried it through the church. Suddenly he felt very alone, and he could only hope that the idea David had just mocked was true. He hoped God carried him now.

"Have you been to your apartment?" the priest asked.

David finally stood up from the pew and turned around. A large army surplus coat hung on his skeletal frame. He looked even worse than he had on Sunday. "Have *you*?" he asked. "Did you go there looking for me?"

Father Jimmy hadn't intended to lay all of his cards on the table, but his creativity failed him. "I was worried about you." And now, after seeing the abomination hanging from the outside the hotel, he was a little worried about *himself*. "I think we need to finish that talk we started on Sunday. I think I'm ready if you are."

David narrowed his eyes. "Ready for what?" He took a step closer, and Father Jimmy resisted the urge to take a step back. "You've seen these things, haven't you, Father? You were there, too. You know what I've done."

Father Jimmy had never believed that confession should be confined to a little box during a specified time of day, but he wasn't ready for this one. Even though he had suspected as much, to hear it outright when before he only *suspected* that David had been involved somehow, changed the course of the conversation. But again he wondered if it was really David. He really looked into the young man's eyes, but realized he wasn't sure what he was looking for. Maybe fear had caused him to imagine the malice he had sensed in David on the previous Sunday.

"I think you need help, David."

"Are you going to betray me?" Another step closer.

"What are you talking about?"

"Goddammit, old man!" he shouted. "You know *exactly* what I'm talking about. Have you already called the police?"

This time Father Jimmy did step back. David's shoulders dropped, and he shrank back as well. He bumped into a pew, then sat heavily. He lowered his head. "I'm sorry," he said. "It's just this anger. Sometimes I can't control it. It scares me, Father." He paused, wringing his hands in his lap. "Sometimes I think even when I'm in control, I'm *not* in control. Like I've let it get inside me. And during those moments I wonder, 'Shouldn't I be able to be in control *somewhat*?' It's my body, goddammit. My free will. Shouldn't I be able to control *something*?"

Father Jimmy moved down the aisle, stopping on the other side ahead of David. What did he have left to lose? "How can I help you, my son?"

David looked up forlornly. "You can tell me where your god is." He pulled a Bible from the back of the pew in front of him. "I know you can tell me where He is in *this*, but where is He now?"

"God is with you always."

"You're wrong. If there is a God, *He* has been anywhere *but* with me for a long time."

Father Jimmy sighed and shook his head. "I don't know what has happened to you, David. Or even what you might have done to others. That's not important now. You can make a difference now. The Lord can help you. He's been with you all this time, just waiting for you to ask."

"Waiting!" he said and laughed. "How stupid of me. All of this time, and all I had to do was ask for help."

David stood up and moved as if he was going to leave.

"Wait, David," Father Jimmy said. "I can help you." He put his hand on David's arm, unafraid this time of the visions he might see. "God can help you."

David jerked his arm away and spun around. "God can help?" he asked and advanced toward the priest. "Your God isn't here today. But I am."

And there it was, the look Father Jimmy had seen before. David backed him toward the pulpit, continuing, "I am the light. But my light comes from the flames."

"David?"

"Do you really believe that God will do anything to help? Where was *God* when all of this started? Why hasn't *God* stopped all of these things, prevented the things I've seen and been a part of, but have been too weak to prevent myself?" He reached into the pocket of the large coat. "Too pitifully weak."

When David pulled his hand out of the coat, Father Jimmy saw a glint of light reflect off metal, and his first thought was *knife*. Then he saw the blue handle and realized what David actually held. It was his own gardening spade. It looked much sharper than when Father Jimmy had used it last. And was that dried blood?

At that point, the priest realized his stupid mistake. There were two exits out of the chapel, but David was blocking both of them. His mind raced for anything that he could use as a weapon, but the best he could come up with was a candle holder. He cursed for the first time in eight years. "Shit."

"Where was your god then?" David asked. "Where was he to save an innocent boy from the fires of hell? And where is he now to save you?"

David lunged forward, and Father Jimmy felt a burning sensation as the well honed tool found its target in his belly. He sucked in air, and then he felt a yanking from his stomach as David pulled the spade out. All of the priest's energy seemed to spill out with the tool, and he dropped to his knees, crumpling forward.

David knocked him on his side and leapt on top of him, with his hands around the priest's throat. Father Jimmy was too stunned by the stabbing, and his resistance was draining with his blood. He was rapidly surrendering to the unknown.

Then David jumped up and backed away, gasping and staring at his hands. Father Jimmy lifted his head from the carpet, but no words came. David looked down at him in frightened confusion, then he turned and ran out of the church.

CHAPTER 29

Jeannie bolted awake, lunging upright and knocking her head on the inside roof of Dr. Brandt's car as the last images of the dream shredded away.

The stabbing of the priest had really happened. Of that she felt certain.

Father Jimmy, Jeannie thought. *His name was Father Jimmy.* Her stomach balled up in pain, and she wanted to cry for the man who looked so kind, but she pushed it away. It was getting easier to do. Dr. Brandt would probably have something to say about that if she made it out of this.

That's when *I make it out of this.*

She rubbed her heavy eyelids, feeling sticky and dirty. Parked in front of the cabin, Jeannie barely slept during her first night back in Montana, even with the backseat of the Subaru put down, but she couldn't make herself try to sleep inside the cabin. Even during the moments cramped in the back of the vehicle when her mind would finally race itself into circles of incomprehension and exhaustion would take over, dreams filled her sleep and kept her running. Dreams and nightmares about both the past and the possible future. But Jeannie knew that the last vision, experienced in a sweaty and fitful stolen moment of unconsciousness sometime after the sun had risen over the mountains, wasn't just a dream.

She took a drink from one of her water bottles, then climbed out of the car. She stared off into the dry grass, where she could hear the stream trickling. The voice of her father echoed in her head as she stood in the silence of the wilderness surrounding her. Only the sounds of a slight breeze could be heard.

She walked through the weeds, knelt down and splashed the cold water on her face. The effect was instantaneous, shocking away her drowsiness, but the terrified look on the priest's face wouldn't leave her mind. She looked back at the cabin, wondering again at her role in all of this. Everything that had happened over the two years had all started here.

Am I somewhat to blame for it all?

She tried to tell herself that it wasn't her fault. If she was going to believe anything, this all started long before she, or even her parents, were born. Still, the thought brought little comfort because she now played a key part in ending it. Her thoughts started crashing over each other again, and Jeannie splashed more water on her face.

She stood and tried to stretch out the aches from the previous night, then walked back to the car and grabbed the toothbrush and toothpaste she had picked up the day before at the travel center in Salmon, Idaho. She had also bought a couple blankets, a Styrofoam cooler and what she hoped would be enough food to see her through, either to the end, or to the point when Dr. Brandt would send the police looking for her.

Jeannie had stopped at the travel center when she realized halfway through the day that, with the exception of the dagger, she was completely unprepared. This realization didn't help her already frazzled nerves and a gnawing doubt that she had any right to be anywhere other than safely at the Rose House.

A thin, brown haze had hung in the sky over Salmon when Jeannie drove in, and when she stepped out of the car at the gas station, she picked up the faint smell of campfire. She filled up her tank and went inside to pick up the short list of items she had scribbled on the back of a receipt she found in Dr. B's glove box.

Jeannie gathered her things and walked up to the counter where a rugged looking man in a cowboy hat and Carhartt overalls was chatting up a pretty blond cashier.

"C'mon, Kim," he said. "How many times I gotta ask you?"

"Maybe just a couple more times," she said and smiled. "Go on, now. I got a customer."

The man turned and raised the brim of his hat to Jeannie. He stepped back from the counter as "Kim" rang up the total.

Jeannie took out her money and handed it to her. "Is there a fire somewhere nearby?"

Kim blinked at her in surprise and then pushed a couple of buttons on the cash register. The drawer slid open, and she counted out Jeannie's change. "More than just one, doll."

The guy in the hat leaned his elbow on the counter. "Haven't you been watching the news?" he asked. "There's fires all over this place. Fire season started early this year. So many they don't even know where to send us."

"Donny's a smoke jumper," Kim said, and the man tipped his hat again.

"Really? Wow." Jeannie had never heard of a smoke jumper, but she could guess what he did for a living.

"Where you headin', miss?" Donny asked.

"Montana," Jeannie said. "Kind of toward Painted Rocks."

"You're not planning on camping, are you? Most of the drainages out that way, especially in the Bitterroots, are closed for fire danger. It's super dry out there, and I hear they're expecting lightning storms the rest of this week."

"My family has a cabin southwest of Darby." Jeannie hoped the cowboy wouldn't ask her any more questions.

"Well, I'm sure your folks would know if it's safe or not," Donny said. "Just keep your nose to the wind, and if you smell smoke, you and your family better hightail it outta there."

Jeannie had thanked the two and left the gas station. At a few spots on the remainder of the drive, she saw what Donny had been talking about. Thick dark clouds over the mountains that she might have mistaken for a storm if it wasn't for the brown tint mixed in with the gray. Some places she could smell the burning trees, but she kept going, and by the time she took the turn off the highway toward Painted Rocks in the late afternoon, the sky had cleared completely to a deep blue backdrop behind the dark green of the lodgepole Pines.

Even though Jeannie had only been to the cabin once, much of the drive through the narrow, winding valley felt familiar. After about ten miles the road widened again as the trees receded, but Jeannie didn't have to consult her odometer to know that she was almost there.

Five minutes later, she had broken out of the mountains into the open meadow, but it wasn't the lush green she had expected. The dry winter and unseasonable early heat had turned the field into thigh-high shoots of dead weeds and grass. As Jeannie drove closer to the cabin, she reached over to the passenger seat and flipped open the snap on the thigh sheath, even though no other vehicles were visible. She slowed as she approached, scanning the thick weeds for movement.

After the death of her parents, the cabin went up for sale, but technically, it belonged to Jeannie. She had used the internet to keep an eye on it over the past couple years, but so far, no one was buying. As she drove up, the disparity between her memories of the cabin and what she saw now struck her first. Obviously no one had been up to look at it since the previous spring. Sheets of plywood had been screwed into place covering the windows. The stain on the logs was faded and discolored on the side that must have received the most weather, and some of the spindles on the porch were either splintered or missing entirely. Jeannie saw a few bottles with faded labels on the ground by the porch. Probably a hangout for local kids.

When Jeannie had pulled to a stop, she was still very aware of her surroundings, but she hadn't seen any movement yet.

Hey, y'all. I thought you'd never make it.

Barb Stack's voice echoed in the back of Jeannie's head. She could almost picture the realtor standing at the cabin as she drove up. Jeannie turned off the car and stepped out cautiously. A gust of wind blew into the valley, rustling the dead grass surrounding the house. She drew the dagger and rounded the cabin first. As far as she could tell, none of the plywood had been removed from the windows. The backdoor was still locked. Returning to the front, Jeannie looked around again, still half expecting a surprise attack, but nothing came. The boards of the porch groaned under her feet as she climbed the steps and approached the front door. Nothing moved behind the small panes of glass on the door, and she stepped forward to try the handle. Locked. She looked around the porch for something to break one of the panes of glass on the door. She was about to search out a rock when she noticed the horseshoe hanging over the threshold. One of the nails had fallen out and the shoe hung sideways.

Spilling out any of the luck it might have held.

Jeannie reached up and yanked on the rusted shoe, popping out the other nail. She tapped it a couple times on the glass pane closest to the deadbolt before striking. A web of cracks spread on the glass, and Jeannie hit harder, sending pieces into the cabin. Then she jumped back, dagger held above her head, ready. Only silence answered her action. Where were they?

Still wary that the demon was waiting for just the right moment, Jeannie stood on her toes without getting too close and tried to see if anyone was crouching behind the door. Then she used the horseshoe to clear away the smaller pieces stuck in the frame. She started to reach her hand through, but she paused.

She knew that it wasn't too late to turn around. She could just hop back in the car and drive away. After all, who did she think she was? Jeannie knew that she could be setting herself up for her own suicide if she stayed. Who was she to think she could take on a force this strong?

This time she didn't let the despair take over. "Someone who doesn't have any other choice," she said aloud.

The demon was only growing stronger, and she knew that she was only standing in its way. Where could she go that it wouldn't find her, and how could she live a normal life knowing it was still out there? "I can't," she answered.

Jeannie reached through the pane of glass and turned the deadbolt with a heavy *click*. She swung the door opened, again jumping back, but she didn't hesitate as long this time before entering into the great room. All of the furniture had long since been removed, but Jeannie could still picture the couch that had been shoved next to the fireplace in the greatroom.

With the windows boarded up, the only light in the cabin filtered through the skylights, settling on empty space, framing a section of dusty hardwood floor. It was the same spot the police had found Jeannie, a day after Barbara Stack was reported missing. The first officer on the scene, just a small town deputy, had crossed himself when he saw her curled up in a ball between her murdered parents. From the report Jeannie discovered later, it took them almost another day to bring in a canine unit and discover Ms. Stack inside the roll of carpet in the garage.

Jeannie checked the rest of the cabin before deciding she was alone. She sat on the floor across from the fireplace and watched the frame of light in silence. The spot moved away from her as late afternoon slipped into evening, sliding up the stone chimney as the sun made its journey west. She shivered when it finally disappeared as the sun slipped behind the nearby peaks and the temperature dropped in the mountain's shadow. The house felt smaller suddenly. Scarier. She could only see partway down the hallway into the darkness. That was when Jeannie decided that she would sleep in the Subaru.

Today she was regretting that decision, and if she had to stay another night, she might reconsider her accommodations.

After Jeannie cleaned herself up as much as possible, she forced down an orange and a banana, and then started weighing her options. Because she had anticipated seeing David much sooner (like as soon as she showed up), she hadn't really formulated any sort of plan besides "hope for the best, face the rest if it comes." This morning, with her nerves calmed a little, Jeannie realized that, while she had run through a hundred possible things she might say, she had barely touched the dagger since buying it. She retrieved it from the Subaru and tried various positions for the blade and sheath, finally settling with it attached on her left thigh under a pair of baggy cargo shorts, with the hilt pointing down. It seemed to be the most concealed place with the quickest access if she needed it. She practiced the maneuver until she felt as comfortable with the tactic as she probably ever would given the circumstances. The idea of plunging the seven-inch blade into a person's body, even if that body was possessed, made her want to reconsider the purchase of a handgun. With that settled, Jeannie set her mind to where she wanted to be when he arrived.

he? they? it?

The closest tree was over a hundred yards away, and after circling the cabin and considering each of the rooms inside, she ended up sitting on the porch, watching in the direction of the only road leading into the narrow valley. Certainly it was the only way they would come in. By what she had witnessed, she didn't think it was the demon's style to hike through the mountains the way David had originally entered her life.

Unless it's actually David coming to meet me, Jeannie thought. *What if he* has a plan?

Jeannie dismissed the idea. Even if it was David, she couldn't be certain of his mental state anymore. Maybe it had already started. The End. Maybe she wouldn't be the first person he had killed. She wanted to believe that it had been the demon that stabbed Father Jimmy, but maybe David had learned of his unfortunate lineage. He seemed pretty angry with God.

"Just the death of the body," she said aloud. "But a freeing of his soul."

Sometime after lunch, still with no sign of anyone, Jeannie went into the cabin and found a broom and some cleaning supplies which had probably been left there by the new realtor. Judging by his picture on the website, Jeannie thought he looked like a nice guy, but probably not as much of a character as Barb Stack.

She started cleaning the cabin, finding comfort in the task, occupying her mind with something controlled and contained. She was going crazy waiting, and who knew when

or even if

they would show up.

The question was answered in the late afternoon when she heard someone driving up the road. She dropped her rag and ran toward the door, trying to compose herself as she opened it. Her breath caught in her chest when she saw the forest green Jeep coming down the road. She had the crazy thought that it had all been a dream, that it was actually two years earlier, and her Daddy was coming home.

The fantasy shredded as she stepped out onto the weathered porch. The Jeep drove slowly up the road. Jeannie descended the steps and stood behind the Subaru, trying to look tough, hoping like Hell that he... or it... or whatever wouldn't see through her act.

As the Jeep pulled up, Jeannie was able to make out the face behind the steering wheel.

It wasn't her father.

* * *

Earlier that afternoon, Mashart was driving the dead apartment manager's Jeep (such a tasty coincidence) along Highway 93 out of Missoula into the Bitterroots and reflecting on how well everything was working out.

Even though Mashart sensed David's presence, his awareness, the boy hadn't made a peep since Las Vegas, even when they were sticking it to that priest. Somewhat surprisingly, he hadn't struggled to regain control of his body. Maybe he had finally accepted the things the demon had told him, even the lies. They were so close now.

The boy had no idea of the power he possessed, the power that Mashart would use toward his own ends. The demon could put thoughts in the monkeys' brains, but with David around, they felt more comfortable, more convincible. The doubters could believe, and the crazy ones stopped doubting themselves. Even the good ones wanted to do better just to please him. Mashart first saw it in the retirement home. The way they flocked to him, one last bit of life before he dealt them their deaths. Jeremy had taken it a step further. They would all listen. And the weapon that the demon wielded the strongest against the boy's resolve was that, in an undeniable way, they would be serving Justice.

Using David, Mashart could overflow the tombs of Hell. Or even better, they could create a Hell on Earth. Only one thing still stood in his way. The girl.

Somehow the girl had found the boy in the mire. She was even stronger now than when the demon took her body the first time. Somehow she was connected with the boy, and just when Mashart thought he had him beaten, the boy had a vision of her failed suicide attempt. But something else beyond strength drove her forward. The demon had tried convincing David that her motive was purely revenge, but there was something else. Mashart suspected that the girl knew that it wasn't really David who killed her parents and that she knew she was on her way to try and kill the demon.

"Hell hath no fury like a woman scorned," he said aloud as he drove. "So the little girl is all grown up but still wants to play."

Mashart could tell that somewhere in the vast wilderness to the west, not far beyond the mountains, a forest fire raged. The sky was black and thick smoke seemed to be oozing out of jagged valleys before being captured by the wind and smeared through the tree-lined slopes closer to the highway. Yes, this was good.

Mashart had spent almost a century planning for this day. A hundred years of wiping out the bloodline from The Seed. Tormenting them with their deepest terrors, just as he had done with his charges in the pits of Hell. Then he had killed them. Or found a way to have them killed. Wars, genocide, mass suicides, right down to a mindless, drugged-out-mugger with an itchy trigger finger. Thousands of deaths orchestrated by the demon to wipe out the last shreds of the monkeys' hope. Until this last.

A cold fire burned in his chest and he wrapped his fingers tighter around the steering wheel when he thought of how the boy had escaped from him. Twice. And now the girl thought she could free him again. The demon thought that those two shared the same affliction. The only emotions they sensed in others were weaknesses. They could only see the injustices in others' lives and then feel pity for them. They failed to see the bad intent in the animals, the bad that is in every one of them. Mashart didn't always put evil thoughts in their heads. Sometimes, he only brought them to life. Formed and fed them and gave them names or faces.

Or maybe the girl was actually coming to kill David, justice for the death of Mommy and Daddy. She might not have any clue of that with which she was coming face to face. Either way, Mashart wasn't quite ready to give up his prized possession just yet. The demon had come too far to be beaten by some child. Mashart had convinced a Catholic priest to firebomb a medical clinic in Dublin in order to kill one of the Bloodline. The girl shouldn't be any problem. Maybe he would convince her that it was her fault that her parents had died. Maybe he would make her kill *herself*.

Mashart sped through another small town, and then the highway curved around a mountain and into a narrower valley filled with smoke. Mashart blinked his eyes as the acrid smell blew in through the vents, and he had to slow the Jeep. A bead of sweat broke on his forehead and ran into his eyes. He scowled and wiped away his blurred vision as a couple of other drops trailed down his cheek. Although he hadn't noticed a drastic change of temperature in the Jeep, Mashart was rapidly getting warmer. He reached over and switched on the air conditioner, but the cool air barely pierced the surface of the flesh, making his insides seem that much hotter.

His heart started beating harder, the very blood seeming to boil through his veins, and it was everything Mashart could do to keep the sweat out of his eyes and maneuver the vehicle. Bile rose up from his stomach and Mashart's vision blurred. Something was happening.

The boy.

Something…

* * *

David fought for control with all of his strength. Even though the demon had been in control since Las Vegas, it hadn't pushed

David completely into blackness, allowing him to witness his own actions from the backseat. When he knew they were getting close to the cabin, he tried to get his body back. He visualized his nervous system, the passageways from the flesh to the soul, imagining his energy surging through those tendrils stretching into muscles that felt cold from lack of use. And it worked. When he could feel his blood pulsing through his body, he punched forward with his mind, pushing through the hole in his vision toward the life on the other side.

The return to his body caused David to jerk the wheel of the Jeep to the left. A pickup truck trying to pass him swerved away, the driver honking as he let off the gas. David clutched his fingers around the steering wheel and pulled back into his lane. The truck sped up to pass again. The driver had his middle finger up as he passed, but when he saw David he dropped his hand and quickly looked away, accelerating even more.

David loosened his grip on the steering wheel and relaxed his tightened muscles. He took a deep breath and slowed his pulse. He could still feel the demon's in the back of his mind in the form of a flood of rage that threatened to pull him under, anger and pain so strong it pushed against the backs of his eyeballs. He needed all of his strength and focus to keep it back.

David tried to convince himself that he had been saving his energy since losing his body again to the demon in Las Vegas. While not in control, he had been aware for most of the past day. There were moments when it seemed that he certainly had slipped into his nightmares, but he had been just below the surface, watching as though through watery glass as the events unfolded. He had witnessed the events in the little Episcopalian church in sickened horror. Maybe he could've done something to help. But he didn't try. He didn't want to hurt anyone, especially Father Jimmy, but he also knew that the priest wasn't the key to his freedom. It had to be the girl. He needed to be in control when he saw her. Despite what the demon had told him, maybe she really could help.

Unless she's coming to kill me.

Even with his temperature dropped and his heart slowed, David's body still felt sore from the force of regaining control. Or maybe it was the effects of the demon. The muscles running through his neck from his shoulder to the base of his skull refused to unknot, and it pained him to turn his head much more than a few inches in either direction.

He tried to think about everything that had happened over the past six months. Everything he had done. It scared him to think about how easily the demon had used him. But the pain served as a good reminder of the feel of his body, helping David stay focused on holding on, and he pushed the limits of his physical resistance as he drove, craning his neck slowly until the strain brought tears to his eyes.

He wondered if what the demon had told him in Las Vegas could be the truth. Certainly they were lies. There had been so many lies. If nothing else, David now believed that he could actually see into the minds of others, their own deepest secrets. He still remembered when Jeremy had grabbed his arm that Friday night in the Atlantic. Maybe what the demon had said was true. Maybe he had seen into the dark corners of Jeremy Leavitt's mind, just as he had with the other people in the hallway.

But why? And to what end? David had never pictured himself as some sort of avenging angel. The demon had been right about him not believing in the same god that Father Jimmy believed in. If there was a god, why wasn't he doing anything now? No one had stepped up to help him. No, the priest didn't have the answers he sought.

However, the girl might. If David really did have a connection with the whole human race, Jeannie had been the first. And the strongest. If he could just get to her first, maybe they could figure a way out together.

A steady headwind nudged against the truck as David drove south, but that same wind cleared the smoke from the worst of the Bitterroot fires. Twenty minutes later, David was given a glimpse of the bluest sky he had seen in years. Not a cloud blighted the horizon as he continued along the highway, skirting the edge of the towering peaks, and even though David knew the lack of clouds meant a lack of rain to stop the wildfires, the depths of the sky, the beauty of the calm, gave him comfort. Maybe there was hope after all. He slowed when he saw the sign for Painted Rocks.

As he turned off the highway onto a side road, David's body jerked back in the seat as the pressure burst in his head. His leg spasmed and his foot pushed hard on the pedal, the back wheels of the Jeep spinning on loose gravel and swerving the vehicle into a ditch. The force of the stop threw David forward, hitting the bridge of his nose on the steering wheel with a flash of white.

* * *

Mashart opened his eyes and looked around the Jeep. He quickly geared into reverse and backed out of the ditch. Then he pulled off to the side of the road. His eyes were watering. He looked in the rearview mirror at the purplish-black spot swelling on David's nose.

"Fucking kid," he growled at the reflection. "Fucking amateur! I should have known you weren't ready. So weak. Well, now you're finished. Playtime is over."

Mashart grinned. He reached under the seat and pulled out a pack of cigarettes. He took one out and lit it, inhaling deeply before releasing the smoke. He took two more drags before flicking the cigarette out the window into the dry grass. Mashart watched the thin trail of smoke rising from the brush for a moment before putting the Jeep in gear and starting down the road.

The boy had been strong, stronger than the demon had suspected. Mashart had been confident that even if David still had any fight, he didn't have any strength, and the demon had been caught off guard. Mashart was not one to be fucked with. If the boy wanted to see *real* power, he was about to be shown.

"Let's see if you remember this," Mashart growled.

CHAPTER 30

David regained consciousness expecting to still be in the ditch but was surprised to see he was on the road. Driving, in fact. He wondered if he had imagined the whole scene, but a sharp ache from between his eyes reminded him of hitting his face on the steering wheel just before going unconscious. He tried to reach up to touch the sore spot, but his hands wouldn't leave the steering wheel. He tried to look at his reflection in the mirror, but his neck wouldn't turn.

David needed to pull over. Something wasn't right. But when he attempted to let off the accelerator, he found that his legs wouldn't respond either. He could feel his heart pumping in his chest, breath filling his lungs, every change of the muscles in his body, every force of action, from his foot on the gas to the minor adjustments his hands made as he navigated along the dirt road, but he had no control over them.

Dirt road? Wasn't it gravel or at least paved when I turned off? How long ago did I black out?

Then he felt something else. Nausea bubbled in his stomach and rose to his throat, and he heard a voice gurgling up at the same time as his jaw opened.

"You want to *fuck* with me, boy?" The demon spoke through David's mouth, spitting bile with the words. Stomach acid burned in his nasal passages. "I wanted to do this the easy way, but you aren't ready. I'm tired of waiting. Now I'll finish it." An acrid belch erupted from his mouth. "Did you know the little girl can still feel the sensation in her hand from shooting her father? Well, I've got a special treat for you. Your own special little memory to take to hell with you. I want you to feel firsthand the taking of a life."

The road seemed to be getting hazier in front of him, and David thought he could smell smoke. The demon must have shared his physical senses, because David's head rose beyond his control and he looked in the rearview mirror at a thick black cloud swirling behind the Jeep. His lips curled into a grin. He looked away from the mirror, his gaze directed to a pack of cigarettes on the dashboard, and the demon chuckled. The wind carried a fire up behind them, and David knew the demon had started it.

The Jeep broke from the narrow valley into the meadow with the cabin at the other end. Over the ridge on the horizon, dark clouds rolled in the sky. They didn't look like smoke clouds. David could only hope they were thunderheads.

The wind rolled through the brown grass in the meadow, like waves carrying the Jeep to the cabin. A gray Subaru was parked in front. David's leg let off the accelerator, and the Jeep slowed as the demon drove nearer. Jeannie walked out of the cabin, descended the porch steps and stood rigidly behind the vehicle. Standing in her defensive posture, David thought she looked more wild than wounded, and again, he wondered at her intent.

The Jeep came to a stop behind the station wagon, and Jeannie moved to the side of the two vehicles. David stepped out of the vehicle.

"David?" Jeannie asked. She sounded leery.

Good, David thought. *Be suspicious.* He wanted to shout out to her to run, but knew he couldn't. He could only watch the scene unfold and look for another opportunity. He still felt strength that he hoped he could use. However, underneath it all, he also sensed an anger welling up inside him, the demon's hatred for Jeannie poisoning his flesh. "It's me," he heard himself say. "It's David. It's been one helluva ride." He could feel himself forcing a weak smile and wincing, then he reached up to touch his bruised nose. "I had to trick the demon, make it think I was going along with his plan. I've been waiting to act, but I didn't have the strength until today. The most important day. Our day." He started to step toward Jeannie, but she backed away.

The tips of David's fingers tingled and the rage grew stronger inside him, but the demon managed to subdue it in his voice. In fact, his tone sounded calmer than David had heard before, soothing.

"I'm so sorry about everything," he said. "I'm so sorry about your daddy. I didn't mean for all of this to happen. You have to forgive me."

David reached his hand toward Jeannie as the valley grew thicker with the smoke, but she cringed away, her eyes narrow.

"I don't believe you," she said.

Run, David thought, but instead of shouting, his body doubled over and he clutched his stomach as if in pain, but it was still an act. His right hand shot sideways to steady his body against the Jeep. Slowly he straightened out. The demon pulled the strings masterfully.

"Jeannie?" he heard himself whisper. "Is that you? Where am I? What's happening?"

Jeannie took a half-step forward and looked at him. "David?"

"Please help me. I can't keep it away for much longer."

Don't listen!

Jeannie shook her head. "Is it really you?"

David's body was wracked again, and he fell against the truck. Then he righted himself. "I'm going to kill you, you interfering *bitch*," he said. "I've had enough of this shit. The boy is weak, and he'll be mine completely once you're dead."

Jeannie stepped back again. "I'll kill you both if I have to."

"You don't have the balls, little girl." The demon stepped toward Jeannie and she gripped her pant leg again. Then David's whole body shook and his head whipped from side to side as the demon faked another transformation. "Leave her alone," he heard himself cry. "Jeannie, you've got to run. Let me die here. It can finally be over and you can live your life."

Jeannie's mouth moved, but no words came.

"Please," he said and looked away. "Mashart will kill you. He's too strong."

"I can't leave you," Jeannie said, her voice shaking. "We've come too far. I can help." She sounded uncertain, confused. She wasn't the only one. David couldn't figure out why the demon was putting on the show.

His body spasmed again. He stood straight, and his voice dropped to a growl. "You really should listen to the boy," he said. "What do you think you can do to me?"

David fought for control, but the demon had given him just enough physical sensation to trap him in it. He heard himself start screaming and dropped to his knees. "Please kill me." His arm reached out and grabbed a softball-sized rock and hefted it toward her. "Bash my head in. Quick! Before the demon comes back. I've got a hold of it, but oh God, it hurts!" He dropped forward on his hands gasping for air, but in reality, the demon watched Jeannie's shadow through David's eyes. She took a tentative step toward him but didn't bend over for the rock.

"David?" she asked again. "What about the priest? Why did you do that to the priest?"

"The priest..." David heard himself say. "The priest was..." in David's head, the demon finish the sentence. *Fun. The priest was fun.*

He lifted his gaze, one of his hands rubbing at the smoke in his bloodshot eyes. "The priest was wrong," he said and coughed. "Just like Jeremy Leavitt. I saw things, horrible things that Father Jimmy had done. He was hiding behind his God, behind his scriptures. He won't do those things again. I've seen to that."

Jeannie clenched her jaw and looked down at the ground. At the rock. Suddenly, David understood. The demon believed it would win regardless of whether or not she stooped for the rock. More than a choice of weapons, the demon knew that her anger would overwhelm her compassion. Although David didn't understand why, Jeannie had finally abandoned hope, and rage took its place. He thought he could even smell it, more acrid than the smoke filling the valley.

Her wrath makes her weaker, he thought. *The demon wants her to act in fury.*

"I know I shouldn't have done it to the priest," he said and dropped his head. "But I can't contain the anger anymore, even when I'm in control. Please, Jeannie, take the rock. It's the only way."

Her shadow stepped closer, then blurred as the dark clouds passed over the sun. "There has to be another way," she said, but David thought she sounded less compassionate this time. Colder. "You can fight it."

The tears came from David then. Jeannie was almost to him. She took another step and then lightning flashed on the hillside behind Jeannie, exploding a pine tree on top of the ridge. Jeannie jerked around, and the demon seized the opportunity. When she turned back to David, he was already halfway up, his fist following his momentum in an uppercut. He caught her on the jaw, and she flew back on the driveway as the grasses up on the ridge surrounding the stricken tree caught fire. The demon jumped on top of her and wrapped his hands around her throat. David could feel his fingers digging into her neck. She struggled, grabbing his arms and trying to claw his face, but he pinned his knees over her shoulders. Her attacks grew weaker. The veins in her neck bulged, and her face changed from red to purple.

"You silly bitch," the demon spat. He let go of her neck with one of his hands and punched her in the face again. Her body slackened, and her eyes blinked and started to gloss over. "Sappy emotions," he said. "The downfall of humans. I told David once, love is the greatest four-letter word of them all. Just before I killed his bitch. And just in time, too. She was in heat. Couldn't have *another* one running around now, could I?"

Jeannie's eyes rolled back in her head, and Mashart laughed. "I really am sorry about your daddy," he said. "Sorry that he wasn't more innocent. But I guess I can't blame him. That other woman he was fucking sure was a tasty dish, let me tell you."

David knew Jeannie was dying, that he was killing her, and he thrashed with all of his strength. When another bolt of lightning struck the hillside, he surged again and shook free of the demon's reign long enough to push himself off Jeannie. He fell on his back, panting, but could already feel the rage returning to his hands, the burning underneath his skin. His hands still clawed out for death. The desire to kill the girl coursed through his blood like an infection, mingling with his own emotions. It was too intense for David. The demon was too strong. David couldn't fight him.

Lightning struck again, and the valley filled with the sounds of crackling flames on the ridge. David hefted himself off the ground. He had to run before the demon overpowered him again. Maybe he would be lost forever, but at least Jeannie would be safe. He started toward the road, but the fire started by the demon was eating at the constricted pass through the mountains. The flames lit the trees like birthday candles, jumping from one to another, black smoke billowing into the sky. He turned and ran toward the base of the slope. It would be a brutal climb, but maybe the pain of exertion could keep the demon at bay. He looked up at the ridge. The lightning had set fire to most of it as well. A ring was forming around the cabin, the exit gaps closing rapidly. David looked back at Jeannie. She had rolled over on her side, coughing violently. Maybe he could make it to the top of the ridge before the fire completely closed in, but there was no way she would make it. He couldn't leave her to burn alive. David watched her push herself to her knees.

"Jeannie!" he shouted. She looked up at him in terror and then started groping around in the grass. David started over toward her, breaking into a run. She started to scramble backward. "Don't run! It's me! It's David." But his voice carried away from him into the wind that fed the flames on the ridge behind him. He waved his arms frantically at her. Jeannie found her feet just as he caught up with her. She whipped around to face him as he reached out to her.

"It's me," David said. "We've got to get-"

His voice was ripped from his lungs by a searing pain through his gut.

And then all of the answers came to him. Suddenly it all made sense.

The demon screamed in his head, and David smiled.

* * *

Jeannie had been suspicious from the moment David stepped out of the Jeep, but she held her ground. If he tried to rush her, the dagger would be out in a flash, but she wanted to keep that card face down for now. If it was actually the demon, she wanted it to think that she was as unprepared as she actually felt.

She should have listened to the subtle little signs, the first of which being that he avoided looking too much directly at her. He looked everywhere *but* at her. The eyes were the windows to the soul, and maybe if she really looked, she would see the blackness. But during the fleeting moments when their eyes locked Jeannie still thought she caught glimpses of the man inside the flesh, and she wanted to believe that she wouldn't be forced to kill him, that she didn't have to destroy the last physical evidence of Good in the world in order to save it. Something didn't seem right about that.

Two years ago, Jeannie had watched David's interior struggle to maintain control of his body, to force the demon down long enough that her life would be spared. The demon obviously remembered as well. The quick "transformations" on this day didn't surprise Jeannie. In fact, they gave her a little hope that David still possessed the strength and the will to fight.

Then she asked him about the priest and felt a pang of defeat when she heard his answer. At that moment, she believed that she was speaking to David, and what hurt the most was that she didn't believe what he had said. Not all of it, at least. Jeannie didn't think Father Jimmy was a sinner. She believed that the priest couldn't satisfy David's questions, and the anger had taken over. He had been infected by the demon. Jeannie felt her own anger rising, the emotion crushing the little voice at the back of her head saying *maybe it wasn't him.*

David was almost certainly lost, but when he started weeping, Jeannie realized she didn't know what to do. Her hand went to the sheath on her thigh, but she paused. Her anger had balled her hand into a fist, but her heart still doubted that she could carry through. An image of herself pulling out the dagger and plunging it into David's back flashed in her mind, and she shivered, her hand poised, just touching the handle.

But she had to do it. One death to save the lives of the others. She didn't think she had any choice.

Then lightning crashed behind her.

Jeannie should have listened to her instincts, and she cursed herself when she turned back from the flash to see David quickly shooting up from his previous position on his hands and knees. When his fist connected with her jaw, her whole head snapped back with a loud crack and her teeth crunched together. In that flash, a realization struck her almost as hard. Even the moments when she thought David had control were faked.

It was all an act. David is gone.

And then she felt weightless. The force behind the demon's attack lifted her off her feet. She landed hard on the gravel, and then David filled her vision as he leapt on top of her. She tried to defend herself, but she was still dazed from the punch, and now the demon had David's hands around her neck, closing off her air, crushing her voice box. She lashed around underneath him but couldn't reach the dagger.

"You silly bitch," the demon said through David and let go long enough to punch her again. This one caught her left cheek, the pain shooting across her face like razor blades. "Sappy emotions. The downfall of humans. I told David once, love is the greatest four letter word of them all."

The demon raged on at her, spat something about her father, but darkness was closing around her senses. Lightning flashed again, and David's silhouette burned into her retinas before everything went black.

Then air rushed back into her lungs, the blood pounding in her head, as color seeped back into the world. Jeannie rolled over on her side and started coughing. Her larynx still felt like it was folded inward. She pushed herself onto her hands and knees, and breath came back to her. She lifted her head and looked toward the end of the valley where the road ran. Smoke was rolling in, and the wind gusted across the plain.

But she couldn't hear any sound. Jeannie shook her head, but still there was only silence. Until a familiar sound sprouted in her head. It started as a buzzing at first, like bees somewhere in the distance, swarming closer. The noise quickly grew in intensity, sounding more like heavy radio static, and just as it reached an almost unbearable point, the racket dropped to a soft drone like white noise that bled into the sounds of the ocean.

The demon will be expelled with the blood, and we will take him back where he belongs.

Jeannie looked out over the waves of dead grass blowing under the gray, rolling sky, like the sea on a rainy day, and she understood the message that the carpenter in Hawaii, Steve Avery, had misinterpreted. Sometimes the only peace is found in death. Steve just hadn't known the right person to kill. But Jeannie did.

"Jeannie!"

She looked back toward the voice. It was the demon. It had to be. She wouldn't be fooled again. Jeannie clutched her thigh for the dagger, but it had been knocked out. She started groping around in the grass, but couldn't find the weapon. David shouted something else from behind her, but she couldn't hear him in the wind. Just as she saw the glint of the blade in a thicket of brush behind her, he started running toward her. She clawed backward and grasped the dagger just as David reached her. She sprang up and twisted around to face him. He tried to grab her.

"It's me. We've got to get--"

Jeannie's hand shot out. David's eyes widened, then he looked down. Jeannie leaned forward. "You killed my father, you son of a bitch," she whispered in his ear.

David smiled and then fell into her body as she plunged the blade farther into his stomach.

As David's body sagged against hers, Jeannie cried in pain, as if the dagger were in her own belly. Her arm was pulled down by his weight, and he slipped off the blade, dropping off to her side. Jeannie stood stunned, looking down at him. He rolled over on his back and looked up at the murky sky. A spasm erupted across his stomach, and with it, a spray of black, viscous blood spouted from the wound, but instead of spattering back down on his body, the fluid hung suspended above him, a thin trail still connected to the puncture in his stomach like afterbirth. It tugged up on his body as if it was wrapped around his spine. It seemed to pull his very insides out with it as it spread out into a wing-shaped canopy over his body, something between a bat and an umbrella, pulsing and quivering. David gasped, his body arching up as he clawed the dirt.

Jeannie couldn't move, couldn't take her eyes away from the abomination. Then a rumbling sounded in the distance behind them, like the earth itself opening up. She turned away from David and looked up the slope. The ring of fire had closed together on the ridge, and the flames took a focal point, starting down the hill. She watched in amazement as the hillside seemed to be slowly unzipped like a coat to reveal the flaming underbelly of the mountain. The fire turned a brighter orange, then blue, and finally gray as the fiery zipper took on the form of a person walking rapidly down the hill. Jeannie rubbed her eyes, but the burning figure remained, breaking into a run and leaving a wake of flames behind it. Burning embers drifted down from the raging ridge, one landing on Jeannie's shoulder. She quickly brushed it off, leaving a smoking black spot on her shirt.

Then she heard a pained shout from behind her. David writhed on the ground, clutching the black stream from the wound in his stomach. The demon seemed to be trying to jerk free. David's body lifted off the ground with each attempt. She looked back at the hill. The flames were almost upon them. Jeannie threw herself on top of David, tearing off the bloody thread with a final yank. David cried out in pain, and in the moment that they made contact, Jeannie saw everything that had happened to him, starting with the night he had lost his fiancé.

Her name was Ann.

She felt all of his pain and loss.

Then he took a deep breath. "I'm sorry," he whispered, and his body went limp. Jeannie barely heard him over the roaring of the fire. She couldn't believe what she was seeing. The blazing figure ran directly at them, flames rising fifteen or twenty feet into the sky. The figure was featureless, but caught up in the fury behind it were hundreds of other forms, tormented faces who cried and tore at their flesh as they were dragged through the fiery aftermath. Jeannie's face grew warm, then quickly hot. She blinked, her eyelids sticky. In a flash, Jeannie thought she saw her father in the tortured throng, and then the faceless leader leapt over their bodies, his own form disintegrating as the flame arced over the two and lit on the black aberration still suspended over the ground. Jeannie dropped her head on David's chest and braced for her incineration, but the flames surrounded the two in a small, unscorched circle, forming a dome over their bodies. Just above their protection the filmy, black mass caught fire with a high-pitched screech. It bubbled and popped in the heat, and the shrieking grew louder.

Jeannie covered her ears and started screaming, half from the horrible sound of the expelled demon and half from the searing heat of the flames that surrounded them. The fire stretched away from them in all directions. The flames danced on the tall grasses and then broke up into curls, joining the larger mass of the inferno. Distance was indistinguishable as the fire seemed to rage even over their heads. It blocked out the sky and cooked the thrashing form above them. The heat burned so intensely that Jeannie repeatedly beat at both David and herself to put out flames that weren't there. While the fire spared them a live cremation, it raged close enough to sizzle their hair to black smoldering stubs. The burnt smell mixed with the smoke of the grass and the putrid scent of the black mass over them, now crisping and crackling and breaking away with the fire. The stench filled the air, stinging Jeannie's nose and throat and making her gag.

Still she clung to David, and while he didn't move in her arms, Jeannie could feel a changing in his body. She had already felt her own clothing and hair turn brittle and fleck away into the flames, but this was different. Jeannie dared to open her eyes just a slit, and the scorching intensity threatened to dry her very eyelids.

David's scars were changing. The pink color of the scarred flesh was dying and turning brown. Like a marshmallow in the campfire, the scars deepened to black, but instead of catching fire, the ridges on his damaged body finally turned gray. As Jeannie watched, they rippled with the consistency of tissue paper before being whisked away from his naked body, incinerated in the fury. The wound she had inflicted to his stomach had been cauterized shut. Somewhere in the chaos of sounds filling her ears, Jeannie thought she could hear the sound of a freight train grinding to a halt, and she shut her eyes as the demon gave one last shrill cry and then exploded into speckled, flaming pieces.

Thunder boomed down from the ridge, and the clouds finally burst, dropping a mass of rain over the valley, scattering the fire with a loud spattering of hisses, including on the bodies of Jeannie and David. It fell so hard that even after it cooled her heated flesh, it pelted her exposed back. Soon she started shivering as the wind blew over her naked, soaked body. Her body shook so much that she thought she might crumble apart. Then the rain softened, and instead of stinging her, it felt like it was soaking into her skin. A warmth spread in her nerve-tangled stomach, and Jeannie gasped as all other sensations, all awareness, disappeared save the feeling in her core.

Then it was gone. Jeannie blinked a couple of times as the downpour tapered off, extinguishing the last small patches of flame around the cabin. Jeannie shuddered, then reached a tentative hand up and ran it over her head. All of her hair was gone. She wiped her eyes. Eyelashes gone. Eyebrows as well. She looked down at David. With the exception of the spot where she had stabbed him, his scars were completely gone, the light rain washing off the last bits of ash. She gently wiped the soot from his face and saw that, like her, he also was cleaner than a newborn.

But he wasn't breathing.

"David?"

He didn't move.

"No," Jeannie whispered. She placed her fingertips on his throat. Nothing. But maybe her hands were shaking too much. She just needed to calm down. She clenched her fists, took a deep breath, and tried again. "Not this way."

Jeannie put her head on David's chest and listened, but nothing moved beneath his ribs. No heart. No breath. "No!" she said, and pounded the muddy ground with her fist. She raised her face to the sky where patches of blue already showed through.

"Was this part of your grand plan?" Jeannie screamed. But only silence answered. The meadow was still. She looked down at David. Then she wept.

EPILOGUE

Jeannie woke with a start and bolted upright in bed, covered in a sheen of sweat. She glanced around the unfamiliar bedroom through blurred vision for a few seconds before she remembered where she was.

The cabin, she thought, and dropped back on the sheets.

She rubbed her eyes. The dream of the fire had been less frequent over the past few months, but Jeannie doubted she would ever stop having it entirely. She reached up and scratched the shoots of hair on her head that had grown back since the fire.

The autumn sun was just peeking over the mountains, shining into the bedroom loft through windows that needed cleaning, now that winter had passed. She rolled her legs over the side of the bed and winced from a darting pain in her stomach as she pushed into a sitting position. It had been this way ever since that day. She took a series of short breaths until the nausea subsided and she could draw a full breath.

Jeannie slid off the bed. The hardwood floor was cold under her feet, and she hopped over to the closet and put on her slippers. She walked downstairs and into the kitchen, where the aroma of coffee hung in the crisp morning air. Lately, she only allowed herself the indulgence on Sundays. She filled a cup, turned off the coffee maker's timer and headed toward the front deck, stopping at the dining room table to pick up the newspaper she had bought in town two days ago. She had barely looked at it since then. She wasn't as concerned anymore with keeping up-to-date on the state of the world, even though she knew she should be. Especially now.

However, with the horrible headlines almost every day, she understood why she didn't want to read it. She didn't like the direction in which the world still seemed to be turning. But still she checked out the news when she got the chance, even if it was just the local paper. Not a single story had struck her in the past three months, not like the others. Only her own thoughts filled her head as she read the newspaper and magazines. The grinding sounds had never returned, but she still feared that they might. She had to make sure.

Only sadness affected her this morning as she looked at the front page. More death and depression. She flipped the first few pages, skimming the content. Another car bomb in the Middle East. Wilderness drilling proposal closer to approval. Jeannie shook her head and was about to close the paper when one of the stories grabbed her attention. It was the headline more than anything else. *Bizarre Shooting of Beer Manufacturing CEO.*

> Milwaukee, MN. Police are still looking for the unidentified man wanted for questioning concerning the disappearance of R.T. Jacobsen, CEO of the Mil-Town Brewing Company, from his office mid-morning yesterday. According to reports, Jacobsen's receptionist, Amanda Stern, apparently let the man into his office, claiming he had an appointment. After a few minutes she heard shouting from behind the door, followed by two gunshots. However, when security broke through the door, both Jacobsen and the unidentified man were gone without any signs of a scuffle.
>
> Mil-Town Brewery has been under fire recently for the release on the controversial Lucy's Fur Pale Ale. For the first time since their opening in 1987, they claimed a loss in the second quarter. Police believe the suspect may...

Jeannie closed the newspaper. She didn't want to read anymore. She didn't need to read anymore. Just another day in the world. She stood from the table and walked out to the porch.

The meadow was still blackened. The grass had been burned down almost as close as her hair, but while the hair was growing back, the cooler fall temperatures in the mountain valley would probably block most of the new green shoots until later in the summer. This wasn't something to be quickly overcome.

The only two spots in the valley spared from the fire were a small circle where David and Jeannie had been cowering together, and the cabin. A ten-foot unscarred perimeter surrounded the cabin. Both spots were already showing grass and wildflowers. When the realtor met Jeannie there a week after her eighteenth birthday to sign some paperwork, he had stared at the unburned patches. Jeannie told him that she was able to completely douse the cabin before the flames reached it.

"Hmm," he said. He didn't seem overly concerned about the state of the cabin, but obviously took notice of the strange condition of the Marrick daughter. But even this was merely a passing concern. After signing over the cabin, he had thanked her, and might've even mumbled something about an albatross before speeding off the property. She had been there ever since.

Jeannie stood on the deck in the cool morning air and looked out across the meadow. The morning sun glinted off the stream, calmer where it pooled about fifty yards from the cabin. A couple months earlier, she had dug up a wider space around the stream and spent each morning of the next two weeks working on the pond, often searching out as far as a mile back on the road for the rocks to complete it. She had taken her time, and it set her mind at ease to have something to do.

Jeannie set her coffee on the porch handrail. Repairs were needed on the deck as well, but she thought the project might have to wait. Maybe Father Jimmy would be able to help her. After the attack, the priest had moved out of Missoula into the Bitterroot Valley.

Ex-priest, she reminded herself, even though she knew that he still held God close somewhere in his heart.

He had been very kind to Jeannie, coming out to visit her at least twice a week. He also made sure that the road to the cabin had stayed plowed in the winter. But more than that, he just had a way of making things much less scary.

As did the woman who came out from Missoula to see her on the weekends. Kate Osbourne. She was a great cook, and when she came out, they usually ended up staying up late into the night and talking. Jeannie knew that something awful had happened to Kate, and that "something" probably had to do with David. But out of everything that they talked about, Kate never mentioned what had happened, and Jeannie never asked.

Neither Father Jimmy nor Kate could say why they sought Jeannie out. Of course, the story in the local paper had been the original impetus. The realtor had apparently been talking to his friend in a bar about how the cabin had been spared from the flames. A writer from the paper overheard them and came out and interviewed Jeannie. However, with fires *destroying* homes across the West, Jeannie's story wasn't a big one, only getting a spot buried in the back. But both Father Jimmy and Kate found it and read it… were drawn to it almost. Even though the story never mentioned David, they both said that something about the article caught their attention.

"I know it sounds cliché," Kate had said, "but it was like a mosquito buzzing in my ear. And I knew I had to meet you."

Even Dr. Brandt had been out a couple of times. The first trip, when Jeannie was staying in Missoula, had been a little strained and awkward. Something about a charred Subaru. There was also the issue of release from the Rose House, but since Jeannie had turned 18, Dr. Brandt had been able to make things work. She still seemed to be struggling with everything that had happened, and after Jeannie told her the most recent news, Sam repeated her comment from back in the hospital parking lot. "Tell me again how I had a choice that night."

Mostly, Jeannie was just happy for the support. After moving into the cabin, her first few trips into the small town of Darby drew stares from people like she was either from the cancer survivors ward or starting up a new Manson family, but it hadn't taken long for most of the locals to warm up to her. This was a good thing. She would need all the help she could get. Especially come spring.

Jeannie stepped off the porch and crunched across the gravel driveway. Her stomach still gave her a little grief, so she took her time. She smiled when she reached the pond. It was a little wider than a child's swimming pool. She hadn't dammed it up like her father had suggested, but rather made sure that there was a way in and out. She had already seen a fish in it during a break from her work one afternoon. She didn't think she would ever try to catch one, but they were peaceful to watch.

As Jeannie turned back toward the cabin, movement on the ridge caught her eye. She squinted in the morning sun and hooded her eyes with one hand. A buck stood at the top of the ridge, poised among the blackened toothpicks that were all that remained of the tree line. The distance made it difficult to tell, but Jeannie thought the deer had spotted her as well.

All the help I can get, Jeannie thought. Then she put her other hand on her belly. She looked down and smiled. *Or rather, all the help* we *can get.*

Jeannie looked up the slope, but the buck was gone. She knelt down slowly and splashed the cool mountain water on her face, running her wet fingers over her scalp. She let out a deep breath, stood and started back to the cabin.

Something had happened that day three months ago. Jeannie had suspected something the very next morning, while she still mourned David, but she had denied it. When she finally accepted the fact that she was pregnant (Kate had insisted on her going to the doctor to find out for sure), she took strength from a growing hope for the first time since the death of her parents that everything might be okay, that the world still had a chance. She didn't know how things were going work out for her and her child, but at that moment she didn't worry about it. There was one thing she did know. She had made it this far, survived, and been given new life. Twice.

Jeannie didn't know if it was fate or circumstance that brought her and David together. After all, he could've stumbled into any cabin three years earlier. Why hers? But even with these questions, she felt sure that it was more than just luck that kept her alive since that day. And if it was fate, she was willing to see where it would take her next. She had choices now.

They had choices now.

The End

ABOUT THE AUTHOR

Paul D. Dail is the author of *The Imaginings* as well as numerous other short stories. His collection of flash fiction, *Free Five,* has spent over a year in the top 50 Kindle Horror Short Stories since its publication in 2012. He also has a piece appearing in the upcoming anthology *No Place Like Home* from Angelic Knight Press, where he will appear in the company of veteran Bram Stoker Award winners.

Currently Paul lives with his wife and children in southern Utah, amid the redrock, sagebrush and pinion junipers. He teaches Language Arts and Creative Writing at Tuacahn High School for the Performing Arts.

MESSAGE FROM THE AUTHOR

Thank you so much for reading *The Imaginings.* I hope you enjoyed it. I would welcome any comments on the novel. You can contact me via email at pdail73@gmail.com. And while you're waiting (hopefully anxiously) for my next thrilling story, be sure to check out my website and blog:

www.pauldail.com- A horror writer's not necessarily horrific blog

OTHER TITLES*
BY PAUL D. DAIL

* Available as of Jan. 2014 where most ebooks are sold